The shaft itself was no pa
like sticking your face i
at a crematorium. Somethin
serious, and from the smell, still rotting eagerly away. Jonathan's
face tried to close all ports in a tight pucker; even his surprised
pores slammed shut.

Rats. Perhaps they had crawled into the bottom of the shaft
to eat, and got trapped down there, or drowned.

Or a cat. Maybe a cat fell in and was bitten to death by all
the rats. A *big* cat ...

THE
SHAFT

by David J. Schow

Time heals no wound.
It merely
Cauterizes the scars.

One

Chicago is Hell, and Hell is freezing tonight.

Boner uncaps his bigmouth silver marker. PUNK DEATH SQUADS BONER A#1, he writes across the port window of the El car, drowning the other proclamations there.

Marginally female, a ragbag watches in fear from the far end of the car, eyes like wet black seeds, body a huddle of scarves and threadbare castoffs. She gathers her shopping-bagged junk closer and shuffles for the door before the guy writing on the windows can notice her and work some petty violence. She has a lot of trouble hanging onto all her garbage while battling the handle of the hatch that connects the cars. Nothing on the El moves or works with subtlety.

Boner signs off with a flourish; his mark. The newer El cars are some kind of graffito-resistant aluminum from Japan. Paint pens, Outliners, nearly anything hoses right off. It'll be fun outfoxing progress. It always is.

He has already dismissed the ragbag from his notice. She represents zero potential for gain or sport. Neither does the wino passed out in his own chunky vomit. No goodies; no cash. Boner recognizes the stench of hydrochloric acid and recycled green beans. The puke mixes with the black slush tracked all over the floor of the car. Finding traction is a big challenge.

Nobody rides the late trains if they can avoid it.

Car by car the train bucks over a junction, dislodging clots of snow; Boner fancies he can hear the snapping of electricity. The fluorescents let him preen. He peers past the fuck-yous and gang codes and spiderweb ruptures marring the window's thick plastic. He slips off his mylar shades and cracks his gum.

He is gaunt and ectomorphic, blade-thin with prominent, red-rimmed aquamarine eyes—a feature that never fails to startle citizens who expect dark eyes on a nigger. His hair is a quarter-inch of buff-dyed bristle. It does little to conceal the two parallel crescent scars on the back of his head, souvenirs of a childhood ritual he survived. Thin wrists, long fingers, no nails except for the pinky, which is tapered, spatulate. His Adam's apple is the size of a golf ball. He is gangly despite his layers of clothing and his down moustache tells strangers he really isn't very old. Little three-point spaces separate each of his front teeth. When Boner smiles it is not a pretty display. Boner rarely smiles while on the prowl.

His split lip from the fight still stings. He can't sneer so he keeps his face neutral and frozen, and death to anyone who fails to notice how sullen and pissed off he is. Tonight he is wearing his red-laced combat boots, and a shredded Levi vest over a biker jacket with a pyramidal green leather back. Studs and chains hold everything in concert. He jingles when he walks, like a belled ocelot. *Stay clear or eat pain.* Inscribed on the industrial denim are arcane mojo. KILLER PUSSY. D.R.I. STONER'S EVIL. No one comes close enough to read.

Boner was worse than bad.

He grins at his reflection, then grimaces as a dot of bright red blood interrupts the maroon scab on his lower lip. His gloves are fingerless, so he dabs, squinting at the blood as though trying to decode it. Then he touches the fingertip to his tongue.

The world was black scuffmarks, and dark snowmelt that stank of burning tires, and a wind howling off Lake Michigan that bludgeoned the chill factor down to minus twenty and falling, and the sharp sparking of the third rail in the night, and a wino unconscious in a bog of his own barf. Boner thinks Chicago is pretty cool.

He hustles out a bescummed hash pipe and fires up the button in the brass bowl. His lungs grab a harsh full pull without spasming to drive out the dense fumes. His eyeballs tingle; his brain spells relief.

Smokables, shootables, snortables—Boner is a connoisseur by virtue of broad mercantile involvement. He vends the best, only and always, because he is connected, notorious, and coveted. You be illing? If you don't know Boner, you don't know shit. He smiles at the thought, more cautiously. His lip holds. The cold helps anesthetize the slow throb of pain there.

Light glances off the ice crust on the township sign as the El lumbers past. Only locals know the sign reads OAKWOOD and boasts population stats a decade out of date. All Boner cares to know about Oakwood is that it is the hub of a cluster of woodsy suburbs for the highballers who pull the nine-to-fiver in the skyscrapers downtown. Old houses, here. A lot of Frank Lloyd Wright and tree-lined avenues and cutesy names intended to confer a feeling of turn-of-the-century stability. Too goddamned many churches and not nearly enough bars. In fact, Oakwood is a dry township, which means you can't buy so much as a beer at the 7-Eleven. To Boner the drink racks in the convenience mart coolers look comically crippled. On a street map, Oakwood is a dead rectangle of upscale real estate completely engirded by bars, liquor stores and nightspots—the surface streets forming Oakwood's border are a literal dividing line. Your right to drink begins and ends on the double yellow stripe. Boner thinks this is a big giggle. So do the entrepreneurs holding the alcohol licenses on the leeward side, all around.

But somebody has to staff the dry 7-Elevens, and collect the garbage of the wealthy, and provide reaffirmation of caste, so the State Street El tracks form another of Oakwood's many dividing lines. To the south—the other side of the tracks, yes—is the scullery in this house of the privileged. Every township, no matter how pristine, has its low-rent quadrant, and Oakwood has Garrison Street.

Boner lives on Garrison Street. It puts him within striking range of Oakwood High School, one of his principal sources of income. Business is good.

He unleashes a cloud of acrid smoke and thinks about bashing the wino, since it is nearly time to debark. A quick laugh, as a sign-off. Two steps and he jacks his boot hard into the wino's midsection. Yeah. The man contracts with a woof. *Urrg.* Bile bubbles from his slack mouth. It steams in the chill air of the car. Still alive. What a miracle, thinks Boner.

He writes EAT ME on the wino's forehead with the silver marker, stepping daintily to avoid getting puke on his boots. Next stop is his. He scoots off.

As far as he knows, wino-tagging is his own unique innovation.

The Garrison Street station is deserted at three in the morning. What a surprise. The front door glass has been replaced with industrial plastic, still intact so far, but one door is cocked open against the fierce wind on a broken closure arm. Some frustrated commuter has ripped the receiver out of the pay phone again. Boner doesn't check the slot for change. What for? He is holding more than five hundred cash, in neat fifties.

No one is sleeping in the shelter of the station tonight. Or dead.

Boner sucks the last of the life from the hash button, then stows the pipe. Its warmth leaches through his pocket. He keeps the pipe in his left Levi's pocket. The right holds his Mexican switch, a white bone handle housing a seven-inch, double-edged vampire fang. In his upper pocket are his silver pen and his Zippo. His belt features several dozen keys on a chain pull, plus the leash to a zippered billfold with Harley wings. Mounted against the small of his back beneath his coats he carries a larger Special Forces survival knife. Somewhere within the leather he also packs a coil of razor wire on ring handles. His mirrored tong shades hang now from a button slit. Boner is wearing enough metal to freak out an airport alarm system twice over.

Besides the five hundred bucks in mad money, Boner's biker wallet contains a letter-perfect fake ID for Illinois State, three attorney cards for emergencies, American Express from his boss, ditto, and a smattering of Polaroids: Here is Cynder, going down on him (from above, out of focus). Here she is spreading her legs for the lens. Here she is with a wine bottle jammed up her twat, fucking the mix of whiskey and codeine that made her so photogenic in the first place...

Snapshot: Here is Boner, crunching alone through a four-foot snowpack to the building on Garrison Street. Too much party. He is tired and has to piss.

The building is four stories of ancient red brick befouled by a dandruff of dirty snow. Thick stalactites of cloudy ice hang to frame the east doorway. Above the door, vague shadows suggest the name in granite intaglio beneath. KENILWORTH ARMS.

Boner does not bother with keys. The east door is usually open. So much for security. The foyer is no warmer than the tarmac of Garrison Street, unplowed and cold as the balls of a corpse. He notices names on strips of embossing tape, pressed into slots on the vandalized gangbox. Not his. He does not check for mail.

Dead ahead, a loose caul of musty carpet patches the narrow stairway. It is the color of dust except for a dark, wet stain on the second and third steps that looks like blood. Boner's boots leave cleated footprints all the way up to the second floor landing.

In his wake, sleet slashes in through the skewed east door and makes that weird keening it reserves for after hours. The old building shifts and creaks. Boner thinks of thumping around inside a palsied dinosaur finally settling down to die. It is no longer called Kenilworth Arms on the lease forms. Long in advance of Boner's residence it was bought out by a corporate realtor. Currently it is administrated by a grubby foreign landlord whose cubbyhole door, in the basement, reads BUILDING MANAGER. One day the realtor will vend the property or flatten it for redevelopment. Until that day, Kenilworth Arms will continue to slip through the cracks. Boner appreciates this. He shares a kinship with anything that survives on the outskirts of polite civilization.

He hears water dripping.

Kenilworth's single-wide elevator is rocky, claustrophobic, unsafe. It has been stalled at the second floor for weeks, reeking of Lysol and cat urine. From Two, you had to hike up anyway. The stairs are not a configuration original to the building; they seemed tacked on, too narrow, with oversharp corners. Boner can touch the walls to either side as he ascends. A fat person could not make it. The cheap paint smothering the wallboard is blackened from all the hands before him.

Down the second floor hallway Boner can see the elevator

doors are open a crack. The forty watter inside has burned out or, more likely, been broken. In addition to the urine smell, the air wafting down the corridor carries the thick miasma of fried food, plus an odor like dirty socks that makes Boner think of jail.

Up one more confined flight. Boner's on top, on Three. Technically the basement level is a floor, but no one seems interested in documenting this with room numbers.

Across from the dented elevator doors on Three is a little table holding a coffee can containing plastic flowers shrouded in dust. Above this, an oval mirror is miraculously unbroken. Up here the floorboards groan with the sound of incontinent old men squeezing out painful farts. TVs babble mindlessly, ceaselessly, hot deals on used cars in the predawn. Halfway down the hall one of the yellow bulbs is dead. Boner passes through the pool of darkness and hangs a right past a head-high column of icebox doors built into the wall. Most of these have been nailed up. Some still open and close. They were installed during a time when the iceman could make his deliveries without dragging huge drippy blocks over your nice kitchen linoleum.

The icebox doors no longer have a function. Nobody makes linoleum floors anymore.

Because Kenilworth has been subdivided so often, its schematic of rooms has mutated from the original blueprint. Today it is a haphazard warren of so-called "studios" and "singles" littered with sealed doorways, casement windows that slide up to reveal plywood or brick, and interior walls at unexpected angles and locations. Boner must unlock two doors to enter 307. The first is thin masonite, decades younger than the building's vintage paneled doors. It opens into what was once the common hallway of a large one-bedroom apartment. When opened, the door totally blocks the little passage; Boner has to dance around and shut it before he can proceed. Enclosing each end of the passage is another door, secured by a cheesy knob lock, strictly for show. Boner can slip it with a comb. Behind the far door lives a plump, stringy woman who keeps cats and works, Boner thinks, as a part-time telephone operator. He has never been interested enough to ask. What would he gain? As it does for most, the building is merely a downscale way station. From here, people either moved up-market, or were cast in TV-gray oblivion.

Boner's neighbor got the half of the original apartment containing the kitchen. He got the half with the bathroom. Not a bad trade-off. What she uses for a bathroom is probably a nightmare, and Boner prefers not to cook. Instead of a kitchen, he got an extra closet. From the tall corner windows overlooking the intersection of Garrison and Kentmore, he knew he'd also gotten the original living room.

He has to force his own inside door. It is unbelievably tight tonight—as though the frame had decided to shrink an inch all around.

Inside, the wall switch does nothing but click. And click. Fergus the super—*building manager*—has been clicking around, turning on too many things at once again. The breaker box is in a basement corridor near the laundry room. This has happened too many times for Boner to raise a decent mad, and before he fixes the lights he still has to piss. Boner believes that dope has made his bladder contract to the size of a pack of Luckies.

It *stinks* inside. Like ammonia or stale hamburger; like toilet leakage. Terrific. If the sewage pipes have frozen, ice plugs would have to be torched out. If the plumbing and electrical foul-ups are related…well, then maybe this whole firetrap could be history by morning. A good conflagration would warm everybody's buns for sure.

Boner's aquamarine eyes adjust to the darkness as he picks his way around the corner. The window shades across the room are matte white rectangles, backlit by the luminescent combination of streetlamps and reflective snow. Boner can see the shadow-shapes of his bed, his dresser, his ghetto blaster, even the little space heater on the floor, plugged into a temporarily useless socket.

There is a silver glow of ambient light in the bathroom. Boner knows the window next to the bathtub does not open to the outside world. The light he sees is residual, akin to the afterimage of a flashbulb, yet faint and cold, with an organic quality that makes him think first of dead fireflies, fading out, then of ghosts.

Boner's bladder is hollering for relief. He sweeps aside the shower curtain and unholsters his weapon. He will whizz in the tub so as not to miss the toilet in the bad light. Look out below. He cannot really perceive his own arcing stream of pee.

The tub is even darker, as though clogged up with black water. Boner wonders if this is what stinks so much. He imagines the largest turd in the world, bilirubin-black, coiled up in his very own bathtub, smelling richly enough to steam the windows. Waiting, as the world's largest, to have its picture taken, perhaps. Boner thinks again of his Polaroids.

He giggles. While his laugh is still echoing off the bathroom tiles there comes a flurry of fast, dark motion in the tub. One of Boner's fingers is bitten off and swallowed, along with the tip of his cock.

Boner falls backward, piss and now blood squirting, his legs a-tangle in his dropped jeans. The pain of amputation slugs in. The arm he throws out to balance himself is seized by a wet mouth the girth and ovoid shape of a football. Needle fangs slide through the ligatures of his wrist, slipping between the fine bones to mesh with a silver razor hiss. Arm-first, Boner is snapped back toward the tub, keys jangling, rills of blood coursing down the inside of his jacket sleeve. He cannot see the blood but he can feel it. His dick feels as though an icepick has been jammed through it. More blood. He remembers the wino's fresh puke, how body heat made it steam when it came out.

Boner does not have a lot of time to ponder these sensations individually. In five seconds he will be dead.

His boots thud into the wall hard enough to wake people in the basement. Before he can cut loose his first yelp his face is engulfed by something cool, chamois-soft and blubbery, packed in an inch of sliding goo. His last thought is of the gel they use to pack Spam. It doesn't smell so great, either. Boner is reeled in.

Past that, it was no contest.

Two

The window panels on the Greyhound bus were made of some kind of tough plastic. Scratch patterns stood out in three dimensions, causing passing city lights to halate and issue rainbow coronas. Just now, the streetlamps of anonymous towns were not coming too frequently. There was no moon tonight and beyond the windows it was dead dark.

"No."

Jonathan stripped off his featherweight headphones. He disliked cutting off music before it was finished, but he had lapsed into a doze and now the outer rims of his ears were throbbing. Truncating music was a matter of personal control; when it was done for you, it was called commercial radio. The regret he felt as he poked the STOP button was trivial but genuine. Tangerine Dream ceased to exist in mid-bridge. Jonathan had been rotating the Walkman's batteries. Long haul, no spares, poor foresight. When you need to conserve your batteries you should at least stay awake for the performance.

The running noise of the bus soared into his ears, unmuffled and crisp. They were cruising at a dull and steady fifty-five in the slow lane. Jonathan's overhead reading light was off and no other passenger cared to differ this late at night. Their driver was a robot, a professional white-line jockey who had not uttered a syllable past his pro forma departure spiel about all the things you were not supposed to do on a Greyhound bus.

All there was: Night and blackness and time and bus noise, and Jonathan, all by himself now.

"No."

He remembered the last time he had slept with Amanda.

Wine with dinner always felled them both on workdays. They had snuggled for an hour before coasting down into sleep. He thought he had undressed her. Sometime after midnight he had awakened and gone to work on her. Their progression had become almost ritualistic.

He scooted down, turned on his side, and insinuated his first and middle fingers between her legs, so gently. Amanda slept soundly on her back—a trick Jonathan could never duplicate—and he was in a position that allowed him to monitor the meter of her unconscious respiration, even her very heartbeat. He set up a soft rhythm, rubbing, using his saliva as a buffer, teasing the periphery of her perception for half an hour or so, until he could tell she was floating up from sleep to vague doze.

His first reward came in the tiny moan that escaped her, and the way her legs drifted apart across cool blue sheets to permit him better access. This was the time when pressure and tempo became important.

Her clitoris fattened beneath his fingers, swelling up firm and prominent as she began to assist him with sleepy, tidal movements. Another fifteen minutes passed. Jonathan watched the digital clock tick over as Amanda was jolted through a pleasantly fuzzy, half-asleep orgasm.

Now his index finger was inserted and he kept the beat with his thumb, feeling her contractions bam bam *bam*, the familiar fluttering in the ring of vaginal muscle. He saw her fingers grip the sheets and tighten, then relax as the afterburn warmed her extremities. Fingers, toes, forehead hot now, body demanding breath. When she rolled over, cocking one leg, she was so wet that Jonathan's fingers barely recorded the friction of her rotating pussy.

His erection was excruciating by now.

He guided her ass slightly higher. She was in focus enough to help him. Only just. She arched her back.

"I don't know why I love it so much this way," she had told him so long ago. Before they had moved in together, back when it was imperative for them to hump their brains out every single night, no gaps. Every time she mentioned this, and she mentioned it almost every time, her admission was seasoned with her characteristic guilt.

"I don't know why I like it; I just...I jussst..." She usually dissolved into sibilance, far beyond words.

Amanda loved being entered from behind—her spine arched, face hugging the mattress, hands hanging on, her splendid rump pointed perkily up at her lover. She could never articulate why she favored this position over all contenders. It was a thing of sensation, not logic. Or her mind just refused to analyze it. Sometimes it was possible for Jonathan to nail down isolated details: The comfortably possessive grip of his hands on her hipbones; the optimum penetration; the freer rhythm that came from bearing straight into her instead of heavily atop her. But mostly, Amanda treated this as an exceedingly guilty pleasure. Maybe Mommy had warned her this was something nice girls did not do. Or worse, maybe Amanda had told herself this.

Jonathan could never fathom who Amanda thought she was apologizing to. She had discovered a position that made her senselessly happy. Thousands had not.

He remembered sliding into her, feeding those first few inches with no thrust at all, and the last thing he had anticipated was her voice. Amanda's voice, in the dimness, resolving to wakeful clarity to tell him no.

Amanda enjoyed waking up in a state of sexual high-burn. He was not taking advantage of her sleeping vulnerability; no way. No fucking way. If she even thought that, she would have stopped the sequence much earlier. She had pounced and taken Jonathan by sleepy surprise just as many times. More. Predawn was one of their mutually approved favorite times for lovemaking. It offered a nice buffer of sleep, a couple of hours to either side, followed by the deeper slumber of the satiated.

"No."

Lately their bedwork had become sporadic, by rote, sometimes almost a matter of resigned duty. An exterior reflection of internal problems that Jonathan had hoped would never find their way into the king-sized that he and Amanda had agreed to share for two straight, monogamous years.

He was, he saw, a fool.

Here he sat, northbound on a Greyhound redeye in the middle of the night, with a truly Olympian hard-on straining against the button fly of his 501s...with dead batteries. He was thankful for the dark, which obviated public embarrassment. He was not thankful for the night, because it made him think endlessly of the last time he had slept with Amanda...and not made love.

It had happened the night Jonathan had hoped to jump their lives back on track.

That night, it had not been a Dinner from Hell. That was what he had come to call the stiff social intercourse they shared on their nights out—a mostly spitless meal punctuated by migraine-inducing silences and overpolite non-conversation. *No.* That night, things had gone swimmingly. No arguments, almost no snapping. Amanda had even laughed out loud once or twice, and it hurt him to think that he might be responsible for stealing the laughter from her eyes.

Back at their place he had drawn her a hot bath dense with oil and scented bubbles. She sank in to the tip of her nose and simmered for half an hour. She surfaced just to kiss him with a mouthful of Cabernet Blanc. When she stepped from the tub to the shower stall, he joined her. They lathered each other in familiar ways and she ducked out first, to change CDs on the player in the living room. He emerged from a cloud of steam, wound into a towel. She wore her favorite blue silk robe, her hair free and damp and shaggy. The robe's hem brushed the floor, but the topography emphasized by its sheer, slinky fabric was almost too much for any mortal man to bear.

They were tired. At least this was detente. She instructed him to lay on his stomach, on the cool blue sheets, and she straddled him to work the kinks from his back with strong and practiced fingers. Her crisp, close pubic thatch teased his butt. Then he did her. She suffered a touch of Marfan's Syndrome, a looseness of ligaments at the joints. It was perpetual bother. She could pop her entire skeleton like a trucker cracking his knuckles. Her shoulders and hands ached much of the time; Jonathan feared incipient arthritis. In ten more years those joints would begin to swell.

For her to rub him down was a matter of caring, of saying *I still love you despite our problems.* For him to rub her was a matter of knowing from experience what to massage, and how rough to be with each area, because she was hurting.

Afterward, they had fallen asleep, entwined in each other's arms, and a stranger would have said that these were two people in love.

Until Jonathan was halfway inside of her, gliding easily into the embrace of her musky orchid cunt. Until she told him no.

"No, Jon. Don't. Hurts."

He backed off, reining himself, fighting not to be a Visigoth about how badly he wanted her just at that moment. He parted her vulva with his thumbs, so gently, and tried again. No strain. She was as wet as a thunderstorm.

"No."

She had jerked down and away. It was a definite physical rebuff. She had not meant that his *angle* hurt. She had not meant *not now but in a minute.*

Jonathan popped free of her and felt a speck of moisture strike his cheek. His treacherous cock had catapulted a droplet of her lubrication right into his face. It was damned near symbolic.

Amanda had meant *no.* Period.

And Jonathan had suddenly seen himself as ludicrous. An absurd man on his knees with a hard-on jutting toward space like a cruise missile with no target to blow up.

Useless then, useless now.

The Greyhound's tilt-seat was a classic, slickly grimed in the manner of a doorjamb that has suffered a million filthy hands. A disinfectant tang lingered in the cabin. It persistently reminded Jonathan of a bar men's room in Mexico. Dingy place. He had logged an unlovely half-hour or so there, hooting into the big porcelain megaphone, in another life. No hard liquor since *that* adventure, no thanks. Just some wine, or beer with lime at dinnertime. Amanda had smoked dope to relax for as long as he had known her. Jonathan had found that if he smoked enough to get dizzy, it made him frisky, then leadenly tired, and he would spend the next day and a half with a sore throat. He lacked any taste for the permutations—hash, bongs, half-and-half. Amanda was a browser, a sampler who used drugs infrequently and socially. She only did coke at parties. Jonathan thought sucking powder up your nose in order to be groovy was genuinely repulsive. His drug of choice was caffeine, plus that other white death, refined sugar. Jonathan was a coffee achiever.

Smoking dope helped Amanda knock down some of the barriers she habitually cast in the path of her own sexual pleasure. She almost never orgasmed easily; it took caring effort and a commitment of time from both partners. Most of the guys in her past had never given half a damn about working at it. Accordingly, Amanda had matured thinking herself to be frigid, or otherwise personally at fault. She seemed most fulfilled when she could blame both herself and her partners, with the bad old world at large thrown in for filler.

More than a hint of meanness there, Jonathan accused himself. Egg her on by telling her she enjoys being a victim. What an understanding fellow you are.

The erosion of their relationship had become palpable at the point where Amanda insisted on smoking a joint before fucking. Rainwater patters against a marble tombstone and at last begins to wear the epitaph to unreadability.

Unbidden, a parade of images from the past marched through his head. Mostly silly. The way she used to playfully grab his ass in the supermarket, or merely tell him what a cute butt he had. That winter drive to Birmingham during which they held a crazily civil discussion on how movies are rated— while his hand was delving into her khaki shirt and making her nipples come to attention. Or Amanda, grinning like a gremlin and going down on him at four in the morning, midway through a night flight to LAX. The groping and giggling in the clothing store changing booths at the mall. The oh-so-salacious phone calls at work. Hawking computer mainframes had never appealed to Jonathan's romanticism. That one evening he had sulked home—he was to quit two days later—and found Amanda waiting in his bed, wearing the most maddening black lace nightgown conceivable. The way she had smiled and said, "Jonathan? Do me a favor...?"

They began playing house shortly after that one.

He snapped to. Bus. Night. He was wallowing.

It wasn't just the sex, of course. He was dwelling on that aspect because the sex had been so good between them, and it had been so goddamned long since he had made love to her. To anybody. They had suffered a few bouts of generic lovemaking as their relationship burned down. It had plowed on, grim and unsatisfying, for nearly a year. Somewhere along the line they'd given up making love and settled for having sex. Problems replaced caring.

Just now he was randy enough to turn goofy whenever a pretty waitress smiled at him.

Sex wasn't it. Nothing was *it*. It was...it was so damned complicated, so tangled, that trying to peg a specific catalyst or culprit would trivialize everything they had shared. Right this minute it had gifted Jonathan with a Clydesdale of a cluster headache that felt like a cinderblock being dropped on top of another cinderblock. It overran the left side of his skull, causing his eye to tear and his nose to drip. There was sweat in his eyebrows. The pain was consuming, and past meditating away. Time to grab for the Excedrin.

He twisted his rucksack around on the vacant seat beside him, unzipped the largest pocket and pulled out a half-empty bottle of Calistoga water that still fizzed. He had an apple and some Hydrox cookies left, lost amid the cassette cases and other junk down in the pack—his Nikon plus zoom, loaded with color film at a thousand ASA, his toilet kit, his address book, a flap pouch protecting his dense, dark pilot shades. The bottle's twist-cap went *fssss*. He dry swallowed three of the white pills. The fourth got stuck. He tilted the bottle to his lips and felt the pill disintegrate in the grip of his throat. He tried to relax, eyes shut.

Nope.

It had all gotten perverted. It had all turned so complex. There were so many beginnings and endings to it that it was impossible to lie it into a nice, knotty, front-to-back narrative.

Once upon a day he had phoned Amanda at work. Just to make contact, hear her voice, ask her how she was.

"Pregnant." She had said it just so, on purpose, and hung up on him.

After that had come the argument. Doom-laden, with dug

heels, it started with talk of abortions, salaries, and practicality. It ended with nebulous notions of what constituted growth in a relationship between two human beings. Amanda wept a lot. Jonathan thought he had won the argument.

Jonathan lost.

Sharp she was, canny and diverse. It frustrated Jonathan that the apparent goal of her life was to subjugate all that made her unique, to melt into the commonweal and become what his good buddy Bash had dubbed one of the Butt People.

Said Bash: People who watched titty channels and hung out at the Silver Bullet. People who reproduced irresponsibly and nattered about their desire to get back in shape someday. People who thought winning a lottery would solve all their problems. People to whom life improvement meant affording a more expensive pickup truck. People who counted on God to fix their plumbing, their shortcomings, their existences, because they were too lazy. Lite Beer people. The massmind, the calculatedly ignorant, the lower spiritual castes. The sort of good folks who under the right circumstances would happily form lynch mobs and book-burning parties.

The Butt People.

Amanda's upbringing had been different. Children had always been a part of her scenario. But too many birthdays had passed for maternity to remain a foggy, sometime-but-not-now notion. She slid down into an exitless panic. Jonathan thought seriously for a while about playing Daddy to some small someone. He was shocked to realize he did not despise kids as much as he feared he might. These miniature human beings were *intriguing*.

They were the most intriguing, he found, when they belonged to somebody else, when they could be observed at will with the repulsive parts edited out.

Too many friends insisted too fervently that everything *changed* when you became a parent. No big surprise there. Jonathan heard the solidarity of the trapped, seeking to seduce him. He asked Amanda why. Her response had been heated, cast in steel.

"Because it's what people *do*."

Not enough, not for Jonathan, who did not believe in building families by accident, the way a pioneer constructs a shelter not out of choice, but out of necessity. And that was not enough for Amanda.

It had been a slow income year, and Amanda had gotten an abortion. Jonathan wondered if he would ever be forgiven for his complicity.

Amanda chanced upon a gray hair, then another. Then a stretch mark or two on her thighs. Jonathan noticed varicose veins on his own ankles. He did not mention them. For Amanda, a time bomb had begun ticking. The prospect of whether she had actually pinpointed a flaw in her mirror was a no-win exchange. If he noticed, it hurt her. If he pretended not to, she felt overlooked. And if he did nothing, held at neutral, her eyes silently damned him one more time.

She stopped smiling. She erected an automatic denial response against any proposal of Jonathan's. She entrenched for a long tug o' war. This irritated Jonathan. Waste pestered him. He reluctantly supplied whatever pressure was required to keep the tension equalized. Nobody was going to budge. There were egos to be preserved. He thought of the joke about the self-protecting fuse—the one that protects itself by crisping the entire circuit rather than burning out.

Lovemaking? Call it nightmarish.

So now Jonathan's cute butt was Chicago-bound, with Texas dwindling to the rear, Tangerine Dream tapes to supply a highway soundtrack, and pills for the headaches that whacked chrome spikes into his brain. He brooded about the end. The damage Amanda could wreak upon him with a look, or a stolid silence. He moped about the practiced and incomparable way they had moved together, melded into one seamless, primal being, giving and receiving pleasure. Two folded into one.

"Take the job," she had told him. "Sure. Go have fun with Bash." Jonathan fancied he heard the *wham* of a gavel. "You will anyway, right? You can probably make some money, so why not? Get away from me because I'm such a bitch, anyway."

There came times when the acid certainty in her voice made him want to start flinging wild haymaker blows. "Well." He had shrugged, still frustrated. "What about you?"

"What about me? Don't make any big sacrifices on my behalf." Her tone said: *You fucked up again, ace. What you should have asked was what about US? See? You don't really give a damn.*

They could predict each other so well. Why wasn't that a good thing, a healing, strengthening, positive thing, instead of the nastiest form of ultimate weapon?

And where do you get off being so goddamned naive? a tiny, impish voice shot back.

Chicago offered work. Chicago offered *distance.*

Jeffrey Holdsworth Chalmers Tessier—of the New Orleans Tessiers—was burly and bearded, slope-shouldered and large of tooth. His eyes were a mellow golden-brown, radiant, absorbent, constantly storing input on his mental video recorder. His line was freelance graphics, his patter rapidfire and ceaseless, and he had been Jonathan's best friend of record since their first encounter at a university film club meeting in 1977. Jonathan had been chasing an architectural degree, Jeff had been loafing away a liberal arts scholarship. Somewhere amidst the womanizing and pool-playing he acquired the nickname Bash. He still maintained a loving hold on his Deep South accent. He told Jonathan that Amanda had been a "shayme." To Bash, ladies might come and ladies might go, but there were always more ladies, and if the universe worked right Jonathan would forever be able to blubber on his big shoulder.

Male bonding was critical to Bash's diagnosis of the world. Give him a screening of *The Man Who Would Be King* or *Heartbreakers*, with Nick Mancuso and Peter Coyote, and he gladly slid into Nirvana. Bash's life was not hampered by marriage or kids or health insurance or devolving into a Butt Person. Such worries never seemed to be on his plate.

"So blow town, Fed Ex your rosy red asshole up here, and help me steal some of Capra's capital, m'boy." He pronounced it *boah.* He always talked like that. "I'm snug in a position at Rapid O'Graphics, snug enough to swing my considerable personal influence and even more awesome charm. Hell, you're a shoo-in as soon as I say so. Think of it as your first step on the

Big Ladder of Life, from Ronald McDonald to Dom Perignon."

Bash had even sprung for bus fare.

Jonathan was no computer salesman; at least he and Amanda had agreed on that. He warmed to the idea of breaking Rapid O'Graphics under the wing of someone as big and loud and life-embracing as Bash. For now, he'd had his fill of bleakness and ashes.

That, at least, was his rationalization. There was no way to express it that did not make him seem petty, self-serving and brutal. It was the ancient pep talk: *We need to separate for our own good*. A venerable old standard that had already failed to work for millions of dissatisfied customers.

There was, as it turned out, a single event in Jonathan's memory. The event he could point to and say *this* is what split and splintered them, a nasty and mordant thing like a caustic chemical sloshing around in his mind and burning the emotions there.

Northward rolled the Greyhound bus, ignoring one small town after another, preparing to hurdle the line into a new state.

The cluster headache still sheeted Jonathan's vision with wetness. He closed his eyes, ringing down his own personal nightfall A tear streaked freely along his cheekbone. He thought once more of the most horrible thing he had done to Amanda, the woman he still loved.

Three

C ruz made it to the rail just in time to see Chiquita destroy an umbrella table, face-first, five stories below. She missed the pool by a good ten feet. Until he saw her brains splatter all over the sun deck, he hadn't realized the bimbo had *had* any.

Cruz would see her fall thousands of times more before his life was over. His ears were cracking constantly and he had a headache. Over the cabin com, Captain Falstaff of Eastern Airlines announced to the passenger complement of the 737 that there was turbulence a-coming; they should belt up. Cruz sat gripping the armrests. One was loose. He stared out over the starboard wing and wondered how these double plastic windows could possibly get marked up on the outside. Was the wind shear that nasty thirty thousand feet up? He thought of fat gremlins riding the wingtips and working their alien vandalism.

He got a pillow, he gulped aspirin, he marveled at the fact that less than six hours ago, his life had been pretty goddamn smooth. He tried not to worry about dying, but that was stupidly optimistic. As of six hours ago, and Rosie's party...

Cruz was still watching Chiquita fall. Down and over, one full turn, then *splat* into the apron of the hotel pool.

Rosie humped across the suite on his bum leg while the party's zombies were still puzzling out what had gone down. Besides Chiquita. Cruz was hanging so far over the rail he almost got sucked over. His mouth was agape and a snow-white droplet of saliva unmoored from his lip and tumbled. Same trajectory.

The party had definitely cratered.

"Back off the rail, Cruz, c'mon now." A textbook of cool in a shitstorm, that Rosie. He was Emilio's big fixer. He caught a fistful of Cruz's flapping aloha shirt and hustled him off the balcony and into the only empty bedroom of the presidential suite. A lot of coke was smeared across Cruz's upper lip and most of his right cheek; he looked like a punk in a cheap Santa Claus getup to whom some attacker had dealt a hard left-handed slap. He had been drinking and snorting all day. Now his eyes had filled with something a bit more potent and permanent, and he was drunk on it. He clomped fumble-footedly along, letting Rosie lead him.

"Yee-HAH," somebody said. "Rawwww-*hide!*"

The suite's other two bedrooms were noisily taken; five in one, a trio in the other, all sweaty, higher than helium and fucking like minks. Seven other mouth breathers were still gawping at the eleventh replay of the *Star Wars* videotape on the big Proton monitor. Most of them had lent applause to Chiquita's brain-dead strip act. The kicker to the act was her jump. Most of the droids laughed. By now half of them had managed to forget she had ever existed at all.

So much glossy black hair, Cruz thought. Her feather earrings. Emilio had paid for the diamond in her front tooth. Her dark Brazilian eyes. All of it had impacted with concrete at about seventy miles an hour. Stone defeats flesh.

"Rosie, she..." Cruz hadn't collected his wits. He squeezed his eyes shut, blinking out white grit, then sniffed mightily as tears freed and rolled. "Fuckin' jumped."

"Shut up a minute." Rosie lent the idiots in the next room a quarter-second of disgusted checkup. No one would pull any shit for at least five minutes. On the video the special effects fireworks had revved up. He slammed the door and in three crooked strides got right in Cruz's face. Cruz was still staring at the shut door, wondering where Rosie had got to.

Rosie was notorious for his efficiency. Efficiently, he yanked Cruz nose-to-nose and backhanded him twice, bouncing him off the wall with a split lip. His footing went away. A tiny cloud of cocaine dust hung between them as Rosie hauled him back up.

"Stupid," he muttered. "Why didn't you keep your jaws

wired? What the *fuck* is wrong with you?" He stomped his good foot, then rushed his hand through his thinning bronze hair. His businessman's tan was perfect. He needed to blow off his mad, and had only moments in which to stitch this rancid mess into order.

"Asswipe needledick birdshit! Goddammit!" One more slap, more a cuffing, an admonishment. "Why for fuck's sake did you tell Chiqui to jump when you knew she was stupid enough to do it?"

"Didn't *tell* her." Cruz's slur betrayed his brain's impaired ability to track. *"Dared* her."

"Wonderful. I'm sure Emilio will appreciate that." He backed off and rubbed his face, winding up with his hands in a prayerlike attitude as he doped out a plan. Cruz could see Rosie prioritizing.

Any second now would come the sound of sirens.

"Okay. Five minutes for them to come unglued about the meat pie all over the terrace. Ten minutes for them to guess which balcony, unless somebody up here has already bitched about the party noise." He assumed yes. He rummaged inside his Verri Uomo double-breasted jacket—two large, retail, easy—and emptied his leather billfold. Into Cruz's trouser pocket he wedged a fat wad of Franklin notes, bent double. Then he fished up a cloth-covered ampoule, holding it beneath Cruz's nose and crushing it with thumb and forefinger.

"Oh...*fuck!*" Cruz convulsed sharply and held his nose as if his sinuses had just snapped aflame. His skull was on the verge of explosive decompression.

Rosie stepped back. Vomit on his Guccis would be *très* uncool.

While Cruz fell to his knees to hock and gag, Rosie continued. "Cops will turn over the whole building. It's not them you have to fret. It's Emilio. Know what will happen if Emilio rolls in and you're still here?"

Bap on the side of the head. Cruz looked up. He was hurting but his senses were home. He nodded, sickly, his black brush cut bobbing. Lucidity had met him like a hit-and-run wreck. "One of those dial-tone dickheads in the next room will tell

Emilio I told Chiqui—*dared* Chiqui to jump. And then *I'll* go off the balcony."

"And, my boy, if you are stupid enough to still be here when Emilio shows, I will fucking *help* him toss you. You know how things are. How they have to be."

Cruz knew, and nodded. Affirmative.

When he found his Numero Uno squiff spread all over the deck on Cruz's dare, Emilio would be torqued. He hated interruptions in his sex life. Cruz could envision Emilio storming in. Catching him with a warm tit in one hand and a cold Chivas in the other, sucking up the complimentary blow and watching *Star Wars*. Playing nonchalant. Yeah, Emilio would have his bones broken in alphabetical order for appetizers. The party would crank. Cruz would bounce out the window and join Chiquita the way peanut butter joins jelly when you squish the bread together.

"You've gotta tear ass outta here, pronto." Rosie was not making a funny. "Wipe off your face. Hail a cab downstairs. Get the fuck to Miami International. Call me." He fast-drew one of his cards. Cruz knew it read *Ross M. Westervelt—Business Investments Counselor.* He scribbled a number on the obverse. Cruz felt absurdly honored. At last he was privy to one of Rosie's top-secret emergency numbers.

Rosie spot-checked his Rolex Presidential. "Call at *exactly* five o'clock. You're catching a plane."

Time seemed to be accelerating now, and Cruz had no mouth for this new taste. "Rosie—listen to me, man. She was on the rail before I could get ahold of her...and...I didn't mean she should *jump*, seriously, but she was on god knows how many mikes of that shit Telstar brought in from—"

"Cruz."

"—that shit was *not* stepped on, Rosie...and she was way over her ceiling for chemical input, if you know what I mean, and—"

"Cruz."

"I wasn't fucking serious, Rosie!"

Rosie hit him again, not so hard. Cruz copied and understood.

"Cruz. We have no time for this. And I don't have time for a speech. I like you. You're a primo runner and I don't want to see you become hotpatch for the Don Shula Expressway. I know a fellow in Chi. You can hole up there."

Rosie was the only person Cruz had ever known who could call it *Chi* and not sound like an imbecile. It sounded natural, coming from Rosie, who Cruz saw as old-fashioned, yet someone to look up to, to emulate. Rosie had this pet expression: *When the shit starts flying, be careful you don't inhale any.* Cruz caught himself using it one day, and it sounded natural for him, too.

"I'll grease Emilio out. Couple of months, no heat, I'll bring you back in. Emilio will chill down when he gets a new bitch. But right now you've *got* to get out of here, before the shit starts flying."

Cruz returned a sad grin. "Don't wanna inhale none."

"*Don't* go to your apartment. Hear me, now."

"But Rosie, what about all my stuff, and—"

Rosie overrode. "No and no. Don't even stop at a 7-Eleven for a bubble water. Phone no one. Go straight to the airport and don't do anything except stay low till five o'clock. Then call me. By then I'll have tickets straightened out. After that, you were never here this afternoon, despite what the dummies outside will say. They're wasted and I'm not. *You were never here.* I need half an hour to cook up a plausible excuse as to your absence, but don't worry about that." He glanced at his watch again. "Our first five minutes are gone. You're outta here, kiddo. Now."

Cruz's hand sought his pocket, where the thickness of cash bills bulged.

"No buts," said Rosie. "Git."

No tears, no strain. Cruz shut the door quietly behind. He was a pro, too.

By the stroke of midnight Cruz was freezing his *cojones* off at O'Hare Airport, already thinking this alien turf truly gobbled the canary.

He tried to sip turbid automat coffee. It seared his tongue. The PA announcements were absurd. *Nondenominational Sunday morning services will be held at 6:30 in the chapel, basement level.* Baggage claim was in the next area code from where the Eastern flight had debarked. He had no bags to claim, and no idea of where to wander. He'd never been a fugitive before.

This airport had a *chapel,* for fuck's sake.

He thought of his cab ride to Miami International, a nervous trip that let him savor the tang of one hundred proof paranoia—utter, bug-eyed, a distillate of all the fear he had known in twenty-one years walking the surface of the planet. He saw the cabbie notice his frequent glances out the back window, and sat rubbing his palms against his pantlegs.

He imagined the telephone at his duplex ringing, ringing with one of Emilio's bad boys on the calling end, sniffing. He built a fantasy picture of Emilio's iron-pumping goon brigade turning his home inside-out. There went the Audio Technics turntable, the one with the twelve-pound professional deejay platter and the solid carbon Black Widow tone arm. *Crunch.* There went the CDs. *Crack, crack, crack.* The belly of his Aqua III waterbed would be gutted by Buck knives. *Splooch.* He saw his wardrobe systematically shredded asunder. His collection of gas station and bowling shirts, with names embroidered in red on the pocket ovals, none of which had ever seen a day of working-class labor...all gone now. Emilio's apes loved destruction almost as much as straight rape and no-frills murder.

It would all come to pass if Rosie's story sprang a leak. If Emilio tipped.

Cruz had locked eyes with Emilio's lady through a freebased cloud of blur. His line: "You're probably wasted and stupid enough to jump off, Chiqui. Go on. I dare ya." Snappy patter that had changed his life in an instant.

He had tried to estimate five stories of height when the 737 had lifted from the runway. Terminal velocity was thirty-two feet per second. Had Chiquita achieved it before her dazzling smile and boner-bait body had flattened into a meatbag of pulverized bones?

Five o'clock. His hands had been shaking when he dialed Rosie's secret number. Relays dealt with the call; the timbre of the ring abruptly changed and answered within one buzz.

"Cruz. Okay, listen. Number's routed through to my carphone. Emilio probably has the stationary phones bugged, and I don't have time to sweep and fry the exterior taps just for one call."

Cruz had watched Emilio's debugger do just such a trick once. His equipment kicked a megavolt surge through the phone lines. Phone company equipment handled six volts, which is why you could never kill anyone by dumping a phone into their bathtub. The surge did to the line taps what a blowtorch does to a strand of hair.

"A first class ticket is waiting for you at Eastern. It's prepaid. Had to messenger it to the desk. Used a two-stage, filtered credit card so it can't be traced back to me."

"First class? Whoa, Rosie, I—"

"Don't kiss my butt. It was a last-minute booking. No coach seats were open. How much money did I give you?"

Cruz never lied to Rosie, not about anything crucial. "Seventeen hundred. I had another two-forty in my back pocket when—"

"Right."

Right. *Bash!* Chiquita hit the pool apron and broke. Blood reddened the pool runoff gutter near what used to be her scalp. Her hair spread out like crimson seaweed in a shock corona around the disintegrated crockery of her skull. Cruz kept seeing the picture. It never got boring.

"Buy what you need. Don't buy anything ostentatious. Let my man in Chi do that for you. I'll call him once I know you're in the air."

"What name is the ticket under?"

"Ramon Aguilar." Rosie spelled it out. Cruz had been typecast as a greaser again. "Copy?"

Cruz recited the spelling.

"Now get your ass over to the gift shop and buy a shoulder bag. Toothbrush, toilet kit, you know. Buy a razor. When you're in the air, lose the moustache. Buy some magazines and junk. Maybe a camera, so you don't board the plane naked. We don't want anybody to remember you had no baggage."

"Rosie. I—" There seemed to be a big script Cruz needed

to work his way through, for the benefit of his mentor. A lot needed saying.

"Shut up. Check your pockets. Any blow or pills, flush it down the john in the men's room. Don't be holding when you board. Hear me, now."

"Yeah, right." There was a gram vial on a gold dogtag chain around his neck. His hand sought its shape beneath his shirt. He actually managed a tiny smile. Rosie's sheer competence was loosening him up.

"You don't need to think about what happened to Chiqui until a lot later. Just remember you weren't even here."

"What about the other dudes at the party?"

The hissing whine of cellular interference made them both wince. Perhaps Rosie had driven his Porsche beneath an underpass.

"Simple to keep them loaded," Rosie said. "Asked if any of them recalled seeing you lately. Most of 'em wondered why you weren't at the party."

Cruz nodded. Fucking droids.

"So far so good, kiddo. Try not to fuck up, hm?"

The last thing Cruz wanted was to rack the receiver, to break that vital connection with Rosie. Already he felt bleakly isolated, cut off and scared...and he was not even clear of Florida yet.

"Hey, wait! What's the name of the guy I'm supposed to meet in Chi? Chicago, I mean."

"Not your problem. He'll find you." The hardball mien of Ross Westervelt shucked away. "Only one brand of dingdong would wear an aloha shirt into a blizzard. Chuck it. Spill something on it. Lose it. Buy a shirt; buy a jacket—a heavy coat, if you can find one. Go to the white zone outside the Eastern baggage claim and loiter until you're picked up."

Cruz wanted to interject, to give back something significant. "Thanks." That was all he got out. He felt like crying.

"Let's just hope nobody loses dick skin over this, kiddo. You go now. I'm already gone."

"Hey, wait."

Rosie held on the other end for one beat, two...

"Shit's flying, old man. Don't inhale none."

There was a quick, breathy snort that might have been laughter under better circumstances. Then the connection was severed.

Cruz had toddled forth to play secret agent. He tasted the differences between purgatory and paradise, the tiger and the Lady…steerage and first class. There was no way he was going to trash his coke vial. It had been a gift from Rosie, along with the novelty dog tags in solid 24K. He was not about to throw it away…or empty it. Certain miniscule disobediences could validate your own control over your life. Cruz maintained this sort of rigid self-discipline by deciding not to toot anything until *after* he was on the plane.

He was most jazzed by the boarding call that permitted him, as a first class passenger, to board ahead of the rabble, just after the feebs and children. The normal passengers (the cheapskates) were thus compelled to stare at him sitting in his extra-wide seat, giving the hostess his drink order while they were still jostling and grunting and packing themselves in. The first class hostess, whose name was Tawny, had legs that could tempt mere human men to commit vehicular homicide. She seemed to have a shorter uniform skirt than the coach stewardesses. Tawny smiled without end at everything—every dumb executive bon mot, every crumb of leering chat, each conversational triviality. Her teeth were so perfect you had to stare hard to see the lines separating them. Up in the front of the plane, the service was linen and glass instead of paper napkins and plastic cups. Tawny constantly and happily recharged Cruz's Cuernavaca. It never did hit bottom. He was dismayed to discover, as he attempted the shave Rosie had suggested, that he had gotten quite blitzed.

The jet slam-danced over pockets of turbulence en route to colder northern climes. The alcohol Cruz had dumped down suffered a head-on collision with the adrenaline blowback from Chiquita's swan dive. He cut his upper lip with the safety razor. At the sight of his blood in the 737's stinky chemical bathroom, his metabolism finally tossed the towel and he spent the next fifteen minutes vomiting into the oblivion pit of the airline toilet. The stench of the blue freshener kept him heaving long after he was empty. With jittering hands he did two medium lines from the coke vial to stabilize, then asked Tawny if she could scare up a bandaid.

Of *course* she could. Right away. Smile.

Cruz's genetic makeup had never favored body hair. His chest was as unhirsute as that of the average Japanese. His moustache had been one of the great triumphs of his late teens, though he had never been able to coerce it into being more ambitious and to travel, say, down toward his chin, perhaps to seed a beard. He had been proud of what he had been able to raise.

Gone now; razed rather than raised. A little something turned into nothing. One more check drawn on Cruz's pride account, made out to Emilio and payable on demand.

He rinsed down and dabbed his face with water, pale and still shaking. The mirror did not lie: *You have the pallor of a ghost in need of a strong fix.* He applied the bandaid to his upper lip; his lower still hurt from where he'd bitten it when Rosie smacked him. He had been too high to feel genuine pain then. Now was rawly different.

He slumped on the still open toilet seat and rubbed his face hard to urge forth blood and bring back some color. Amazing, how your whole fornicating life could unravel in fast-mo. If Emilio ever suspected him, Cruz's life would not be worth the sock on a wino's foot.

Would Emilio see *why* Cruz had blown town? No, Rosie said he'd deal with that one.

Cruz ached to punch the rewind button on the whole day. Go back and change the story in the telling so that it was exactly the same...except that it would leave that dumb cunt Chiquita alive and him on the ground in Miami instead of midair, somewhere over Tennessee.

His aloha shirt was besmirched with puke. He balled it up on the stainless steel micro-counter. After swabbing out his pits and smearing on deodorant, he wriggled into a pink *Miami Vice* T-shirt he'd purchased at the airport's souvenir shop. It was crisp and stiff. No airport ever seems to stock clothing without slogans or signs on it. He had picked up a sweatshirt that read LIFE'S A BITCH, THEN YOU DIE. He reversed it so the white seam stitching showed and pulled it on. He thought of Boris Karloff's sheepskin jersey in *Son of Frankenstein*. Start a trend.

He stuffed his aloha shirt into the blue nylon gym bag he'd bought. It read NIKE TEAM in cheap silkscreening. He didn't want to throw away the shirt; he'd gone unexpectedly sentimental about it. Maybe he could keep it, save it, wear it on his eventual return home...if everything worked out. Already the idea of flying in the opposite direction was swooningly seductive. Sometimes the future was just one big come-on.

Captain Falstaff announced their gradual descent into Chicago. Local landing time would be 10:45 p.m. Tawny smiled and checked his belt. She had to have a boyfriend who was a blond hunk, probably a karate instructor. Cruz wondered if she smiled that way when Kung Fu was banging the tits off her.

Did people this cheery ever *have* sex?

Upon touchdown at O'Hare, Cruz found himself reluctant to surrender the warm cocoon of the plane. It would be another link severed. There were two edges to the blade Cruz was riding: For every ounce of homesickness, he knew Emilio was that much farther away.

He wondered what Emilio was doing, right this minute, as he searched in vain for clocks in an unfamiliar terminal. He felt absurdly glad he had kept the coke vial, the aloha shirt. They reaffirmed his identity when he felt he might be losing his mind.

Chicago had only looked good from thirty-three thousand feet up. During descent, the patches of snow and ice dotting the nighttime landscape grew ever more ominous. How many times, he wondered, had a scab of runway ice frozen at the right place to wreck a plane? The only thing that might slow down a gigantic, ass-skidding jumbo jet might be a nice, solid building full of people. Maybe that was why they called them terminals.

Back in Miami he had swapped four hundred in cash for a cherry Minolta 35mm camera. It weighed down one end of the Nike bag. Big airports always had a gift shop plus other, more serious venues, generally labeled *shoppes* so customers would expect astronomical prices. A card of AA batteries costing a buck could run four or five times that in an airport gift shop. The cheap ones. Cruz had used the camera to smuggle his coke vial on board, tucking it into the film bay and handing the Minolta over for hand inspection at the metal detector. No problem.

He supposed he could teach himself how to operate the camera sometime. Fill those hours.

Most of the Eastern passengers retrieved their baggage from the assigned carousel and evaporated. He felt the air traveler's usual stab of worry: Would the sentries at baggage claim request a ticket for luggage he had carried onto the flight? It had never happened in the nearly one hundred air trips Cruz had taken, but he always thought of it. Strange. He smiled in passing at the uniforms, the same way he'd smiled at the armed and unsmiling folks back in Miami, the ones staffing the metal detectors. Who, me, guilty?

Electronic-eye doors ground slowly apart and Cruz got his first whiff of Chicago.

No new snow was falling; that condition had permitted Cruz's flight to land on time. He saw old snow bulldozed onto a row of curbed cars. It gradated from white to gray to slushy black at the bottom of a four-foot pack. The air smelled like engine lubricant. The wind had at him, blasting, wind-tunnel cold, rattling the heavy sliding doors in their tracks. Unmelted flakes lifted from the snowpack and swirled in the air, grains of albino sand. The in-flight weather update had let everyone know that the wind-chill factor was minus twenty and dropping. Cruz's first inhale felt like tossing back a straight shot of Everclear. Once fully outside, with the cold carving through his sweatshirt, he inhaled again. His nose hairs froze together. They thawed when he exhaled. Now they were damp, icing up even faster with his next breath.

He had seen his breath condense before. The twin plumes of vapor jetting from his nostrils were the consistency of locomotive steam. That seemed weird and a bit thrilling. He leaned on a trashcan to check the traffic in the white zone. It was the surface temperature of the moon, and touching it was like immersing his bare hand in liquid oxygen.

Cruz was just beginning to feel truly lost and miserable when a flawless 1971 T-top Corvette sliced slush and nosed its way into the available curbspace. It was beaded with water and its billowing exhaust was the same color and density as Cruz's breath.

The horn beeped twice, curtly. Cruz bent down to look and saw his own face in mirrored glass. Then the passenger window buzzed down and he got his first glimpse of Rosie's Chi-town pal, Bauhaus.

enough without a linear explanation. *Bash.* It *sounded* like this big man. Everyone Jonathan had ever known had come attached to some sort of nickname...except, of course, his own self. Amanda had been Cookie and Green Eyes and Gorgeous, depending on how sexy the phone chat had to sound. They both addressed the shorthaired terrier next door as Dog Face even though his tags announced him as Doc. Amanda called her cat Pookie; its real name was just as cloying. While sloughing through pick-up electives in Classic Philosophers and Anthro 101A at the University of Louisiana, Jonathan would gang over to Grizzly's Tavern to tip back Mason jars of beer with Bash and Stretch and Fungo and Mad Max...and apart from Jonathan, he had never been called anything else. In grade school he had been Jonathan-plus-initial, to differentiate him from all the other Johns in the classroom. He fit in with the plague of Mikes and Jeffs and Cathys and Debbies, all boringly named in those fabulous Sixties; he supposed he was lucky not to have been named Glyph or Rainbeaux or Sativus. His real last name was stunningly prosaic.

Just Jonathan. Hey you, shithead. Yeah, you.

He thought now that everyone possessed another name, an alternate face. Sometimes you caught a glimpse of the flip side of a person you thought you knew five-by-five. Sometimes it wasn't pretty. Some people spent lifetimes not seeing the ugliest aspects of those closest to them.

Bash was talking about beer, deftly manhandling the truck's stick shift and correcting whenever they began to hydroplane or slide ass-backwards in the slush. Jonathan hung on.

"...how you say, *interesting* local breweries close by the city. That's the single aspect of provincialism I enjoy. Regional beer. Can't wait to introduce you to Quietly."

"Who's she?"

"No. Quietly Beer." Bash was a good comedian; he paused to let it sink in.

"Quietly Beer." Jonathan couldn't stop his face from breaking an honest smile. It felt unfamiliar. It almost hurt. "Quietly *Beer?*"

"Absurd, ain't it?" Bash was grinning like a talk-show comic. "You haven't let Jesus into your heart, or anything dumb like that, since the last time I saw you. Have you?"

"No. I like beer fine."

It was wine Jonathan could not bring himself to drink anymore. He had invested the last parts of his twenties in carefully cultivating a casual taste for basic wines. He enjoyed knowing what to order when restaurants did not have his first choice. No longer, not now. He did not drink wine anymore because...

"Gotta give you the skinny on Quietly Beer," Bash was saying. "You'll laugh till you cough up a lung."

Jonathan nodded. The smile set on his visage like drying cement. The smooth, velvet undertow of memory dragged him under and tried to drown him one more time. It had made him weep on the bus, and locked his throat shut just now.

Jonathan did not drink wine anymore because...

It was one of their last Dinners from Hell, and it was going badly. Too many ossified silences.

Jonathan thought you could always tell married couples in restaurants. They're the ones not talking to each other, paying more attention to their plates than their partner's eyes. Ditto for established relationships—the ones heading at high speed for the septic tank of spoiled human emotions.

This goddamn meal will cost fifty bucks, exclusive of tip, Jonathan thought, and Amanda has got her brat knob turned up full crank. She doesn't care. And neither of us can taste the food.

Tonight Amanda ran her full menu: She was getting old. She was getting fat, wasn't she? She wasn't making enough money. Jonathan didn't care that her job in home mortgages was not paying enough and never would. Jonathan didn't care about anything but Jonathan. Nobody had ever truly fallen in love with her, her alone. Nobody ever would. She was closing fast on thirty and had not yet reproduced. If Jonathan cared he would have *done* something by now. She hated her entire fucking life.

And—oh yes—Jonathan didn't really care. Did he?

At which point he was supposed to protest that yes, he gave a damn. Several damns. His concern had ruined his meal.

But she cut him off, certain he cared not at all, and by the by,

I've been thinking a lot about suicide lately.

Forever unspoken, her accusation was that she was nailed to a cross she loathed, and Jonathan was the guy holding the hammer and spikes. Amanda despised culpability, even for her own lot in life.

He knew what was coming out of her mouth next.

"You don't want to hear this shit, Jonathan. Why don't you just tell me to fuck off?"

Too goddamn easy. It was exactly what she wanted. If she could goad him into saying those words, then *he* could be blamed for terminating their relationship. One more little death. Amanda's view of a hostile and destroying world devoted to crushing her would be reinforced another degree if she could successfully drive someone as tolerant as Jonathan to the boiling point of rage.

Amanda was an on-off smoker, a knuckle popper. She picked at scabs until they bled anew.

Jonathan would never give her the satisfaction of easy rage. Allowing her to piss him off would not solve any of their problems. He told her this.

"Oh, great. So you're saying that I'd be happy if I could make somebody who cares about me give up. Terrific."

His hands vised shut on air. It was like trying to build a computer from ectoplasm. Or fuck tears.

No, he told her. But it seemed as if she could only be fulfilled if life was as miserable as she persisted in believing it was. She nurtured her unhappiness because it was familiar turf, and bitching was easier than actually doing something, taking action. He expected her to snap back with the usual rejoinder: *Never mind, Jonathan; it's no big deal, right? You don't care, you don't understand and you never will.*

Instead, she tossed half a glass of white Bordeaux in his face. Maybe she had been watching too many movies that week. A bit of televisual melodrama.

He spluttered while she stomped out. Ambient conversation in the restaurant switched instantly off.

The atonic white wine seeped past his eyelids with a disinfectant sting. He heard Amanda walk away while his eyes flooded. Everyone was looking, all right. Somewhere behind him he heard a laugh, abrupt and feminine. Then came hushed whispers. None sounded sympathetic.

He had not let Amanda's party line gnaw at him. Congratulations. You won. Big fucking deal.

He mopped his face. Their waiter brought a fresh napkin. Jonathan ordered a cappuccino. Maybe he could sit here until all the witnesses finished their meals and went home. Five minutes later he was drier and no longer blushing. The cappuccino tasted like barium. He overtipped.

He walked all the way home, fifty minutes of putting one foot in front of the other, thinking, then brooding, then fuming.

When he used his keys to unlock the deadbolts he found the security chain latch engaged. He smiled to himself. Then he kicked the door brutally just to the right of the knob, snapping the chain and tearing the screws from the lintel like pimentos blowing free of a thrown hors d'oeuvre.

She would be expecting him to tarry guiltily by the bedroom door. They could exchange more meaningful silences, more useless apologies, and proceed with the erosion of their lives. One more day paid up in pain and wear.

Jonathan did not stop at the threshold.

He grabbed her by the throat, gripping her neck with the same familiarity her pussy had enclosed his cock. He was remembering a time when, dinner completed, they would be making love by now, laughing, wrestling, sharing. She thrashed and made a noise but he was stronger and she was badly positioned.

Then her frightened eyes saw what was in his hand. He had brought it from the kitchen.

He had never struck Amanda and did not strike her now. She yelled for him to take his hands off. Then she focused on the weird light in his eyes and shut up for her own good, like a trapped cat resigned to an oncoming beating.

Jonathan knew what she was thinking: *Go ahead. Do your worst. You'll pay later. In guilt.*

Almost perfunctorily, he asked her just who the hell she thought she was. Holding her tight to the pillows by the throat, he emptied a one and a half liter jug of Rhine wine, ice cold, all over her. It gushed from the bottle, foaming from her mouth and nostrils and soaking her hair.

Amanda tried to scream.

This was what it had finally come to. Making her feel pain in response to the tiny agonies she thoughtlessly manufactured and dispatched to sting him every time they spoke. She did it automatically, almost without malice. Jonathan's response, now, was automatic in the same way. Robotic. Almost inhuman. Someone else was at work here, using Jonathan's skin as an envelope.

He made her hurt because he could no longer make her feel pleasure. Any emotional response was better than the arid vacuum of stress and the slow poison of their decomposing love.

She sucked huge, husking breaths in watery gulps, sobbing and quivering on the bed. Jonathan left the wine jug on the dresser intentionally. She would be forced to touch the awful thing, feel the memories of her humiliation, if only to start the jug's journey to the trash dumpster.

He had lost control at last. No doubts here. A big door had slammed and now they were on opposite sides of it. It was time to leave. Only an imbecile—or an even bigger masochist—would have needed a brighter GO light.

In concept, his act was dazzling. Never again would Amanda be able to look at a bottle of vino without remembering what she had brought down upon herself. But the effect had reversed on Jonathan unexpectedly. Now wine would remind him endlessly of what he had done to her.

Beer reminded him he was no longer drinking wine.

"...maybe a third of the suburbs to the east and south of Chicago are what they call dry townships, can you swallow that? One place you can buy liquor; two blocks away it's against the law. The local heat has beefed up the open container violations, all that kinda horse piss. The public issue is 'decency.' The bottom line is cash flow. Y'know—guilt, *wrongness* is the stalking horse. The paper tiger. What they've really got big boners for is..."

"Tribute," said Jonathan. His throat had unlocked. "Your money in their pockets."

"Rightee-o, Felix. But I'd never *seen* a dry township until I landed in this corner of the world."

"What do they have instead? You don't have bars and liquor stores, what do you fill all those empty lots with?"

"Churches, my man. Loads of God condos. Come Sunday you'll think you're celled up in a Pavlov ward, for all the ringing bells you'll suffer. Enough to drive you straight into the embrace of the demon alcohol."

"Which you have to sortie out of the dry township to buy, yes?"

Bash grinned. Jonathan had rarely seen individual teeth so large. "Now you're getting some notion of how this place functions, my son." He stomped brakes and skidded to avoid a darting mongrel. Wet, ragged, freezing and starved, the dog shot a look of feverish panic toward the truck that reminded Jonathan of the wino in the bus depot. Maybe this was the bum's lost mutt. Dogs often assumed the traits of their masters…

There you go again. Running.

He had not mentioned Amanda to Bash yet. He could predict Bash's feelings on the topic: You *enjoy* eating that brand of cow patties, he'd say. Good old Jonathan softens up and goes *no, you're not being a bitch, darling,* Bash would say. You fall for it every goddamn time, he'd say. Then he would yell that *he* gave up doing guilt a long time ago. Guilt doesn't exist, he'd say. It costs too bloody much and you never have anything to show for it, he'd say.

Not mentioning Amanda was another kind of flight. Running away could be a cleansing, declarative act. Also cowardly—a child's response to a grownup problem.

Vehicles wallowing in snowbound lanes honked in the night. Water diffused the passing streetlamps into bold splashes of primary color.

Without noticing, Jonathan had begun rubbing his palms heavily along the legs of his pants. *Out, damned guilt.* His feet were roasting inside of his Justin boots as Bash's heater blasted.

The streets that ambled past the truck windows were dark, icy, sinister. The truck thrummed, wipers squeaking. Bash kept eyes front.

Jonathan cleared his throat, which seemed coated with a double scoop of thick gunk. "So. Anyway. What do they call a district where you can buy liquor legally? A *wet* township?"

"Ho, ho, ho. I can see you're really gonna love it here. Near as I can reckon, the newspapers call them 'depressed neighborhoods.' They roll over to Division Street and shoot tape of derelicts whenever they need to emphasize our civic need to contravene urban decay."

"Downscale?"

"Strictly." Bash rubbed his lip with his index finger, as though miming brushing his teeth. "You know that when winos freeze to death they turn black? No matter what color they were when they were alive. Weird. Like bones in an archeological dig. Spring thaw always unmelts a hundred or so every year— sterno and ethanol drinkers who sat down on a curb or a bus stop bench and got covered up by snowfall. When the snow goes away, you see loose clothing washing along the gutters when the sewers overflow. Some of 'em just melt right out of the clothes they were wearing."

A glance in any direction confirmed that the snow here could bury or erase nearly anything. Jonathan saw featureless dunes of hard-packed snow, weeks old, with car bumpers sticking out. Sometimes the snow lifted the automobile from the street, like a glacier on the rise. It was simple to envision corpses, heatlessly entombed beneath the unyielding drifts of white.

In the surface streets, gray slush. Black ice. Oil-slick colored frozen puddles, and the waffled grain of a thousand thick-treaded tires. Fangs of snaggletoothed icicles depended thickly from every eave, dripping venomously tinted water. They fattened like stalactites, broke free and plummeted to the ground to assimilate into the frozen Arctic topography, to evaporate and rise into the filthy air. To condense again into new icicles.

"How the hell do you *live* in this?" said Jonathan.

"Stay indoors. Drink a lot." Bash negotiated the first of several narrow turns. "It's really odd to watch the locals when snow season starts. They try to pretend nothing important has changed. They're determined. And they go sliding around in their bigass cars and crashing into each other at intersections, and the expressions on their faces never change. Like this is all some act of God and it's not their station to comprehend."

Bash had chosen the surface streets because the highway had become a nightmare of vehicles jumbled together in HO toy chaos, not so much an orderly, frozen row of taillights as a mad, Modernist neon sculpture: Black pavement, sliced from an ice frosting in double strips; police flashbars winking pink to crimson on the snowbanks; whirling frost-blue from the tow trucks; the brilliant glare of high beams pointed in the wrong directions for progress on the road. And everywhere, white, descending from the sky like a hex of legend to bedevil mortals foolhardy enough to attempt travel. White, blanketing all, the starched sheet on the corpse, the non-tint of bloodless leftovers, the visual expression of absolute death.

Bash's eyes memoed the freeway deadlock with his usual bitter bemusement. "Like I said, they *all* try to ignore the snow. Stupid. And...congratulations. You have just made your first successful excursion through the township of Russet Run without getting robbed." His voice dropped into his deadly Rod Serling impersonation. "And *survived.*"

"Russet Run. Sounds like what you get when you eat too much Tex-Mex."

"Your first dry township, me bucko."

"So that was one, huh. I noticed it looked a touch haunted." Actually, Jonathan hadn't, but it sounded good.

The streets began to shed their commotion of crowded brick buildings, metamorphosing into a series of woodland suburbs linked by scenic roadways lacking many streetlamps. In moments it was all trees, shadows, and snow. Jonathan fantasized the nighttime eyes of forest creatures, chatoyant, monitoring the motorway and trying to figure out what automobiles were.

"They're heavy into oaks in this neck of the woods." Bash was still in tour-guide mode. "Oakland, Oakdale, Oak Run, Oak Park, Oakwood. The mighty oak, lending a touch of spurious class to the progeny of gangsters and bootleggers. You'll see more Frank Lloyd Wright architecture here than in any other part of the country. Actually, I dig the hell out of the houses—there's very little ticky tacky here. The houses aren't all falling down or rotting, like in New Orleans. If I never see no more Spanish moss in my life, it'll be a lifetime too soon, you know what I'm saying?"

Splash! Jonathan had sunk back into fugue and was jolted to reality by the truck's obliteration of a genuinely awesome puddle of ice.

"Sorry," he said. "I'm phasing out. Too much time on the white line."

"Mm. Road fever. Classic case. What you need is some Terminal Turbo from Uncle Bash's killer espresso robot."

"Or a Quietly Beer."

He regretted missing Bash's anecdote about Quietly while busying himself in misery. If he waited a respectful distance, he could probably coax the story out again; Bash loved rattling on, never more so than when the talk involved one of his personal theories on why the world was so fucked up.

"What the hell is a Terminal Turbo?"

"Santy Claus—in the voluptuous form of Camela—hath bestown upon my pore white head a Krups Espresso Novo. Top of the line, state of the art. When I first got it I spent a week trying to figure out how to froth milk for cappuccino. It looked like the Amazing Colossal Man had ejaculated all over my kitchen. Whitewashed it. Now I'm pretty good at driving that ole foam nozzle. I had to drink all my experiments. Espresso is too expensive to waste. Speed while you learn. I spent the next week or so grinding my teeth to sleep. Once I got the espresso right I crossbred it with a Hot Shot. You use four measures for two and a half cups; really strong. Add a shot of Bailey's. A shot of Kahlua. Add inspiration of the moment in the form of amaretto or Frangelica or chocolate or whatever. A hybrid is born. Voilà—Terminal Turbo."

"The Doctor Frankenstein of coffee."

"It's *aliiive!*" Bash's Cohn Clive really sucked.

"It knocks you down and wakes you up at the same time." Jonathan wondered how many Terminal Turbos had greased Bash's tubework already.

They slalomed into the oncoming lane to dodge a fool trying to parallel park in a snowbank twice as tall as his Le Car. The traffic moved at fender bender velocity and that was about it.

"Hey squirrel dick!" Bash bellowed. "Get a license! Get a brain! Get some motor control! Buy a fuckin' American car!"

"Where are we now?" Fleeting panic hugged Jonathan. Irrationally he thought that alone, he could never pick his way to the bus depot through all this Bosch.

"Elmwood Park."

"Wet or dry?"

"Wet. I think."

"Then there *is* a God."

He watched the artful way Bash would shift down and cut speed preparatory to hanging a turn, utilizing the truck's momentum against the treacherous bushwhack of ice. They ski-turned onto a smaller side street. Neat houses smothered in snowfall paralleled to meet at some infinity point in the darkness beyond Jonathan's vision. An Exmas card view, with the cold light of a television fire in each parlor window. Life in the cadaver locker, the calm of bloodless blue-white flesh, the stability of rigor mortis.

The alley into which Bash cranked the truck was stopped up with a two-foot drift of snow. In the dim light it looked like a concrete wall. Tire ruts had been excavated and were half full of falling snow already. The Toyota's jacked chassis swept on through. Jonathan thought how frustrating this passage would be for a conventional auto, like trying to jog through waist-deep water. Bash slammed into first and floored it to negotiate a steep concrete ramp leading to a second-level parking slot. The garage was open to the weather; the space into which Bash slotted the truck overshot the edge of the building above by several feet. As a consequence, each parked vehicle had won a neat mound of snow on its hood, a foot or so.

"Yesterday the wheels froze to the concrete," Bash said. "It was hysterical. I finally jarred the truck loose by jacking it up and then knocking out the jack." He smacked his bare hands together and got an echo from the far side of the parking bay. "Can't go nowheres if your wheels don't go round."

When Jonathan opened his own door the frozen wind tried to shove it shut again. He gawked at the door in mild surprise. When he tried again he put his foot into it. Above them the apartment building shot upward for five floors. More TV light up there, from windows blurry with condensed moisture.

"Is this it?" he said.

"Home Sweet." Bash rolled his big brown eyes. "Welcome to Hell."

Five

"Welcome to Paradise, sailor. You've got to be Cruz."
The Corvette must have been carrying around at least eighty coats of lacquer; it looked as if it had been dipped in blood-colored liquid glass. Cruz tried to see through the window crack.

"I'm Bauhaus, and I detest idling among the peasantry." The voice came in a draft of warm air through the crack. "You get my drift? Jump in before your balls turn to ice."

Cruz tossed his NIKE TEAM bag onto the floorboard, got his legs around it, and crimped himself into the low-slung suicide bucket. Water pooled on the rubber floormat. His hair dripped condensation in the heat of the 'Vette's cabin. First freezing, now soaking.

"Christ-o-mighty, kiddo, we're gonna have to procure you an overcoat if you plan on staying in *this* distribution zone a spell."

Bauhaus stuck out a powdered and uncallused hand. He was large and fleshy-pale. Cruz saw Armani lapels tucked into a big London Fog trenchcoat with a hefty fur liner. The guy probably wore colored silk underwear.

Cruz tried to warm his hands in his armpits and nodded a quick acknowledgment. He wanted Florida, Rosie, and his bowling shirts. He did not want to make new friends. The Corvette peeled out of the loading zone to the chatter of Cruz's teeth. Bauhaus withdrew his unaccepted handshake and peered briefly at the road unwinding ahead of them, pretending to concentrate on his driving. The interior of the car stank of some top-end lime and woodsmoke cologne.

Once his teeth stopped, Cruz's split lip began to throb. Warmth brought the pain of thaw. He stamped his feet on the floorboard to restore circulation and soon it felt as though acid was coursing through his veins down there. His nose leaked. When he cleared his throat, the snot came up the temperature of ice cream. It was totally repulsive.

Bauhaus reached across and poked open the glovebox to reveal tissues. Cruz saw a crooked stack of compact discs and what might have been the butt of a revolver.

As Cruz hocked and ventilated, Bauhaus said. "So. Feel more human, kid?"

Talking to Bauhaus was going to be unavoidable. Rosie would tell him it was all for his own good. "So," Cruz said. "Why Chicago?" He'd been dying to ask that. "And don't call me kid." Now that his moustache was history, he was more sensitive about his looks than ever.

"Sorry. Off on the wrong toe." Bauhaus rummaged around in the depths of his coat. Every movement brought the backwash of cologne. Cruz's eyes stung, then watered. "Thai stick?"

Cruz accepted and fired up, using the dashboard lighter. After dusting his nose and pounding down airline alcohol, he welcomed the draughts of sweet smoke. It was another kind of warm air. Bauhaus refused the pass and dug out a chrome breast pocket flask with imitation Deco engraving and a blued dent in the cap. "Got my own insulation." He swigged and chuckled to himself.

Jolly dude, this Bauhaus.

They zipped past a spotlit welcome sign featuring the signature of the current mayor in three-foot neon script. After a few more inbound miles, Bauhaus sighed and said, "Okay. I'll tell you why Chicago, kiddo. I mean...*sir*."

That sounded even worse. Inside his skull Cruz saw Chiquita tumble, and rupture redly, and change his life.

"Had another boy. Man, I mean. Another runner by the handle of Jimmy McBride. Did his summertime rounds on skates, for godsake. Too too bad to the max. He's currently in the slam for porking some thirteen-year-old junior high school squack from Oakwood. In Oakwood they take Ash Wednesday *seriously,* slick, you copy what I'm saying? No liquor. No sense of humor. Jailbait offense is worse than cannibalism there. Just the pits. Doesn't mean dick that his little quail was totally wasted on Peruvian flake and Lite Beer. She and Jimmy did it four times on her parents' heirloom dining room table. Ma and Pa walked in on Act Five. Girl wins herself a bellyfull of bambino—strictly dark meat, if you hear what I'm saying? And Ma and Pa, being standup local God freaks, don't have a clue about how to unsmear their precious except maybe lock her up in a nunnery after she drops. They have money, they have community standing, they have a kind of exposure that I can't afford to pull. So poor Jimmy goes away for awhile, because even if I slid him free I couldn't run him in Oakwood again... and the Oakwood High footballers need their dope to go ten-for-ten this season. Shit, man, I made fifty grand off those guys in side bets last year. Paid for this bucket you're riding around in now."

Cruz held in his toke and grimaced.

"So guess who called me on the phone with a solution to my little conundrum? Go on, guess."

"Rosie." Rosie had a way with logistics, making something that was useless one place real important in some other place. Rosie had been apprised of the vacancy in Bauhaus' chain, and had efficiently tucked Cruz in where he could serve as something better than guppy chow for the Gulf.

"See, it's warm enough to talk. We're gonna be pals, you and me. You'll like the setup here. Less pressure than all that urban narcotics kingpin crapola. Fewer Cubans. Ain't some hitter shoving a MAC 10 in your back every time some Columbian dickhead overblows and gets paranoid."

In Emilio's sphere, Cruz, as an entry-level distributor, would have done a quick pickup-dropoff in the back of a Mercedes limo. He would have spoken to Emilio's second or third under Rosie. Bauhaus' web was out in the Chicago suburbs. He had come to collect Cruz at the airport personally, marvel of miracles. Cruz wasn't sure yet whether this was outback hospitality or merely the pull of a phone call from Rosie.

Bauhaus' neighborhood was well-plowed. In this neck of

the country you measured status by how clear your roads were kept when it snowed. A winding upward drive, distant city lights, a lot of trees. The Corvette was kept in a heated shell inside of a stable-like four-car garage.

The House of Bauhaus was a textbook of cash without class. The entrance door was a double-wide portal in carved, weatherproofed oak. The brass handle, center-mounted, resembled the go-grip of some medieval torture device. Cruz's eyes went first to the Cutlass box mounted flush with the brickwork. Its crimson LED telltale winked on the half-second, an electronic sentry tapping its foot with boredom. Below the box was a metal speaker grille and a lighted doorchime button. Bauhaus, sniffling, vast breaths steaming in the chill, bent to punch in his code.

Next came an oblong foyer with mirrors and a lot of hanging draperies in cancerous red. Lacquered Chinese tables bracketed the far end and intricate gold-painted molding was suspended from the ceiling. One inlaid door turned out to be a closet. Dead ahead were sliding doors of thick, smoky glass that parted with a hum and a grinding noise when Bauhaus played the proper tune on the keypad of a second Cutlass box.

Cruz examined the ceiling of the foyer. Good, thick heat billowed toward him. He was starting to feel damp and sticky. He looked closer.

"Cameras?"

"Yeah." Bauhaus yanked off his heavy gloves. "If I dislike what waltzes through the front door, I can detain it inside my little airlock, here." He indicated the foyer. "The entrance doors throw titanium bolts, two up, two down. The glass doors fracture along cleavage lines—they're more like stone than actual glass—and they'll deflect a point blank .44 Magnum round at a forty-five degree angle of entry. No way a second or third shot can be on target. By the time the rude awakening occurs, I've weighed options and moved. We've had fire drills. We can dispose of, or conceal, what the cops call 'evidence of illegal substances or merchandise on the premises,' see?"

Bauhaus enjoyed his speechmaking. Cruz wondered how many times he'd delivered this one.

"Don't forget that Chicago is still Gangster City USA. A lot of law enforcement in the Southwest still behaves in cowboy terms, yes? Well, a lot of the syndicate heavies here are still convinced this is 1930, and they swing enough clout that nobody's going to hurry to contradict them. So this is a terrific little hamlet for security procedures—authorities don't blink a lid when you install bulletproof windows. You hungry?"

Cruz's stomach sloshed with acid, and the hunger-kill of the coke had worn off. "Food would be good...if I could grab a club soda and some Rolaids first."

Bauhaus patted his shoulder. "We have everything. *Attendez vous.*"

Beyond the glass doors was a large central room designed as an L-shape with the foot bent outward and floor-to-ceiling windows making up the outside corner. Cruz drifted into the pit of the central living room, imagining how a firefight might tear it apart. The lush ebony carpeting on the floor made footing unsure in the dim light. There were three levels: Two steps up to an oval dining area near the windows, two down into a padded circular pit full of built-in sofas and curved tables and inset entertainments. The conversation pit was circumvented by an enameled rail and organized around a gigantic projection TV screen. It reminded Cruz of a large Jacuzzi or a very small swimming pool. Tubes of blue neon delineated the steps. Red neon ran the circuit of the entire room at the junctures of floor and ceiling. On the side of the dining area opposite the television was a wrought iron spiral stairway. The play of light off the dark walls indicated a pattern that mimicked the orientation of the neon—alternate slashes of smooth and textured surfaces that dashed around the room like racing stripes on a car. One entire wall featured a row of doors, close together, leading off to other chambers. More center-mounted doorknobs, ornate. The interstices of the doors were Yupped out with fake holes revealing fake brickwork, lit by garish Depression-era theatre sconces.

Organ music seeped from speakers Cruz could not see. Classical stuff; almost liturgical.

Bauhaus ignored messages and clattered about the kitchen,

seeking imported beer. The kitchen area was offset by a stretch bar, also L-shaped, with onyx countertops, leather stools, and a big brass hurricane lamp mounted at each end.

The dining room table was two-inch glass. On it Cruz saw at least twelve cartons of Chinese take-out and a couple of pizza delivery boxes. The smell of food almost made him swoon.

One of the back doorways clicked shut and a woman wandered out to pick pepperonis off a still-steaming pizza. She was not exactly naked. She wore a gauzy wrap that seemed designed for no purpose, except maybe local background color for a sci-fi movie. New World. Against the light from the dining room windows it offered her silhouette in a nimbus of blue. She possessed a round, sassy ass, strong legs, and breasts like two scoops of vanilla with halved cherries at ground zero. She wasn't much taller than five feet and didn't seem to notice Cruz at all. She posed by the window, nibbling a pizza slice. She did not eat the crust. Her blonde hair was unbound, flat as string cheese, butt-length. Cruz tried to imagine Bauhaus on top of her. It would be like a walrus raping a sparrow.

"One of my executive assistants," Bauhaus said unnecessarily. His tone pointed her out as property. "Dumb as lumber."

Cruz knew this drill. It was this woman's job to be a toy. *Woman*, if she was of age, which Cruz doubted. Certainly Bauhaus wouldn't use this nymphet as an arm doily in public. He probably tapped one of her older co-workers. In return, they got to shoot more snow up their snoots than Santa Claus had seen in his lifetime. Nobody *forced* these people to be sexist caricatures.

He thought of Chiquita again.

"Hey, Chari—set us up over here, willya?"

Cruz counted seven barstools, and saw that the hurricane lamps flickered with electric fire. The leeward end of the bar was padded leather against burnished black teak. Facing the windows was a hearth of glazed tile big enough to spit-roast a Volkswagen. Concealed vents blew out heat from crackling cedar logs. Diaphanous curtains interrupted the smooth, blank flow of window glass like gossamer pillars. The moving heat stirred them hypnotically.

Cruz sorted through containers of spicy eggplant and chicken in mustard sauce, napalm-hot. Bauhaus joined him and handed over a bottle of Grolsch. "So—what do you think of the ranch?"

Cruz's eyes followed the bouncing Chari. He skipped cost estimates and said, "A lot of security." His vision had adjusted enough for him to pick out at least two of the camera eyes lurking over the living room, plus motion sensors dutifully blinking green-to-red whenever somebody moved.

Was Bauhaus expecting loud compliments? He probably thought Cruz was playing blasé too hard. Impress me? Naah. He had no way of knowing how stunned Cruz still was. Pure physiochemical shock had not yet waned. The events of that morning were still less than a day distant.

So he supplied praise himself: "Yeah, I tell you, kiddo. You and me can sit down, relax, discuss what kind of business arrangements we need to make. We can scope the great view, when it's not so overcast and the snow's not battering the windows. We can swill Veuve Cliquot at a hundred bucks a bottle and Chari will suck our dicks while we count money. And I can videotape it from almost any vantage in the room."

"How do you compensate for the light?"

"That's for the Japs to worry about, not me. Dig in."

Cruz lifted a morsel of shredded Szechwan pork to his mouth with chopsticks. "You sweep for bugs?"

"Twice a week." Bauhaus swigged half his bottle of beer and wiped his mouth with the back of his hand. He had a belly his silk shirt did not care to hide. The belt fighting his waistline had a cast bronze buckle far too big—embossed fighter planes in commemoration of some forgotten World War Two battle. It made Cruz think of Texans.

"Easy enough to toast outside taps on the phone lines," Bauhaus went on. "Government-issue sniffers can't penetrate the electrical interference I've set up inside my walls. We modify before the good guys can budget improved equipment. Two jumps ahead, always. The window glass over there has a chemically-disrupted refraction index; that means nobody standing outside can photograph us standing inside."

"Like polarized glass."

"You got it. And all the guy outside gets is a sheet of gray." He wolfed a large, drippy bite of kung pao shrimp and chased with a plastic forkful of wok vegetables before the first mouthful was chewed. The greens were swimming in garlic. "Potential entry areas have vibration trips in the floor. Suspect movement when the house is empty kicks on the video surveillance. I have large, ugly, and very faithful enforcers ninety seconds from either side of the house."

The shrimp was good but too peppery. The food began to soothe the steel-spike aspect of Cruz's headache. Time for maintenance.

Bauhaus conducted him to a large bathroom off one of the guest bedrooms. Here the throb of the neon could finally dissipate. Cruz rifled the cabinets and used a bottle of chilled Perrier to drop a hundred and twenty milligrams of commercial decongestant, five aspirin, two ibuprofen tabs, four Rolaids and a multipak of vitamins. He plugged in extra Vitamin C, plus a B-complex to activate it. His head would turn right in twenty minutes.

He stood under an extremely hot shower, letting the massage spray pound him. He scrubbed hard and emerged red as a stop sign. Pills sloshed in fizzy water and his stomach invented a rude noise. His feet felt good out of their shoes. Muscle aches that had begun to deep-seat were headed off by the aspirin. He pulled on fresh underwear and socks. His aloha shirt was still wadded up in the Nike bag. He left it there. Bad mojo to re-don that shirt now. It was tiring enough dressing in his other used clothes.

When he came out, the big video projector was going. Freddy Krueger was chasing dream teens and delivering the blade between one-liners. Cruz stuck to the blander Mandarin dishes, knowing that between the vegetables and the vitamins his urine would come out phosphorescent. Another jailbait snow princess floated out to join them after regaining consciousness in another of the back rooms. This one had brown bangs and heavy, flashy earrings. Stunning eyes, video blue, in a blank china-doll face. Her aspect was feline and sinuous. Bauhaus sure liked his home stock young. She wore a shortie terrycloth bathrobe and did not say anything. According to Bauhaus, her name was Krystal.

They were always named Krystal. Or Chaka or Suki or Lolabelle or Star or Tanya or Chari. They always wound up overdosed, discarded, burned out. Or off the nearest balcony...

Chiqui did her trick again in Cruz's mind. *Splat.*

Cruz moved closer to the movie. Bauhaus was feeding noodles to the girls. A bean sprout clung to the two-day stubble on his chin; Chari purred and licked it off, chewing lasciviously, her impudent little tits bobbing and weaving with every motion of her aerobicized bod.

"You ready to perform?" Bauhaus said. He stood and ignited an overpriced Cuban cigar, puffing furiously until an inversion layer of gray hovered in the dining room lights.

"What you got?"

Bauhaus jerked his stogie in the direction of the bar, where Chari had set things up as instructed. Three neat pyramids of white powder were arranged on the onyx. Track lamps spotlit them dramatically.

"Rosie recommends your awesome nose," Bauhaus said. "I'd like to see you do your stuff. Do *my* stuff."

Krystal giggled like an axe murderer.

Cruz quickly scoped the coke. It looked fresh from the brick. Chari had laid out two clean mirrors, some single-edged razor blades, lab spatulas, atomizers, cotton swabs and several cork-stoppered glass vials. It looked as though surgery on an alien lifeform was about to commence at the bar.

"Door Number *One*, Door Number *Two*," Bauhaus enumerated the piles. "And Puerto Numero *Tres*." This time both girls laughed and settled in to watch on either side of him, behind the bar.

Cruz inhaled through his nose. Both barrels were clear. He raked up a stool and sat, facing off with them.

"So tell me about this stuff here," Bauhaus said.

He took a pinch from the leftmost pile and rubbed it between clean fingertips, dusting most of it back onto the pile. He touched his finger to his tongue-tip.

"Got distilled water in one of these?" Cruz said, indicating the squeeze bottles.

Bauhaus nodded. "Got Vitamin E oil if you want it."

"Not yet." Of the first pile, he said, "Offhand, I'd place this cut at about forty percent." Using blade and mirror he chopped a thirty-milligram line exactly two inches long. He looked around until handed a glass straw, and hoovered the flake up his left nostril. He let the mix burn, then cocked and shot an aftersniff, pinching his nostrils shut alternately.

"It's cut with baby laxative and speed." Some mystery additive was numbing his nasal tissues; not the anesthetic freeze of pure coke, but more likely the psychoactive saltiness of procaine or the coffee boost of benzocaine. As blow it was hardly potent enough to raise Cruz's blood pressure. But it would pass on the street. "Five or six lines at least, to jump start. You sell this stuff to high school kids? Figures. They wouldn't know any better."

"Baby lax for babies." Bauhaus gloated. "Right...babies?" The bimbettes tittered.

Cruz used the inhaler to blow back stray particles. He hung fire a moment—rinse cycle—then turned his attention to the middle pile, snorting a sample up his unpolluted nostril.

"Oh." He jerked his head back, half-surprised. He sniffed again. Several times. "Mm. Wow. Purer. Eighty-two percent or better." He lifted one of the glass vials and uncorked it, smelling to verify Clorox. "These clean?"

Bauhaus looked offended. Cruz would not put doctoring test materials past this guy, not on the flavor of the acquaintance they'd shared so far.

Using one of the petite lab spatulas, Cruz held the vial level and dumped in a pinch of Pile Number Two. It hesitated on the surface, then about half of it began to course downward, a milky tail still linking it to the pooled amount topside. Each particle emitted its own opaque vapor trail. Cruz thought of Magic Rocks. A few grains veered off and wandered through the bleach like an errant platoon of spermatozoa. That was the cut—probably pseudocoke. It beat the real stuff to the bottom of the vial. Pseudocoke was reputed to stump the bleach test.

Cruz knew better. It was generally marketed as incense, its mix granting it the legendary status of being a "legal" alternative to cocaine. Same junk as the first pile, only more artfully mixed, with a higher degree of bonafide blow.

Some people would snort fucking *incense.*

"This is pure enough to bring two, three times what you probably charge for this shit over here." He grabbed the inhaler again, repeating his routine.

The teacher approved. Bauhaus nodded, making puppy noises as he stroked his party babes. One of Chari's breasts had become undraped, and Bauhaus was squeezing it so the large brown nipple strained in Cruz's direction. His free hand slithered into Krystal's robe, to ditto.

Cruz ignored the sordid grade school shit taking place within two feet of his eyes and took on the last pile of powder. Bauhaus had begun his mindfuck: Beat the Expert. Or distract him, if your coke mix isn't subtle enough.

Somebody moaned. The drug-enhanced cycle of autopilot passion had commenced.

Pile Three turned out to be some creative twist on coke-plus, the nasal equivalent of a mixed cocktail. Yes, Bauhaus' pure coke base was impressive. Here it was cut about seventy-thirty with either ground-up Demerol or Methaqualone. The combo of coke and ludes was supposed to interbalance, cutting the sharp edges off the coke boost and replacing it with a high in another direction. Like popping barbiturates to ease off speed.

Cruz knew how efficacious *that* could be.

He began to get into his role, stroking his chin and pondering. "I'd say the first pile is for street bindles and back alley deals. This one's for regular customers you want to fool into thinking you love 'em, so they're getting something special. And the middle pile is for real."

Chari's face was in Bauhaus' crotch, trying to milk him. Krystal swayed on her stool as though someone had slipped her some catnip. Bauhaus applauded.

"Atta boy. Good. *Damn* good. Trust old Rosie."

There was close to twenty large in street bucks on the bar

between them. Only the ladies were mesmerized by its holy white light.

Bauhaus yawned bearishly, almost oblivious to the pumping and suction going on below the fighter planes on his belt. "Just great. Sold! Listen: Tonight you stay here. *Mi casa es su casa,* right? *Mañana* we go for a local tour. You want one of these?" He meant Chari or Krystal.

Cruz returned a dour grimace. Only one woman he thought of lately. "I want to eat for real. You think I'm sleepy after this?" He indicated the trio of piles.

Krystal seemed to hinge at the waist, hungrily dropping her face into the middle pile, scattering it, making clouds, sniffing and snorting and rooting about in it as though starved for breath. When she surfaced her face was kabuki-white.

Bauhaus lumbered off to the rear of the apartment, Chari in tow by one wrist. No formal goodnights. Krystal passed out on the kitchen floor and started snoring.

Cruz's day had begun with a party a thousand miles or so away. He had hated the unconscious drones there, and he hated them here. The day had ended with another, more intimate party. Hell of a way to drag down a living. Rosie had known how good Cruz's nose was, like that of a wine connoisseur. He had seen what a waste, to terminate talent such as Cruz's for the sake of an impassioned gesture. New Chiquitas would soon be lined up for Emilio. Noses like Cruz's determined the local gold standard; how many of *him* were available?

He hoped Rosie was pulling strings apace. The sooner he could jump from this place...

He managed a few more bites of food but the cocaine had beheaded his appetite. That came with the job. He took nourishment anyway, knowing he'd need it later.

He moved closer to the smoked glass windows and gazed reflectively toward greater Chicago. Snow rolled past in dust devil clouds, swirling and restless. The lights of the distant city were fire, seen through ice. It seemed compelling and romantic somehow. Cruz knew it was probably just the drugs, fucking with his head.

Six

It occurred to Mrs. Elvie Rojas that she might have been possessed by her apartment this night. The alternative was that she had gone bad in the head, and the word *senile* had never been an acceptable vocabulary-builder.

Elvie was stout, barrel-shaped and thick of calf. A penguin waddle had governed her stride for the past twenty years, but she made sure and steady progress whenever she opted to be a pedestrian. Elvie Rojas was not an old lady who fell down, dim and blinking, to bust her bones. Her bowed and sturdy legs had seen her through life's travails. Back during the War she had been nearly a foot taller, almost willowy for her era, dark-haired, coffee-eyed, attractive enough to draw more notice than most attractive women would need in Francophile Spain.

She had spent her nineteenth and twenty-first birthdays ripe with child, and squeezing out those first two had started the irreversible pelvic spread, like tectonic plates drawing apart inside of her. After Emilio and Cristina had come three more children. Her first husband, Esteban Mercurio, had been a battle casualty of the final poisonous year of the Good War, and in his wake had come an American sergeant named Bryce Cannom Welch. She had experienced her first real orgasm with Bryce. He brought her to America, legally, just in time for the McCarthy witch hunts. Once a staunch old war buddy from Bryce's Army Air Corps unit decided that Bryce's studies in comparative sociology were hot copy, Bryce found his qualifications as a bonafide war hero (two Air Medals, two Purple Hearts) less important to investigators than his newfound role as a Commie. Some bitternesses never went away, or paled. Betrayed by his own country, Bryce drank himself to death by the time Kennedy was elected.

Elvie persevered, marrying a third time.

Carl Rojas had been a grocer; had not gone by "Carlos" in over three decades. Leukemia had knocked him down ten years past. Bryce's eldest, Robbie, had fathered two grandchildren and gone on to die in the acidic flames of a chemical detonation at a Dow plant. His last wife, and children, were well compensated, so the attorneys said. James, named after Bryce's father, had eaten a Bouncing Betty mine in Vietnam; half of him died in the bush while the other half hung on for thirty hours in a field hospital. Elvie had no idea what had become of the middle child, Loris, except that like her mother, she had gone through many husbands in her life.

Elvie could enumerate such minutiae of her personal history lucidly, at whatever depth of scan civil conversation required. She was clear-headed. No tumors, no strokes. She had not needed glasses until her sixty-second year. Her diet was conscientious and she cooked most of her own meals. Knowing Carl Rojas had provided an unanticipated windfall later in life, when it came to eating healthily.

Not being able to open the windows in her room had been the first thing leading Elvie to suspect godless presences. Instead of complaining or lamenting, the incident caused her to sit and evaluate herself...to insure that a potential problem was not with *her* before taking such overt action as blaming other people or agencies.

The building's windows were large casement jobs with swivel latches. From the day Elvie had moved in, the uppermost windows had been too thick with paint to budge. Temperature could coax the lower ones to swell or jam. True, this was the thick of the winter season, but the turkey casserole she had prepared in the apartment's cubbyhole kitchen had rendered the air dense, and she craved ventilation. Snow could do such marvelous things to the air one breathed! It could be so cleansing. That was why it was frequently soot-colored by the time it stopped on the ground.

Oomph, and nothing. The window was unyielding. She

got out a little pry bar, one of those special tools that evolves from years of residence at a single location. That was when she noticed that the gouge in the sill—the fulcrum of her custom-fitted lever, also the product of years—was no longer there.

She made a small, inquisitive sound and ran her finger along the sill. She no longer painted her spade-shaped fingernails, although she lacquered them to prevent splintering.

Nothing.

It was as though the sill had been patched, sanded and flawlessly repainted. Her searching fingernail proceeded upward. The frame of the window had joined with the wooden track as an uninterrupted surface.

A cursory eye would have dismissed this as a slapdash paint job, clogging the groove Elvie knew to be there. But this was too perfect. Each detail of the window and casement remained, except that now they were not separate. They did not manufacture good casement windows like these anymore, she knew. Nowadays they touted thin sliding glass in harsh aluminum track frames. Component windows with no molding, no detail work, no pride, only mechanistic repetition. Perfection in ceaseless encore. She wondered how the craftsmen so common in the 1940s fared today.

On tiptoe she peeked at the top of the window that worked. The brass hasp moved freely enough, hampered by the thick gluey quality of the cheap paint that drowned out every other detail of this building; no pride, no pride at all. Elvie had patiently scraped the foul stuff away so the latch could do its job. But now there were no distinct sections of the window to lock or unlock. The grit-filled gap separating upper from lower had vanished, or been erased. Sometimes that gap had proven so annoying that Elvie had stuffed it with newspaper to evict the seepage of chilly air. That shortcoming no longer existed.

She could not have opened the window any more than she could enlarge her tiny apartment by pushing against the walls.

She scrutinized every surface accessible to her. Even the dust lay in a homogeneous coat, mocking undisturbed snowfall. Diplomatically she chided herself for not dusting more often.

Defeated for now, she returned to her cane rocker. Her

hands sought surcease in her rosary and crucifix. After a while she ate more of the casserole, which tasted even better at room temperature. She'd cut the spices by nearly half without harming the flavor. Eventually the television was switched on and the outside world rolled on without her, as usual.

It had become immeasurably quieter in her corner of the building since the young hoodlum upstairs had relocated. Elvie was over-tolerant, a believer in the status quo and not making waves unless provoked beyond manners. She tended to mind her own business even on weekends when things got noisy. Many of the tenants were young; weekends were for the young. She had seen the upstairs occupant a grand total of twice in her life, and had never spoken to him. He was what they called a punk these days. The word was freighted with entirely different connotations for Elvie: Jimmy Cagney in *White Heat* was a punk. Richard Widmark in *Kiss of Death* was a punk. Bryce had loved action movies, and had instructed her well. During the time federal goons were poking into Bryce's genealogy and hobbies—he had married a foreigner, after all—he had told her that Marlon Brando and any booger-nosed brat who wanted to emulate *The Wild One* was, de facto, a punk. As in punk kid.

Today punks were still kids, but looked more like the storm troopers of a bizarre alien strike force, their costumes complex and reeking lethality, their eyes metallic and sullen. Elvie saw the kid upstairs as brash, brassy, loud, probably terrified of human interaction. He wasn't *even* a punk to her.

He had generally thumped in about four in the morning, and Elvie was usually roused by his stomping around. She decided that she generally needed to get up to visit the bathroom about that time, regardless. Sometimes talk seeped through the ceiling, too loud, possibly accelerated by narcotics. Nothing was comprehensible to Elvie's ear; her hearing was unimpaired, but her schooling in slang had come from a past era. She could hear fine. The spectacles she wore were a very mild prescription. Her hair, even now, was more iron than snow. Her fingernails were not brittle from a lack of calcium.

Sometimes the upstairs rhumba got rhythmic enough to shake or sway the dusty light fixture depending from her ceiling. She deduced body heat in collision, and if a whoop or gasp bled through, often smiled to herself. A vacant niche of her heart, mostly dormant but for memories, had forever been overseen by the taste Bryce had given her for lasting, vigorous sex. It lent her a tiny pang whenever she guessed the people above her were copulating.

Lately these predawn commotions had stopped—Elvie instantly noted any disruption in the calm waters of her daily routine. The world might not notice she existed, but she maintained a certain succor in her own careful custodianship of one small and inoffensive life. So long as bad things were not her fault, Elvie felt at peace. For now it looked as though her quiet sufferance had paid off. The upstairs quakes and blarings had calmed on their own.

The boy who thought himself a punk had moved on. In this class of building, they always moved on.

Except, Elvie thought, for folks like me. Another of her roles was to keep some aspect of this building eternally stable, and she cherished it. As an elder tenant she outdated those who came and went, fading like matchflames on a moonless night. As an anchor, she balanced the building's occupancy against the transients. The world needed Elvie Rojas and those like her, even though they would never be noticed individually, like gravity, like air to breathe. As far as she was concerned, she played her part.

The matter of the noisy adolescent had been resolved. Now the matter of the windowsill distracted Elvie from her enjoyment of the television. During commercials, her frustration magnetized her back to the sill. Both windows, her eyes onto the world at large, had changed identically and without a clue or suspicious noise. She used a reading magnifier to squint at the smooth commingling of sill and sash and windowframe. It was all a single piece, as seamless as her ordered life.

Perhaps this was a punishment.

The only disruptions in the settled grit were made by Elvie's gently tracing, questioning fingers. She had spent her life refining her life, as a woodworker sanding and beveling and varnishing, and now that life, completed, needed no more work. She was left with an existence. Life had been evacuated; pride remained. Pleasure in the detail work. A vast canvas painstakingly committed with a three-hair brush, relegated to a dim corner of a dismal building with no audience and certainly no appreciation. Three husbands, she thought. Five children borne in sweat and pain, taxing the nether regions of her femininity until they sundered to yield new life. She felt phantom stabs of memory in her abandoned womb. The pain of childbearing always ran in inverse ratio to the pleasure of their seeding. Her harvest of offspring had edged her to the brink of death. For James and Robbie the clock had begun ticking with their first draw of breath. Elvie could not even name where her other children were today. She had outlasted three husbands, yes, but not by effort. She had not intended to survive them; it had simply curved out that way, planless. Without making the careful accounting of each plane and angle of her residence here *important*, she had held onto nothing. So perhaps obscurity was her lot. Old women on modest incomes never enjoyed a wide breadth of options.

They also tended to complain a lot, she chastised herself. Like *old* people. She could casually dismiss the vanishment of her obnoxious neighbor, above; why worry the mystery of the windowsill? Dismiss it, and it will be right by sunrise.

The punk upstairs had probably moved in with a dolly who received her junk mail at a much more private address for sex. Who the devil would want neighbors in three directions overhearing every grunt and giggle of good deep penetration, the intimacies of lust-balming? She had noticed the absence of the boy the way a clock is finally noticed when it stops ticking. A girlfriend, that was it. Another bedroom, with fewer eager eavesdroppers. Fine lovemaking, energetic and moist and exhausting. Purgation by perspiration, the benediction of heat and motion and contact...

Now, stop it! A smile creased her face, softening the weathered look. She was too old to giggle outright.

All right, fine. The window.

She had levered it open halfway just last week. It had not always been painted shut. Now there were no gaps, no shadows, no evidence that this window or its partner had ever been opened a millimeter.

In this building, things always went wrong in the middle of the night.

Possibly her mind had changed, not the window. It was as it had always been, except now she could not see this. The notion put a prong of fear into her recently satiated stomach. But that word *senile*...

Damn it.

And damn the building, for cruelly trying to fool her, and damn any God that would harass an old lady this way.

Outside the wind marshaled like a backswelling ocean wave, then hit the building broadside, sandblasting it with hard pellets of sleet, making the noise of salt sprinkled on tinfoil. Elvie fancied she felt the structure heave, saw the pane before her nose bow inward with the assault. She fetched up a handkerchief. Lace-bordered and monogrammed, she had had it nearly twenty-five years, and it retained the nicotined tint of aged cloth. She used it to buff a spyhole in the icy condensation fogging her side. Beyond was blackness.

She put her eyes closer to the glass. The frames of her spectacles tapped the surface. It still *sounded* like glass. The viewport she had wiped in the middle was still utterly dark, admitting vision of nothing Elvie was used to seeing outside— the streetlamps, the plowed mountains of snow, the buried automobiles, hunched-over figures doggedly walking their pets, or the flash-frozen coproliths deposited by those animals, like dark dots of random punctuation on a vast, blank white page. She could not see the houses and buildings across the street, disguised, she knew, in their funhouse beards of matte white and icicle muttonchop sideburns. She could perceive only blackness. The spyhole rapidly surrendered to the temperature and the pane was reclaimed by frost, an eye cataracting in an instant. It was extremely cold out there tonight.

Elvie's questing finger sought answers on the surface of the glass. She could panic and break it of course, and freeze by morning. She could lose control, try to find a phone, and summon the building's superintendent—somehow. He was a foreign fellow whose actual name was beyond significance in her memory. He would certainly be eager to remedy the tiresome complaints of an old woman at this hour.

Or: She could solve these strange portents in her own way, to her personal satisfaction.

The pane of the sister window reacted identically. It was as though light-impervious black paper had been affixed to the obverse of each window. When she wiped away the frost, all she could see was the reflection of her own face. Her eyes were sunken behind the tiny windows of her bifocals. Elvie Rojas still had all her own teeth. In her image she could precisely deduce the shape of her own skull.

Across the small room the network movie gave way to the eleven o'clock news. The odor of leftover turkey casserole loitered in the air, which was thick with the warmth of steam heat. And Elvie's windows admitted no view, and refused to open.

She had tired of standing by the windows. Her own schedule had been disrupted. It was past her bedtime. And now the punk would not be along, come four in the morning. She might not make her early-morning bathroom call on time.

Elvie sighed, making a sound like the steam heater. Big changes could be so unworthy of note; microscopic things could disrupt the world in which she moved. Life's big mystery. Catholics were satisfied with keeping *everything* a mystery; faith did not cleave to a desire to solve equations. This aberration had evolved before her own unhindered gaze. It was stimulating and maddening, but now it was not anything that could not wait until morning, and morning's mystery-dispelling light. Even if the apartment itself was working mischief on her, Elvie herself was not possessed. Her mind was her own. Her identity was concrete.

She turned off her ancient, tube-powered Magnavox and prepared to retire.

By the time her head met the pillow, her front door was gone. There remained a door-shape, and a knob, but no access, not even threshold cracks. From her bed, especially without her glasses, she would have been able to see no difference.

The slats of the floorboarding melted together, fusing to a smooth and uninterrupted surface. Hairline cracks etched themselves vertically on the east wall.

Behind their old drapes, the front windows faded out entirely, leaving black rectangles denser than lead shielding. The steam radiator hissed and flicked as it shut down. It never had provided sufficient warmth. Without street light, from outside, it was totally dark.

Elvie, her identity intact, consumed what oxygen remained in the now airtight room in the even, measured respirations of untroubled sleep.

Seven

Jonathan had composed a legit stage review for his own life.

A pleasant, if trivial, rep company production of a minor effort by a deservedly obscure playwright who failed to engage a popular audience in his own lifetime. Technical aspects, though unabashedly amateur, seem promising. The drama fills adequately...but fails to nourish. It is all too emotionally uninvolving, spiceless, and would play as well to an empty theatre—a work whose very safety is offensive during times when risk-taking is de rigueur. Two stars.

You are the star of your own life, his mother had informed him, what seemed like centuries ago. But what if your life was a play nobody cared to watch?

So what? C'mon, kiddo—dazzle me.

On the shelf at eye-level was a wind-up pterodactyl skeleton, one of Bash's little "Welcome to Hell" gifts. At his desk, Jonathan had been paring his cuticles with an X-Acto knife. By now he had drawn blood twice. He let the knife roll down to the retention border at the bottom of the layout table, which was a solid four-by-three surface of opaque plastic illuminated from beneath. Two long strips of Compugraphics galley proof were taped to the table, blue with Jonathan's handwritten tweaks and corrections. He twisted the windup knob on the prehistoric proto-birdie and set it to climbing the slope of the table. Its rubber wheels slipped on the smooth white plastic. One skeletal wing flapped slowly; its opposite was lame, the tab that operated it stuck in a rib strut. Jonathan removed the wing and trimmed the tab with the X-Acto, but the prognosis was not optimistic. He thought of pterodactyl remains, of ghost dinosaurs recently reborn from a

David J. Schow

glacier and fighting to negotiate the icy incline. No go.

Bash had a faultless taste for toys and owned all the best ones. He was still the caretaker of a lot of the fallout from his childhood—a Robot Commando with most of its projectiles, a James Bond Attaché Case (missing the exploding codebook), a set of Rock 'Em Sock 'Em Robots and a whole first string lineup of vending machine Rat Finks. To Jonathan, Bash's most intriguing trifle was a snow globe, the kind filled with water that simulated a blizzard when you shook it. The scene within was a miniature cemetery: Tiny gray headstones jutted from a hillock in painted plastic with part of a rotten picket fence at the rear. When you looked straight down from above, you saw the little graves were open, all occupied by little corpses, their skulls showing jeweled eyes, their cerements clutched about their bones like the clothes of dead pirates. Snug in their tiny graves, they formed a microcosmic necropolis. When the snow settled, the graves were evenly filled again, their tenants concealed.

Bash still had his Magic 8-Ball. Flip it and a mystic answer would bob to the surface of the circular window on the bottom. *It is Not Certain. Outlook Good.* When Jonathan had owned one, and asked it about meaningful things in his life, he had usually gotten the dreaded *Ask Again Later.* But Bash, predictably, had grown bored with this bargain hocus pocus. Too tepid, too conventional. In the layout room of Rapid O'Graphics he had designed and glued together his own tetrahedron of answers. With the resources of the shop and his own fine touch it was simple for him to dismantle the Magic 8-Ball, substitute his innovation, refill the glass globe with water, and deftly reassemble the sphere. After Bash's meddling, it was constructed better than it had been off the shelf. And here came Jonathan to Chicago, picking up Bash's Magic 8-Ball off the shelf, utterly sans clue, fearing *Ask Again Later* after all these years.

Bash had taken a bathroom break. Jonathan asked it, sotto voce, whether things would ever get straightened out between him and Amanda. The reply bobbed forth.

Fuck You, Asshole.

Bash cruised past to monitor the handicapped pterodactyl's climb. It was hopeless, backsliding.

"Yo, bro, how it be?" Big hands clamped Jonathan's shoulders. It was a proprietary sort of gesture he had come to quietly appreciate. Almost like being adopted.

He waved the X-Acto toward the copy sheets. "This is done; I'm just dicking around. It'll be ready to fly out of here in five minutes. Ten at the outside."

"No sweat. Most everybody's taken off; it's close enough to El Quitto Time. Wanna hear some office gossip?"

Jonathan's eyes stayed with the windup robot, hopeful. Then the copy. Never Bash. He steeled himself. The wrong answer was going to bob up. "Shoot."

"Capra says to Charcoal: 'Y'know, Charcoal, I've been nursemaiding cripples for so long it physically pains me to see competent work done so *fast*.' He holds up an ad dummy. 'I am in *pain*,' he says.

"Charcoal looks at him and says: 'We'll do our best to keep you from hurting, oh bossman.' Then Capra, like, petrifies. And says: 'You'd better do your durndest to make sure I get regular pain as good as this dummy, Charc, or guess who's gonna get your pay rises next quarter, hm?' And they both laugh. But Charcoal doesn't look all that amused, and Capra doesn't look like he's joking. And guess whose work they were talking about. Go on, guess."

"Your ownself, naturally." Jonathan swiveled on the drafting stool and met Bash's eyes. "The Big Bwana of layout."

"Nope. Guess again." Bash was beaming. He really was like a great big daddy bear.

Jonathan lost a bit of color. He could not spare it. "Seriously?"

"Serious as a heart attack, my man. The boss is impressed. That ad was for Krueger's magazine. Krueger was impressed. He phoned Capra. Can you add or do I have to spell it out for you?"

"He said, gleefully mixing his metaphors." Most of Jonathan's ripostes were funny only to him. "Jesus—you're not kidding. He was *that*...?" An ember of pride stoked up in his breast. Of course he had been trying to dazzle them, but consciously, quietly, he thought unobtrusively. Recall modesty. Try not to gloat. "What about Charcoal? Isn't he going to be pissed? Am I going to be the recipient of sullen glares from afar?"

"Nah. No skin off his dick. His sinecure at Rapid O'Graphics is a given, *mas o menos.* He worked his way up the ranks, too. Every so often, new blood's a fireball, and all the happy dancers suddenly remember that they're supposed to be on their toes. It's good for business. Last time it happened was when yours truly signed on. Nobody got shitcanned because of my illustrious presence. I told you you'd dig it here."

Rapid O'Graphics was headquartered in a five-bedroomed house on Saffron Way, two blocks distant from Oakwood's northeast corner, bordered by Russet Run to the north and Elmwood Park to the east. Capra had gutted the backyard garage to make a carport for his employees. Heavy snowfall had collapsed the structure two weeks back, burying Capra's Baby Beemer and forcing all and sundry to park on Saffron Way, battling the implacable wet white stuff and the lunatic, unreliable plowing schedules. Jonathan's first task as the new hired hand was shoveling out parked berths on the street. Bash had shrugged. That was life's great pageant in all its tawdry tackiness.

Capra owned and resided in the house next door. It had been sheer bad luck that his BMW was not in his own treelined drive on the day of the cave-in. The Rapid O'Graphics house did not thrust a business nose outward to deface this residential avenue; it joyed in blending in. The downstairs kitchen was a disaster area of each employee's favored work beverage. There was a restaurant coffeemaker with three hot pots—normal, decaf, and hot water for one of twenty teas. There was a fridge full of soft drinks and a case or two of Freixneif for the frequent after-hours toasts and the odd birthday. There was a freezer the size of a casket stocked with Weight Watchers entrées and pizzas and a host of microwavable munchies. Nobody at Rapid O'Graphics "took lunch." The plastic eateries within striking distance all served Denny's style vomit on a plate, and who the hell wanted to tough it out back in the White Nightmare?

Upstairs, three bedrooms were crowded with slanted drafting benches, files, and unboxed supplies on steel component racks. Downstairs was a darkroom with a revolving blackout door, plus a roomful of typesetting and photo reduction gear. Capra was clearing floor space for a monstrous Xerox machine on which he'd just closed a thief's deal. The living room was sofa-grouped into a comfy general-purpose staff meeting area, relaxation zone and slouch-a-rama. An offset press had been set up in a utility room formerly used for gardening storage until Capra weatherproofed it and moved in space heaters.

Littering all available wall space was paper. The first reaction Jonathan had felt was of mad bunting, of shredded party crepe with the detritus of a ticker tape parade hurled in for extra chaos. Stapled, taped or otherwise stuck to the walls was enough paper to supply pulp for a run of the Chicago phone book, white *and* yellow pages. Cutouts, cartoons, dummies, galleys, strips and snippets. Film and photos. Maps. Graffiti. Posters and ad art. Memos and menus impaled on thumbtacks, pushpins, cocktail swizzles, even tournament darts. The closer you got to Capra's office, the more frames you saw: Awards, commendations, appreciations. You could conceivably sit and read the mosaic of any given wall for hours.

Jonathan liked the atmosphere. Capra's place of business was an outpost of common sense in a world of corporate waste; funky, homey, vaguely subversive. Capra had been a product of the Sixties with his eye turned—no boast—toward the Nineties.

Jonathan's corner was next to a laughably unneeded air conditioner blocking a second story window. Once he had nested, and arranged his tools to suit his reach and temperament, he quickly felt as though Capra's was a place he might *belong.* The stool was locked to accommodate *his* height. The work surface was slanted to *his* taste. Bash had presented him with a coffee mug, a Gary Larson job in color featuring cigarette-puffing dinosaurs. Its home was on a slim doodad shelf Jonathan had erected beside the air conditioner. This was where the lame pterodactyl perched. Jonathan had gagged the cooler's vents with gaffer's tape to block the wisps of frozen outside air that shimmied through. When he checked in on the third day of actual time-clocked work, he found that someone had stationed a blue plastic brontosaurus on top of the cooler, with a Post-it note word balloon: SAY HEY DINO BOY.

The culprit had been Jessica, who made her living in the darkroom downstairs. She possessed an incredible thundercloud of frizzy black hair, flawless chocolate skin and a symmetry of facial features that suggested to Jonathan that there was Oriental blood lurking in her mix. She always wore heels to work and quickly cultivated the ritual of hugging Jonathan hello, or socking him on the bicep en passant. According to Bash, Jessica's divorce papers had come through spot on her fortieth birthday, and she had not stopped smiling since. She had the most generous mouth Jonathan had ever seen. It was intended to smile.

After that, Jonathan attracted dinosaur mementos as though magnetized. The walls of his corner were decorated in no time. The nickname Dino Boy stuck—unfortunately. More than once, Jonathan jested that he'd sleep behind his desk at Rapid O'Graphics if he could get away with it.

There was a biting reason for this.

His first night in Chicago, Jonathan had been assigned to Bash's living room couch. At seven the following morning, he listened in a semi-doze as first Camela, then Bash bought consciousness in the shower. Then came the whirr of his and hers blowdryers. Camela emerged after a half-hour regimen of cosmetics, grinned large, and ordered Jonathan to call her Cammy—everybody did. There was no way he could climb into his pants out of her sight. She hovered while he choked down two hard-fried eggs edged with char. Camela explained how *crazy* she was about General Foods International Coffees. Jonathan convinced Bash to steam him an espresso for breakfast. He did not wish to insult Cammy's cooking, and so avoided telling her that when he woke up, the idea of eating food was only slightly less repulsive to him than soaking his head in the shower. Jonathan was not a morning shower person. He usually did it before retiring. The sheets lasted longer that way. If you had a bedmate, it was pulse-quickening to slide in next to them all smooth and clean and radiating heat from a late night shower. Frequently this could evolve into a capital reason for making the bedding sweaty and tangled.

No problem so far. Just adjustments. Real coffee Jonathan

could get at work. If you knew the elixir of life was waiting at the far end of a commute, it was easier to slap yourself awake. Showers at night, after Camela retired, were acceptable. He was careful not to make any noise. He was amused to discover that his old buddy Bash was a confirmed eater of breakfast cereal. It was two bowls of Frosted Flakes or it wasn't a new day.

They rode to work together.

Camela was Rapid O'Graphics' interface with the outside world and ringmaster to the switchboard circus. She deflected intruders, greeted visitors, kept up a pleasant phone face, oversaw anything that lived in a file folder and tried to keep workaday bullshit out of Capra's flight path. She ran errands and distributed paychecks. She was the butt of cautious little jokes by the upstairs crew, who were privileged not to have to share a floor with her. Jonathan sensed the brand of group hostility that never truly grows, goes anywhere, or catalyzes action. Camela was easily the most officious of Capra's employees.

She, Bash and Jonathan rode home together.

He was good with reassuring banter and kept on his company manners. Past Day Three there were no more complimentary breakfast eggs to worry about; she was just so *busy* and he would understand, right?

Six days in, Camela began going to bed earlier. Sometimes she would clearly summon Bash to attend her. Jonathan thought of a slice of spoiled Suthrin whitebread, snapping her fingers for a slave. The second time it happened, Bash lumbered out of the bedroom and gave Jonathan an exaggerated shrug that said he did not really fathom what was going on, either. Then he switched on the ceiling fan, ostensibly to circulate the building's costly heat more efficiently. Jonathan realized the fan was supposed to mask the noise coming from the bedroom. The building was newer; the walls were garbage. Camela woofed like the Little Engine That Could when she was being fucked. She was one of those romantics who had seen too many soap operas and not enough porn, concluding that a definitive moan should accompany each manly thrust...as though to earmark it for later filing.

Jonathan's gut untightened only after Camela had gone to

bed. He and Bash burned oil, working their way through Bash's
CD collection and many sixpacks of Quietly Beer. By the third
week it was clear that a competition for Bash's attention and
leisure time was afoot, and that Jonathan was winning.

"She wants to have your babies," Jonathan said. Quietly
Beer had a nice, nutty afterbite. It was light enough to permit
consumption of several bottles without a breath-stealing bloat.
An overproduced synth tune called "The Killing Love" was
rolling out of Bash's Quattro monitors.

Bash shook his head. "The one thought that turns my morbid
attention toward Mr. Vasectomy. I know that if I brought that
back up, she'd talk about adopting kids. She's got the next thirty
years all blueprinted."

"With or without your consultation?"

Bash made a face. "What do *you* think?"

Long swig, held and swallowed. Jonathan cleared his
throat. "I think Camela's cruise control was engaged a long
time ago, and nobody ever bothered to disillusion her while she
was laying plans, and now all of those plans have stacked up,
accumulated weight, and are about to tip over and squash one
or both of you."

"Mm." Bash's hyper-talky persona had stepped out. He
groped around in the clear plastic bag at his side and brought up
a fortune cookie, which he cracked and devoured. He glanced at
the slip of paper without reaction and tossed it into a clamshell
ashtray on the coffee table. Filling the ashtray, amid dead butts
with Camela's bubblegum-flavored lipstick staining the filters,
were enough fortunes for a crowded busload of people. Some
were half-burned. Bash bought the cookies by the bagful from a
restaurant supplier. He could plow through fifty or more while
watching a movie on videotape, always checking the fortunes
before he threw them away, as though on a quest for some
ultimate revelation, or a single prediction more perfectly suited
to his life.

Bash's reaction to the expression on Jonathan's face had said:
*You are the only person who finds this compulsive consumption of
fortune cookies weird; I bet lots of people like 'em. So there, kimosabe.*

"Camela strikes me as the sort of woman who was

meticulously programmed to snare herself a husband," said Jonathan. "As though the only way anyone would want to spend time with her was by being lured, tricked. Mommy says learn to apply makeup well enough so that your prey does not see the pit covered with jungle leaves."

Jonathan was being cruel and he knew it. He had seen, from Camela's wardrobe, that she had hit the stage in her twenties where strategic concealment was more important than diet. The dressy stuff she wore to work was layered to hide the runaway widening of her thighs. Scarves with brooches would come next, to cover up the chin collection. The straight cut of her suit coats diverted the eye from the sprawl transpiring in the butt zone. Jonathan kept this observation to himself, along with a few meaner ones. Bash was pretty large himself, no skeleton. But surely he saw that Camela was not the sort of woman to deny herself anything, from double desserts to a prefab family.

Perfectly fine, if that was what Bash wanted. His discomfort and reticence suggested otherwise.

"She was bugging me about when you were going to leave," Bash said. "Find a place of your own." He killed his Quietly and rose to fetch two more, taking along a fortune cookie to fuel his kitchen run. Jonathan did not get to see the fortune. When Bash came back he was rubbing his forehead as though he was nursing an alcohol headache.

"I wish there was a slot in *this* damned building," Jonathan said. They'd had this talk once before. "That would be the best of both worlds: I wouldn't be in her way, we could still mesh for work, and everybody gets a little more privacy."

"Last vacancy was a studio, two months ago. But you might be too weird for the management. In their eyes Cammy and I are an upwardly mobile *couple.* But if I was by myself I don't know that *I* could get in here, either."

Jonathan and Bash had investigated several of the local rental agencies. Most held some very strange conformities in high priority. One desk jockey had emphasized that approvals for listed units were based strictly on availability...and that Jonathan's haircut, of course, had no bearing on any decision that might or might not be made. Jonathan had been struck slackjawed. Bash, livid, had loomed closer, throwing the rental agent into a large shadow, and had gently opined that perhaps the agent's receding hairline and bad vision were a consequence of fucking too many barnyard animals as a youth.

Scratch one more agency.

Week Three bled into Week Four. Presumably Camela had hit her period in one of these four weeks. Jonathan noticed no difference. Was she this hostile *all* the time?

"I mean—I *like* having you, Jonathan," Bash said. "Hanging out and catching dinner at restaurants and seeing movies at grindhouses downtown is my language. Cammy always knew that."

She had started calling him Jon, knowing it annoyed him. "Maybe she chose to ignore that. Doesn't fit into her master plan."

"Yeah." Bash cracked another fortune cookie and dropped the fortune into the ashtray.

Beware of offers that are too generous.

"She's local, right? I mean, you met her here?"

Bash nodded. "She applied for the desk job at Rapid. She had a fiancé in the city, Robert Somebody, who dumped her. All her furniture was in storage. I was looking at a rent bump in Russet Run I really couldn't afford solo. Melanie and I had broken up; I was going out with waitresses from the Apple Pan, for godsake."

"Yow, jailbait city. You one daring dude." Jonathan decided to have a fortune cookie. *A man is known by his deeds.*

"So, Melanie was gone, anyway. Camela shows up. We took lunch. We did bed. She said, wouldn't it solve a lot of problems if we moved in together? Partners. Maybe a genuine relationship could develop here. You know, a relationship is what you do while you're looking for someone better to come along. I thought her little-girl lisp was cute. I still do, sort of. I don't know. Somewhere between takeoff and landing this plan to grow old together popped up...and to date, I have done nothing to countermand it."

He unleashed a beery sigh, gathering air in his big hands as though trying to mold it into a shape, make his problems physical so he could wrestle them, fight to win. Bash had always disliked if-come, blue-sky shit. He massacred another cookie.

Marriage requires much serious consideration.

"Amen," he said to that one.

"Is this a woman you look at and say, 'I'd like to spend the rest of my life with you'?" Jonathan fiddled with the snow globe. The dead were reburied by snow.

"Nope. Not at this moment."

"You're hedging." Jonathan exhumed all the dead with a shake of his hand. The snow resembled whirling curds of cottage cheese.

"Yup."

"Then both of you guys are waiting for the penny to drop. You're trying to outlast each other, because nobody wants to take the actual responsibility for terminating the relationship."

"Doesn't everybody do that?"

Jonathan conceded. "I'm beginning to think it doesn't do any good to stand and watch a relationship shrivel and rot and finally drop off the tree. Even when it turns to compost, goes back into the earth, you try to convince yourself that it's *still* there, and nothing really has changed. Hope springs eternal. Guilt, too. But when it's over, it's *over*—I'm still not very good at it, but I'm learning."

"You're worse at it than I am," Bash said. His new beer was drained to the dregs.

"We're talking about you and your roommate, big guy."

Bash had a new sparkle in his gaze that said he was ready for a Terminal Turbo. "Don't obfuscate. I *am* bigger than you, squirt. Half squirt."

"Oh yeah. Beat me up. Change my opinion."

"I didn't say *taller*, needledick."

"Uh-huh." Jonathan aimed his Quietly bottle, lapsing into his demented Oriental voice: "Mister, you trying to drive car wif no gas, and car a Datsun, anyhow."

"Wrongo, chuckwalla." He rose and made a rude monster noise accompanied by a pelvic thrust. "Watch Truck-Zilla crush *buses!*" He was hale and valedictory now.

Jonathan toasted back. "You mean watch Hindenburg crash, white boy."

Bash proudly displayed the international greeting he carried between his index and ring fingers. "Terminal Turbo for two?"

"Yowzah." Jonathan replaced the snow globe and picked up the Magic 8-Ball, inverting it without actually thinking of a question.

Eat shit, pinhead.

Bash stoked the Krups and spooned up his quadruple measures. Unscrewed caps for liquor bottles. He hummed.

Jonathan had another cookie. Better than playing a loser's game against the Magic 8-Ball.

Be prepared for unexpected new developments.

"Did you see that xerox Jessica brought in?" said Bash from the kitchen. "The hairless cat? Some rare breed. Supposed to be only a hundred of them in the world. A cat with no fur. It looked like a demon, all pointy-eared and wrinkle-skinned and hungry-looking. Feral. Ugly fucker."

"I missed that one."

As a fifth grader, Jonathan had fed cats. It was too presumptuous to say you *owned* a cat, since they always vanished or got killed in messy ways, and with either the departure was permanent.

He had hated Amanda's cat.

She had named it Puff, of all things, back in the early days before a normal person would realize what a stupid name that was. Puff was an orange tabby. Amanda used to let it sleep between her legs. Dozens of times, Jonathan had watched Amanda part her legs in sleep to accommodate Puff, who rubbed against her, supplying warmth and pressure and, Jonathan supposed, a gentle purring vibration, in a kind of loathsome surrogate of sexual union and childbearing. The invader would monitor Jonathan through half-sleeping, slitted devil eyes. It insinuated itself into the warm saddle from which Jonathan had found himself, more and more often, rebuffed.

Thinking of cats now was just one more thing that demonstrated what he had lost. He *was* worse at this than Bash.

"I've always supposed that dogs and cats have the same degree of raw animal intelligence," Jonathan said. He had to say something, to prove his mind hadn't gone a-wanderin' again.

"Cat people say cats are smarter. Dog people ditto. It's probably that dogs are much easier to anthropomorphize. They lead the blind. They pull drowning infants from frozen creeks. Cats... cats stare at invisible monsters."

Invisible monsters. That had been Amanda's rationale for Puff's habit of sitting and staring into a blank corner for minutes at a stretch.

"It's the way they toy with their prey that unnerves me." Bash demonstrated just how good he'd gotten at frothing milk. The Terminal Turbo ship was about to land. "They bat it around and torture it before they dismember it. All fun and games. Mundane sadism. It's innate, keyed right into their bones."

"I think cat intelligence is unsettling just because it's so *alien*." Jonathan could not resist thinking some malign point was being made whenever Puff did his thing between Amanda's fine legs. Her taste for good sex had waned, but Puff never had to do without *his* nightly berth. At least, she had told Jonathan that sex with him had been good sex...

The espresso machine gurgled and wheezed. There is no sound quite like it. The kitchen was filled with its wracking, asthmatic toilet noise.

If Jonathan brought up Puff with Amanda there would be another argument. Of which there had been too goddamned many. The arguments always led to Amanda's stonewall views on children and life in the real world and what *normal* people did. It never failed to degenerate into a nightmare of tension and tight-lipped disagreement.

Ask Again Later. Fuck You, Asshole.

Things were too damaged to ever work out. Jonathan and Amanda were so *wrong* for each other. There were basic things that they would never agree on. He knew all that. He also knew how much he missed her. Her absence was a hole in his stomach, eaten by acid, that never went away. All the times he thought about her. The things he saw in stores that he knew she'd like. It hurt that he missed her; it hurt that she didn't miss him. And if she did she would never let on; that would be exposing a weak side. Any conversation between them was like an Egyptian tomb full of booby traps. It was fucked up to an extent made possible solely by long and intimate knowledge of a fellow human being. He would miss her right now, and he would miss her tonight when he curled up on the couch.

Cookie. *The time is right to make new friends.*

"Here," said Bash. "Fill the hole in your soul." The cup of Turbo was almost beer mug size, pulsing heat, topped with a creamy whitecap.

Jonathan sipped, and thought he felt the world change. "Bash, about me and Amanda, I..."

"Whoa. Whoa. Whoa." The humor had fled from Bash's face. "I don't want to hear any more Amanda stories. No. That's a bad habit you've gotta break. No Amanda. There is no Amanda. You copy?"

He hadn't expected such a total rebuff, but Doktor Bash probably knew best. He was as good at reading mindwaves as anyone.

"Okay. How about the box score between you and Camela."

"My dear heart and bed-pal Cammy, I fear, is decaying into one of the Butt People," Bash said sourly. He'd had enough to drink that coarseness was no longer a concern. "Breakup is imminent. But it ain't gonna happen tomorrow, and it ain't gonna happen this week. Time is required." He quaffed and won a white moustache atop his black one. "My personal sense in this matter is that she'll get pissed off and move out. Which means you can move in. But first, I think you've gotta vacate, so she and I can finish up. Your presence has imposed a stiff and mannered detente; in a weird way it's put the deterioration of my relationship with Cammy on hold. Now she's trying to prove to me that she's more fun to live with than you are. Therefore, squire, we have gotta find you a place. A way station. If only for a while. So I can knock down these dominoes my own way, and build 'em back up to suit. I *know* Cammy and I are going nowhere fast. It's my problem. I see it. And I've gotta deal with it in my own way."

Jonathan dealt with it. He'd sensed it coming. The too-polite ultimatum from the embarrassed friend. He should ease Bash through this, not shovel shit at him for saying the wrong lines. "Well...if I could find some cheap place...with the idea that it was temporary. Well, almost anything could be withstood, yes? I might even find a place you can escape to when things get too hot at home." The Turbo was sharp and strong and Jonathan's palate could not get enough of it.

Bash looked relieved. "After that, it'll be the Bash and Jonathan Show. That's a promise you can take to the bank, Dino Boy." Bash's Louisiana accent was creeping back, as it generally did when eroded by alcohol and inspired by caffeine.

"Remember that place we checked last week? It's as basic as you can get without pitching a tent. I can lie and say I'm gonna be cooking in there, so they'll stick in an oven I can use as a heater. Looks like that place isn't too lavish with the steam heat. You'll have to loan me your ghetto blaster for a bit." The compromises were stacking up in Bash's favor, and Jonathan now felt entitled to make requests. "That building does have one advantage."

"What's that?"

"It's walking distance from Rapid. Even in the worst weather I could hoof it to work."

"Worst?" Bash sniggered. "Bro, you ain't seen the worst *this* place has to offer. Yet."

Eight

It was a three-story drop, easy, and Cruz thought Jesus *fuck*, campers, somebody could *die* down there.

Fergus, majordomo and greasebag super extraordinaire of Kenilworth Arms, had informed Cruz that this abyss was a ventilation shaft, though Cruz could not see how in hell it ventilated anything unless maybe you savored catching a whiff of your neighbor's potty waft. By standing in the bathtub you were able to look out a cramped two-by-one casement window. About ten feet distant across the sheer drop you saw another sealed-up bathroom window. Others were staggered above and below on all three sides, black and cataracted the way windows next to the shower usually grow, fogged by mildew and strata of soap scum.

The shaft itself was lined in rusty corrugated steel. Whenever anyone in this leg of the building washed up, Cruz could hear a tinny dripping noise. From his vantage on the top floor it was impossible to see the bottom of the shaft even with a flashlight, but from the smell it must have been lousy with bilge and mulch and toilet leakage. It had been a weightlifter's challenge to pry that teensy damned window open even halfway, and all that had won him was an odor kind of like humid fertilizer.

Past the sill it was impossibly dark, suffocatingly close; Cruz could not perceive a bloody detail up *or* down. On the roof, the mouth of the shaft had been tarped over, probably due to the snowfall.

"Ventilation. Right." He banged the window down and flakes of paint jumped from the runners.

It was a pit. It was home insofar as there was no place like it. Best perk: No Bauhaus.

Hanging at Bauhaus' overblown wet dream of a bachelor pad held all the appeal of a Drano enema. Bauhaus was not merely a coke vendor; he was the dealer cliché loudly personified. He *played* at being a player, spending half the day with his ear in a mobile phone and the other half bragging and braying. The man was piggish, lethargic, overfed; in seconds Cruz had stockpiled a lifetime of hatred for Bauhaus' donkey laugh. He was the sort of spud who would huzzah his own stupid jokes with a half-assed chuckle designed to cue all brown-noses within range that they'd better laugh along, loud, or else. Bauhaus cut loose that laugh a lot in public, dropping five hundred on dinner, wasting good bubbly while parading his catch of the day from the teenybop coke whore zone. It was all smoke for his urban contacts—a bunch of beard-stubbled fucksticks wearing bolo ties. All smoke.

That first night, Cruz had done the AM Creep, peeking into Bauhaus' inner sanctum. He found Bauhaus beached and naked, snoring like an asphyxiating whale and wrapped around a thirteen-year-old who turned out to be a boy.

Cruz had not been introduced.

He had finally cleared the snowstorm from his brain enough to lapse out on the sofa in the circular pit. Two hours later he woke up; the revived Chari was busily mouthing his cock. Once she powdered her nose she was like something out of a monster movie. Oral-Zilla. He had not felt his pants being peeled to his knees. Escape proved hairy, not that he made all that knightly an effort. He settled for trying to get his eyes to focus and track. A pinch of nasal espresso would bang the room into full color resolution—sort of like whacking the top of an uppity TV set to make it work. Chari continued sucking his bone with demon fervor. Prone feet were visible beyond the onyx bar; Krystal was still out of it on the kitchen floor. The soles of her feet were dirty. White granules clung to Chari's upper lip, making Cruz think of inept makeup, like a child practicing. She was so boosted that sleep would be impossible for hours. She had probably been up all night, gumming kitchen utensils and humping bedposts while Bauhaus cornholed his best boy.

All that titty-squeezing and raw alcoholic-daddykins

innuendo had been for Cruz's benefit. Oh joy. This was a nest of stale eggs breaking open for sure.

Cruz needed his own haunt; he knew this instantly. A place away from this center ring pig circus. A place closer to the promised Oakwood High School action, where he could bolt his doors and not suffer Bauhaus' omnipresent alarms and cameras. The neutral expression on Chari's face as she gulped semen had probably been recorded. White stuff, thought Cruz—maybe that was all she needed it to be.

He had shaken his booty inside snow queens aplenty; enough to turn ten concupiscent rock 'n' rollers gray. No thrill no more; barely distracting. Chari had been like jerking off into a mannequin—spasm and voiding, slight pain. Her mouth was dry from too much blow. It would take something much more potent to distance him from the day that had begun with Chiquita's moist one-point landing. Cruz did not wish to learn any more about the ways a human body could come apart.

Especially not *his* body, at Emilio's vengeful hands.

Around his neck Emilio wore a folded straight razor on a chunky chain. It was a keepsake from his gang-banging days. More recently he'd had it immortalized in platinum, and it was sharp enough to carve visible patterns on air. Cruz had heard all the stories about the tricks Emilio could perform with his pet razor when piqued. Like the Vanishing Tongue Trick. The Disappearing Balls Trick. So real you'd swear it wasn't an illusion.

No thank you.

He had to make Bauhaus find him a place. Any place.

In two days Cruz had been billeted as Kenilworth Arms' newest tenant, a reasonable jog from Oakwood High.

His first shock had been Fergus, the "manager," whose job description would read "pusbag" on some document if there was any justice in the cosmos. He lived in clothes that looked scrounged off dead winos and smelled as if he drank a pint of Aqua Velva a day...perhaps to pickle his flesh, which was doughy, and spotted like overripe fruit. His ratty Converse All-Stars were slick and grimy; they had been white at the beginning of time. Maybe. Things had *hatched* inside them,

Cruz thought, and Fergus had slipped them onto his plump, horny feet while the membranes and afterbirth were still warm. Gnomish and dull of gaze, he exuded the aromas of stale dates and sour sweat from beneath his megadose of aftershave. There were brown gaps between each of his teeth, and even in this freezing climate the tips of his hacked-off and slicked-back hair were perpetually gravid with droplets of some opaque liquid. Cruz would learn that the guy only understood English clearly around the first of the rental month. He had informed Cruz—in English—that rent would be acceptable only in the form of cash or money orders, the ukase new and the fault of newer tenants, who were unreliable in such responsibilities.

We have standards to uphold here, Mr. Crooze. Fergus had not said this out loud. Cruz would have herniated from laughing.

Cruz's room-plus-bath had been designated a "studio." The floor covering was to carpet what a scab is to healthy flesh. He had gotten the refrigerator he requested. It now crowded a doorless alcove that had once been a bedroom closet. Two big casement windows overlooked Garrison Street from three stories up. When the steam heater wheezed on, the windows usually clouded up. It was a sweatbox, even in winter, sifting the rising heat from lower floors in a structure built long before insulation.

Unexpectedly, the bathroom had been recently retiled and all the faucets worked without dripping. The toilet did not gurgle. That part, at least, was basic but civilized.

Cruz had been duly unveiled as Bauhaus' new runner. The Oakwood boys were a yuppified zoo of blond-on-blond *palomitas* with firm handshakes, PR grins and Aryan eyes like video snow. All bound for med school or law degrees. You could sense the zippers on their girlfriends' vaginas. Cruz pushed Bauhaus' 70 percent cut another ten with ground-up aspirin; the Oakwood dildoes never caught wind and the extra income was always welcome. Cruz accumulated a backstock of the prime cut, the middle pile, for personal use.

Within a week his ass was bored fartless. He had hit Chicago head-on, in combat mode, and outfitting himself in two days had proven no strain. Downtown he picked up a ghetto blaster and forty tapes, boots, new clothes, and winter gear including a crisp fatigue jacket in nightfighter black with an Arctic zip-in liner. He fantasized Schwarzenegger, suiting up. Tough interior music footnoted every move.

And then a whole lotta nothing happened.

He had powered up on pink Peruvian flake and decided to start cleaning his bathroom like a maniac. That was the first time he had heard the building's ghost, moaning.

One-thirty in the morning. There had been a riot of peripheral noise tonight in Fergus' three-story firetrap: Battling stereos, slamming doors, angry Hispanic voices doing doppler riffs in the corridors. Cruz heard a high shriek that meant the black-and-tan newlyweds in 314 were re-engaged in slapping themselves toward court or jail. Some derelict old white mofo lumbered down the hall, bitching about how the Jews were infesting our great land. Cruz had first seen this occupant down by the mail gangbox. He always seemed to wear the same outfit—argyle socks and bedroom slippers, trousers hoisted high, shirt and tie. His face was mapped with drinker's tattoos, organized around harsh, mint-blue eyes and topped with lush white mad scientist hair. When the mail ran late, it was the fault of the Jews. When it came, it was only bills from Jews hungry for his money. When it was junk mail—you guessed it—Jews again, plotting to flood the country with advertising to brim their coffers. The mailman was undoubtedly a Mossad assassin. Cruz had been advised of all this hot poop when he had offhandedly answered no to the old man's first and only question.

Are you now or have you ever been a...?

Miniature stokers in Cruz's brain pan sent down an urgent request. Cruz express-delivered a load for their tiny shovels, one Left, one Right, a little extra for Left to balance. The staging area was the back of his hand. He used the leftovers to work his gums. Sneeze and relax at 78 RPM. He chased each nostril clear with a pinch of tap water, and every tile in his bathroom *kaboomed* into lucid deep focus.

He had known righteous blow monkeys who suffered hallucinations with what doctors called a "clear sensorium." That meant whatever the mind created for you to look at *seemed* deathly correct because it was not overtly strange or psychedelic, like when you did a tab too many of sophomore lab blotter and the room filled up with cheeseburger-breathing Jell-O dragons doing the frug. Cruz had forgotten Spiderman's real name, but his fate stood as parable. The dude had gotten it into his head that there were little spiders crawling all over his skin. Normal little spiders. Lots of them. It was perfectly believable, from his chemically-enhanced viewpoint. When he found he could not brush them away—he had some kind of bug phobia in general—he tried to burn them off his arms and legs with a propane torch.

Spiderman later died in a burn ward, his lungs collapsed and fried by freebasing. That trip had taken seven days.

Spiderman was past tense. Cruz knew an object lesson when one was thrown at him, and so at first lent the sound of Kenilworth's ghost no serious attention.

Velvet hammerblows to each temple eased the tension headache he was getting from grinding his teeth. He made a mental note to score some Librium from Bauhaus. His brain promptly misfiled the memo; it dropped into a convolution, lost. The stokers shoveled merrily away, grunting and heaving spadeloads of Great White into the open furnace door of his cerebral cortex. Mister Heartbeat notched from bugaloo to slam dance and Cruz's bathroom got more spit-shined by the microsecond.

Past the building's ambient chaos, his ears were able to vacuum in the errant sound and dissect it, pronto.

A moan?

It rose and fell, anti-rhythmic, with enough caesurae to render it almost imperceptible amid the banging doors and blasting salsa music. Cruz knew the coke had fine-tuned rather than stupefied him. He froze like a hunting dog on point and waited. The moan teased the periphery of his notice. Each time he thought he heard it, he flash fed new info through his mental channels. Eager neurons gobbled it up. Synapses were discharged. The first equivalent that reeled out on his mental ticker-tape was that this might be a street sound, more a groan than a moan, deep in the gut, a belly-hugger, the sort of digestive lament a back-alley grapehead makes after blowing a quart of

Mad Dog out of an empty stomach.

Somebody flushed a toilet and Cruz heard the intruder noise no further. His dark eyes glinted with a spark of reflex hostility. He was revving just high enough to punch a stranger. Badge or no badge.

Ghost, the busy worker bees in his head ventured. More likely some brain-dead junkie, circuits toasted, adding rainbow puke to the floor patterns in the hallway. Typical Saturday night action.

Outside he could now hear that guy Velasquez's brat yowling and galloping up and down the hallway. Cruz wanted to shove the little diaper-fuck down a long flight of metal stairs. The high pitch of baby screams made his teeth throb.

He had seen Velasquez's wife and litter his third day at Kenilworth. They lived close to the dysfunctional elevator. On the same day he discovered his refrigerator was schizophrenic. It could change its batty Freon mind without any sort of malfunction noise or warning, and shift internal gears from *chill* to *roast*. This tended to happen whenever Cruz laid in supplies like ice cream or cottage cheese or anything else that reeked like a decomposing corpse when inadvertently heated. He gauged the bullshit potential of trying to wrangle a better box out of Fergus Le Pusbag, and decided that he had probably already been assigned the best fridge the basement storage had to offer.

A trot downstairs, past said storage rooms, through two creaky doors and along an outside corridor, brought the erstwhile tenant to Kenilworth's pathetic excuse for a laundry room. One coin-op washer and one dryer, one of which was usually out of order. It was open to the weather. Total loss, there.

Tonight the upper floor clung to the stink of cheap whitefish. Cruz's brain pictured some pollution-poisoned aquatic casualty, dragged from Lake Michigan with oilslick intact, plunked into a hot skillet to cremate. Phew.

He pulled a bottle of Quietly Beer from the fridge and found to his relief that it was frosty. Quietly Beer did not have twist-tops. He took care not to slam the door of the fridge and perhaps bring on the curse. If it malfunctioned again, he could always chill his beer in the snowdrifts piled high against the windows on the outside ledges...provided the windows were not frozen shut. After two long, wet, lifegiving pulls on the bottle, he dabbed up the lees on his coke mirror with the pad of his middle finger. Devil dust for the gums. Finger-lickin' radical.

His ears strained for the sound of the ghost but got only the Velasquez brat. Then the page beeper clipped to the pocket slash of his jeans went off. It would have trilled, but the knob was cranked to eleven and the abrupt summons nearly launched him to cling from the light fixture on the ceiling...which was rusty, cobwebbed and bare-bulbed, and totally incapable of supporting his weight, freaked out or not.

Fucking Bauhaus.

Time and convenience had been subjugated by the vicious Chicago winter. Availability was akin to Russian roulette. So Cruz was presently the on-call victim of a procedure concocted by his Midwest mentor. *That fat baby-groper.* At the call of the pocket pager Cruz was to tromp three blocks north, to the Oakwood post office. There, in Drawer 100, he would find a surprise. A callback to one of Bauhaus' tap-proof numbers from a payphone in the post office would verify delivery and clarify special ops instructions. Until Cruz scored a more secure address or got a telephone, that was to be the drill. Bauhaus enjoyed the control this gave him. Payphones were SOP when you were security conscious. Cruz's digs, no matter how upscale they might become, would never be as paranoid as Bauhaus' little Nazi fortress. And a US postal drawer was one of the safest drops to be had in a place like Oakwood.

He chugged the rest of his brew, swallowing foam. He laced up his new boots—leather broken in but not worn, olive canvas sides, good thick cleats. Snow salts and chemicals had already done a job on the shine, but Cruz had sprayed them with water repellant. He husked into his nightfighting jacket and knotted the waist tie to lock out the cold. Clasps were snapped and the zipper run full up. A hood was available from a zippered pouch in the collar and a Velcro flap sealed snug around his neck. Outside he knew it was at least ten below.

He jiggled the knob of his inside door to make sure it was locked, patted for his keys, and moved into the stale-smelling inner hallway. His neighbor's door faced him. He stepped out the center door of the airlock and made sure it was locked, too.

He looked down. A thin black cat looked back at him, as though expecting to be let in.

Cruz neither tolerated nor disliked cats. The only time he had bothered to think about them, he concluded that the only real difference between cats and rats was that cats had learned the art of soft-soap politics in regard to human beings. He wondered if this one belonged to his airlock-mate, Linda something, the fat woman whose locked door was five feet distant from his own inside their makeshift, shared ex-hallway.

He stepped around the cat, who sniffed the air inside the airlock as though it knew what it was doing. If it lived with Linda, it could fend for itself just dandy.

He clumped to the narrow, twisting stairwell, knowing full well that Fergus was never going to repair the damned elevator. Velasquez's rug roach rioted around before the door to 314, boisterously lead-footed, thud-thud-thud. Clumsy little dick. Was everyone supposed to tolerate this headache samba because kids were too fucking stupid to know better? The diapered terrorist petrified to assess Cruz, clad in black. They faced off. The kid fled through the open door to 314 with a howl. Good. Cruz imagined using his gaffer's tape on the little fuckwad. Seal his foghorn maw and pin his legs and pitch the whole bundle of joy down the elevator shaft so they could all get more sleep.

The pedestrian ruts on Kentmore, northbound, had filled with fresh white snow. At this time of night, when there was no traffic, Cruz could almost see the beauty of winter. Swirling twisters of blowing snow threw the street into gauzy soft focus. Ugly buildings were rendered indistinct and Gothic, and clunky, battered automobiles with their clotted wheels and grilles were interred beneath a smooth, flowing, uniform layer of pristine non-color. White, Cruz had been told, was the absence of all color. In the form of snowfall, it bleached away identity, and on Kentmore Street that was a good thing. The streetlamps had become nimbused in blue, like sconces in dreamland.

He crunched along on Kentmore with emphatically big strides. He had quickly learned how to tread fresh snowpack.

Near the El tracks he passed the 7-Eleven whose dark sign read OPEN 24 HRS even though it closed at midnight. What was the difference when you couldn't buy beer there at *any* time of the day? It was a block past the El to the post office. The underpass was dark and wet, the stones hashed with graffiti. Cruz was the sole life on an avenue of lightless houses. At the first cross-street a blast of wind rocked his balance and pelted him with snow so cold it did not liquify on contact with the warmth of his skin. It was as hard as sand, or extremely tiny hail; like glass dust or grains of pepper. His eyes teared.

It seemed colder in the underpass, though windless. Sounds here were hollow and haunted. He thought again of the ghost, his imaginary ectoplasmic pal. While in the shelter of the underpass he snugged the drawstrings on the all-weather hood. His ears felt frozen and brittle.

The post office in Oakwood was intriguingly Old World, all Doric columns and marble floors, sculpted archways and real wrought-iron grillwork dating from the Coolidge administration. The counters were topped in brass sheeting, painstakingly affixed by craftsmanlike rows of brass-headed nails. On the arches were Latin inscriptions, and the vaulted ceilings bounced back your voice in a resonant and mellifluous way. A chamber of the gods...now conscripted into service as one of Uncle Bauhaus' dope drops.

He ascended the steps carefully. He'd slipped the first time here, almost cracking open his head on the ice and granite. The huge brass-framed door swung ponderously back with a *whoof* of air. That door was as heavy as it looked, and took a bit of muscle to bully open.

Heat rushed toward his cheeks. When he opened the inside double doors he saw a woman in a long, burgundy coat striding his way with a wool glove full of fresh mail. He tarried a beat, then decided to hold the door for her. She met his eyes quickly, with a confined, tight-lipped smile, noncommittal but acknowledging the courtesy. You never knew *who* you might catch lurking around the P.O. at this hour.

She had a cheeky, feline face half-hidden in the winds of a truly heroic muffler which looked hand-knitted. Her snubbed nose peeked cutely over the top fold. Her eyes were widely spaced, bright cornflower blue, with a slight bulge that lent her a little girl aspect. She probably still got carded at drink-ordering time. Framing her face was a cloud of black, frizzy hair restrained below by the muffler and above by bright red fur earmuffs. Her hair had trapped snowflakes, and droplets glistened magically like Christmas ornaments.

She hiked her muffler over her nose without breaking stride as Cruz let her pass. A double row of gold eagle buttons ran down the front of the coat, and she wore brown leather boots with two-inch heels, as if daring the snow to try spilling her. Even with the boots she was petite, five-five or thereabouts, with just enough rounded bottom contouring the coat to give her away. She plodded into the snowscape with an aggressive step that made Cruz imagine the muscles in her legs, and smile.

Now heat was boiling up from his shirt collar as well as from the sanctuary of the post office lobby. He cracked the door to peek back out. She was southbound on the same side of Kentmore he had just come up. He had not noticed footprints. She lived in this neighborhood, it looked like, within easy reach of the P.O. even this late at night. Or maybe she was going home from somewhere else. He could most likely see where she lived from his own corner windows.

The sudden horniness boffed him like a double whack of Jack Daniel's to the occipital lobe. Sometimes desire could clout you unawares. He knew, as he watched her grow vague in the weather, that he was going to spend tonight with a tormentor of an erection unless measures were taken. He was by himself, defenseless, and the brief sight of her had unhinged him. His buttocks clenched sympathetically with the need for below-the-belt nourishment.

There was only him. And the Kenilworth ghost. And Frosty the Blow Man, there in his dresser drawer.

Whoo, lord!

Upon examination of Drawer 100, Cruz found that Bauhaus had made his walking weight heavier by an entire kilo—a guaranteed no-shit felony bust for dealing, should anyone wearing a badge opt to play poke-and-pat. Never mind that there was another baggie just like it already stashed back at 307. Yesterday's pickup, still sitting. Not smart.

His headache surged back, trying to unsocket his eyes from within. Son of a bitch!

He plugged change into one of the payphones, which were situated within small alcoves near the brass double doors.

After riding out Bauhaus' stupid answerphone message (backed with the *Thus Spake Zarathustra* riff Cruz knew from *2001: A Space Odyssey*), he punched in a digital code that cued a line test. If the line proved clean, he would then speak to a real live person. Somebody had to be home, or Cruz would not have been beeped to call this number.

A bit more electronic freeform. Then Chari's voice, sniffling and bleary: "Uh yeah, hello?"

"Get Bauhaus. I didn't drag my ass out into glacier land to try talking sense into *your* dead ass."

Chari hiccupped and chortled. The receiver hit the bartop with a *thunk* as Sugar Doodad was paged. Cruz's bullshit threshold had maxed at critical mass already...

...and the image of the woman he had just encountered burned above and below. He could see a small puddle of snowmelt, where she had been standing, near the smaller mailbox windows.

"Howdy, kiddo. How's the ole hammer danglin'?"

"Why the fuck have you loaded me like this? You want me to wear fucking *bells*? Maybe get a tattoo on my forehead that says DOPE?"

"Calm it a notch, boyo. 'Tis the season to increase the traffic flow. Supply. Demand. You know? *Profit.*" Bauhaus let go of a boozy sigh. "Makes ya hard, don't it?"

Cruz was having a hard time tracking this amateur hour owlflop. What would an operator like Rosie say? He tried to draw even breaths. Rosie would say. Rosie would. Rosie...

"The Future Politicians of Oakwood need gassing up for their round of holiday parties," said Bauhaus. "Family fun, a bit of wife swapping, dirty secrets out of closets, shared cognac with Grandpa, that brand of happy horseshit. To relieve themselves of the tedium, they arrange *other* parties, where they can assemble with their peers to partake of illicit substances. Which is where you and I come in, right after the procurers who supply the tarts who'll fellate a whole fraternity for one price. That stash will be out of your hands in a matter of hours. Trust me. Weight that doesn't *move* doesn't make me a nickel."

Rosie would say...*take advantage of the 24-hour party going on inside the skull of this piker. Do what he wants but get what YOU want. That's as far as you have to pollute yourself. You'll be around when he's history.*

"All right. I don't want two bricks in my life after tomorrow night." Oh, god...before the cut, before markup, it was still nearly a hundred in flake under Cruz's wing. He held even. Try to hold cool. Try not to blow Rosie's faith. "But two *kilos*, man..."

"You'll have to pass a lot more by the end of the week, believe me. Hey. Don't pop a vein. I know what I'm doing."

Cruz heard one of the Jailbait Twins laugh in the background.

"Which reminds me. You've run girls before, Bauhaus. Well, you're gonna run one right over here. Tonight. Not one of those brain-dead twinkle twats like Chari or Krystal. Someone above the age of consent."

"Here's to...uh, whatever his name was. McBride!" Cruz heard ice clink in a highball glass. Jesus, but Bauhaus was a moron.

Thinking of Bauhaus made him think of Emilio, with his slick Miami network, his hotshot Marielito pilots, his paramilitary trucking chain in Bolivia. Emilio could be *très* scary. No false fronts there.

"Pay attention and just *do it, por favor.* And one more thing." He consciously kept from swearing or demanding. Bauhaus could probably have people snuffed, too...only up here it was done differently.

"What else do you need, Cruz?" Not *kiddo.* Cruz was treading a line, yessir. Careful; don't judge a dweeb by the flash of his plaid.

"You want me to handle this much blow, I think I'd better have a piece."

"I presume you mean a gun, son, and not a piece like you

already asked for, to wit, a twit." Bauhaus had regained some of his ho-ho. "A gun. *La pistola.* Yes?"

Cruz decided to push it one more notch. "Anything nine-mike-mike not made in America, preferably with better than a mickeymouse eight-round clip."

Bauhaus harrumphed. "I'll call Marko. Yo, homeboy!"

Cruz wanted to start smashing the receiver against the wall, imagining both to be Bauhaus' cranium. The coke tipped him over.

"Do you *read* me? And a party girl. She'd better not have any exotic infections whose names are, like, acronyms, you dig what I'm saying? Don't smoke me and don't pull my dick. Otherwise you can pound your stash up your loading dock with a mallet!"

"Chill out, kiddo. Cool it off. Freeze it."

"And don't call me kiddo."

A moment of measured silence. Then: "No hard feelings, right? Right. Okay. Got it all jotted down on Chari's butt. Girl. Gun. PDQ. Now, if you're ready to listen, *Mister* Cruz, I'll give you the whens and wheres."

"Yeah. Sorry. It's just..."

What was it? Frustration, mostly, at the quick flee and the alien digs. Anger at giving up Rosie for Bauhaus. Irritation at the Oakwood High dips. The decaying orbit of life in general. How could he put this into words for someone like Bauhaus?

"Forget it, Cruz. This place is getting to you and you need a little R&R. My specialty. You hear me? First aid is on the way, troops. Now write this down..."

Cruz dutifully recorded vital stats and hung up without amenities. He bundled the sniffproof package of cocaine into his battle jacket and prepared to meet the night again. It would take all of the beer in his fridge, probably, just to get to sleep and he did not feel much like drinking alone.

Enough of the mystery woman's new footprints remained in the snow for Cruz to trace her to one of the houses bunched together on the east side of Kentmore, half a block past a side street actually named Kenilworth. Perhaps, he thought, the backside of Kenilworth Arms actually reaches to the next block; the building was so sprawled it was difficult to tell. The trail of rapidly filling depressions led to a skinny two-story place with an ornate porch and unshoveled driveway. No car. Maybe there was a garage backed onto the alley. Etched cameo glass distinguished the front door, which was sheltered from gale force by an uglier and more functional storm door. Cruz estimated that if he squashed his face against his Kentmore window, he might just be able to see part of her front yard. The windows above him were all dark. To home and to bed.

He could hear himself breathing, his body laboring against dehydration in the cold; felt his breath leave him in unraveling clouds. He thought of his hands, warming the hemispheres of her ass. He wondered if the hair on her pussy was as curly, as black.

Time for another jolt, nasally speaking. To keep the pornographic movie in his head unreeling headlong toward the Good Stuff, which starred Flagpole Cruz penetrating every orifice into which he might conceivably fit. Oh god, Bauhaus had fucking well better not nod off before making the right phone calls...

Back at the Garrison Street door he kicked snow from his boots and hit the stairs. Halfway up he nearly collided with someone headed down at twice his speed.

Cruz was lugging enough nose candy to make him instantly reactionary. He sprang back a step to cut himself some striking room. The last toot had tuned him tight.

The guy on the stairs jerked backward, flinching. He did not drop the Del Monte cardboard box he had in both hands. He was wearing thick gloves in yellow leather—trucker's gloves, thought Cruz, the kind with the red balls on the wrist fasteners. A knit cap was sleeved down to the guy's eyebrows. He wore an off-green parka, hood down. It had a lot of zippers and pockets, like a space suit. The big floppy hood was fringed with some kind of genuine fur. It looked really warm.

Cruz let his fists open slowly. The guy three steps up relaxed, not panicked, just startled. The time for attack had rushed past.

"Whoa. Me friendly." His green eyes seemed mildly inquisitive, not frightened, almost disinterested. Preoccupied. He held his position, aware he was blocking the stairwell.

"Sorry," said Cruz, his hands still up in supplication. "It's late, you know?"

The stranger nodded.

In the box, Cruz could see the tops of manila file folders. A lot of paper. He dismissed the guy as a burglar. "You uh moving in?"

"Yeah. You could say that." The green eyes examined the planes of Cruz's dark, now-moustacheless face. Perhaps searching for an attack breach.

"Kinda late."

"I like being unobtrusive," the guy said. "I just couldn't resist freezing my nards off in return for a fabulous view of everything buried in snow. Or, I'm just the slowest and most methodical home invader in Chicago. I've never been caught because I put stuff in instead of stealing it." His eyebrows went up and he shrugged. Sense of humor...or not?

Cruz decided to stop being such a dick. "Like Santy Claus." Every tenant was a potential customer, he thought. This guy looked jumpy enough to perhaps crave an occasional piece of the Rock. "Moving in, huh?"

"Yep. 207, that's me."

"You're right under me. 307. If I party too loud, just come on up and join in."

"I'll remember that." He shifted the box weight to his opposite hand.

"You get the tour? Meet Fergus, all that good jive?"

"Oh yeah." The newcomer's lip curled, exposing incisors. He rolled his eyes. "Pretty scary. I was thinking maybe that guy is dead and he preserves his body from decay with all that cologne."

Cruz grinned. "Only it don't work so good. I'm Cruz."

"Jonathan. Meetcha."

Cruz screwed his face funny, as though unused to people having names so long or highborn-sounding. *John-a-thon? Eeuw, thenk you veddy much.* The thought didn't rate more than a half second.

They shook hands, gloves crumping together with that badass saddle noise.

"You need a hand with any of this stuff, Jonathan?"

"Not really; I'm almost done. Noticed the elevator was shot."

"It's always broke. Forget it. Forget the laundry room, too. It's like a waiting room in Hell."

Jonathan snorted. "Only time I could borrow a truck to move my junk was this late; that's another reason I'm creeping in and out right now. You a night worker or something?"

"Sort of. I'm just up late a lot." He looked at Jonathan's feet and saw Reebok hightops, soaked fully through. Not from around here. "Lotta books and papers and stuff. You work in an office?"

"Sort of." He'd run dry fast. "Listen, I'd better finish up before I drop. I've got to roll in to work at nine. Who knows, my truck might be buried already. Cruz."

Cruz watched the green eyes go vague, like green computer type blinking impatiently until data is squirreled into the proper hidey-hole. This Jonathan guy was storing his name.

He backed down the stairs to let Jonathan pass, and dusted the remainder of loose snow off his battle jacket before it could melt and soak in.

If Bauhaus delivered tonight, poor Jonathan might be kept up till sunrise.

"Guess I'll catch you later, then. Jonathan."

Jonathan nodded one more time, and they went their ways.

Guy probably thinks I'm an idiot, thought Jonathan as he dropped the box into the back of Bash's Toyota truck. While clearing out he'd accidentally taken one of Bash's fileboxes, how comic. Now it had to go home. He needed to make one more trip anyway. Then his move, such as it was, would be finished.

He lifted the last two boxes of this run, mostly goodies purloined from Rapid O'Graphics, and headed back for the Garrison Street entrance. Half in jest, he thought to himself that that guy Cruz looked sort of like his idea of a dope dealer.

Nine

M ario Velasquez heard the bad man coming back, and hid. The biggest event so far in Mario's short life of two years had been his recent promotion from toddler phase to a new frighteningly exhilarating mode of locomotion. Not yet potty trained or articulate beyond urgently loud monosyllables and parroted commands from Mama, Mario tarried in Kenilworth's third-floor corridor, packed into didies, a food-stained T-shirt and miniature track shoes with reflectorized insets on the heels. He was pretty grimy but it was not his mother's fault. Not old enough to read his second-hand shirt, which proclaimed I'M A LITTLE STINKER, he nonetheless tried to live by this maxim.

When he heard the tread of boots and voices on the stairs, he made a bubbly whine and retreated to the open door of 314. He never resisted peeking. There was a crack in the doorjamb, so peek he did.

His Papa had called the bad man a *chingon* but Mario did not retain the word. He saw snow-crusted boots and black clothing. The bad man scanned the hallway in both directions before digging out a set of keys. Mario heard the keys and instantly coveted them more than anything in the world. Safe in his hiding place, he duplicated the motions the bad man made with the keys. So shiny, so gloriously *noisy*. The lightweight Masonite door opening into the hallway made a hollow noise as the bad man bumped around it. As it closed a skinny black cat darted through just in time to keep its tail from getting truncated. The door thunked shut. The cat glanced quickly rearward, hit full stop, and sat to lick itself in case anybody was watching.

Mario immediately forgot the key ring existed and visions

of the *gato negro* consumed the grabbiest portion of his mind.

Usually, when Mario decided a thing should be his and his alone, and he encountered resistance, he gave vent to a shriek that could gasify brain cells. Then charge: Hands in the air, barrel forward, scream until all breath is gone. His signature gallop made the third floor sound as if it housed the largest and most clamorous rats in Oakwood. Whenever Mario was conscious, he ran, and whenever he ran he squealed.

His mother, frustrated at her first son's wanton demolition of the few good family hand-me-downs within reach in their tiny apartment, had finally let Mario run around in the hallway. She admonished him to never go near the stairs, as if he could understand the consequences. The elevator was no danger. It never worked, and the third floor doors seemed permanently shut. Letting Mario loose was a compromise. He was quiet in general but now she had to monitor him every minute or so to ensure that the reason for his silence was not the brand of infant death she now spent most of her waking hours fearing. Apart from Mario there was Eloisa, and after Eloisa…well, she and her husband had not decided on a name, yet.

Mario knew that Mama was occupied with kitchen duties, the steam industry of bubbling pots and hot skillets. A late meal for Papa, who was soon due home. The meal was not yet ready for Mario to gleefully fling it in all directions. Mama's head poked around the kitchen alcove, saw Mario near the front door where he was supposed to be, and withdrew. Mario watched her. Right on time. Only Mama could perceive the invisible barriers inside of which Mario had been remanded.

All Mario could see or care about was that cat.

He crept beyond the door, into the animal's sightline now. He saw it, he wanted it, so he squealed. It was an uncertain interrogative, not yet pitched to shatter Plexiglas. Almost a coo. The cat crouched, unsure of whether a chase was about to commence, unwilling to move if there was no attack. The creature in diapers was not that large, but it emitted weird screechings, and the cat had long ago learned to dodge the questing paws of children.

Mario determined that if the cat of his desire could not be

nabbed before Mama did her next forty-five second surveillance, the prize would be lost. The cat would run.

Mario unleashed his forward-ho scream and blasted off, thud-thud-thud.

The cat did not dally. It accelerated claws to carpet, puffs of rotten fiber flying in its wake. Its sleek speed easily aced Mario's clodhopping gait. It zipped around the hallway's western corner.

Gone!

Mario tried to hang a speed turn, but his top-heavy momentum tipped him over and the pursuit cut short with a *clonk* of impact as he fell, palms slapping the floor, forehead bouncing off the nap. His big brown eyes welled with easy tears. He sucked in a breath destined to be expelled as a shriek of historic volume. Mario fall *down*.

He hesitated.

One of the icebox doors in the next corridor hung ajar. Generally they were nailed shut, drowned in paint. Mario was used to seeing them closed. He forgot his abraded knees and disposable pain. His plotted caterwaul leaked forth as an upward-curving peal of fiendish delight. He scrabbled to his feet and thundered over to the target. The *gato* had to be holed up in there. Foolish *gato*.

"Mario! Mario, *donde esta?*"

Poop. His cover had already been blown. Mama had no way of knowing that he was just around the next corner. Her next step would be the usual maternal freakout. The next cry of Mario's name was strident.

The *gato* would be lost in seconds if Mario did not drag it out of its lair. He knew from experience that the tail part was the best when it came to *gato* dragging. It was sort of like a furry suitcase handle, almost unbreakable. Almost.

His next screech was victorious. He jerked open the bottommost icebox door. *Oho, gotcha furball, now you're gonna eat some torment, for running!*

The *gato* was not hiding inside.

Marisole Velasquez knew that one of the calculated gambles

of motherhood was leaving one child unobserved so that another might be rescued. Baby Eloisa was swaddled on the couch, busily trying to plug a pacifier all the way into her mouth and waving her legs like fat antennae. She would not roll off onto the floor in the few moments it took to collect the wayward Mario. Probably. If she did, the whole building would share the event in a hurry, but in the meantime Mario had once again pulled his jailbreak routine and needed rounding up. Marisole could track her first son like a bloodhound, correctly picking his most likely trajectory, her motherly seventh sense guiding her. She continued calling his name. Her tone would suggest that for mounting a sortie alone he would get his *cachetes* whacked.

She rushed into the corridor, trailing fulsome cooking smells. Once she was gone little Eloisa made a face and filled her cloth diaper with essence of infant, a double scoop. Eloisa smiled toothlessly at the abrupt burst of warmth. She was happy to keep her mother so busy.

The swell of Marisole's third pregnancy was sufficient to list her weight as she heeled around the west corner. She had to clutch the wall for support. Already she was breathing hard, panting. A voice behind the door of 320 shouted a general order to shut the fuck up out there. Such imperatives rarely came with backup. To Marisole it was the same as street noise, something to be ignored. If construction workers whistled and hooted at you, you paid them no mind. Marisole had not been whistled at in quite a while.

Sweat, mostly from the kitchen, speckled her neck and forehead. She called again, but only the first two syllables of her errant son's name made it into the air before she spotted the single, Mario-sized track shoe. It was lying on its side near one of the disused, flush-mounted icebox doors. The laces were still tied.

Eloisa, back in 314, would begin crying any second now.

Marisole ran to the shoe as best her pendulous belly would permit, and petrified when she saw the blood staining the floor. A wide, wet slide trail had mixed with floor dirt to make thin mud. It began next to the abandoned shoe and swept straight into the icebox door, which hung wide open and was supposed to lead no damned place at all except into a one-by-one cubbyhole lined with sheet metal.

Which it did, Marisole saw.

More blood was pooled on the floor of the tiny box. So much more blood than Mario's birthing had brought.

From the corner, a black cat watched, not very interested, licking itself methodically. Mario was nowhere to be seen. Worse, he was no longer making any noise.

Marisole heard Eloisa begin screaming back in the apartment; hitching, gulping baby bleats that might signal colic. By then, Marisole was pounding on the door to 320 for help and screaming herself.

Mario's tiny foot was still inside the shoe.

Ten

Jonathan felt dead below the ankles, his gym shoes slushed, his socks saturated and freezing, his toes like cocktail ice cubes. Okay, okay, Bash was right, Capra was right; he'd buy some boots. The winter was not going to recede in time to spare his footgear. Okay. I give. Chicago wins this round.

And some paranoias never rinse clear. He decided to lock Bash's box of stuff in the cab, despite the fact that it was late at night and no passing thief with any sense would be tempted by the boxes of books and junk awaiting the offload. It was snowing, for godsake. The only other person he'd seen for hours had been Cruz, his neighbor to the north.

He did two flights of narrow, angled stairs with his last load of this trip, feet squishing along. This box had the towels. He could use a basin of hot water or the steam heater to thaw out.

Several other boxes were stacked next to the outside door of 207. One at a time they would have to be lifted through and placed to the left of the door in a pile. Then he could shut the hallway door, open the *other* door to 207, and repeat. U-Haul aerobics. Technically, the tiny airlock's other door, the one to his back now, was 205. His neighbor, who had not yet manifested, also had a key to the outside door. It seemed a needless and labyrinthine complication until Jonathan figured out how the older apartment had been subdivided.

His hair was damp. He should've worn the parka hood. He chided himself that he was new to this climate and could make his body sick fast by being too casual. He'd gotten ill enough Texas summers by walking from century-mark heat into a refrigerated supermarket.

The parka had been his father's, long in the closet. This was its first opportunity for practical use. Jonathan wiped his face, shucked the heavy coat, and searched up towels from the box circus.

The bathroom light was a naked bulb on a pullchain, spattered with thick slops of white paint from the apartment's recent and indifferent makeover. The el cheapo latex lay thick as barnacles on the switchplates and had blocked up some of the electrical outlets, not that plugs were in abundance to start with. This building's circuitry would probably scare the ass hair right off any sober electrician.

Jonathan set a dish drainer loaded with kitchen implements into the bathtub. It was a freestanding clawfoot tub with one of those circular shower curtains. He twisted the hot tap on the two-faucet sink and noticed the sink had also been painted, probably to make it look more like porcelain. He snapped up a blade on his Swiss army knife and gouged down until he got rust. Judging by the paint strata, the sink's factory surface had last been exposed to air sometime around the Great Depression. The paint job in toto clogged the air with its stuffy industrial fumes. Jonathan had done time in enough low budget residences to accept an indifferent paint job as a norm, but who was this half-assed cosmetology supposed to fool?

The whole move stank of the depressing and inevitable. He felt suitably cast away by Bash, who was full up with his own problem. Jonathan already knew what *her* name was. Bash had promised, awkwardly, that the whole rancid romance would be old news within weeks. Two months at the outside. The prognosis was not happy-making.

Meanwhile, life at Rapid O'Graphics had to move on. Bash's homefront situation was now stressed to the point that Jonathan was required to telephone prior to returning the truck, even at this hour of the night. Camela would not lift the receiver, he knew. Bash would wait out front and taxi Jonathan back to Garrison Street. That way, Jonathan and Camela would not have to trade any more tight silences. Bash would apologize again. Jonathan hated that part most.

Dead of night. Amanda would be sleeping by now. He

wondered bitterly if she was sleeping alone.

Movement caught his eye from the bathroom. He dropped a moldy Rubbermaid plug into the sink drain as soon as the water ran hot.

Oww; his feet were beginning to tingle.

The passage to the bathroom from the studio's central room was formed by a dead space across from a doorless closet. He traced fingers along the wall as he looked out. The hair on his arms scared up and he felt immediately that he was not alone in the apartment.

Some paranoias...

He saw a curl of blackness wisp around an encyclopedia box and vanish.

In Texas one summer night, Jonathan had been washing dishes, wearing swim trunks and thongs. Those were the days before he or Amanda could afford an air conditioner to knock back the temperature. They sweltered, invented shade, and compensated. Were things really happier when people were broke? Every so often Jonathan would wipe his face with a rinsewater-wet hand. The sensation of air evaporating moisture was a noble, simple pleasure. Puff, Amanda's wretched cat, was aprowl and Jonathan could feel its tail brushing the backs of his bare calves. Several times he kicked without looking to shoo the damned beast. The ticklish intrusions did not curtail. He finally stopped what he was doing to boot the monster well and soundly...and discovered a tarantula as large as his hand making the slow climb from knee to thigh on the back of his right leg. Jonathan reinvented the St Vitus Dance in the next few seconds. His taste in clothing refocused toward long pants.

He thought again of the tarantula, and shuddered. Spiders, big spiders, *noo thanks.* Ghosts of spiders past, come to haunt him?

It was, he saw, a cat.

It peered, golden-eyed, around the boxes, awaiting a decision. Fuck, feed, fight or flight. The intrusion was not that much of a bother. Without Amanda he did not have to be so instantly reactionary. This was not Puff, that obnoxious little orange shithead.

"Well."

The cat was slim, the blades of its hips apparent through thin fur. Except for an unambitious white shield delineating its breastbone, it was entirely black. The front door was still open. The sound of Jonathan's voice did not launch it into escape gear.

"What're you doing in here, fuzzface?" He crouched down. "Who do you belong to?"

Cats don't belong to anybody.

"Sorry, right—cats don't belong to anybody." He watched the tail switch idly. No panic moves. This was getting funny. "I suppose you wouldn't care for a midnight snack? Unlike most pussycats?"

Look close. Do I look like Morris or Garfield or one of those overfed numbfuck cartoon cats to you?

"Right." Most of Jonathan's food supply was in the last load of boxes, yet to be transported. He did have some luncheon meat and makings for brown-bag specials already in the refrigerator. A sliver of turkey loaf was no biggie. Jonathan moved closer and went down on his haunches to offer it. "Check this out. Come on…"

Trusting enough, the cat ambled across the room and after a perfunctory sniff, ate.

I suppose now you want me to rub against you or purr or some lovey-dovey thing to prove you're not such a rotten son of a bitch human being after all, right? Jesus, are you sunk.

"Welcome Wagon," Jonathan shrugged. "I don't suppose you could stand guard over my junk up here while I catch the last load?"

No way.

"Thanks ever so much." Best not to rile the natives. This quaint hovel was no home base. "C'mon—in or out." The doors had to be locked.

He peeled off his frigid wet socks and soaked each foot alternately in the sink until circulation was agonizingly restored. He changed into two pairs of fresh tube socks, *ughhed* back into his wet shoes, sealed up his parka and dug for Bash's car keys.

In the airlock, the cat waited, sitting Egyptian style, tail

flicking. When Jonathan opened the outer door it slinked into
the hallway.

"So what do I call you? Do you have a name?" He was
abruptly embarrassed by the thought of some other tenant
hearing him.

Cat is fine.

"*Dawg*, maybe. I never did get around to getting another
dog." He was babbling, and deserved the flash of cat anus he
got as the animal strolled off.

By the time Jonathan returned with his final payload of the
night, he would find Kenilworth Arms girded by police cars.

Eleven

Her opening line was: "Bauhaus tells me you're a Chivas man at heart." She hoisted the bottle for inspection.

Cruz's eyes lent the jug the millisecond it deserved, and hurried to catalogue the ups and downs and ins and outs of his after-hours visitor.

His brain replayed the line about how the first fifteen seconds of physical attraction were the most vital. His heart and glands woke up. Adrenaline flushed clear. Her knock on his outer door had catapulted a bolt of panic through his midsection. There was more snow inside his apartment than outside. With such a big taste of coke, a bigger taste of hair trigger xenophobia floods in naturally—like gasoline seeking its own level when you were siphoning it out of some stranger's tank.

The snowflakes spangling her shoulders and shoetops hung in the phantasmagoric instant between crystalline and droplet. Cruz's eyes busied themselves. He had expected some skittish and sleepless *mexicana*, hollow-eyed, ready to suck or engorge anything in trade for one more snort of angel dust, or maybe a wink of jobless slumber.

She was faster than him. "You're Cruz. I guess that makes me Jamaica. Hi."

She had a purple streak job and Isis eye paint speckled with highlighter frost. The aggressive cheekbones and slash brows made Cruz think she might be Italian, maybe second or third generation Brooklyn, lacking the slovenly walk or the baby maker hips. She was wearing a long car coat, black roughout suede, with a lush collar of real mink. She began thumbing loose the glossy ebony buttons.

"I'm sort of like Count Dracula," she said. "You have to invite me in the first time."

Cruz cleared the way. She seemed to find the maze of the airlock charming, like a maladroit but unbearably adorable puppy.

When she opened the coat her special aroma was released into the room. Jasmine, Cruz thought, maybe Objet D'Art with a pinch more spice. Chiquita had always doused herself in Love Crazy. She had left a vapor trail en route to the concrete. Whatever scent Jamaica had dabbed on made Cruz's erection get serious about embarrassing him. Beneath the car coat was a snug leather skirt, a chromium cartridge belt and a Madonna album's worth of tramped out rock 'n' roll lace. Her spikes had gold heels. She dutifully drew a Kleenex from her saddlebag to wipe off her shoes. A hundred fifty bucks, easy, on those slim feet.

Cruz felt coarse and slovenly. His hand wanted to ensure his zipper was full up. He regretted not casing the bathroom mirror to deter obvious zits from humiliating him. He saw Jamaica's smoothly beveled hipbones declare themselves, molding the leather, and felt something icy leap between his lungs. Her legs were sensational. He found himself thinking that such legs were too upmarket to ever wrap themselves around Bauhaus' piggy torso...then he corrected. Of course they had. She had boned him and blown him and left him gasping. All in the line of duty. The duty of lines.

As she shucked the coat she handed him the Whitman Sampler box she held crooked beneath one arm. "This is for you. Another little forget-me-not from Uncle Bauhaus."

The weight was all wrong. It held either a clinker brick or something a lot deadlier than gooey cordials and chocolates. Cruz posted the box on the dresser. No rush.

"Uncle Bauhaus." He laughed.

"Everybody's daddy. 'No prob, kiddo; anything ya want— it's all free and it's all cool.'" Her imitation was good. "Kiddo" translated as anyone inferior to Bauhaus. A dogsbody, as they were called in jolly old Great B.

"But tomorrow," she said, "when bill collecting time rolls

around, you've gotta watch your ass to make sure you've still got both buns and a hole. Bauhaus is the elephant that never forgets anything he's given you, or loaned you, or done for you. Because it's all for him, really."

"He seems too eager to give everybody everything they want."

"Absolutely—if it's dope or sex or money. Try for position. Try for power. You'll wake up face down in the Chicago sewer with rats gnawing on your eyelids." The recitation seemed to amuse her, but hardened her features like cast metal being tempered.

"Is that why you're here tonight?" said Cruz. "A payback? Red to black in Bauhaus' ledger?"

"No other reason for a strange woman to visit a strange man after midnight, babe."

Cruz nodded. All business. He was going to get what he had asked for. Every passing second of his life put him deeper in Bauhaus' debt, and he wondered what *his* payback would be. He enjoyed the talk, however. Jamaica was more articulate than any of Emilio's *cuinas,* and better looking than most of them. When Cruz inventoried Emilio's stable, all he ever thought of were brand names: Physique by Ironworks Body Coaching. Billboard teeth by Ranson Hale DDS (a coke-sniffing maniac who gave his regulars free jolts of nitrous oxide for referring new patients). Tans by Uva-Sun. Tits by NASA. Brains by Looney Tunes.

Despite the makeup and flash, Jamaica came by her assets naturally. Her teeth were not perfect. Her dark complexion was marred by a Y-shaped scar beneath her lower lip—a charming flaw that affirmed her realness more strongly. Under the dusky polish those nails were her own—tapered and pointed yet businesslike and short. No fakes, no bull. Her snide hinted that she shared Cruz's fine opinion of their illegitimate uncle.

Maybe a friend lurked here.

It took them a while to get around to fucking. Cruz liked talking to her, and his fascination made him hesitant and clumsy. She fancied what she took for shyness in the same way he found her scar compelling. At least he didn't whip out the bogus suavity or try to act supertough.

She told him she wanted to chase the dragon. Cruz set up the fixings.

One of the things he had done with his overstock from cutting Bauhaus' cocaine was to extract a stash of freebase, using baking soda to filter out the impurities. Pulling pure cocaine hydrochloride out of a cut that was barely stepped on was pretty simple.

Jamaica said she enjoyed it best when smoked through a bong full of rum. Cruz had heard of this in Miami but had never tried it personally. He lacked a water pipe, at any rate. Instead, he lit a candle and set about folding a small square of aluminum foil. The trick was to dodge the bad carbon taste that spelled the line between cooking and burning the freebase. He played the foil and flame like a fisherman, drawing out the contest. She sniffed in the milky wisps of smoke that curled upward. He saw her pupils dilate with impact.

"Whoo!" She sat backward too fast, breathing to break up the concentrated rush with a hit or two of air. Cruz watched the lace bodice of her camisole top whomp away. They would definitely be up through most of the night.

He put on a Circle Jerks tape and took his turn, going easy on the potent smoke. He was the host.

About the time "Love Kills" revved up, he asked her to keep her spikes on while they did it.

He tore the double stitching in her pantyhose and felt how moist she was already. Freebased into the ionosphere, she subjected him to vigorous use of her extremely motile pelvis. Everything seemed overhot, urgent, just out of reach; fulfillment confounded by the hyperclarity of their mutual high. Internally she must have been distracting herself like a pro. She soon rollicked through an arched-back, toe-curling orgasm, or at least mustered a passable fake for Cruz's benefit. She opened up his back with her fine brown nails, shallow furrows that stopped just short of bleeding. They hurt so good.

Once Cruz came, matters turned slicker and simpler down below. This excited him so much that he got hard again without withdrawing from the fervid grasp in which she held him. She paced her breathing nasally, like a distance runner, and broke a sweat at last. The room seemed to run short of air. It became a game to see who would be the first to run out of juice.

She straddled, and began ramming herself onto him, reddening their pubes, baiting him to madness, until he dumped her onto her back and planted his knees wide to deal her lustier, deeper strokes. She clawed at the mattress, came again, and glided down with a dazed satiation glimmering wetly in her gaze. Such depths there, in green, impenetrable.

The candle had burned down and the tape had run out half an hour back.

Cruz's metabolism roared and broke beach. He felt more and more awake, an acceleration that stressed the limits of his envelope and threatened to burst him from internal pressure. It was as though he had missed sex for a year and was venting a hundred per cent in a single glorious overload.

Her pump now primed, he went to work on her with mouth and tongue. Her pubic hair was immodestly lush, a fragrant triangle that cushioned his face and pointed the One True Path. No bikini depilatory here. It was brazen and unusual. Cruz was reminded of the challenge of uncut dope: *Can you hack it without dilution?* Small labial folds, almost petite. The blood-flushed randy bud waiting there like a mine ready to explode, touchy and swollen, ripened to the point of near pain. He teased and tested and flicked and then backed off. Then it was a full commit. He laced fingers to hold her hips down, and nibbed and suckled until she was ready to scream.

Jamaica lost count.

Cruz hung in there primarily because he did not know if the coke would let him get it up again. She stopped him and took that fear away, too. Her eyes were almost chatoyant in the candlelight, and as the wick drowned in its own wax, they finally called a timeout and clinked rejuvenating bottles of Quietly Beer.

Still the coke denied them genuine sleep. She mopped her forehead and told him she had really been climaxing. Cruz drank deeply, and, like a fool, believed her.

When she hit the bathroom to eliminate some of their

collaborative effort, Cruz checked out her saddlebag.

Mixed amid a nightmarish jumble of cosmetics he found a pinky vial barely dusted with lees of coke. He did his gums with the smidgen and found it a weak mix. There was a sample-sized bottle of mouthwash and a plastic case of good old Ortho-Novum, plus an Illinois State ID that assured Cruz had not just made the same error in judgment as his predecessor, the dishonorable Jimmy McBride. Jamaica's name was really Loretta Paxson, and she had turned twenty-two three weeks ago. The ID mugshot made her look green, like one of the living dead. Cruz refilled the amber vial from his own ample stash. He tried not to be a bad guy, generally.

He broke the tape seal on the candy box and lifted out a matte black Sig Sauer 226 with three clips of Luger ammo. Nasty enough. He replaced the lid when he heard the toilet flush.

She came out barefoot, shredded hose clinging, unwilling to let go of such sleek legs. The symbolic hymen rent asunder; a good start for them as a team. She poured lukewarm beer on his cock, making him jump and soaking his groin. The tape got changed to Slayer and in moments she had lipped him back to stiffness. She shoved his shoulders down, pinning him and stepping over in one fluid move. He felt himself part her and slip in to the hilt; she was so damned warm there. She locked him down with her forearms and cut loose more below-the-waist moves than a snake dancer.

He awoke with his most recent erection easing out of her, slowly, slowly. She was still on top of him like a blanket, lightly dozing.

The tape was off again. Might as well give it up.

"Hear that?"

"Mm." Her eyes opened, slim fissures. "Hear what?"

"Sound." It was back, capering just beyond the limits of his perception, but the building was much quieter this time. He tried to approximate it for her and fumbled; the noise he made stank of Hallowe'en haunted house records. *Weeeooo.* That wasn't it. The signature of what Cruz had come to think of as Kenilworth's pet ghost was subtler. Not a puking wino groan, but the type of noise someone might make when stroked or petted, with a weak downward curl at the end, a shift of timbre that carried just a hint of cemetery corruption, of lives and opportunities irreclaimably missed, of woe and regret that came of losing one's way in the darkness. Or having lost everything.

"I don't hear anything except that fucking samba music." She rolled off and lost him. "Oops. Sorry."

Cruz's vague fix on the sound had been lost. Now all he could hear was the calliope beat of dust-brown *danceteria* music, muffled by doors and walls. A bit of clanging and dripping going on in the airshaft. Thumping footsteps above and below. Latino singing, all in one unvarying key, wailing, abrasive enough to blot out the more fragile texture of the ghost noise.

Somewhere in the building, the old anti-Semite would be in auto-bitch mode on his favorite racist topic. He did not need an audience. Perhaps he spoke to the ghost.

Jamaica got up with the idea of opening the Chivas, untouched so far. While she peeled and uncorked, Cruz asked about her name.

"When one pulls down a living with one's pussy," she said, mock-lectorial, "it helps to have a lot of pseudonyms. I used to be Cyndi—yeah, with an i. Short for Cynder, which was short for *burnout.* Today I'm Jamaica, which is far away. I'd like to be far away. Someday I will be. I'd call that an improvement, wouldn't you?"

This was not the first time she had told this story. She swigged directly from the bottle and passed it to Cruz. He took a fair knock, swallowed and let it burn all the way to his balls.

She dipped a finger into the bottle and massaged between her legs, repeating several times, allowing the sensitive clitoral tissue to absorb the alcohol directly. Using cocaine was headier but more hazardous. Cruz knew people had applied it to their genitals to retard orgasm, but it was too easy for it to get into the urethra or vagina; from there it was sucked pellmell into the bloodstream. Instant overdose. Rosie had told him about witnessing such a blowout live. The only thing pretty about it was the robust skin tones the mortician applied to the corpses before they were planted.

She drew his tumid cock between her lips and stroked it

with her tongue. He was rubbed raw; the residual whiskey in her mouth stung. The irritation quickly subsided into a prickly buzz, making his dick feel more or less the way his arm did when it fell asleep. The pain peaked out and evaporated while he fought to collect a surprised breath. Jamaica was astonishing. He felt mated, well and truly.

Screams, outside, in the corridor. The Velasquez *mamacita* yelling for her brat. Responsible parents would have bedded the little bastard by this hour.

Mars wasn't even an upper limit. Together they could fuck beyond mortality. He chopped a few lines to insure they stayed at this high ebb. The stuff on the mirror did its vanishing act and they climbed back aboard each other and rode, using spit and beer when matters needed lubricity. Her heat baked him, and for the first time since arriving in Oakwood, Cruz forgot about the omnipresent snow.

Outside, past the condensation fogging the windows, flakes as big as the palm of Cruz's hand began to meander down from the sky to bury the city anew.

They traced cartoons on the panes. A serpent. A heart. FUCK YOU in reverse, a message to the outside world. He almost heard the ghost again, crooning softly, pining for god knew what.

"Cops," Jamaica said, not kidding.

Her eyes were unblinkingly targeted through one of the clear smears forming the snake head on the bedside window.

Three Oakwood cruisers blocked Kentmore near the eastern entrance to the building. Cruz checked the other window. Red and blue flashbar light bounced up and down Garrison as a fourth car nosed closer through the snowfall.

Cruz's brain hastily registered two hundred new definitions of the word *panic.*

Buck naked with a hard-on, he sat up here on the third floor, no back door, with better than four pounds of cocaine, an unregistered handgun and a page beeper tied to one of the biggest drug dealers in the area. Now was not a time to stand a pat hand, bluffing.

"Shit!" Cruz snarled the word between clenched teeth, using the force of his abrupt anger to propel him into motion.

"Seven uniforms, total." Jamaica had seen action like this before and was unrattled, calm and alert. "Four just came in the downstairs door."

Cruz heard, or thought he heard them clomping up the steps, talking. *Shit!*

"Number Five just decided to mosey on in. Looks cold out there." She re-rubbed her spyhole.

"Do they have their guns out?"

"No. Wait. Can't see."

Shit, shit, shit!

Tonight's script did not read *fade into the wall and whistle innocence.* Deflecting the enforcers of law had always been Rosie's lookout. Cruz and his cronies rarely got speaking parts. They enjoyed lines, but no words, if you can get behind that. Now Cruz the understudy had to perform under pressure. It was bad and by surprise. Maybe it was some sort of test Bauhaus had cooked up for him. Maybe Jamaica had been prepped to see the police cars. Maybe...

Maybe you'll have mucho federal time to sit like a fucking Greek statue and passionately review your life options for decades unless you kick your bare butt into overdrive and fucking DO, he thought. Use that clear sensorium or none of it is worth gull shit.

Ninety thousand dollars in refined cocaine smiled at him from the dresser drawer. Screw "street value." That crap was just to make drug busts sound more impressive on the six o'clock news. Ugly pictures piled up in Cruz's head and he knew the one place he did not ever want to be was on local television.

Trying to flush more than a kilo might hurl his ass to the tornado. What about the plastic, the tape? Could that much blow clog the pipes? Should he really trust Fergus' Cro-Magnon plumbing to keep him innocent?

He whip-cracked a Hefty bag and swept in mirrors, foil, matches, candles, paraphernalia, dope and all. After half a heartbeat of nervy deliberation he tossed in the box containing the pistol, too. He spun the neck of the bag, tied a firm knot, then unfurled a second bag and repeated, making his own impromptu double-ply. It had to be watertight. If coke got wet you might as well try to peddle cooking lard.

He popped a few rings when he tore back the shower curtain in the bathroom. In the black reflection afforded by the window to the airshaft, he could see his own sweating face. It was not a picture of innocence. He smacked the frame with the heel of his hand until the crookedly-mounted, rotting casement squeaked reluctantly upward. Three inches up, it skewed in its track and jammed. That was comic enough to stomp hard on the big red button in Cruz's brain. He began to bash that fucker solidly with one fist, pretending it was a cop's nose, and the greasy face of Fergus, and the throat of the yowling brat down the hall, and Emilio's entire body. Bash, bash, paint slivers jumped and *bash* the lower window wrenched full open and he piled the whole package—oh great god of coca leaves, let it be gently—through. Into the shaft. It made a faraway splash when it hit bottom. He hoped nothing pointed had waited down there, to jab a hole. He hit the window again. It slammed down squealing, tight as a vacuum can, with a bloody handprint on top of it.

He wiped off the blood with toilet paper, hit the bowl on the first shot, and flushed.

Husking air, arteries throbbing, he stepped out and drew the shower curtain slowly shut. Rosie was not around to compliment his initiative.

Primo job. Now you get admitted to the inner circle. I present you with your own secret phone number.

He had just enough time to towel his face before the police knocked on the outer door. Jamaica was wiggling back into her leather skirt.

The officers, as it turned out, were conducting a door-to-door Q & A. A child, Mario Velasquez, had suffered some sort of accident and was missing. Had anyone seen or heard…

Cruz's manner told them he knew the drill, that he had run similar laps too many times before. They heard the toilet, stubbornly running. It had flushed as soon as they had knocked.

When they took a friendly peek, they recognized Jamaica. And when they peeked again, just as friendly, into her saddlebag, they discovered Cruz's belated birthday gift to her and busted them both.

Twelve

Once he saw cop cars girding the corner of Kentmore and Garrison, Jonathan guiltily reviewed the crimes of his entire existence. *His* door; *his* building. Badges all over, porcine eyes to scrutinize the new suspect in town. Bright reds and blues a luminous botulin on the snow. Their swagger a rude, officious dare: *Do something about us. You won't. You can't. Coward. Wimp. C'mon, NOTICE us—we love to ask questions.* The sight of uniforms had stiffened Jonathan's stomach muscles for as long as he could recall; since before kindergarten, the time he'd strolled over to McCoy's Market in Fort Worth for a Choc-O-Pop and gotten rounded up by the police.

"You live here, kid?"

Sour recollect and present reality collided face-to. He struggled for invisibility. His tongue thickened. *Don't let the teacher catch you; don't let the class hammerheads see what you have; never, ever embarrass yourself before the girls.* Feminine ridicule was worse than the Death of a Thousand Cuts.

Jonathan's gaze rushed—guiltily—to the carton in his grasp. He tried to redefine contraband. Who in Hades knew what was legal in a place like Oakwood? He acknowledged the officer, eyes darting nervously. No points for cool.

The shoulder emblems told Jonathan that Oakwood paid for its own law enforcement. The cop wore a thick nylon coat with a blue pile collar and fireman's buttons. Above the shield mount an embossed plate read STALLIS.

Officer Stallis reminded Jonathan of a lizard. His nose was beaky and the flesh around his eyes reddened, as though blood vessels had tried to break dermis there, to aerate. The splits that accommodated the Lizard Cop's eyes looked stressed, tender; the eyes themselves, disinterested in alibis. They were the color of bank mud, the kind water moccasins burrow under for naps.

"The hell is that." The Lizard Cop's eyes indicated Jonathan's cardboard box. It might have been an inquiry.

Jonathan's balls puckered. The box contained deli ham and swiss cheese for sandwiches. More smoked turkey loaf. A mess of Tangerine Dream movie soundtracks dubbed onto cassette at Bash's. Jonathan's jittery nerves reminded him that unauthorized tape duplication was AGAINST THE LAW. More index cards, white-out and office doodads appropriated from Rapid O'Graphics. STOLEN. Six novels from Bash's paperback shelf. CENSORED! Did Oakwood have blue laws? Were books, like alcohol, illegal here? Would they even care about *The Drive In* or Westlake's *The Man with the Getaway Face?* Or the moon mug borrowed from Bash? His mind raced to catalog the other potentially incriminating cargo in his hands: A pair of insulated plastic coffee cups with regrettably stupid sayings on them. An aluminum dripulator. Two bags of coffee, courtesy Bash. Compass and X-Acto knife sets in padded draftsman's cases. LETHAL WEAPONS. Jonathan gave up. Absolutely nothing incriminating here even though his expression said *box? What box?*

"Moving in." He shrugged. It had come out muttered, undeclarative. It sounded made up on the spur of the moment. Now the Lizard Cop would say...

"Funny time of night to be moving in."

Rat piss redneck pederast baked and glazed stormtrooper chancre go harass Officer Piggy's sphincter with your big bad baton and mind your own fucking business turd-smoking coprophagic squirt of pus...

"So you and I both are on the late shift. What can I say?" He saw more uniforms in the foyer of the Garrison entrance. One cop, bulked out by coat and gear, was questioning a white-haired older man in a bathrobe. Probably still pretty cold in the foyer. The cop didn't care, slowly jotting memoranda in a big flop-over leather ticket book. He looked like a bored waiter taking a small order. Jonathan realized now that most of the lights were on across Kenilworth's northern face. He was getting his first glimpse of many of the other tenants. It looked as though everybody was being rousted. On black and brown and white visages he saw the fear that had just nestled frigidly between his heart and his right lung.

He moved foot-to-foot, in a holding pattern. "Can I go inside now? I'm uh, I'm uh, I'm freezing my tits off out here." A sense of jolly familiarity never worked with the police. Try courtesy. "Please?"

Jonathan could not go in now, please.

Not before he had surrendered to the Lizard Cop his full name and apartment number and valid ID and period of residence; how goddamn stupid, here he was just moving in. A hundred other bits. What was his relationship if any to the child Mario Velasquez, currently missing, presumed seriously injured or deceased. Why wasn't the Toyota truck registered in his name? Who was the rightful owner? What was the owner's name, address, home and work numbers and relationship if any to the child...

Jonathan droned monosyllabic answers. The Lizard Cop scribbled, disliking Jonathan's attitude. Jonathan fantasized jamming a twelve-gauge between the Lizard Cop's teeth and blowing his entry-level brains all over the snow. At least that would cut the glare from the flashbars. Neighbors were peeking through drapes now. Jonathan popped a sweat in spite of the near-zero temperature. He smelled coyote terror spiraling up from his own pits. His dick had tried to telescope into his sternum. The thing that abraded him most was being called a kid by the Lizard Cop, who topped 27 at most.

He was then herded toward the foyer, and more scrutiny. It was announced that Jonathan had been in and out of the premises before, during, and after the pinpoint time of the event. But not on the third floor. So he claims.

Stallis reported to Reinholtz, the bulky one. Reinholtz's expression said that Jonathan's story was wet toilet paper.

Reinholtz was the Bird Cop. He had his cap off and Jonathan could see a gleaming bald patch that had forced scant, grizzled occipital hair rearward. It looked like a glob of mashed potatoes full of pepper in the process of sliding off the back of his head.

David J. Schow

His eyes were diluted blue, like drinking water that assumes the hue of its container. The Bird Cop carried a bowling-ball belly. After four Pabst Blue Ribbon tall boys, he talked in bars about shooting people like Jonathan on sight.

Wind howl cut down as the foyer door closed. The old man being grilled by the Bird Cop turned on Jonathan.

"You," he said. "I ain't-a never seen you here before just now. No sir." He sidled closer. Jonathan caught a whiff of canned spaghetti sauce as he was inspected. "Nope." Light from the unshaded bulbs careened off the old man's blue eyes, making them harsh and adjudicatory. "You some kinda Jew?"

Near the mailboxes another officer sniffed loudly, as if to protest his heritage to this elderly bigot. A group of people came thudding down the stairs and Jonathan saw his new upstairs neighbor, Cruz, in handcuffs. Behind Cruz was a girl in lace and leather; streak job, caramel skin, elliptical, almost Japanese eyes of bottle green, a stone fox from scalp to soles. Just now her eyes were clouded with hassle and ill temper.

"Well, hi-dee-whore," the Lizard Cop smirked. "If it isn't our old darling Cyndi the Choad Chomper."

"Now who in hell is *that* little slut? I ain't-a never seen *her* around here before neither!" The man in the bathrobe was moved to the sidelines to play more guessing games with the Monkey Cop, who was clearly at the limit of his competence just restraining the old fart.

Cruz and the woman were being prodded along by a Robot Cop. Jonathan spotted sergeant's hashmarks. The Robot Cop was the oldest officer present, the largest, the slowest-moving. False teeth, too even, browned by decades of rotten coffee.

"Didn't think we'd find any new faces in this shithole, but here I found Cyndi, who says her name is Jamaica *this* week, stuffing her turkey with this spic hemorrhoid. Third floor."

The Robot Cop's silver nametag flashed. BARNETT. His steel-rimmed glasses put Jonathan in mind of Gort's visor, just barely restraining a death ray gaze from frying everyone standing. More metal was involved in badges and decorations. The Robot Cop clinked when he moved. Inside his unzipped coat Jonathan could see the shoulder epaulettes peculiar to Chicago's finest.

"Christ on a Wonder Wheel," groused the old man. "I don't know *any* of these damned brats!"

"These two were holding," said the Robot Cop. "Traces all over the apartment. Found a page beeper." He gathered Cruz's collar in a meaty fist. "You flushed quite a wad, didn't you, dickhead?"

"No, sir," Cruz said, eyes down. Police and animals with rabies dislike direct visual contact.

"Toilet was stuck and running; I think he introduced a kilo to our sewer system and now the rats are all racing little rat speedboats. Probably one of Bauhaus' new butthole buddies. What the hell; we need to update him anyway, and that goes for this sweet piece here, too, whatever her goddamned name is today."

Each enemy of society was jostled forth.

"Hey, Reinholtz," said the Lizard Cop. "Tell the spic how much police nightstick this bimbo has sucked."

The Bird Cop warmed immediately to the game. "Aw, hell, Stallis, hard to say. You'd have to tote it in board feet. Right, hotpants?"

Jamaica shrugged free. "Yeah. One board foot means I must've made it with ten of you dung flumes, and you know what? Cops can't fuck for spit." She smiled brilliantly; America's Sweetheart gone to porn.

Jonathan wanted to edge nearer to the stairs.

"Wait a second, you." It was the Lizard Cop, his keeper. "You hang fire with Miss Candy Cunt, here. Nobody said you could go." Jonathan's bicep was vised and he was escorted to the corner by the mailboxes to join Cruz, Jamaica and the old man, under the watchful eye of the Monkey Cop. He was still holding his box of possessions.

"Welcome to the neighborhood." Cruz acted like his bracelets were no biggie.

Jonathan's eyebrows went up-down. Too unbelievable. Too late for this outrage.

Cruz leaned closer, notching his voice down. "674-2779. Call it. It spells a word. MR HAPPY. Call it and let them know what happened to me. Cruz. Right? Do it. Tell them what went down."

From the stairs the Robot Cop ordered Cruz to shut his trap. Cruz yessired. Then, to Jonathan, he added: "*Do* it." He was serious, urgent.

Jonathan had not said yes or no, but Cruz turned his mouth downward and nodded, as though assured of their pact.

Jamaica was browsing Jonathan. Not bad for a white boy. "You live in this place?"

He nodded again, like a marionette or a court jester. He admired her fire, the way she'd unhesitatingly mouthed off to the police when she had to know it could only buy her trouble. It injected him with another dose of self-loathing. Good old Jonathan. Given the manly option of doing something and doing nothing, you can rely on good old Jonathan to spring into inaction. Why risk the tarnish of involvement? Civilization had been custom-fitted to Jonathan, offering thousands of civil rationalizations that could easily document or justify any weaseldickery. Stay dead neutral. Do nothing. Avert your eyes and the irritant will magically rinse clean. Blame Amanda and flee to Chicago, where no one will suspect what a chickenshit you are. When confronted with that nagging inability to muster backbone, do it again—run. Whenever you try to take action it's too little too late, so don't bother. That stunt with the wine bottle had sure worked out in your favor, for sure, Sir Jonathan. So pretend it never happened. Blame others. Fault the fucked up universe at large.

Do anything...but for godsake don't actually *do* anything.

"You gonna help him?" she said.

"Uh." His brain was finding elementary tasks confounding. He wanted to stare at her for hours. She was exotic, enigmatic, sensual. He realized her *smell* was making him crazy. She smelled like sex, recent friction and humidity, lots of it, robust and deep-dish. "Uh. I." Seeing her expression downshift into resentment helped clear his board. "Yeah. I guess. That is, I mean—"

"Last warning, fungo," barked the Robot Cop. Jamaica, not cuffed, sweetly offered a single-digit salutation.

"MR HAPPY," Jonathan said.

"You got it, babe." Her gaze was still leveled at the Robot Cop, plotting vengeance, mutilations.

Jonathan had just joined the ranks of the underworld. If the cops did not throw him back, he would balloon fiercely out, a blowfish of spines and stingers and concentrated venom. His aggressors would go *yah!* and spring back with only a hairsbreadth moment to regret their poor pushy judgment before the swift slash and tear of fangs and poison and the slow acid suffering of justified death.

A child had vanished from the third floor, leaving behind a screaming infant sister, a befuddled father newly home from the graveyard shift, and a pregnant mother nearly grand mal with shock. Jonathan felt relief, knowing that whatever had happened he could not be incriminated. He knew already that he was innocent.

The old man was released first. He lived on the first floor right underneath Jonathan. When he shut his door he was bitching about how Jew babies cried the most.

The Lizard Cop and the Bird Cop engaged in a quick confab concerning how Jamaica might work off the time it would take them to book her. Jamaica spit on the Lizard Cop in fury and was formally arrested.

Cruz was conducted to the back seat of one of the patrol cars by the Robot Cop, who did not care if Cruz bonked his head while being shoved inside. Jonathan remembered that he had just assumed residence on Mayor Daly's old stomping ground.

After leeching him of useless minutiae, the police permitted Jonathan to resume his lawful private business, sans apology. Free at last to hump up the stairs, Jonathan felt as though he had just gotten away with something major.

He found the black cat waiting for him outside of 207.

This time he noticed the stink of fresh paint permeating the second floor. That would be Fergus, sloppily rejuvenating some other recent vacancy. Jonathan smiled when he remembered that *landlord* had been an epithet, a pejorative during the days of the Colonies. The phylum sure hadn't matured much since.

Jonathan's bathroom was a sterling exemplar of Fergus' overwhelming inadequacy. A half-hearted attempt to retile it had been aborted. Periodically, poorly glued tiles would disengage to shatter on the floor or in the tub. Chunks of stale grouting crumbled free to hamper those who dared go barefoot. Vermin used the resultant trenches to conduct nighttime troop movements, like Viet Cong in their tunnel mazes. Now and then a drowning bug would make a desperate leap for life during a shower and land on a naked human being. If you hazarded a hot bath in an attempt to bypass the never-ending cold, you might spot the same bug, swimming, hellbent. Downdrafts of frozen air rattled the metal lining of the ventilation shaft and sneaked goosebump fingers through the crummy seal on the bathroom window. If you went wet in there, it was enough to spike your temples like a mouthful of ice cream.

The bathroom ceiling was another effort of Fergus' that had not been a success. Jonathan could estimate the building's horrendous seasonal plumbing problems by looking up. Some twenty months back the ceiling had rotted out and been replaced with crookedly sawn sheets of gypsum board stamped *Sheetrock Firecode.* Rather than plastering and painting, Fergus had sutured the seams with fat swatches of duct tape. These soon peeled under gravity. The overweight wallboard grew moist and gray from seepage about once a week. It was beginning to sag like parachute nylon. It stank of mildew. Jonathan had already fabricated a nightmare image of it busting loose to shower him with sump water and bloated insects and other tenant's flushings.

Face it. The bathrooms in most places where people pulled the old nine-to-fiver were generally worse. Cracked concrete floors. Wobbly toilet seats. That one-and-only stench of spattered piss.

Feed me.

"Free ride. You little parasite." He fished up his keys, not yet used to knowing which came first in the game of locks he had to beat. He set down the box and his fingers unclenched, achingly. The cat sauntered over to sniff the swag, then rub a shorthaired cheekbone against one cardboard corner, rasp rasp.

Come on. We're pals. Feed me.

Just stay clear of my legs, Jonathan thought. What might be a cat might also be a spider inching up your leg, hunting for a warm place to empty venom sacs.

Jonathan's inner/outer door arrangement was identical to Cruz's, in 307. To the immediate right of Jonathan's first door, however, was one of the old iceboxes, a vertically stacked row of three small doors. The latched cooler doors still worked, making the solid click-lock noise of an industrial butcher's cold room. Chicago was once termed the Hog Butcher of the World. Thanks to Fergus' artistry with the paintbrush, the fit of the small doors was too tight, and sticky. The cream-colored paint had intimidated the corridor lights down to a baleful yellow.

Kenilworth Arms was like a latter-day House of Usher, its shafts and passageways actually the convolutions of a lunatic's brain. Somewhere near the center, that feverish glow, the burnout-flare of something ill, something dying, something not entirely normal. So much paint, bulbs so lightless, floors so creaky. Shut-down elevators. Obsolete freezers. No doubt other aspects of the structure that worked did so in abnormal or unanticipated ways. Jonathan thought of rats in the foundations as potential roving hematomas; black cats, free-stalking tumors waiting to perch. All the tenants just the passing fictions of a crazy person's imagination—here now, gone tomorrow. Errant thoughts, facts to be misfiled by an unsound mind whose memories were sepia-toned and sugar-coated by extreme age, perhaps even by dreams.

Be a good little corpuscle, he thought, or the antibodies will getcha. The spark of a single synapse was never noticed as an important event by itself. Or missed.

Hey. Food time.

"I won't forget, you little putz. Who else am I going to complain to about the po-leece?"

I'm innocent. I wasn't even there.

"You're lying." Said casually, with no oomph. "MR HAPPY." The intrigue of codes committed to memory was seductive. Like Cruz, Jonathan had not bothered wading into the quicksand of local forms that would gain him a phone for 207. He did not plan on being in residence that long, Bash willing. A telephone was an unneeded luxury inside a stopover for transients. There were phones at the post office, three blocks away. Apart from Bash or Capra's office, who was he going to call?

Just now the prizewinning question: Was he going to call
MR HAPPY?

He imagined Cruz's glare, should he do nothing to get him
out of jail. How inclined toward physical retribution might
Cruz be? Jonathan had watched him hang stolid in the face of
cops and cuffs and baiting.

How had that fiery girl known what she could get away
with? Jonathan did not admire her so much as wish he could
emulate her on an autonomic level. Respond without thinking;
trust your reflexes. She had bigger balls than he did.

Scuze me.

The cat slipped ahead of him into the room. Most cats are
thinner than most human beings and the door had only been
opened a crack. He had left a lamp on inside. By the time he
got to the windows all but one of the police growlers had
departed, leaving the overlapping scrawl of multiple tire tracks
in the snowy streets. The near-hysterical Velasquez tribe had
been loaded into one of those cars and hauled away for more
paperwork. It was a fair bet that Oakwood's white-on-white
constabulary presupposed that this beaner mama had decided
she had one *niño* too many and needed to trim her workload.
The question in which the authorities would be most interested
tonight was: *Okay, what did you really do with the body, you dumb
Mex or Puerto Rican or whatever the hell you are.*

That was why Kenilworth was not overrun with searching
cops.

The cat resumed its investigation of Jonathan's other
boxes. Bash had loaned him a collapsible camp cot that folded
out bigger than a single, not quite a full. Jonathan would not
trust his spine to anything that Fergus might scare up as
"furnishings," although he did thieve a wicker rocking chair
from the wreckage in one of the basement storage rooms. 207
had come with a hot plate, refrigerator, a mirrored bureau and
a card table.

Something stank.

The fridge was chugging, pump laboring with a sound that
suggested duress. Maybe the motor was busily frying its coil.
But the smell was not electrical or mechanical; it was organic,

a hint of decay. It was too cold inside. Jonathan could hear the steam heater in the corner sibilantly delivering warmth. He knew the knob was opened all the way. Definitely too cold.

A knock of chill hit him next to the closet. By process of elimination, he called the place with the tub and toilet the bathroom; cold air was coming at him from the bathroom, then. Carrying the smell with it.

Had the john overflowed? His lips retracted to tighten his face at the odor. His body requested he breathe orally unless he enjoyed the spectacle of regurgitation.

The stink was similar to maggoty meat, a lush bouquet that again took him back to his Choc-O-Pop days and his discovery of a decomposing squirrel in the fireplace flue. He had yanked the sooty steel handle to vent the hearth. It resisted, screeching open when outmuscled. And the tiny corpse had tumbled out to burst open at his feet, loaded with wriggling white grubs. Yuck.

Jonathan wondered if other tenants had to put up with this smell of fresh dogshit and suppurated bandages. As he reached for the pullchain over the sink, moving air hit him in a rush and for one second of bugfuck terror he was sure that someone or some thing was in the tiny bathroom with him.

The window next to the tub was broken, most of the sharp, reflective wedges scattered inside the tub. Raked onto the sharp fractures still clinging to the frame were gelid clots of reddish-black matter like bloodstained feces. It was in the tub, too, a lot of it, slopped onto the sides as if a dump truck of sewage had been emptied there through the window and most of it had bubbled down the drain, leaving semisolid chunks and crimson, inviting flies. Who knew where the flies had been drawn from, in this cold?

It was a fastidious mess, considering.

Jonathan turned the hot tap to full and engaged the shower plunger to dissolve and sluice away the detritus. Only four or five viscid droplets of muck had glopped onto the floor outside the tub. He tried not to imagine what it actually might be. It was just sewage, backup. Bloody sewage. The stuff in the tub was slightly redder than the stuff on the window.

Mrs. Velasquez's child had been taken in blood. Jonathan's heartbeat fired and missed.

Leaving the water running and the doors open, he hurried up the next flight of stairs and came out on the third floor. Here was Cruz's apartment, 307, locked tight. Several doors down, near the stilled elevator was the Velasquezes'. Past it, just around the western corner near another set of disused icebox doors, he found a bloodstain on the carpet. White tape had been laid around it.

When he returned to his bathroom he found the cat lapping at the coagulated gunk on the floor. He swept the animal aside, using his foot but not kicking it. It took no offense and kept its eyes on what it thought was food.

"Get the hell away from that, stupid, you want to poison yourself?"

You said you'd feed me.

"I did *not* say I'd feed you. Just hang on a second."

I'm hungry now.

"You gotta be kidding. *I* was hungry until I saw this shitstorm here." It smeared when he attempted to scrub it, releasing a riper, subdermal sourness. "I *was* hungry until I had to fuck around half the night with the goddamn police; before I practically became an accessory to a drug bust and an infanticide!"

Fortunately for Jonathan, Bash had bestown a six-pack of Quietly Beer. Those first cold gulps would rinse down a lot of strife.

Jonathan no longer cared who might be disturbed at this hour. He redonned his trucker's gloves and used a wrench to break out the remaining pieces of glass, which plummeted into the dark netherworld below and splashed. The shaft itself was no paragon of olfactory pleasure. It was like sticking your face into the smoke from a chimney at a crematorium. Something had *died* down there, something serious, and from the smell, still rotting eagerly away. Jonathan's face tried to close all ports in a tight pucker; even his surprised pores slammed shut.

Rats. Perhaps they had crawled into the bottom of the shaft to eat, and got trapped down there, or drowned.

As he pulled his head back to safety he heard a slight noise, beyond the dripping water and the steel acoustics of the shaft itself. Sort of a tuneless hum, truncated. Maybe another of Fergus' hapless tenants, weeping in the night.

He emptied a box and cut it apart with his Swiss army knife, sizing a square that would block the hole for tonight. After work tomorrow he'd try to beard Fergus and complain. Doubtless he would get new window glass, a protestation of innocence, and no clues. He'd tell Bash about it at work, and Bash would listen. But he had no obligation to explain the night's events; he had his own problems to wrestle these days. Camela the Butt Person, for one.

"MR HAPPY," he said. An observation. A curiosity. A reminder. A possible path to some facts he could utilize.

As a name, I hate it. Stick to Cat.

"You cause any more problems, you become a rectal nuisance, and I'll yoke you with a stupid name, kiddo." This was not a toothless threat. Too many people he'd known had handicapped their pets with imbecilic labels derived from Tolkien or *Star Wars* or comic strips.

Or a cat. Maybe a cat fell in and was bitten to death by all the rats. A BIG cat.

Cruz could enlighten him. This sort of mystery was completely beyond Jonathan's ken.

"Tell you what. I'll leave you in here. Live bait. If you're still here when I get back, we'll try something else. No sense in trying to sleep right now, anyway."

He left the cat a dish of skim milk and some smoked turkey, then bundled up, bound for the phones at the Oakwood post office.

Thirteen

This cell just wasn't big enough for Cruz and the guy who wanted to mangle him.

Routine nightly bullpen follies, he thought. No one in the block could know what time it was. There were no windows, no clocks, and no public servant was about to waste his or her life by playing cuckoo-bird for the lowlife soiling the cages. Along about dawn, Cruz got to see the result of one of Officer Stallis' forcible restraints. The glimpse was too detailed.

A guy nineteen or so. Hard to tell past the blood. Divested of a biker jacket, shorn of insignia plus anything with a solid or sharp edge, shaken free of smokes and change, belt and shoes confiscated, he was hammerlocked, handcuffed and staggering. He had gotten his nose skewed sideways and a tooth or two was lost upfront. He had bitten through his lower lip. Or fallen and accidentally struck his head on a curb, several times. He had been revived with Officer Stallis' baton, at which time he made a gesture both officers Stallis and Reinholtz interpreted as threatening. He had probably been trying to hold his face on and figure out which way gravity was pulling. Fortunately the rear door of the patrol car sprang open and prevented the suspect from inflicting grievous bodily harm upon either officer. Several times.

Cruz had been abstracting past the barwork, hands stuck through the interstices and into the freer portion of the cellblock, when Stallis had dragged in his catch of the night. The guy tried to clop and pace the duty officer's bring-along, but the cop was in a hurry and the arrestee still didn't know what planet he had just landed on. There was no time to compensate for the new and unusual G-forces and atmosphere. On this alien world you were expected to breathe your own blood. Midway past the bullpen the new prisoner lost it, doubling over and coughing.

"Wait, wait...oh, god!"

The duty officer's face flared with annoyance. He executed a classic ten-hut! stiffarm, grabbing scruff and cuffs and straightening the crooked captive the way you'd unfold a deck chair. He wheeled the guy around to fling him headlong into the bullpen's grid of metal. Cruz thought of the way he would flop a top-heavy mattress against the nearest wall to keep it from tipping backward and overwhelming him. He jerked his arms in too late. Droplets from the Oakwood station's newest guest, unimpeded by the bars, speckled him. A deathly draft of beer-breath hoicked at him, stinging his nostrils with the rotten-tooth odor of congealing blood.

"Fuck!" Cruz spat mostly at the uniform. He was behind bars now, and free to say just about any damned thing he cared to, since he was no longer in control of his immediate destiny. He wished for a teeny pinch of blow to put him on Cruz Control until escape time. He was, right now, glad he had kept his head and not smarted off to look good in front of Jamaica. She knew the score, anyway.

The new arrival was billeted in solitary, a few doors down the stone corridor. That made him a minor; otherwise he'd be in with the general population. They were going to unload on the poor sumbitch: Obstruction, assault with intent, impeding officers in their lawful duty, resisting arrest, and whatever garni du jour they could add to whatever it was the guy had done in the first place. Bail would be astronomical.

Big deal. Cruz knew his own bail would top four figures, easy. They had 24 hours to charge him. The way police logic worked in Oakwood, until Cruz was charged he was not entitled to any phone calls. If he complained about this later, they would simply respond that he was offered his calls, but had refused them. Once you're in that cell, shine the bullshit some cops will tell you about getting to use the telephone.

Once you're in that cell, they have you, and the only rights *you* have is the rights they feel like giving you.

Never let 'em see you sweat. Cruz was still lucid; he still had all his parts. Most people lost it when confronted with arrest and detainment. TV had not prepared them. Only on cop shows did the knightly minions of law and order swap rough-and-tumble *mots* with their justly bested foes.

When your survival imperative was no longer wired to your mouth you ended up in the shoes—socks, rather—of the dude just booked, who had probably said something stupid like *I know my rights* or *You can't do this* or, worst of all, *I pay your salary.*

MR HAPPY. Jonathan had the number. Would he do anything with it?

He remembered Jonathan's eyes, uploading. Green eyes, but not like Jamaica's. An unfathomable subphylum of green, more yellow near the pupil, with sharp bits of brown that came and went, a murky blend like agitated pea soup. Cloudy. Dense. Jonathan struck Cruz as too upscale for the likes of Kenilworth Arms. All that paper stuff, to move in. This guy was a thinker, a planner, the sort of person who devised stratagems and wrote down lists before making focused, surgical moves. He aimed *before* he fired. Probably destined for some high rise, an office with Danish furniture, a health plan and a savings account. He would spend years amassing the perks that Emilio or Bauhaus could summon right now with a fingersnap...only to waste. Jonathan was real people; he fit into the bourgeois world of people who drove Nipponese compacts and paid taxes. Cruz was a fringe dweller, a maverick virus; he slipped through the cracks and hung at the edge of proper civilization. Like a predator, he fed off the norm. Columnists wrote inept articles on what they called "the drug subculture." People like Jonathan read them in Sunday supplements, having one of two reactions: *How can people LIVE like that?* Or *Jesus; must be goddamn nice.* When you boiled it down to business structure it was all the same. Profits, losses, hostile takeovers, power raiders. The veepees eventually slid into their boss's vacancies. Corporate America; just say no. Cruz took pride in his outsider status, whose risks included the cell in which he had landed. Average people craved vicarious and riskless excitement. Maybe Jonathan's presence on the opposite side of the fence of social respectability would serve to balance out the fact that Cruz lived and breathed.

Maybe Cruz could do Jonathan a favor someday.

From what he overheard, Oakwood cops called their collars "alleged individuals" when in the presence of Sergeant Barnett. Otherwise, arrestees were known as hemorrhoids. Or bugs. The benediction of the Oakwood station, as you were thrown into a cell, was:

"Welcome to Club Paradise, bug."

It was what the duty officer had told him as he opened the bullpen door. Enter by yourself, hemorrhoid—or do it my way. Cruz heard it coming hollowly from down the cinderblock corridor, followed by the sound of the new prisoner being cuffed to a Murphy bunk. Then the slide-slam of the cell door, not barred, but a solid core job thick with industrial gray paint like the bulkhead of a battleship. The new guy had been isolated in one of the solitaries. One tiny square window, no glass. One food slot. Silence.

One of the bullpen's bugs was hunched on the steel toilet, liberating a blatting, diarrheic shit. Cruz tried to ignore the acidic aroma that enriched the big cell. When the duty officer came back, he saw flecks of the new bug dotting the starched uniform blouse. Good. Cruz wiped a palm down his own face and stuck his hands back through the bars. Your clothes got stale quickly in jail, and he could smell himself. Awhile back he'd unzipped to piss, and the updraft from his pants was like the den of a randy puma. Jamaica's juices still scaled his thighs and starched his pubic beard. His penis, tender now to the point of pain, did not wish to see the outside world and shriveled, withdrawing toward the sanctuary of his torso as soon as he had relieved himself.

Some of Jamaica was still with him. He was happy for that.

The head of his dick had been cold between his frozen fingers, and his toes were dead in socks too thin. In the bullpen it was probably lower than fifty degrees; cops knew that the temperature could help keep prisoners quiet, bundled into themselves instead of overheating and pounding each other. Each incoming hemorrhoid was issued a 4×4 square of Army roughweave that left fiberballs on any clothing it touched and was inadequate for real warmth. Cruz could almost see his breath condensing. The air around him was fetid. Nobody ever washed their feet, foreseeing incarceration.

They would want him to talk about Bauhaus. He might have to stay here a spell. Due process would never be expedited on behalf of someone like Cruz. He knew this and prepared to mentally cocoon until Bauhaus could spring him. The concrete bullpen floor was as cold as the metal grid of a soft drink cooler. The bunks were all taken. The King Kongs of the cell had already relieved the lesser bugs of their blankets and were mummified on the topmost shelves of steel. Other bugs were wasted enough to pass out on the floor in fetal wino's curls, oblivious to time, temperature, pain and life. Cruz hung on to the square of floor he had staked out, and did not stray except to rub cold water into his face from the push-tap sink mounted above the cell's single toilet. If he had to drop his pants and sit, eleven pairs of eyes would be aware of his vulnerability.

He sat lotus, tucking his frigid feet behind his knees to try and thaw his toes, which felt like particles of ice from Saturn's rings. The chilly floor instantly buzzed his butt numb. A toot would have kept his metabolism more attentive. Another rockin' Friday night.

His very familiarity with police procedure had irritated Stallis and Reinholtz, the arresting officers. They had heard the secret word—drugs—and wanted an excuse to cripple him. He kept his face shut and did not respond to taunts or threats: "You got some kinda *problem* with this?" Best to say nothing beyond no, officer, sir.

Jamaica knew the limits to which she could badmouth her lawful abductors. The social dynamic was charged, primitive, and its innate sexism was both a boon and a drawback. It was part of the game of insult played by all cops with all prostitutes, including males. Including female cops. The downside was running afoul of a cop not fond of games...in which event you sometimes got raped with a nightstick, or worse, for mouthing off.

His spine was beginning to ache. He sat, legs folded, arms wrapped tight, head down and jaw clenched. His teeth wanted to chatter. The afterburn of the coke had blown away, leaving bleary insomnia. His joints were packed with iron filings, muscles striated from his mattress olympics, brain pulsating and trying to crack his eggshell skull and push through like expanding bread dough. A ground glass feeling in the creases of his eyes. A sewage deadness thickly veneering his tongue. Neck tendons like the wire of a spiral binder yanked into uselessness. He nodded heavily but could not sleep, his sinuses packed, his head top heavy, a bowling ball tottering atop a drinking straw.

He could not remember whether he had actually kissed Jamaica, once, during the whole night. Just kissed her.

Officer Stallis had checked him into the holding tank, a box with two payphones and a bench as cold as the floor. The bench was splintery and etched with graffiti. Two big fractureproof windows overlooked the corridor leading to the cellblock. To one side Cruz could see a window of wired glass and beyond it, the police day room. A fat cop with a flattop sat watching a portable Sony TV and checking the security monitors, trading lewd jokes and tall tales of arrest and valor. No female field cops in Oakwood. Cruz had seen a uniformed woman working the switchboard. The property sheet he had signed had been filed by a woman.

In the holding tank he lifted one of the payphone receivers and listened to the dial tone. A sonic barrier he could penetrate with his voice, thereby putting a tiny part of himself back in the world. He had no change. Who could he call? Dialing Bauhaus direct or collect would be *verboten*, not to mention unfulfilling. Why help the cops get for free data they were hoping to frost out of him?

Call Rosie long distance. Sure.

The phones were right in front of him, and useless.

Maybe Jonathan would drop dime on behalf of a total stranger. Maybe Jonathan would think that by helping Cruz he might get another look at Jamaica. Whatever works.

"Rack that fucking phone, shithead, nobody gave you permission to call nobody."

It had been Stallis, hungry for fingerprints and a Polaroid or two. Cruz had signed the arrest form, which was passed through a slot akin to the drawers at a pump-and-pay gas station. Reinholtz had trouble with the camera. Cruz's mugs came out greenish, like Jamaica's ID photo. They did several complete print workups on him, including palms, which meant one set was tagged for the FBI. Great. Cruz had to wash his hands in acrid blue gunk the texture of lard. The stench clung to his hands for hours.

His indoctrination done, he was escorted to the bullpen. Welcome to Club Paradise, hemorrhoid. As the new guy he became the object of disinterest until dethroned by the night's next candidate.

Huddled, shivering, half-in and half-out, snot caked like crushed ice in his nose, cranium hammering in 4/4, Cruz was jolted back to reality at the sound of a voice.

"That cocksucker Barnett say you a drug pusher, boy."

He saw frayed gym socks and smelled bromidrosis. Old chinos. Gut. Lumberjack shirt, thermal undershirt, both grimy with jail time.

Over in one corner of the cell a bug with wild, matted hair and eyes as vacant as clear marbles was furiously jacking off, cock poking up like the heating element of a soldering pencil.

Cruz sighed. "No. Barnett's full of shit." The cell shrank in to crowd them. Here comes the inevitable. Get ready for it.

One of the feet nudged him roughly. A tap to crack the hard freeze of his joints. "Then what the fuck *are* you in here for?"

If anyone had really needed to know, Cruz would have answered such an inquiry when he had first come in. Not now. Now was different. Now defined the asshole before him as a habitual arrestee, a chronic misdemeanor bug whose confiscated shoes would be work boots and whose personal effects baggie would contain a cowboy belt with a brass buckle the size of the grille on a '54 Chevy, and a fat, battered wallet with a two-year-old condom welded to one pocket. Now was time for the first detainees of the evening to stir up some shit, having slept off their binges and needing exertion to get warm and perhaps seed an appetite for the Oakwood jail's continental morning cuisine.

Cruz pretended to be out of it. Two more seconds, to torque up.

The man had abandoned his nest of hijacked bedding, one of the blankets hanging from his shoulders to make a shawl with a bunched cowl. He was fleshy, heavy, but in the meaty, slow-sinewed way a grizzly bear is. Thick neck like the hatchway on a tank, bulging veins laboring under the stress to flush the nose and face red. Visage eroded, sunburnt, deep-wrinkled. Irish spud nose traced with burst capillaries, eyes a brainless blue, hating the world, cataracted against logic with the base rage of the inbred and stupid.

This guy spent a lot of time beating up people.

"Talkin' to *you*, shitface."

A hemorrhoid elsewhere in the cell—crony, or a former victim—laughed. Cruz did not divert his attention from the dangerous beast right in front of him. He kept looking up until they locked gazes. In those eyes he found no slack, no reprieve, nothing.

"So why the fuck you in here with a buncha *men?*"

He was ready now. "I cut the balls off a loudmouthed redneck faggot like you."

As the bigger man bent to wrest this skinny snotball off the floor, to wrench him erect and make him swallow a fist, Cruz reached back overhand, grabbed the vertical bars, and arched one nearly senseless foot into the crotch hovering dead ahead. He rolled. His opponent woofed air and folded, banging his simian brow ridge against the bars with a drainpipe clank.

Cruz hit his feet, wobbling but rebounding in time to smash two solid punches into the man's exposed kidneys. They were packed in fat, well padded, but the guy grunted and crashed to his knees, hanging on to the bars for support now. Street politics had taught Cruz to get his hits in fast and make them count. Lacking his opponent's size and strength, all he had as a backstop was speed and meanness.

Pummeling this monster's Peterbilt body wouldn't even count as exercise. Cruz had to put his lights out, and now, or he was going to get mangled as soon as Moby Dickhead caught his wind.

The cell woke up fast. Cruz snapped around to kick the big man in the face while he was still down and wheezing, one hand cupping his flattened testicles. Hemorrhoids rooted for their chosen contestants. In ten more seconds the guards would tip and charge in, truncheons raised.

Cruz hoped they wouldn't show up just to place bets. Breath rushed in and out of him as he cocked his foot. Payback time, for this day's harassment.

The wild man in the corner whooped and ejaculated, making pig noises.

Cruz fell on his ass before he even realized what had happened. Like water into a pan of hot oil, *ssss*, he could no longer feel either of his legs until the cramps hit.

He tried to roll but felt his vital seconds piss away. He grabbed the toilet and managed to get one leg under him.

Momentum tore him askew as his enemy helped him up. Cruz was yanked backward by the shirt and the next thing he saw was an oncoming fist the size of an anvil with knuckles like rivets.

The haymaker plowed full-blast into Cruz's midsection, tearing loose a hawk of pain and imploding his chest around the fist. He thought he could feel his intestines springing across the cell.

Cruz went down, then up, and saw the cannibal grin of his attacker. "I want you to remember this, you little fucker."

Cruz tried to lash in with a side kick but it was like trying to dance by remote control. Moby had his wrist in a trash compacter grip.

He snapped it sidewise and out. He kicked Cruz sharply in the exposed armpit.

The pain was astonishing.

He felt his shoulder unsocket and his vision whited out. *Crack* like fractured kindling.

The prisoners were cheering and cursing as the duty guard and four other officers piled into the cellblock. Everyone was awake now.

Cruz was airborne.

He saw the concrete floor hurrying to kiss his face. Another gentlemanly contest forfeit in deference to the Marquis of Queensbury rules. If only he'd've had some nasal steroids, he would have won.

The cell flip-flopped. At least he was warmer.

Fourteen

Jonathan's pump was thudding, stressing his ribcage, irising his throat shut. He felt excited, elated.

Hanging up the payphone had been a rush.

The cold air did not seem oppressively arctic, but crisp. Despite the move-in, the cops, and the late hour, all his weariness had drained as though lanced. Relief; he felt good for perhaps the first time since he had stepped out into Chicago—city of bootleggers and Neapolitan knee-breakers and Sinclair's meat packers, the land of fascist mayors and Dillinger and Speck and Gacy. And the snow, the ceaseless, engulfing, choking, blinding, freezing wet devil shavings of alabaster cold, coiling down from the night sky to suck the color from the world and shroud it in the deceptive numbness of a lethal injection, to pack and suffocate the city in a season of death until even the calcimine downfall itself assimilated the city's blackness and stink.

Somehow, Jonathan now found himself able to look across the sweeping dunes of white seamlessly interring cars and phone poles and avenues alike, and feel good. There were times when everything could change that simply.

He felt good on his own terms. No chemical assists; no overdose of Quietly, nor the slingshot rush of Bash's Terminal Turbos. So much easier it would have been tonight, to grumble while shooting the cheesy locks on his two doors, to hit the cot and submerge the late-night roust of Kenilworth Arms in a self-indulgent drunk of sleep. By dawn it would have been someone else's problem.

Instead, he had acted. Now he felt good. Simple.

His internal bias was for talk, not action. He always talked a great game, as Amanda used to say. Sharp insights, the firm glue of potent words, aimed and bowshot with killing skill. Since most other people were all talk, too, Jonathan could therefore verbalize his way out of almost any responsibility. Amanda had accused him of trying to disenfranchise from the grownup world of hurt. If you never stuck out your neck, you never feared the razor.

He ignored television and disdained common pursuits. Most people were unattractive or vapid; if neither, then a timewasting bore, beyond their utility to him. Before Amanda it had been simple enough for him to magnetize transient partners. By the third meal taken in public most turned repetitive, dreary *oh yeah David Lee Roth has the most GORGEOUS bod* or bottomed out in their own shallowness: *You know what I like more than anything in the world? Chicken McNuggets.*

In bed, most were overly passive or conventional. Jonathan's sexual notions impressed them much too quickly. They were strangers to pleasure. And he never got a feeling of hooking up with another personality. Until...

No.

As a former hash-house waitress, Amanda had educated Jonathan on the necessity of proper tipping. Today, if service was rotten, he would withhold. Sometimes he overtipped, not only if a waitress was receptive to him, but if she knew her job and was good at it. The act of tipping itself was a tenuous link back in Amanda's direction.

Of voting, Jonathan's line had always been that he refused to vote for politicians. "It only encourages them." Amanda would sigh, tell him not to bitch because he had not taken a say, and peruse local ballot initiatives alone. He talked about drops of water in an ocean, of corruption so deeply rooted as to be immune to a universe of good intentions. Amanda voted anyway, telling him he had closed off too many avenues. Soon he would be perfectly impregnable, walled up inside his own head.

She would tell him it was pretty goddamned hard to lose anything when you had nothing.

Before Amanda, it had been much easier to evaporate problems by averting his attention. You really *could* ignore it and it *would* go away. It was not a very honorable way of life, but it was safe—a core survival lesson learned long ago by hyenas. Just another verse of that venerable old standard blues, *Don't Get Yo Ass Involved.*

Just now, Jonathan was thinking that Amanda would find the rolling, uninterrupted blankness of the predawn snowfall charming. It was simple to let your gaze blur and imagine a clean slate world beyond hatred and bills and sickness. Permafrost kicked back rainbow points of night lights like thousands of blue-white diamonds. No car tracks yet. No dirty dustmop sunrise. A pristine moment...and right in the midst of it Jonathan caught himself thinking again of you-know-who.

Inertia can be the most exhausting exercise of all. Running at redline without engaging a gear can burn up the most expensive of cars *real* good. Jonathan had jump-started his hesitant glutes, climbed into his parka with a prodding sense of mission, slogged it down to the post office, and done himself a deed. Now he felt a headlong sense of righteousness that was unassailable. He had rejoined the world of human beings through his act. And golly gee...now he felt good about himself. Amazing; like trying to explain to a sofa spud how good exercise can feel.

MR HAPPY.

A flighty female voice had instructed him to wait until sunrise the following day. He would receive money sufficient to post Cruz's bail. He would be handsomely recompensed for this. The voice called it a favor. Then Jonathan was listening to a dial tone.

It stank of clandestine rendezvous and film noir intrigue. The coals of his imagination were fanned, and he achieved a spurious feeling of revenge wreaked against the berserkers of the Oakwood police, who had unhesitatingly adjudged him no different from their arrestees. Conceivably he had skimmed within a microdot of spending the night playing pat-a-cake with Cruz in some dungeon.

He stood in the snow, still free, feeling the tug of obligation and the abrupt yet pleasing solidarity of the commonly oppressed.

Jamaica; that was what the cops had called the woman

with Cruz. Her image defrosted Jonathan's brain and warmed his thoughts. He was thinking of her as he came through the Garrison Street door...so it was a jolt to see her in the flesh, there right in front of him. She was sitting on the stairs of the foyer where all the badness had come down. Waiting, apparently, for Jonathan, as light began to intimidate the sky far to the east.

The night had not used her well. The picture in Jonathan's brain was sexier, less haggard; more the streetwise and capable urban siren and not so much the sleepless, lost woman ODed on too much of the Wrong Stuff. It shone in her eyes. Wiped free of their elaborate makeup, they had shied back into her head to hang like dim lamps in distant caves. She blinked too much in the undiffused light of the foyer's naked bulbs. She hugged her knees, huddled in her car coat. Jonathan thought of a child left to sit too long at a football game.

She saw him and brightened. He stopped where he was and scrambled to recall her name again.

He said hello. His tone said: *A surprise, but a good one; what are you doing here at this time of night and I hope it involves me?*

"God." She cleared her throat. "I was hoping you'd toddle back here. I knocked but you weren't home and Cruz didn't have time to slip me his keys." As she stood, Jonathan caught flashes of the hip-hugging leather skirt, the net lace of her stockings, the legs as long and fine as polished sculpture. She preceded him up the stairs to his own apartment. Cruz must have told her. "Can we go up? It's really freezing down here."

He nodded, clumping up the steps behind her, grateful for the view. He had thirty seconds to collect his thoughts. He fished up keys from his parka while she toyed with one of the icebox door handles.

Inside she pondered the riot of cardboard boxes and what they might contain. She immediately liked the skinny black cat, who snaked into her grasp as though magnetized. "You got any coffee? Or some beer? No, wait—something hot. You got towels in any of these boxes?"

"I'm unpacking." It was lame. Try again. "Uh—towels?"

"Yeah. If you don't mind I'd like to grab a bath. Soak and thaw out my bones. The smell of cop cars and police stations

always makes you want a bath." She pulled off her high heels; it
was an effort. Jonathan noticed that her little toes were turned
outward from too many years spent being stylish. The knucks
were rubbed raw and shiny. Her feet were disastrous.

"Uh..." He resolved to stop saying *uh*. "Sure. I mean,
absolutely. Let me dig out the accoutrements."

"The what?"

"Towels. Soap. More towels. I think I've got a loofa in one of
these mystery boxes."

"Jesus—that'd be fabulous. I feel like I've just run a marathon.
I lost." She let her coat fall to the cot and sat on it, dropping her
saddlebag to the floor and peeling off her wrecked stockings.
The gracilis muscles on her inner thighs seemed as big around
as Jonathan's wrists. They jumped starkly out as she raised each
leg. The second most chewable muscles on the body.

He knew what she was doing, and knew that *she* knew. He
smiled to himself. The trick in dealing with her would be not to
respond like a doggie head in Pavlov's lab.

"How come they let you go and not Cruz?" It was almost
the question he wanted to ask her.

She stood to yank her camisole free of its tuck. "They want
to pin the coke to Cruz, because they don't need me to pin Cruz
to Bauhaus, and they're positively ravenous to nail Bauhaus."

"I dialed that number. I didn't get to speak to him."

This appeared to amuse her. "Yeah, Bauhaus loves his
security, all right. Thinks he's some kinda secret agent. The
Man from B.L.O.W." She was down to the serious disrobing. She
smiled in a charming fake of modesty, and made a move for the
bathroom door.

"Here, wait—let me do it." He rushed in ahead of her, mostly
to insure that none of the disgusting mystery mess had blobbed
its way back to the tub. A faint morgue-slab taint hung in the
chill air, but the square of cardboard he'd force-fit into the
broken window remained unbowed. He spun the spigot and
was thankful to see reasonable gouts of strong steam. She was
behind him, leaning against the jamb to watch.

"Sorry I don't have any bubble bath or stuff like that."

"That's okay." She was barefoot, shorter now, less statuesque, more human. A pleasantly calm smile hinted at the corners of her mouth but was spoiled by the topic at hand: "They'll shitcan Cruz for twenty-four hours before they release him on bail. That's SOP. They'll want to work him for a day."

Water rushed to fill the tub. "How did you handle that?" he asked. "I mean, bail and stuff? Why didn't they just keep both of you?" He felt a blush coming on as he decided to ask what he meant. "That is...how did you get out so fast?"

Jamaica sighed. It was a *what's a nice girl like you?* sound. She concentrated on the tub. "Because some things never change, and the world goes round, and hell, it's not really me they want..."

He saw her shoulders, lace ties hanging from the camisole like cornrowed hair. It was just the answer he had feared. He felt so much younger than Jamaica. He felt like a naive asshole.

She brought her smile back. "Hey—don't turn so blue." Her timbre was philosophical. "Sex with cops ain't like making love. It ain't even like sex with real people. It's the reason the great god Scope invented mouthwash." She let that sink in, then: "So. Is that tub ready yet?"

He tested the water and nearly scalded his hand. "Let me calm it down a little bit." He almost didn't want to look back, to see her one more deadly time. As if he had a choice.

She turned to fetch towels, leaving her camisole hanging from the doorknob—once cut glass, now a paint-clotted protuberance that could hardly turn either way. He saw her bare back, the way the skirt switched when she walked.

"Bubbles are bad for you anyway," she called from the other room.

"How's that?"

She reappeared with one white towel knotted low on her waist, like a sarong, and was otherwise nude except for the cat, which she cradled, letting its purr warm her bosom. The cat looked dopily pleased to be held so strategically.

Get an eyefulla this action, bubba.

"Stupid cat," Jonathan muttered. "He's freeloading here, honest. What did you say about bubbles?"

"They tend to bubble into uncomfortable places. Sometimes

they can speed along things like bladder infections."

"Really? God." He drew the plastic shower curtain halfway, shading the tub in blue-tinted light. "All yours, madame. I shall repair to the conservatory and ring Jeeves to bring up a tea tray for you."

She returned a courtly nod, keeping the cat poised where it was. As before, it was modesty feigned, and Jonathan found it overwhelmingly erotic.

He pulled the door partway shut, not needing to tell her that if she needed anything at all...

The sounds she made as she disturbed the hot, placid surface of the water were not entirely sounds of pleasure. He imagined the water dogging down bruises and scrapes and perhaps worse. Cleansing pain, like the cauterization of a wound. Her muted protests and yelps, echoing off the bathroom's haphazard tiling, finally settled into a drawn-out *mmmm.*

Leaving the warmth of the bathroom made the living room seem that much colder. Jonathan appreciated the glow from the hot plate and the rejuvenating smell of coffee. Bash had stashed small, bargain-sized bottles of Kahlua and Bailey's amid the scavengings in the kitchen box. Bash always seemed to be in host mode; his cabinets contained crap he would never touch himself. Jonathan remembered a time when he even kept cigarettes for guests, until he discovered how fast they staled. Now he ran a nonsmoking household. Jonathan counted himself lucky if he knew to buy coffee before he ran out. Amanda had learned that letting Jonathan stock the refrigerator by himself was a losing bet. Under his administration it would go unreplenished until it contained only a lemon plus several tubs of moldy stuff, unidentifiable food that looked more like failed biowar cultures.

Tonight, he had Bash's bounty with which to tweak the coffee and, he hoped, impress his first guest. He even had *two* spoons, by god.

"How we doing in there?" He curled fingers around the door crack. That was as much of him as dared to enter.

She emitted a long, low sound that announced she was not coming out into the world of cold air and snow anytime soon. "Jonathan? Can you bring the coffee in here? It *is* Jonathan, right, not John? I really want the coffee, but I really want to stay in the tub, too."

"What do you take?"

"Uh. Whatever. Cream and sugar, one each?"

His dino-mug was still at Rapid O'Graphics. For Jamaica's use he reserved a borrower from Bash's, featuring a cratered half-moon and science stats about it enameled in white on grey porcelain. For himself he scrounged a plastic hot mug he knew to be in one of the boxes. He blessed her cup with a generous dollop of Bailey's and hoped the crack in the handle would not offend her. Or make her think him cheap.

He tapped. "Room service. You might want to pull the curtain."

Her voice came back through the half-closed door. "Give me a break, Jonathan. Just get your ass in here and *talk* to me."

Steam escaped. The sink mirror was cloudy and the tiles were fogged; the airshaft window was like a dirty blackboard. The cat was calmly licking the floor where the shit-brown gunk had slopped earlier. Christ, had all this stuff happened in a single night? This morning he had endured Camela at Capra's, fighting not to respond to her smugness and dreading the release of the shaky foothold he had established at Bash's—by extension, the precarious hang he had on the alien turf of the Chicago 'burbs. Then had come a brackishly spicy Italian meal with Bash and his beloved, eaten mostly in stiff silence while Camela wallowed in what she thought was a territorial victory. Then had come the back-and-forth with Bash's truck; the box parade. Three trips—but not three truckloads. Jonathan knew he had stretched it out unduly. What else did he have on tap for the evening? Bash and Camela would be huffing and puffing the rest of the night.

All that had come before he had gotten adopted by the black cat. Before his tub had gotten slimed. Before the raid and the madness of dead babies, before the Nazi police, before meeting Cruz. Before Jamaica.

Bash would shit.

She was submerged to her upper lip; only her nipples broke the surface. Eyes closed, she recharged, her physique preserved

in blue water for Jonathan's scrutiny. In the midst of such a
fierce winter her mocha skin tone seemed unnatural, and was
unblemished by bikini lines. Her eyelids, wiped clean of shadow
and liner, were the same basic color as her toes. Jonathan guessed
at a tanning salon. Midway her dark triangle of ecu captured
his attention, an inviting equilateral on the sea of skin. Then he
noticed, against his will, the catalogue of bruises on her shins,
the marks where her forearms had been gripped hard and
lovelessly, the purpled tracks bestown on the calm swell of her
breasts, perhaps by Cruz, or, more horribly, by others. Jonathan
traced rise and contour and the perfect denotation of aureolae as
big as the circle he could make with thumb and forefinger, the
nipples centered there so much like thumbtips themselves. The
hot water had steamed her to the color of polished rubasse, and
her eyes were weighted and dopey, as those of the cat had been
in her arms. She extended a dripping hand for the coffee mug.
Jonathan watched water sluice down her forearm as though it
was a magic trick he could not quite figure out.

"God, this is great. This is total. After a night like this." She
would have laughed, but strengthlessly. She made a bittersweet
kind of snort. "I'm not making any sense. S'okay. Don't have
to. This is great." She raised to sip and Jonathan watched the
ripples. Her eyes widened, just a degree. "Oh. *Oh*. This is perfect,
too. Are you for hire? What do you charge? Do you do backs?"

"Cheers." He sipped his own and felt the strength spread
in his chest, a bloom of warmth. So far he was doing manfully
in the anti-*uh* department. He congratulated himself on his
aloof deportment in the presence of naked ladies. He was not
thinking about Amanda for entire minutes at a time, now.

"So tell me what happened after all the cop cars went home."

Up-down went her brows. "Hm. I've really gotta learn to
watch my mouth in the presence of those assholes. You don't
truly get away with fucking anything. You have to look your
part. *Any person not presenting a conservative middle-class fear/
respect attitude is likely to be bullied and tested in order to determine
their level of hostility to authority.* I'm quoting a guy named Doc
Stanley. There's a whole psychology to dealing with situations
like the one we had tonight. Stanley calls it 'policemanship.' *The*

whole objective is to avoid getting beaten up, arrested roughly, or shot. Since I'm here now, I guess it sort of worked anyway. I just get so fucking mad I forget my mouth. It always gets me in trouble later. Always." She switched the steaming mug to her other hand, agitating wave patterns that distorted the contour of her body underwater.

Jonathan's eyes were full of her. When she spoke his brain tried to hit the HOLD button. He had to remind himself to intersperse semi-intelligent nods and grunts. Proto-man attempts to indicate he is actually paying attention mentally as well as physically. He hoped the spiked coffee would continue to clear his head and plane the sharp edges off staying up too late. His eyelids felt packed with grit, sore and sanded as though tortured by floodlamps. You *vill* stay awake, he ordered himself. You *vill* pay zee attention.

"Whatever happened to all that *Dragnet* stuff about due process?" he said. "That Miranda stuff about reading your rights?"

Her gaze met his in blinking disbelief. She tilted her cup against the curved lip of the tub against the tiled wall. "I hate to be the one to tell you this, but Mighty Mouse is just a cartoon. Superman is an actor. And the Tooth Fairy was your parents." She grabbed a barely used cake of Ivory and began sculpting a head of lather in her hands.

"And TV cops follow by-the-book procedures that real cops know just ain't so," he said, paraphrasing Mark Twain.

"Plus which, I've had to deal with Stallis before. A real pig, and I don't just mean police brand pork. He's a pervert. Likes to be jerked off while you go down on another cop. He busts hookers so he can grab their ears and come in their faces. He likes smearing it around and making you lick it up. Sorry if I'm grossing you out."

"It's okay." He remembered to bring his cup the rest of the way to his mouth; it had frozen halfway.

"Sometime I'll tell you a horror story about Stallis and a girl named Little Oral Angie, no lie." Foam drifted on the surface of the water as she lathered. "Did you say you had a loofa? I didn't see it."

He rummaged around and uncovered it. The cat had pulled its vanishing act again. "Oh, and by the way, the answer to your question is yes."

"What question?" She sat up in the tub with a slosh.

"'Do you do backs?' Yes."

"Boy, I was hoping you'd say that." She leaned forward, hardly parting her legs. Her knees did not break surface. She was very supple. "Why, here's a convenient back right here. And I'm sure you need the practice."

"Nah. I'm a black belt at backs. Say that fast three times." He held out his hand for the soap. She drank, he scrubbed.

He thought of his own recent past and waxed unexpectedly forgiving. Who in hell was he to judge someone like Jamaica? Everybody did what they had to do to survive, as the cliché went. Once you had that taken care of, you could think about living, not merely surviving.

Without really knowing whether he'd be able to borrow Bash's truck again in time to get Cruz out of the slammer, he assured her that it would present no difficulty.

"Is the sun up yet?" She was looking toward the darkness of the airshaft window. She pushed back, bracing herself against the pressure he brought to bear on the sponge.

It was Saturday morning. Work today was optional, he decided. "It's daylight, but it's raining. The windows are iced up. Streets'll be a nightmare." The snowpack would grow a thick, slippery crust of solid ice. Driving or walking through it would be like trying to juggle while seated on a chair balanced by one leg on an icecube—Nature's response to Jonathan's foolish assumption that the weather just could not get worse.

Her resinous amber-green eyes sought him again. "Mind if I crash here for now? I'll have to check in with Bauhaus later, but that's later. He won't talk to me because of my recent proximity to the cops. You have a cot. Right?"

His heart sped up again. "Uh—a cot." He couldn't help that one. "Yeah. My friend—Bash, that is—got me some sheets and blankets and stuff, plus I've got a good sleeping bag, which works better than a comforter. You can take the cot, I guess, and I'll the take the bag, and—"

"I think we can fit two on the cot, Jonathan." She closed her eyes and smiled at some internal joke. She saw his puzzlement, the facial evidence of turmoil, conflicting signals, hormones and adrenaline rampant. "Stop being so gallant and do me a favor. We did a ton of coke tonight and when I drop off I'll be like a corpse. I don't want to sleep like that alone. I want to be held while I snooze. If you want a more complex explanation, I'm sorry, I don't have one. Okay?"

He swallowed hard. "Sure." His throat clicked.

"Great. Now get out of here because I don't want you to see the red marks this tub has left on my butt."

He laughed, relieved, and handed over a fresh folded towel. "Vintage Holiday Inn linens, stolen by Bash. For guests, strictly."

"Thank you. I'm touched. Do you think you could find me a T-shirt or something I could wear to bed?"

"I doubt it," he said. Jonathan the Glib.

Now would be a good time to see if the space heater Bash had loaned him worked. Jamaica's mention of sleep suddenly twisted his weariness knob to full blast. His feet and shoulders decided to leadenly protest their new, extended hours. Too many chores.

Somebody was arranging to pass cash to him. Maybe they were working furtive setups for Cruz's bail right now. This all might seem more thrilling if he could catch just a nubbin of sleep.

He looked down and saw the cat waiting for him at the end of a trail of dark, wet little cat footprints.

You'll never guess what I just found.

It was fastidiously licking beads of blood from its whiskers. It apparently liked the taste.

Fifteen

Morning.

As suburbs go, even in daylight Oakwood can strike you as being a haunted place. Jonathan thinks it might just be the winter, a ferocity to which he is unaccustomed, but it takes more than snow and cold to make a place this inhospitable. He cannot imagine it warmer, even in fair summertime weather.

The streets here seem as disused as the corridors of a plantation estate abandoned to cobwebs and dry rot. By noon the town's pallor resists the sporadic penetrations of sunlight; by midnight, with the chemical light of streetlamps lending an operating-theatre sterility to the snow and quiet, the shadows rearrange themselves into an unforgiving chiaroscuro that bespeaks not a natural scene, but a still life. Stilled life. The few pedestrians or motorists that dare manifest themselves seem to originate from somewhere outside the dry township cordon, and are bound for destinations nowhere near Oakwood. That imaginary boundary locks out so much of the real. Residents sleep here as deeply as hibernating vampires, cocooned in ennui and insulated by the cobalt television glow of business as usual.

They do not even sleep in a true section of Chicago.

The visages of the houses lining Kentmore and Garrison are as blank of identity as a busload of retards. The architecture is lively and Gothic, but in the manner of a jaunty and ornate tombstone. The designers and artisans had been alive and vibrant…but that time is long past. The houses, the monuments, remain shrouded in their annual quarter of coma. Somewhere, smothered beneath the four-foot snowpack, are paving stones and tarmac and sidewalks, icons of a lost civilization awaiting archaeological excavation. The eyes of the walkers who pass Jonathan look not trapped, but hunted; not totally dead, but fatally brutalized. They dart at the passage of another human being, not afraid so much as shocked into jaded lifelessness. Once passed by, you cease to exist—the better to curtail the bloody fantasies of assault, injury, the swift rape or the blade in the spine. Urban terror refined to the sweet, sealant thickness of country honey.

Jonathan's mind tells him that this is not a place for those interested in living. One can subsist here, as in the Arctic, but beyond the challenge of survival no rewards await. It reminds him of an ancient bastille, gone to ruin and occupied by nomads. Life here had made sense once. Now there was no life, only occupation. Customers shuffle listlessly in and out of markets, clutching sacks. Snow is robotically shoveled from drives and walkways. At the coffee shop where Jonathan takes most of his solitary meals for convenience's sake, the locals seem salty and inimical. Nobody wanted to be bothered. They shuffled to the churches of their choice every seventh day with the same zombiatic lack of expression. It was nearly atavistic, a behavior remembered but no longer comprehended.

When daylight intrudes it lends a funereal aspect to the denuded trees. Still they reach, skeletally, toward a sky that cannot offer photosynthesis. What leaves linger, dead, are bereft of autumn hues and have gone utterly black. When Jonathan considers the iron-colored sky, the frozen mud, the black leaves, he thinks again of Usher's tarn.

Not merely the sky, but the downpour itself is gray—the stained hue of unclean ivory. Fat drops, ice-cold, plash through swirling mist; the combination chills to the very strands of muscle fiber. Jonathan no longer feels the cold and the rain fails to touch or despoil Amanda, who stares down upon him. He is posed all wrong inside a casket that is too small for him. Her eyes flare. They tell him that if he wanted to get horizontal so badly, then this arrangement is fine by her. She plucks the best irises from the floral groupings while rainwater rapidly fills the casket. Wet silk is disgusting. Amanda smiles, keeps the flowers for herself, and continues to watch dispassionately as the freezing water rises to cover Jonathan's open eyes.

Nobody fit in Oakwood. But most stayed. Jonathan does not fit here, and neither does Bash, for that matter. Or Cruz, or Jamaica.

Jonathan wishes he could save somebody.

He awoke spooned into Jamaica from behind, still wearing his pants and socks.

His left arm was draped over her and cradled between both of her forearms. His hand had nestled just under her chin. When first he tried to retrieve it, her sleeping grip tightened. *Don't go.* He could feel her breathing. Beneath the sleeping bag her scrubbed skin exuded a teasing aroma that made him want to close his eyes and return to dreamland, to stay this way forever.

Except that would mean fossilization deep in the calcified heart of Oakwood, and Jonathan would rather die. The sound that had awakened him was itself like a heartbeat.

Boom-cha-boom-cha-cha. He timed it against the noise of blood traversing his vessels, the backbeat of his own heart muscle. *Boom-boom-boom-cha. Boom-boom-cha-cha-cha.*

First it was 4/4, then almost a rap beat. It seemed to vibrate in his direction from the outer walls of the building, sounding distant, easily blanked by the ambient noise of the other apartments. Transmitted, perhaps, via beam and bricking from the rooms on the far western side, in the manner of canyon acoustics. Perhaps from the other floors.

A hard and a soft. Then hard/soft-soft. Then hard-hard-hard/soft/hard-hard/soft. Then over again. Same cadence each time, now. It stabilized.

His mind wanted to explain it so he could forget it. Kenilworth Arms had been sliced and diced into forty or more units by his reckoning, its less vintage walls like pasteboard. Transient tenants and odd hours were factors of an equation whose product was this foundation rhythm, *boom-cha*, hard to soft. Somebody somewhere in the building would be spinning tunes no matter what the hour. Or staring at nightowl music shows on the tube. Someone was always awake, watching or listening or fighting, in a place like this. If Jonathan had hoped for respite by marking time in this place, then he'd better get used to the extended dance mix—uh huh uh huh *boom-cha-cha.*

It was not an authentic part of the barrage of salsa and heavy metal native to the building's constituency, whom Jonathan had seen knocked rudely up just hours previously. Nor was it the raw noise of those occupants or residents themselves moving up and down the narrow firetrap stairways in the metronomic march of life in America below the poverty index. It was not outside traffic. Any sound could obliterate it. But it was always there, like a base coat buried beneath the twenty-plus layers of generic paint that Fergus the super tended to slap all over every wall and door in the joint.

A lone car slushed past on Garrison, compressing snow. Jonathan lost the mystery sound—what he fancied the heartbeat of the building.

Boom-cha.

He remembered coming out of the bathroom and seeing the black cat with fresh blood dappling its muzzle.

Jamaica was going to be coming out the door any second. He had moved quickly, snatching up the cat.

Hey! Now wait just a darn...

Move fast. He ascertained that it had not injured itself. It was not in pain. The blood had come from somewhere else. Probably a rat or other small vermin of the sort cats relish torturing prior to killing.

"You little fuck." Jonathan's pleasant nighttime interlude was in jeopardy of being ruined by the innate sadism of a lower life form. *Wunderbar.* No mewling, he thought. You start meowing and I'll slam your face in the door jamb.

Rub, rub. Want some?

"You don't fool me, you fucking little parasite."

Rub, rub. It got blood on Jonathan's shirt.

I wuvvv you...feed me. C'mon.

He booted it out the first door.

Sigh.

It smoothed its ruffles and began to rub against the wall of the cramped interior hallway.

Jonathan popped a button rushing his shirt off. Great. Jamaica will come out and see me stripping. Wrong ideas all around. Life could be such a sitcom.

She emerged from the bathroom turbaned and swaddled in towels, deep heat radiating from her exposed shoulders, her racing-fine legs, the coltish weave of muscles at her neck. Naturally, the first thing she requested was the cat. Jonathan made a pretense of finding her a T-shirt to wear and she made a joke about him giving her the shirt off his back.

He lamely explained that the cat had wanted to go out. After all, he was not sure whether it was owned by someone else in the building already. He was certain that any second he would stumble over a half-eviscerated carcass in the middle of the floor. Then Jamaica would want out.

No miniature corpse turned up. Things stabilized. They fell to sleep surprisingly fast.

Now Jamaica sighed and burrowed closer, maneuvering her ass into his lap, seeking his warmth the way a plant phototropically leans toward light. He had been conscious only scant moments. He became aware that the button fly on his jeans was restraining a heroic erection from the world at large. He had to disengage himself to take a leak.

The bathroom had gone clammy in the steam's feeble aftermath, and Jonathan felt moving air as he pulled the light chain above the sink.

The shower curtain stirred weakly. Not exactly a gust; most like a deflected breath. He swept it aside and discovered the cardboard square slightly dislodged from the window frame, its top edges bent as though it had been slapped through from the outside. He considered this quizzically, the light from the bathroom's bare bulb stinging his eyes. Too early for this shit. He leaned in and gave the cardboard a tug. It resisted. He had pressured it in nice and tight. From the colder face his fingers collected minute smears of the brownish gunk he'd had to deal with in pools earlier; the crap the cat had tried to lap up, dry and pasty now. It reminded him of vomited bile, of fresh hot bone marrow, of an encyclopedia of things revolting.

He washed his hands. He repeated when he found the stink

was tenacious and clinging. After the rinsewater gurgled down the drain, he thought he heard the heartbeat of the building again. *Boom-cha-cha.* Then an upstairs toilet flushed, the pipes awoke, and the ghost noise hid out again.

The air was fetid, sulphurous and chilly. With care he bent the cardboard and pushed; it snapped back into the windowframe grooves willingly enough.

He thought of swinging by Rapid O'Graphics when his business at the jail was completed. Capra had everything. Jonathan could probably borrow one of the big battery lamps, the six-volters racked in the garage. As for the airshaft, it certainly smelled as though some leprous creature had been half-eaten, then discarded to molder in the soup of freezing sewage and drowned fauna. Maybe he could spotlight physical evidence for some sort of complaint. For now it was sufficient that the ominously sagging bathroom ceiling did not collapse and inundate him in a downpour of watery shit.

Tomorrow, he reminded himself. Tomorrow was now.

It was light outside, and still raining. The snow smoked. Dense fog rose to swirl in the steady sprinkles. 207's steam coil labored, leaking heat like a running nose. Thank the gods for Bash's space heater.

He'd have to ask to borrow the truck again tomorrow. Today.

He ran the sink tap until the water warmed again, and dabbed his face, prodding nuggets from the corners of his eyes. A tubful of mystery diarrhea, then cops, then the cat had come back bloody. A kid had gone missing and a bust had gone down. Now he was awake, having slept maybe a grand total of forty-five minutes, with a hooker snoozing not fifteen feet away on a borrowed cot, on borrowed sheets, after having absorbed a Mason jar of other men's semen in one night. He rubbed his face to scare up circulation; the tip of his nose was cold. He tried to visualize Amanda's face, in the mirror, superimposed over his own reflection saying...

Look at you. Some victory. Some life you're building. Just look at you. Baby, you're so fucked up you don't even know that you ARE fucked up.

"Hell with you," he said to the mirror, whose edges were

blotched from where the silver backing had gotten wet, then
blossomed into mildew and decay. He thought of thick corneal
scars.

"Jesus, you're freezing," Jamaica said when he returned to
bed. She snuggled, grabbing his arm and pressing his frigid
fingertips to her sternum, near her heart. He felt the tempo in her
chest, racing, then relaxing as she eased back into slumber. He
felt her heartbeat and heard no other. He tried to imagine he was
back with Amanda, that she was touching him in this receptive
way, that things had leveled out through some unguessable
alchemy. And soon, lying to himself, he achieved fitful sleep.

Cruz had to be signed for.

The circumstances might have been amusing, but Jonathan
was jumpy and flying solo. Jamaica had zero desire to cross the
threshold of the Oakwood police station again, and Jonathan
realized he had never been inside one of these places his whole
life. He had never even *phoned* the police before, and now he
was compelled to visit their brightly lit lair. All he knew of the
trappings and procedures of police had come from two—count
'em—speeding tickets. And television. Most of what he thought
he knew was tame or mistaken.

Jamaica's camisole was truly stale, and Jonathan had lent
her an Overkill T-shirt and muffler to wear beneath her car coat.
She provided explicit directions and they took the Eisenhower
Expressway downtown. He was told to circle the block while
she ducked into a brownstone near Van Buren and Wells.
Ten minutes later she was out, with Cruz's bail enriching her
saddlebag.

The Oakwood station had plenty of exterior lighting and an
abundance of parking. The lots and walks were clear of snow.
Salts and chemicals had been sprinkled like Parmesan cheese on
the pathways. It crunched underfoot.

He took in the heavy glass doors, the security cameras and
bulletin boards. Flyers featured feted officers and down-home
updates on specially organized social soirees. The waiting
benches were comfortless. There was a revolving pamphlet
rack. JUST SAY NO TO DRUGS. TEN WAYS TO PREVENT

HOME INVASIONS. RAPE IS A FOUR LETTER WORD. The room's centerpiece was a semicircular desk, laminated like the countertop at a McDonald's in a queasy hospital orange, and resembling the throne dais of some Martian monarch. Within were all manner of weird police buttons and phones and consoles. Beyond it was an eight-by-four window whose sickly tint tipped it as a one-way mirror. Jonathan saw himself, fingers steepled on the counter, wondering what in hell to do next.

He glanced behind himself. Nobody home except for him and the payphones. He could be sealed in, no doubt, by the touch of a hidden switch.

A buzzer razzed and a big door behind the dais opened. An identical door was set flush with the brick wall outside the dais. Both had massy aluminum lock knobs and matched the doors Jonathan remembered from college classrooms. Both doors had inset squares of shatterproof, wire-mesh glass at eye level.

"Something you want?"

It was a fully uniformed officer at least seven inches shorter than Jonathan. He had a bald spot for which a handlebar moustache fought to compensate. His eyes were red-rimmed; brown like a Labrador's. Eyes unwilling to consider chat about the weather. His tags read MALLORY but for Jonathan it was too late—this man was the Doggie Cop.

He felt as though his thought transmissions had been time-delayed. Voyager calling Jonathan. He consciously aborted the *uh* command from his speech center.

"I'm here for Cruz." It was out of his mouth. "He was arrested yesterday."

"Charge?"

I didn't bring my MasterCard. He shrugged noncommittally. Not my job.

The Doggie Cop shrugged too, then riffled a card file with supreme disinterest. His tongue worked at his incisors, dislodging stubborn food. He turned to a stack of yellow flimsies on the crescent of desk and paged through. The carbon sandwiches left smudges; they were probably the source of the smeary fingerprints Jonathan noticed on most of the other paperwork.

"Ah. A little nose candy action down at Kenilworth Arms," the cop said—trying, convicting and executing in one sentence. His K9 eyes reassessed Jonathan in light of this new information. Jonathan read suspicion and dislike. He battled to look behind and see if anyone scummier had just entered, some alternate suspect for whom the cop's prejudicial glare was meant instead of him.

"I don't know, man. I'm just here to bail him out." Inwardly he winced. *Man* was obviously doper slang to this minion of justice.

The Doggie Cop surveyed the room. "No bondsman? No judge?"

"Uh—no?" Jonathan had to wet his lips.

Once more the glare, accompanied by a rueful shake of the head. "Hope you brought your piggy bank, kid, 'cos bail for prisoner Cruz is going to run you a couple grand."

Jonathan was prepared for this one. Better than three thousand in Franklin notes padded the inside pocket of his parka. He feigned surprise. Jamaica had prepped him. "How many grand?"

"Coke's two thousand an ounce, give or take. I'm sure it ain't that much to your...buddies. Twenty-five hundred."

Jonathan felt an invisible dragnet constrict his epiglottis. Jamaica had warned him not to respond to baiting or taunts. Stay polite and neutral. Don't insult back or speak when not spoken to. *Winning in a police encounter,* she said, quoting Doc Stanley again, *meant that at its conclusion you were left alone.*

"Excuse me, officer, but it's been nearly a whole day. I suppose Cruz has been booked, and I'd like to bail him out now, please."

That seemed to tighten the Doggie Cop's knob. He nodded, tongue still probing, scribbled on a form, then lifted a receiver and buzzed the jailer, dismissing Jonathan from his notice.

The door behind him opened and Sergeant Barnett, the Robot Cop, lumbered through, recognizing Jonathan with open distaste.

"Ahh, *Christ.*" He was tired; his voice was burry. "See, Mallory? Told you this scumbag was a buddy of the pusher and the whore. Jesus H. fucking Christ."

Apparently he was unaware the Doggie Cop had not been in attendance at the Kenilworth bust. Or it just did not matter. Or all Oakwood cops shared knowledge through instantaneous telepathy. Cop logic.

But harrowing was not enough for this guy. He was a veteran. "Wantcha to do me a favor, sport." He hoisted the hinged portion of the desk and squeezed through, his medals and equipment clanking. "You want to lean up this counter here, and you want to put your feet back and spread 'em. Time for a little pat-me-down."

The Doggie Cop's eyebrows arched. He did not approve.

Jonathan's mouth unhinged. "Do I look stupid enough to waltz into a police station holding?" It was academic. He wished Jamaica had been inside to hear him say it.

The Robot Cop snorted and kicked Jonathan's legs further askew. The search was thorough, professional, degrading.

They made Jonathan wait another forty-five minutes. The clock in the police anteroom was exactly like the clocks he remembered from high school. The sweep second hand moved slower on the 6 to 12 crawl, faster on the 12 to 6 fall. Cruz was released to await arraignment, set about a month from the arrest date. He came out through the companion door to the one the Robot Cop had used.

He looked as though he had been backed over by a bulldozer. He had trouble with the door. He held a heat-sealed plastic property bag in one hand, and did not recognize Jonathan at first.

"Hey, neighbor," Jonathan began, hurting already.

The nod of acknowledgment obviously hurt Cruz. His left eye was welded into a puffy squint, hued like titanium jewelry. His lips were fat. He worked his mouth like a senile man chewing bland food; Jonathan realized he was keeping a running inventory of tongue and teeth. His stride was constrained and cautious. He held his left arm curled against his stomach as though supported by an imaginary sling.

"Thanks." It came out *thankf.* "For coming."

"Looks like I'm too late. You need help—?"

"No. Just get me...out of here." His eyes sought the EXIT door, his grail now within his grasp.

Jonathan lowered his voice as they approached the push-bar. "I've got the truck. Jamaica's with me. Bauhaus arranged for the bail, but she picked up the money." Okay, he thought: Favor performed, humiliation endured, sleep lost. Now came the chaser. "Listen, Cruz. We've got to talk about some stuff—"

Cruz snorted—oh so carefully—and smiled as much as his battered face would permit. It was more a graveyard grimace. "She fuck you?"

"No, it's not that."

Cruz overrode, waving his uninjured hand. The baggie swung. "Let it...hang fire a bit. Now let's...just go." Jonathan heard *lezjest gho.*

In the back, no clocks. In the front, clocks. Have a *nice* day!

Twenty minutes into his enforced wait, Jonathan had given Jamaica the Toyota keys so she could keep the heater and radio going. She wouldn't really steal Bash's truck...he hoped. When he and Cruz came out, the truck cab was thankfully toasty. When Jamaica saw Cruz Jonathan saw her mouth go *omigod.*

"I've got Percodans in my bag," she told him, and that was all Cruz needed to hear. He dry swallowed two and washed them down with a minty swig of her Scope.

"First we gotta. Bauhaus..."

Jonathan felt an evanescent dislike toward not being thanked, and now being expected to play chauffeur. But for him to pussy out on his surge of samaritanism now would be an act as cowardly and illogical as the rest of his life. Besides—hearing about what had transpired in the room above his apartment was entertaining in an unexpected way, sort of like seeing alien TV for the first time.

Jamaica rode the transmission hump, one long leg on either side of the stick. Of course. Jonathan's shifting hand got to brush her knee; that dispelled his momentary pique. So far Cruz had been the night's biggest victim. Relax and ride this thing out.

"You still think Uncle Bauhaus set up that little entertainment last night?"

Cruz shook his head at Jamaica. "They came to see about that kid that disappeared. Not us."

About the time Cruz and Jamaica had been grinding and gyrating, and Jonathan had been loitering at Bash's with truckload number three, at Kenilworth several police shutterbugs, two detectives and a sleepy man representing the Cook County coroner had come and gone. Eleventh-hour bigotry had prompted Sgt. Barnett to turn the rest of Kenilworth's constituency inside-out, to see what sort of incriminating goodies might shake loose and hit the floor.

"If Bauhaus *didn't*...set it up..." Blood outlined Cruz's teeth. He was trying to speak without causing himself any more damage. The bear-fucker in the cell had kicked the synapses right out of his skull. He could still see the jism-stained floor rushing at his face. He'd hit and skidded. That brought surging back the image of Chiquita, still falling. "*If*...then don't mention the dope to him. Not word one."

"I don't get it." Jonathan always tried honesty when clarity failed him. He braked for a red light on Lake Street, westbound. The Toyota surfed the final few feet wetly, and he got to touch Jamaica's leg again.

Good godamighty.

"Cruz had to ditch the two keys Bauhaus stuck him with," Jamaica explained.

"Keys." Jonathan thought of door keys, like the copies of the keys to 207 he'd cut for Bash, just in case things got "domestic" with Camela. When the police said "domestic" they were usually referring to a boxing match between cohabitants.

"He put them in a plastic bag and dumped it down the airshaft. If the bust last night wasn't staged by Bauhaus, to acid-test Cruz, then Cruz can say he legitimately had to flush the whole stash. We can get that shit back, sell it, or just sit on it." She computed. "It's better than ninety large Bauhaus will just have to kiss bye-bye as part of the hazards of doing business."

"Split. Three ways." Cruz tried to grin again as he looked toward Jonathan. "Less small change, that's twenty-nine or thirty grand. For each of us." He was already thinking of FedExing the stash to Rosie for some out-of-state laundering.

"Not counting what Bauhaus had goddamn well better pay Jonathan here, for playing stalking horse." Jamaica smiled.

Cruz had no idea what a stalking horse might be, but nodded in agreement, so far as his sprung neck would allow.

"Uhh...listen, guys." Jonathan kept his eyes on the bob and weave of the snow-encrusted road unreeling before them. "I don't know if I'm cut out for the wonderful world of drug sales. Honest. If it's all the same to you, I'll take whatever this guy Bauhaus cares to spend out of the goodness of his heart. You guys are welcome to the rest."

"I told Bauhaus it'd better be a thousand, at least," Jamaica told Cruz. "Jonathan's all right. Too scared of the cops, but all right. Don't push him. He did you a favor."

"Offer's still open." One of the things Rosie had always taught Cruz was the value of engendering good faith. That translated as making as many people as possible beholden to your disposable gestures and courtesies. The concept was nothing new to anybody who had seen or read *The Godfather.* No strain. The flash of cash usually brought around the holdouts by the time you needed them.

She almost poked Cruz with an elbow, then realized there probably was not a place on his body that did not hurt. "Don't push him. He's nervous enough about this shit." Her tone suggested she found Jonathan's discomfort kind of cute.

Cruz made a pain noise. "Think that guy may have dislocated my fucking shoulder." After Bauhaus, then maybe a hospital. He briefly outlined the fight in the bullpen. It didn't sound very exciting in the retelling. "I'm afraid to actually look at it..."

"Yeah, nobody's gonna want to sit on *your* face for a while, babe." They sparred visually. "Just kidding, Cruz. Christ on a skateboard."

Jonathan's imagination did a riff on the advantages of collecting thirty thousand dollars, tax free, in hand. It was a swift and intoxicating fantasy. He could buy his own car, drive straight out of this hellpit, pull a real Houdini on everyone. Escape. Run to a town where no one knew him...and start fucking up his life all over again. Dirty up that nice clean slate.

Or he could stick with the scenario he'd bought into the moment he picked up the payphone and contacted MR HAPPY. He could wipe the slate he had until it was pristine, then chalk up something that made sense. That seemed more like real honor.

"Turn up this drive, right here, before the street sign," said Jamaica.

"We clear?" said Cruz.

She checked. "Nobody's sniffing our butts. They probably don't know about this truck."

It had not even occurred to Jonathan to worry about whether they had been tailed. They were, after all, suspects and worse.

The notion that his prosaic life had speed-shifted from sordid soapery to sleek spy thriller shot a thrill of excitement though his parts. Except for his stomach, which pestered him endlessly about the throw-up option. All voted in favor of the singing lunch. He might get shot. He could get arrested. That meant he could get beaten up by the cops or the thug brigade that had manhandled Cruz...or both. He might wind up in Lake Michigan wearing cinderblock loafers. Bash would never believe it.

He could also just shut up and make the dark turn to the House of Bauhaus, which he did almost without thinking.

Sixteen

Bauhaus was enrobed pasha-style. He struck Jonathan more as a plump warlock delightedly overseeing his coven of nymphet witchlings. Theme night at the freak tent. Patchouli incense hung cloying and impenetrable; the smell of migraines.

Jonathan gawked too much: At the lavish waste of the blood-tinted Chinese draperies, at the retina-numbing mileage of neon, at the wall of mirrors and the wall of windows, at the amphetamine-injected security measures.

Spy thriller, definitely.

"What's the matter, young knight?" Bauhaus was addressing Cruz. "Forget our tae kwondo? Fell asleep during the lecture? Looks like King Kong used you to scrape out his bong screen."

That elicited titters from the faithful. Chari was pedestaled like a Tijuana Buddha atop one of the barstools, warming her fanny by the fireplace. She was barely draped in some ephemeral little nothing, her sparsely furred auburn muff visible for the world's appraisal. There were spoons and straws and dope galore on the onyx bartop, and she had obviously wasted no time cramming—just in case there was a pop quiz.

Past Chari, Cruz half expected to see Krystal still passed out on the kitchen floor. She was down in the sofa pit, packing away sour cream and onion Ruffles one after another and staring at the big video screen. Her mouth champed like a shredder but her eyes did not blink. She was watching the *Friday the 13th* movies in sequence, on fast-forward. She made mewling noises as assorted fornicating teens got divvied. Cruz realized she was providing her own fast-mo soundtrack: *Whee screech yahh chop...*

Cruz had to sit down; the room kept moving. "Listen," he

said to Bauhaus. "I'm fucking exhausted. I want a doctor to look at my arm. I need a bath and some real food. I want some Percodans, some Talwins and enough blow to level my head."

"First fill me in on the party the police invited themselves to," said Bauhaus. "You can clean up here." Using one of the candles burning at the bar, he fired up a coca paste cigarette in a holder of drilled ebony and gave it a few languid puffs. It smelled like smoldering bathtub mold.

"Five cop cars showed up. You stuck me with two keys. I had to flush it. All of it. Even the wrappers."

Bauhaus frowned. It was the look of someone who has just pitched a paperball toward a wastebasket and missed. No points. "Damn it. All gone?"

"Sorry. But they're dying to tie me to you. They found the beeper."

"Did they find the gun?"

"It was in the apartment when I left; I haven't been back yet. I came straight here." Cruz knew that if he claimed to have hidden the gun, Bauhaus would want to know where, and why didn't he just hide the dope there, too? Better to let him think the gun had been quietly confiscated and had gone into some cop's private arsenal as a fringe perk of not writing up an unregistered handgun report.

"And I wouldn't've made it here if it hadn't been for this guy." Cruz indicated Jonathan.

Krystal had worked her way up to Part Five. On the screen the FBI warning raced past, polluted with scanning blur.

"This is Jonathan," Jamaica said. "The one who called."

Bauhaus sniffed and laid a finger aside his nose, studying. "Good of you."

Jonathan felt himself being visually sized up. He thought of his embarrassment in stores where nothing seemed to fit him. If he sang a long and tedious opera about why he had decided to help Cruz it would bore everybody and make less sense than the bloody misadventures of Jason. His smile was not returned.

Cruz reclined his head, trying to hold his face on. Even rising from the chair would be a chore.

Jonathan wondered whether Bauhaus was stoked on some

kind of drug right now. All eyes in the room—except Krystal's—
turned to record the entrance of the young boy Cruz had seen
his first night here. He crept down the spiral staircase and sat on
the bottom step, bracing his bare feet against the center column.
He was built slender, and the drop of the monkish brown
pullover robe he wore revealed a girlishly round bottom. His
hair was colorless and anemic, and fell in the direction of least
resistance. His skin was very fine to mint, china-thin, revealing
delicate traceries of blue veins. The pink hands and feet were
innocent of physical labor. He seemed pleased to sit and stare
at some nondescript spatial junction, with lemur-pupilled eyes
as blue as the neon in the room...and as empty as a beer can at
a toga party. Jonathan thought of Puff the cat, on his invisible
monster watch. Bauhaus sidled over and fed the boy a white
tablet from a dish on the bar. When the boy swallowed, Bauhaus
petted his head.

"Never mind Lord Alfred, here," Bauhaus said. "He's gone
back to his home planet for the nonce."

"Uranus," Jamaica whispered to Jonathan, grinning.

"Jonathan, is it?" The cigarette holder moved from one
downturned corner of Bauhaus' mouth to the other. "I wonder
if you could help our friend Cruz crutch his way to the
bathroom from here, so he can begin cleaning up. I'll have the
drugs he needs and anything else sent on in, hmm? Use the
blue bedroom." He pointed. A simple gesture done imperiously.
"Oh—and Cruz? Your pal Rosie wants to talk with you. I have
the secret numbers and all that folderol. Take care of it after you
hit the showers. You smell, kiddo."

"Stop calling me kiddo."

Jonathan played candystriper. Not facing Bauhaus' cherry
cordial gaze felt better.

"Man, my body feels like a bag full of broken sticks," Cruz
said. At least he was articulating better. "You know when you
rake leaves and sweep everything into a Hefty bag and the
twigs and branches poke holes in the plastic? That's what my
body feels like."

Cruz had not done yardwork since he was eight, and
Jonathan had not lived in a place with a lawn to tend since age

twelve. Past a bedroom of hedonistic overstatement, he helped Cruz get the massage spray started. The shower was as big as his entire bathroom back at Kenilworth.

"Watch your ass with Bauhaus," was the only caveat Jonathan received. "Be careful."

Jamaica had squared off with Bauhaus during Jonathan's brief absence.

"He's okay, and I think it's time to pay him. At least a grand. He spared you a lot of grief." She stood arms akimbo, legs apart, a referee stance. Bauhaus was in slippers, and shorter. His eyes shone the transparent slate-black of apache tear, glittering in the opium-den lighting, assaying her, then him, then her.

"Absolutely," he said. It did not sound from the heart. "Why not. A little recompense for our good friend, *Jonathan*. Better watch your ass, girl. He might turn out to be a better bargain than you." He turned to Jonathan and brightened artificially. "Well! Why don't you kiddies help yourself to some goodies while Uncle Bauhaus makes a few nasty ole phone calls. Sounds like you did real good, there, Jonathan. Maybe I'll rent you this highbox cooze for the night? Did you know you can do just *any* old thing you want to her? She'll eat the peanuts and corn kernels out of your shit for money." He smiled venomously.

The words hit her like a slap, and were just as preferred. "I'd say fuck you, Bauhaus…but then, we know human fucking isn't to your taste anyway." She was off toward the bar with a haughty swishing of hips.

Everyone's scoring points, Jonathan thought. Bauhaus was probably angry at the loss of his drugs, and venting this via general abuse. He began to think the insults he heard carried no real clout.

Now he faced Bauhaus by himself. He felt himself being sniffed and litmus-tested. Outside, frozen rain pelted the floor-to-ceiling glass and made Chicago decompose into a Symbolist blur of twinkling lights. It all looked so clean and organized from a distance—the view of a hated former hometown as seen from the seat of a jetliner used to escape it forever.

The phony bonhomie was back. Bauhaus swept his arms wide to embrace the room and all that was his—bought and paid for, indentured till death or arrest did them part.

"Make yourself at home, Jonathan. *Mi casa es su casa,* right? Help yourself to anything you see. As our little rent-a-slut Jamaica says, you've saved me a lot of trouble and expense by pitching in. That gesture should be rewarded, since you don't know me from Caligula." His eyes sought Jamaica. She was at the bar, her back turned. "She's a dear. We always spar this way. Just like nasty little pussy cats."

On the big screen, a flash of crimson as Jason split wide a copulating teenybopper. Krystal went *whee, wheee.*

"Ciao for now." Bauhaus was off down the hall.

Jonathan let himself be drawn back in Jamaica's direction. He was uncomfortable in this movie-cum-reality. Since he had come through the front door, none of Bauhaus' three worker bees had spoken a syllable.

"Hi."

"Hi yourself." Jamaica finished her toot and dabbed up the residue to work her gums. "I need a drink."

Voice lowered, Jonathan said, "I need something; this is just all too weird, okay?"

"Mm. Hadn't noticed." She snickered and boffed his bicep. "Don't fret all this showoff shit. Bauhaus was the fat kid in school who never made friends, and now he has power." She found a thick-bottomed tumbler and filled it with Stoli on rocks as clear as medical lenses.

"I guess a beer."

"Permit me," she said, waving him toward a stool. "Never mind Blow White; sit on down."

Whatever Chari was fixated on, Jonathan could not perceive. Occasionally she would run her fingertips over her neck, her thighs, as though feeling up something in the dark and trying to guess what it was.

On the bar below one of the brass hurricane lanterns he saw what resembled a chromium soup bowl heaped with flour. It was close by the fruit-salad dish of pills.

"Jesus. Is that cocaine? I mean…is that *all* cocaine?"

"Bauhaus cares enough to stock the very best." She spoke with her head in the fridge. "How do you feel about New Amsterdam?"

"I'm not sure about *old* Amsterdam yet. Got any Quietly?"

"Wow, I see we've gone native. Yeah, here's one." She opened the freezer and extracted a heavy, frosted mug. Her gaze followed Jonathan's from her legs to the cocaine and back. "Go on, sailor, have a snort. One thing about Bauhaus' in-house coke—you don't have to worry about it being cut with lye. Although the purity sometimes makes it feel the same in your sinuses." She laughed at her own joke.

He dipped a finger and inspected the powder as stupidly as Chari's expression. She continued to stare deep and hard into the gossamer weave of patchouli smoke. Into nothing. Behind her on the bar was an open can of Coca-Cola with condensation beading the lower half. Granules littered the pop-top.

"Looks like our lost little girl has been putting the coke back into Coke," said Jamaica.

"Coke used to have real coke in it...didn't it?" This conversation was tilting into the surreal.

"Yup. True cocaine was removed from the mix around the turn of the century. They substituted caffeine. And there was a cocaine wine once that was really popular—Vin Mariani. Thomas Edison drank it. Jules Verne drank it. Even a President—Grant or Wilson or McKinley, somebody like that. It was more popular than acid in the Sixties." She set up Jonathan's Quietly with a perfect one-inch head, then took stock of the rest of the bar makings. Jonathan stared as though at hieroglyphs. "Speaking of acid," she said, "we got some medium grade blotter right here. Very mellow. Ludes, downers, mixers for the coke, even a touch of Number Four." She was pointing at an open silver snuffbox. A mezzotint of a foxhunt scene adorned the lid.

"Number Four?" Lost at last, was Jonathan.

"Straight out of Chaing-Mai. As close to heaven as you or I will ever get."

She did a peculiar thing, then. She rummaged under the bar until she found a box of paper drinking straws. She poked one into the snuffbox until it filled, then she twisted each end tight.

The icy Quietly tasted just like a shot of Xanadu. "I don't understand a thing you just said." He nonchalantly wiped the smear of coke on the thigh of his jeans. It didn't go away.

"You really *are* a virgin, aren't you?" Again the timbre that said she found this genuinely charming. "Look, it's school-time." She pointed at each item. "Mild acid, for relaxing. Makes you smile a lot. The downers are to take the edge off the coke. And the heroin—mm, baby! Heroin smooths out the rough spots better than any other cocktail. Like, when you overbalance on blow, a little smack settles you right down. Mind you, no needlework—just a touch to toot. Mr. Coke plus Mr. Heroin equals Mr. Speedball..."

"Isn't that how John Belushi died?"

"He mixed too much of it with too much of other shit. Does it really matter? No." She helped herself to a swig of his beer.

"Why the bit with the straw?"

"That's how they sell it in Thailand. Chaing-Mai is the gateway to the Golden Triangle." She stowed the straw in her saddlebag, eyes bright with this unanticipated boon. "Relax, Jonathan. Enjoy life. Eat out more often. What were once vices are now habits, and what was once Pepsi Please is now the White Tornado. Watch."

On the bartop she chopped five or six skinny novice lines from the chrome bowl. It looked as though the black mirror surface had been laid open by a white claw. She selected a glass straw from a squat mug of cocktail pies and swizzlers.

"You pinch one shut." Her voice got a helium buzz as she closed off one nostril. "You Hooverize with the other." The first line wind-tunneled away. She went erect and sniffed several times to blow the magic dust back into her system. She giggled. "Repeat as needed." Another line zipped into the opposite nostril. "Easier than Aspergum. Your turn."

Jonathan bit his lip as his eyes tried to dodge the proffered straw. No go. Surely a blast of this stuff could do him no more internal damage than, say, one of Bash's Terminal Turbos. Bash had done coke before; at least Jonathan felt pretty sure that he had. No big deal.

Or: Jonathan could politely decline. Sit and sip his beer. Quietly. Then sashay out of this den of iniquity as though he were still a quaint innocent, a forest foundling, a walking lie.

He played at making his smile hardy. "Well...here goes

nothing, I guess." If it was good enough for Sherlock Holmes…

"*Not* nothing," she said. "I cut these lines thin to keep you from sneezing and blowing about ten large all over the floor. Ever use nose drops or a nasal inhaler?"

"Yeah."

"You'll *feel* the powder, but don't sneeze. Kind of like tipping liquor toward the back of your throat."

"Like shotgunning a beer." Another college skill.

"Generally. Then tip your head back and shoot some air to get the residue off the top of your palate."

He did it, crossing his eyes in a bullish yet amateur attempt to visually aim the straw. He thought of tyro smokers and their dislike for having fire close to their faces. He caught most of the weak dose and followed instructions, sniffing hard and swallowing a couple of times.

"Take a drink. How's it feel?"

"Funny. Not bad, but…I don't know. Cold, like ice. Nice, though. Sorta numb ice." He hadn't turned into a werewolf.

"You got it. It's crystals—like ice. Only it looks like powder because it's sooo fine."

On the spiral stair, Lord Alfred scratched his hair-free balls. In the pit, Krystal witnessed another gooshy homicide with all the emotional involvement of a mannequin. *Whee, weeee.*

"Now do the other one."

He positioned the straw, feeling like a southpaw attempting to draw with his right hand. The coke achieved ignition and liftoff; it seemed to rebound from the ceiling of his skull and beeline dead-bang for his heart. He swore he could feel it skid past the backsides of his eyeballs. He wrinkled his nose. "Feels like it's gone to sleep."

"You know they still use coke as an anesthetic for plastic surgery? It's supposed to be one of the world's few naturally occurring anesthetics."

All of a sudden Jamaica made him feel undereducated.

Jonathan's serotonin ignored input while his other neurotransmitters jump-started. His pupils dilated slightly. He felt his heart and respiration torque up. He seemed acutely sensitized to motion; the nape of his neck and the backs of his hands became radar dishes feeding his fight-or-flight reflex. He felt alert and controlled, as though he had sought and found cruising altitude.

"Burns now," he said, making the face dogs make when they don't like their dinner.

"Have another drink. Wash that bad taste right out."

He drained his Quietly to the lees. So this was it. It with a capital *I*. The social drug that scuffed up so much brimstone and damnation. It was more or less like a knock of straight gin to the nose.

Jamaica loaded a couple of extra straws with the root canal quality coke and tucked them into Jonathan's parka, which was draped across the ladder back of one of the dining room chairs. That seemed a right neighborly thing for her to do, and for her to flash so much leg while doing it. Jonathan thought Jamaica was pretty swell.

A few lines later, Jonathan was polishing off his second beer, thinking Jamaica was even more than swell, mega-swell, when Bauhaus re-emerged.

"What's the matter, Papa Bear?" said Jamaica. "Lose track of time while you were watching Cruz through the peephole in the shower?" She elbowed Jonathan. "Just kidding. He's got video on every room in the joint."

The fun escaped Jonathan's expression. Had Bauhaus watched Jamaica stashing coke in his parka? Had he taped their conversation regarding him...?

"He's got secret panels, too. Escape doors. Wooo, scary!"

Bauhaus ignored her jibes. "Jonathan, yes?" Was he trying to recall Jonathan's name, or merely sanctioning his presence? "Yes. Jonathan." He handed over a blue parchment envelope containing ten one-hundred dollar bills.

"Thanks. Thank you. Mr. Bauhaus." He had one leg twined tight around the upright of the barstool, his opposite foot bouncing manically, burning ergs. He needed something else brilliant to say. "Have to piss. I mean, uh, where's the...?"

It might have been the beer, or his compact-sized bladder, or another common reaction to the coke, or all three. Jamaica pointed the way.

Bauhaus' rheumy eyes followed Jonathan's wandering progress down the hall. He stopped and started. The framed pictures on both sides seemed intensely interesting. They were abstract canvases, expensive originals. They were signed in arcane, illegible ways. Chaotic splashes of color. Disordered lines. Jarring compositions. Definitely real art.

Jonathan at last ducked through the correct door.

"Now, my dearest. A query or two?" Bauhaus massaged Jamaica's shoulders from behind. She went rigid, and gently replaced the paraphernalia on the bartop.

"First. My coke. Is Cruz telling the truth? About having to dispose of it?"

"Sure." Her eyes were downcast, defocused.

"And did you see how he did it?"

"Flushed it. All of it. Surely you've taken a four-pound shit before. It all went down."

"No doubt." Rub, rub, harder now. "I've rarely taken a ninety thousand dollar shit. Next. What did he do with the wrappings? All that coke-coated plastic?"

"Flush number two. The cops were on their way up the stairs and he had no idea they weren't out to squash him. He thought it was something *you* set up. A loyalty test."

"That's good. I hadn't thought of that." His voice stayed fatherly, succoring. "And the wrappings, dear. What were they made of?"

"I didn't really see, Bauhaus, I was watching the window. Five cop cars at least. And they want *your* big fat ass. That's why Cruz slept in jail." Not exactly true, but it made for a more leak-proof defense.

"And what did Cruz do with the gun?"

Something poked at her skirt. Bauhaus' interrogation had inspired him with a hard-on, which now protruded from his Grand Poopah robe and was bonging the leather on her butt like a metronome. He was revving up to get mean.

"Gun. Is that what was in the candy box?" She had suspected this from the moment she lifted the box, but had not actually verified anything. Her ass was poked again. "Stop it."

He whirled her, fingers digging into her upper arms fiercely enough to make the point. "Don't lie to me, you cunt. Don't forget that I own you. I snap my fingers and your *life* burns to the ground. I won't even leave ashes. If you're shooting me through the grease they'll find your head on a spike in the Plaza." His erection was full-up now, curving toward her, pulsing in time with his heartbeat.

"I didn't see a gun." Her voice had dried up.

"They busted him for the dope in *your* purse. You fucking owe me. You want to keep your public access twat between your legs and not in my garbage disposal, you level with me and don't ever, *ever* lie to me."

"I'm not lying," she lied. "Cruz flushed the dope. I didn't see a gun. Bauhaus…there was no time at all, from the moment the cops dropped out of the trees. Cruz acted fast. If they had tied any dope to you, bigtime, we'd all be freezing in cells right now. The cops don't have shit on you. Cruz did okay."

His grip relaxed, but did not release. The door to the blue bedroom closed and the hallway filled up…not with Cruz. Jamaica did not recognize the man except by genus. He had curly, golden-fleece hair that looked abnormal above the tight tweed jacket. He was gangstered out in a black shirt and a dove-gray tie knotted tight as a hangman's noose. The suit was buttoned and looked ready to burst. No question about the bulge at the armpit; no attempt had been made to disguise it.

"Marko," Bauhaus nodded.

Marko scoped the living room with eyes like ball bearings pressed deep into hot black rubber. He followed Bauhaus' glance and parked himself accordingly on the sofa next to Krystal just as Jason chalked up a fresh kill. *Whee.* His notice was drawn more to the potato chips than to the stalk 'n' slash antics onscreen, or Krystal's boobs.

"Do I pass or what?" Jamaica was impatient and angry. Enough accusations, enough fencing, enough of Bauhaus and his nasty little boner.

"I always liked you, my dear." His voice passed her ear hotly. "You give better head than the children, here. You stay straight with me and it's good dope and fast times and everybody makes out, yes?" He paused to deepen his tone significantly.

"You cross me, and I'll pick up the phone one more time. And when the knifework is done, you'll have a hole in your crotch big enough to *hide* those two kilos in. You understand and approve wholeheartedly, I'm sure."

She let the spark rise in her eyes, heightening the amber there. "Okay, okay, I read you, I'm not stupid." Her retort was tempered by her knowledge that Bauhaus could make good on his vile threats. He could make her evaporate, and no one would ever miss a hooker with a quick mouth.

"Now. Go await my pleasure in the big bedroom."

"Gimme a break, Bauhaus. Not tonight. Not after all this shit."

He smiled and came around to pat her cheek. Not quite a slap; not nearly a love tap. "Ah, I *do* like that. Such fire and defiance. Next time I fuck you in the ass I'll have you sing 'Addicted to Love' while I bugger away." He clapped his hands loudly. Marko did not look over. Lord Alfred, catamite-in-residence, snapped to attention like a pointer. Jamaica ate another face-to-face tap-slap. "All this brutal honesty has aroused me. And Lord Alfred is much tighter than you ever were."

Her expression told him to get on with it.

"Marko will see our friend Cruz to a hospital. St. Jude's, I think. Make sure he's not broken as well as busted. He is two days behind, and as you know, I have a slight operating loss I need to recoup. What is Jonathan's story?"

"He just wanted to get Cruz out of jail."

"Why?"

Lord Alfred drifted past, bedroom-bound, butt jiggling beneath his monk's robe. His necklaces and bracelets clinked and jangled.

"Look—why don't you ask Cruz?"

"I did, dearest. Marko, my stout yeoman, helped. Grilling someone naked carries a tremendous psychological advantage. And if your answers, just now, had deviated from his...well. Never mind. Uncrease thy rumpled brow. But before I go back there to play with Lord Alfred, you, my dear, are going to moisten me up, and Jonathan's going to see you do it. Because you are a whore. And you insulted me in front of him. And I am *not* one of your fucking cops. And because I pay you, and you'll goddamn well do what I demand, or you'll stop breathing right now. Right, Marko?"

Marko nodded. He hadn't missed a thing.

She saw the light. She knew he could make it happen. Her bloodstream was rocking and rolling with Bauhaus' primo drugs; because of him she had had every conceivable orifice breached. She had accepted cash, purloined dope, and if she had ever believed in possessing a soul, she would have pawned it years ago. He could force her to become nothing, make her die and blow into oblivion with the next winter wind.

If he made her disappear, then he won. Bauhaus was one sick ticket.

And so it came to pass that Jamaica was pressed to her knees there on the flagstones of the kitchen, Bauhaus' reddened member waving an inch from her nose like a blind cobra. She was sorry that Jonathan would have to see her with a mouthful: Sorry for him, because she kind of liked him. Sorry for herself, because unlike Jonathan, she needed to act the part as well as speak the lines.

Krystal did not have to get up to change cassettes. *Friday the 13th Part Six* commenced in Super VHS. It was the neatest one in the series, even at silent-movie speed.

Chari kept to her stool, immobile as a sculptor's bust. Marko sat, stayed, did not fetch.

Bauhaus grabbed Jamaica's hair and thrust, making her gag unexpectedly. The occipital ridge of her head banged the bar cabinet; the small fridge there started up at the shock. She felt the purr of its motor vibrating the laminated woodwork. She concentrated on it.

Her saliva oiled Bauhaus up good.

She was sorry for a lot of things. But Cruz still had the dope. That dope could transmute into money just as surely as fairytale spinning wheels made straw into gold. If Cruz could retrieve the two kilos, then most likely he could save the gun as well. She remembered seeing the candy box go into the trash bag before everything was stuffed out the bathroom window.

And if Cruz still had the gun...

Preseminal fluid lotioned the roof of her mouth. An old, old taste to her. Jonathan came out of the bathroom, rubbing one eye. He looked up and then grated to a petrified standstill in the hall.

Just as dope could become cash, Bauhaus could be changed by a bullet or two. Either way, such changes might mean freedom, she thought.

Might they not?

Seventeen

"Well, lookee here what the dawg drug in…"

Bash was flipping an X-Acto knife in the air, trying to see how many times he could get it to somersault and still catch the end that didn't have a point on it. He stopped to swig half the contents of his *Twilight Zone* coffee mug, then spent some time trying to guess why Jonathan looked so wrung out.

"Lemme see. No, don't tell me; I *know* this one…" He was turned up too loud and wrapped too tight. "She told you she was from Salinas and it was her first time in the big city, and *normally* she never *considered* doing stuff like this, but you know how it is when you run out of money, and…"

"And Merry Exmas to you, too." Jonathan's voice was crawling up from the back of this throat this morning. "Ho. Ho. Ho." He slumped behind his light table. All his rubber dinosaurs forgave him. *The world is your squeak toy*, they lied.

"You okay?" Bash shifted to Big Brother mode, just concerned enough not to go mushy. "If you ain't sperm crazy then you look hammerstruck, Dino Boy."

Jonathan grunted. The room refused to resolve into focus. Jessica waved hello from the hallway as she bustled off to xerox something. Always in a hurry to reproduce. He was thankful that her workload kept her from seeing how wasted he was this morning. Or maybe she knew, and was permitting him to save face. He had no mouth for storytelling, not even for Bash.

He told Bash anyway.

He started with his apology, for returning the truck late. He knew Bash would tell him sorries were unnecessary. He made a pallid grab at losing the morning in work. It was difficult to see what purpose all this ant-like industry served. When you completed a job another sat right down in its place. You had to have reservations just to catch a breath. Jobs had backed up. Bash was in his face.

He tried truce mode. "You know when you feel the need to explain something? And it's something you shouldn't really be talking about in the first place, except that it's so big you can't keep it to yourself, you can't contain it all without bursting?"

"Cammy frequently complains that I'm so big she can't contain all of me without—"

"Yeah, right. Well. What happened last night was sort of like that."

"Let's haggle." Bash grinned. Frankenstein's Monster: *Goooood.* "Give me juicy tidbits. Edited highlights. And I'll pull some of that small shit off your desk so you can preserve your sterling rep around here, since you look like you're about to faint and put out an eye on a compass point."

Jonathan was in no mood to play tough; he genuinely needed the help. "Take the proofing," he said, handing across a stack of sheets. "I track the words but they don't mesh into anything meaningful." Layout seemed more accessible. Cutting and pasting the paper maelstrom into a juxtaposition with straight lines; smacking disorder on the side of the head and making it behave. Bash battened gleefully on tales of police raids, naked prostitutes, mayhem in the snowy night. Jonathan veered around most of the drug stuff, and was yanked under by a shock flash of recall that reminded him of several straw-fulls of pharmaceutical chuckle dust still assuming squatter's rights in his parka. There now. The thought stole his wind like a rabbit punch to the sternum.

"Gas pain?" said Bash. "Your face just went as blank as a Butt Person's brain scan."

"Tired." He wanted his sinuses to drain and his brain pan to stabilize. How much had he drunk yesterday? Had he gotten round to eating? Would any damned thing take the dead lead out of his buns this fine, blinding-bright Illinois morning?

The thing really clogging up his head was Jamaica. All sass and steel and aerodynamic curves, a cherished memory perma-bound in a rectangular bloc of blue water, eyes hinting green and streetwise, motions fluid and sensuous, tongue scalding, then, to Jonathan, merciful.

Her mouth engorged with five stubby inches of beet-red Bauhaus bratwurst.

Tougher now, to moon over Amanda. She was gaining a sepia tint, spoiling on the shelf of his memories. Amanda was passing from the ripe blush of guilt and recriminations into the decay of old news.

Senses blunted, he had shuffled away from Bauhaus' bad pad, unable to encompass any more weirdness for one twenty-four hour slot. By ramming his dick into Jamaica's face the overweight drug lord was making some kind of power point. By permitting such a gross violation, she was acceding to some unknown politic. Bauhaus held some Damoclean blade over Jamaica's life, and thus, the privilege to part her bee-stung lips with his crooked little chimp-choker.

Jamaica would have an explanation. Hope broad-jumped eternally.

And through it all, Jonathan thought: *Who are you, to judge?* While he didn't have to judge, he decided he didn't have to witness, either. He took his money, ran, and hoped Jamaica did likewise after paying her own bills.

Truck back to Kenilworth. Keys to door. Head to a pillow still simmering in her spicy scent. Autonomic actions all, prefacing two hours of sickly sleep. No rest. When his faithful travel alarm blew reveille he rose, no more sentient than a coffee-swilling robot. For the first time he noticed the trail of blood on the hopeless carpet.

He had booted out the black cat…Jesus, decades ago.

The pawprints in the blood were still fresh enough to glisten. Definitely cat feet. Passage had occurred while Jonathan was sleeping. The red swath commenced low to the wall next to the wheezy steam heater and meandered past the cot. Jonathan had tracked it to the bathroom. From the smears and skids he pictured the cat's bloody progress: A slippery leap from the closed toilet lid to the edge of the bathtub and thence to the windowsill. Presumably it had hooked its claws into the cardboard sealing off the broken window. Presumably it had slid into the airshaft, seeking edibles, and gotten a long surprise tumble down to a full-stop impact fraught with pain and broken cat bones. Jonathan had popped the cardboard out. It was still stained by the fecal grease, which had dried and crusted now like burned pie filling. He had called into the shaft. No meows. The worst was feared, but without a light, what could he have done?

And he still had no idea of what had become of Cruz.

"I love stuff like that," Bash enthused. "Like having the *Enquirer* read to you. Except it's all so rich you couldn't have possibly tall-taled it together." He was not completely serious, and his face reflected a snap or two of doubt. "I suppose you cleaned all the blood and stuff up?"

"No time. I didn't want Capra to get pissed at me for being late. By now it's dry. I wonder what happened to that goddamned cat?"

"Gone to cat hell."

He peeled up angular hanks of masking tape and worked over his job with an eraser to eliminate a few errant thumbprints. He preferred working with the table's underlight on so that he could see how his paste-up aligned in terms of silhouettes— dark, darker, darkest—as well as hewing to the longitudes and latitudes of the photo-blue graph. Without work on the board the light was too strong. He moved the next job in his stack into position.

"You don't suppose Capra would miss one of those high-powered garage flashlights for a day or two, do you?"

"You going to check out the shaft tonight, bro?"

Jonathan tried to work moisture into his dry lips, feeling skin cracks with his tongue, which was just as arid.

"Damnation," Bash went on. "I'd do it with you, but..."

"Camela?"

"That's a big ten-four. We're in what you might call the negotiation phase."

"What happened?"

"She did the one thing my get-rid-of-Cammy campaign never counted on, swabbie. She went and started being nice to me. No naggery, no face powder and eyebrows all over the bathroom sink." He lowered his voice, aware that the subject of his discourse lurked in this selfsame building, and who knew what walls had ears? "She's dropping weight like crazy. In another week she'll be able to slide into one of those evening sheaths that drove me so nuts in the first stretch of the race. She wants you to come to dinner tonight. She told me to tell you she promises no char. She bought me a hat." He bobbed his noggin in the direction of the coat rack, where hung a floppy, mustard-colored newsboy's cap.

"Maybe she's having an affair," Jonathan said. "Buying you presents to share the wealth."

That squeezed a patronizing laugh out of his big friend. "Or maybe she caught a case of multiple personality, and right now I'm living with Nice Cammy. Soon the Evil Anti-Cammy will manifest in a fart cloud of sulphur dioxide. I don't know which personality fucked me last night, but I will confide one lurid detail, no more: I think we should phone the Guinness Book, or *Believe It Or Not!*, because she banged me like a bullet train. I could barely hang on." His broad Ed Norton grin leveled off. There was some other tasty bit he was keeping to himself. "More coffee for you?"

By now Jonathan knew Bash's pattern. A peekaboo shot of sexual minutiae, just betwixt me and thee, pal o' mine. Behind the crude honesty he was hiding something else. He wanted Jonathan to know he was getting laid, but not the Bad Thing. There was something Jonathan was going to have to drag out of him. Jonathan decided to change the subject entirely, kidding himself that he was sparing Bash some embarrassment.

"Can't do me a Turbo here, can you?" A beer might go down better, but no, not here at work, dude.

Bash had hoisted the Pyrex pot, trying to see how high he could hold it and still hit his mug with a steaming arc of Colombian Supremo. When he finished, with a flourish as always, his cuffs were spattered and his coffee had a head on it.

The stuff was good, potent, newly brewed. To Jonathan it tasted like spitoonage.

He hit the bathroom and inventoried the melanotic bags

under his eyes. They were puffy and insisted on some quality sleeptime. He hesitated, bit his lip, and pulled the straw of cocaine out of his shirt pocket. He'd bent it double to fit it less obtrusively and the paper elbow had split, depositing a good two lines or so in the crease of his pocket. He did not care. He tapped out a pinch on the ridge of his hand, feeling like Dr. Jekyll on the verge of quaffing his tainted potion. Stevenson had written *Dr. Jekyll and Mr. Hyde* in the 1880s, probably during his cocaine treatments for tuberculosis.

Let's see if the booster rocket hype of this stuff is all it's cracked up to be, he thought. Cracked. Ha-ha, he was wielding the jargon like a pro now, even making puns out of it.

Under cover of running water in the sink, he did two healthy toots and flushed the rest, straw and all, down the toilet. He washed his hands, dabbed at his mouth and face, then inhaled small jolts of water up his nose the way Jamaica had told him to.

It took ninety seconds for the hyperdrive to kick in, the way a tank of nitrous oxide can supercharge a race car. He remembered *everything* that needed doing, without using memos. He dive-bombed his work stack, polishing it off along with eight more cups of coffee.

"Never heard you hum music while you work before," Bash said.

Jonathan laughed and shrugged it off. He could handle this kind of efficiency, for sure.

This was easy to get to like.

The sight of Camela's new engagement diamond, over dinner, brought on a depression of Shakespearian overstatement. Jonathan found his gaze morbidly affixed to the ring that glinted from her betrothal finger. He stared blankly, not meaning to, the way ministers stare at a woman's breasts.

With his newsboy's cap on, Bash looked like a twelve-year-old with the world's most overactive thyroid.

Dinner was tarragon chicken with lots of fresh vegetables, a salad of butter lettuce with julienne bell pepper and jicama. Dessert was wide-topped goblets full of sliced strawberries in chocolated whipped cream. Bash marked Jonathan's oblique hold on the evening, sensed that a serious interview would come later, and otherwise ignored his friend's discomfort with a breezy, studied indifference.

Together they watched a rental tape of *Amazon Women on the Moon*. Camela laughed in all the right places. At ten she grandly excused herself, as she said, to "retire." She had worn a one-piece velvet wraparound with a plunging neckline and a broad, fancy belt. She had done the alterations and padded the shoulders herself, and in sum the outfit was meant to impress, showing off the assets of her resurging figure and expertly camouflaging the areas still chalked for restoration.

Bash laughed loud and long—at the movie, at Jonathan's occasional wisecracks, at nearly goddamn everything, reaching too hard to prove he was having a good time. He worked his way through a six pack of Quietly Beer, alternating with double-spiked Turbos, and determinedly crunched up at least fifty fortune cookies.

Hang on to your ideals. A man is known by his deeds.

Once Jonathan heard the fan come on in the bedroom, he scooted closer to Bash on the sofa, speaking low. "Okay, man, just what the fuck is going *on* here?"

"Zit look like?" Bash was half-bagged.

"Just a couple of days ago you were shoveling shit about how Bash plus Camela equaled no way, José. If she'd have aimed that gold at my eyes any more I would've gotten sunstroke. Looks like *your* weekend was pretty goddamn eventful too, stud."

Bash waved a hand dismissively, sloshing the contents of his half-empty Quietly bottle into foam. "Did I ever tell you why Cammy came to Chicago? Not just to waste her life jumping from one idiot secretarial gig to another."

"You told me you guys linked up after her fiancé dumped her."

"Ahum. Well, the nub of our gist, chilluns, is this: She stays poor and on her own as long as she stays single. Her mission, Jimbo, should she decide to accept it, is to return to Mommy and Daddy in Iowa, how shall we say, spoused." His Louisiana accent came out of hiding and made every other word strange and new-sounding, drowned in noble deep-South honeydew.

"*Spoused.* Then Mommy and Daddy give her the three-bedroom in the moneybelt suburbs, two matching Volvos, and one whole year to honeymoon wherever their one and only's heart desires." He said *dee-czars.*

"What are her parents into?" Jonathan had begun fiddling with Bash's modified Magic 8-Ball.

"Computer keyboard manufacture. Third largest in America." He was starting to have difficulty with the harder consonants, and took a shot at rinsing the blur from his speech with a slug of Quietly swished around like mouthwash. "Now your ordinary mortals might opine: Geez, guy, you're kinda selling out, ain'tcha?"

"That crossed my mind, yeah."

"You got it. Invasion of the Mega-Butt Peoples. But just between you 'n' me, Jonathan...I am thirty-fucking-four-fucking years old, this year. And you know what? I think I could *use* a year off, bought and paid for. And I think there ain't nothing you can do by marriage that you can't undo by divorce."

The 8-Ball's two cents worth surfaced: *Bite My Packed Shorts.*

Bash sounded morbid and ingrown, craving exterior reassurances for his less than noble charter. Jonathan felt clear-headed, able-bodied and in control—like he'd felt in the wake of his premier blast of toot-sweet—but very tired, very old. He patted the nearest of Bash's sloping shoulders and felt knots.

"Hey, man, it isn't for me to vote yea or nay. I mean, just look at how fucked up *my* life is—"

Bash nailed him, shiny-eyed. "Don't start that shit about Amanda again. I ain't in no mood, bro."

"I wasn't going to."

"You *were.* Fucking were." He drew breath faster, a bull pawing and snorting, amping toward charge and crush and bright gushings of crimson. "Man, when are you going to just admit that *Amanda*...all that pain and bullshit you put yourself through...is just..."

"Shh, cool it, just calm down, okay?" It was scary to see Bash in such a state—defanged, unboisterous, less than positive. Like lifting Apollo's toga and finding a pea pod penis, below even human average.

"Listen to me. Maybe it's *you*, Bash-man. Maybe you did it, helped make Camela better, or helped her get closer to her own optimum vision of herself. That's not a bad thing. Jesus— so you might have helped somebody; how could that be bad? You sure as hell have helped me more times than I deserve. I might have taken the high dive years ago if you hadn't been around. My other so-called fucking friends sure faded into the baseboards; to hell with 'em. You told me you'd be there for me and the difference was that you *were*. And friends don't ever tell friends that. They tell everybody else, at funerals, when it's too late and it doesn't matter a damn."

Jonathan knew he was babbling, stringing phrases, grabbing for superficial logic. But his performance had enough surface tension to keep Bash from slopping over into big, ripe tears. If for some reason he started crying, Jonathan was afraid they'd both lose it.

"But I'm here because you gave a shit, man, and so I'm here to tell you right now that your life is yours. And if you want my opinion, it's yours, and if you don't, that's fine too. I'll defend whatever you decide, because I love you, man. Anything else is just a fix. Right?"

Bash swallowed and nodded. Jonathan was unaware whether he had just done any good, or which of them was more purged. The emotion passed with the moment, and ten minutes later Bash had slumped into the corner crook of the sofa and was snoring softly.

Jonathan pursed his lips. No use in talking to his knees, or his hands. Masturbation was out. The dinner dishes had already been done. Efficiently, too.

He whispered into the kitchen phone, tip-toed to the door, and caught a cab back to Kenilworth. When he stepped into the fresh snowpack the night cold hit his bare face as hard as a swung plank. He brought the depression home with him. It was more than clinical; it was classic, settling its weight onto his spine and belaboring his temples like an invisible cartoon stormfront. The blue triangle hovering in the mystic fluid of Bash's magic 8-Ball stayed with Jonathan, too. He saw it bumping against the round window and thought of a corpse floating up to the porthole of a sunken ship.

Kill Yourself, Slug Snot.

The funk refused to dissipate. He needed sleep. He overpaid the cabbie and slumped inside to find some.

Eighteen

L ate night in Oakwood.

Edgar Ransome heard the taxi's snow treads mashing through street slush. When the car door *chunked* shut outside his ground floor window he parted the eastward drapes for a look-see. He was Kenilworth Arms' unofficial sentry-without-portfolio, and his vigilance permitted him to maintain a passing mock of security. He did his part, though no one else ever suspected. His vision was crackerjack: he could see individual motes of backed-up dust sifting floorward from the disturbed curtains, even the white lines of dry dermis delineating the print pad of the finger he used to part them. He memo'ed the identity of the cab's passenger as one of those new kids from upstairs, the one who had moved in a day or three ago.

From the ground floor Edgar was privy to the comings and goings of the night. Since Fergus—the joke that called himself a manager—was aloof, unconcerned, probably brain dead, Edgar's role of watchdog was self-assigned. He felt he helped prevent Kenilworth from actually becoming as seedy as it already looked.

When he had been younger, he had been called Edder—short for Eddie R.—by nearly everyone. His keen eyes and powerhouse right arm buttressed his fantasy of one day becoming a baseball pitcher for the majors. He favored the Cubs. During World War Two he organized pick-up scratch lot teams among other Army Air Corps guys whenever they weren't being noisomely unbunked in the dark to go dump bombs on Berlin. His wartime parachute jump over friendly waters—abandoning a lame Liberator that decided to start losing gas and hydraulic fluid like a runny nose—brought him a Purple Heart for a busted hip and membership in the Caterpillar Club. His caterpillar pin had green eyes. If you chuted out over enemy territory during wartime, you got one with red eyes, and most likely an Air Medal to boot.

Television tonight had been the usual hash—sexless fitness nuts anguishing over junior high school crises. Now, *The Equalizer*, there was a program Edgar enjoyed. It depicted a protagonist in advanced middle age, a grandfather almost, who was strong, sexy, proficient and lucid. One of these days, Edgar thought, it would be nice to purchase a videotape deck so he'd never miss an episode. Indeed, he could save up the ones he'd already viewed. Build a library. When current technology didn't disgust him, it still enthralled him. So many buttons that could be pushed.

At 73, Edgar had outlived two wives, these being the only two women he had ever spent the night with in his life. Mae Lynn was the first, and he had never really fallen out of love with her; he'd been doomed, thunderstruck from the moment they'd met as teenagers. She saw him off to war and was waiting for him when he returned from the European Theatre. She had been taken by a violent series of sledgehammer heart attacks; he had watched her die on the day before Thanksgiving, 1965.

His marriage to Glenda had followed within nine months. He needed someone else in the house, someone to relate to over morning coffee, someone to run errands for and react with. No disrespect to Mae Lynn was ever intended. The union with Glenda took a decade to fall apart, and by the time she died of uterine cancer they were only speaking to each other about once a year.

Since then, Edgar had become a sort of caretaker, watching his friends die. His enemies died too. He settled on trying to make no attachments. Emotional involvement only brought you sorrow when death came to thieve its due. He came to see those who populated his life as biological mishaps. Skinbags with too many factory defects. Ticking time-bombs of death strung like deadly jewels along a timeline of mortared arteries, burst hearts, blown joints, blood more like venom, clots and arthritis, ulcerations and assassinating infections, sundered bones, exhausted organs and ruined minds. First feeble, then helpless, then dead. Dead as granite, dead as dreams.

He watched the young man from upstairs pay the hack and enter the building through the Kentmore door. This boy had been a player in the dramatic events of the past weekend. Police cars, Nazi tactics, shouting and madness, Edgar thought that he would not want to be a young person these days. So much more was required of them.

They killed themselves more, these days.

Edgar's backbone was ramrod straight, his posture a fringe benefit of being a veteran. His trousers were belted high; his shirt was clean and starched and tucked. He wore slippers, but neatly, with clean socks. He cultivated fastidiousness. You saw sloppy old people so often, and the assumption was that age made you lax, forgetful, slovenly. He shaved with a straight razor every morning and always came out nickless. He dunked and flossed his dentures every night. Once the Army had taught him how to shine shoes, he'd never forgotten. It was a skill he cherished because it seemed outmoded, now. There was nothing to compare to a good spit-shine. The worst critique to be ventured of his wardrobe was that it was threadbare; pensions only reached so far, even with his frugal accounting. And shirts and trousers were not made so well these days. He could see all that. His eyes were still crackerjack.

Edgar's wake-up and sleeptime rituals had expanded to fill the extra time that came of living alone. Instead of merely watching TV and waiting for either the next pension check or the old Reaper to show up with the new day, he became almost meditatively introspective. He tried to focus more finely on the world surrounding him, to contemplate bigger pictures. He had become attuned to the seasonal rhythms of the building in which he lived. He *listened* to the sounds the structure made. He could read the olfactory hue of the corridors, or the sounds made by the brickwork contracting in winter, expanding in summer, making soft igneous sounds with the receipt of the first rain of spring.

Lately the building had been acting oddly.

The sense impressions Edgar registered seemed queerly garbled, pregnant with hidden information like flyby scoops of some too-distant radio signal. It reminded him of how he felt when he took medication too soon, or drank coffee too abundantly—the tightness in his jaws, the throbbing at his temples, the frustration of useless alertness. The building felt to him like it was wired. Anxious, perhaps. Maybe paranoid.

He wondered if the steam heating had soured somehow, polluting the air, poisoning the occupants with unlikely hallucinations. Just this morning, while his trusty GE percolator was hocking and splurting, he had noticed his sofa had been scooted out from the south wall about six inches. It was actually a secondhand loveseat, but it accommodated Edgar and his magazines and TV snacks quite adequately. He looked at this anomaly and assumed he had been clumsy in rising from it. Then he noticed that the wall was the same distance further back from the gargoyle spiral of the steam grille, which was mounted to a steel floor plate by six rusty railroad bolts that had been new before the Great War. The sofa had not moved forward. The wall had moved back.

Edgar had hung a single framed picture on the south wall, a foxed studio pose of Mae Lynn. It had fallen to await him face-down on floor space that had not existed the day before. Fortunately the thin picture glass had not shattered. He lifted it, paused to play back some memory of his first and best wife, and moved to rehang it.

The nail on which the picture had hung was gone. So was the nail hole. Edgar had spent nine years memorizing the topography of the shoddy paintjob mopped onto his walls by Fergus, that stupid ape. Wall texture trapped dirt and grease and dust in patterns. Those patterns were gone now.

It was as though the building had forgotten the wall, then remembered it incorrectly.

He felt the judicial stab of his own age. A lifetime of snide jokes about encroaching senility and Alzheimer's Disease were loudly restated by memory, bleak now, and unfunny. He was an old man, he was alone, he had tried so hard to maintain a dignity that was important to him…and now he was losing it.

A more conventional senior citizen would have made the nobility of age a weapon to brandish in the sneering faces of young generations. This was not important to Edgar, who rather enjoyed his public face as Kenilworth's curmudgeon. He was in control of the image he presented; my god, wasn't that the whole point? He did not care for the good opinions of Kenilworth's shabby, downscale tenantry and so for their pleasure he performed a role of his own conception. No doubt they all thought him a dotty old snotbag. The last laugh was all his own.

From wartime, he kept to the tenet that the best way to beat an enemy is to get him to underestimate you. What did he care for the good opinion of a bunch of foreigners and dopeheads and tramps like the ones he'd seen during that little Gestapo door-to-door the other night?

Now that Mrs. Rojas, she'd been a nice old woman. For years Edgar had only known her as "207." Eventually he had broken his own rule and struck up laundry talk with her. She was his kind: stout, upright, a survivor. He had been looking forward to wearing his good silk tie for her someday soon when she up and vanished from the building. Another one of the good people displaced by the march of time and Kenilworth's need to grow sleazier. One day she was there in the apartment above him; the next, gone without a trace, a note or a peep. Edgar had suspected the moment the building noise from the second floor shaded differently; the sounds were not hers. Many of the noises Edgar heard, or fancied he heard, were confusing or impossible to interpret. But he knew she had left. Moved on to whatever options elderly women with restrictive incomes might invoke, in their need to escape rat-trap poverty or make their calling address more respectable.

Damn. The swell of her bodice had been quite nice, too.

He arched his spine as he walked to the bathroom and succeeded in popping a few vertebrae. He needed to pat water on his face, clear his eyes and cycle down the worry in his heart before it began to resonate and get destructive. His mind was okay. That business with the sofa and the wall space had a rational explanation. That was a prize that age and waiting and patience got you—the time to figure everything out.

Hell, he thought. If I had everything figured out, then I'd be a *teenager*.

Thumps from above. The new tenant, the guy from the cab, was checking in for the night. Previous night, he'd been up till dawn. He had not disturbed Edgar's sleep, but Edgar knew.

Edgar thought of taking a quick bath to unsweat his pores and clear his head, then decided against it. He had no wish to disrupt his routine that much.

Like the other apartments bunched into the northeast corner of the building, Edgar's bathroom was aired via a small window opening on to a ventilation shaft. He had boarded his up years back, and badgered Fergus until the gnomelike creature made a house call with a caulking gun and more of his endless supply of white latex paint. From the first Edgar had hated the diseased, industrial odor of the shaft. If it was air he wanted, he'd get it in the living room. He was in a corner apartment, and by opening both casements he could recycle his air in two seconds flat, with the help of Momma Nature, and had no need for the ugly little porthole in his bathroom—something he might shatter with an elbow while showering.

Outside the wind marshaled fearsomely. Blowing snow tried to bow the windowpanes with a noise like salt sprinkled on tinfoil.

When he left the bathroom he noticed a new crack in the wall where Mae Lynn's picture had hung until this morning. It had not been there when Edgar had searched for the missing nail hole. Settling crack, he thought. A blizzard rocked the building. Storms could modify interior walls, sure enough. It was a maroon hairline fracture that ran up from the baseboard in an erratic tributary for about four feet. Best to dismiss it till breakfast, then force the Hunchback of Kenilworth to repair it... with Edgar acting the peppery old man, just nasty enough to spice all the proceedings up. Heh.

While he prepared for bed and gloated over this future performance, the crack reached upward another foot with a whispery sound like tearing bread. It split into a snaky-tongued fork at the top and spit out a puff of wallboard dust.

This made Edgar jump, but he rallied fast. Was it an earthquake? Some sort of tremor making the building lurch? Could the blizzard be that merciless?

He peered close and traced the fresh leg of the crack with one finger. It was wet. Two dots of blood traced divergent paths toward his open palm. Edgar knew blood when he saw it.

Rationality told him that one of the upstairs sewage lines had burst again. They had frozen and split before, to drain into the lower walls. He had not cut his finger. Then he remembered that the child who had vanished from the third floor had vanished in a wake of blood...and had not yet been recovered. Only blood marked a trail.

He stopped fearing the erosion of senility. If he could calmly ponder out what was happening right before his excellent eyes, he need not fear going loopy through inactivity. You only got scared of infirmity and absentmindedness when you had too much time to sit around worrying about it. Right now he was switched on, his brain gearing up to be speedy and analytical.

While Edgar was congratulating himself, the middle of the crack swelled apart like an exploding vein and a blood-soaked hand reached out of the wall to seize him by the throat. The grip was not a friendly one.

He made a watery choking rattle. Before he could drag in a breath of shock the hand yanked him forward, breaking his nose against the still-solid wall. He felt a sharp spike of pain as a pointed fingernail pierced his neck near the collarbone, sinking to the first knuckle and cutting loose a geyser of arterial blood that jetted from under his chin to mingle with the free rivulets now squirting from the wall as the crack widened like ripping tissue. Plaster mixed pinkly with wet scarlet, and at Edgar's feet the floor was splattered as though a sponge of blood was being wrung out, dipped and wrung out.

Fingers oozed from the split, found purchase, and began to pull the rest forth. The hand locked to Edgar's Adam's apple was like the teeth of a steam shovel. He was wounded, bleeding, caught fast and at disadvantage. Death was going to cosh him if he struggled like some dope in a monster movie on the late show. He had to turn this around.

He braced his arms against the wall and wrenched himself backward. With pain he bought freedom. More of the blood-drenched arm followed from the wall but he felt its grip loosen a degree. He saw a leather-jacketed elbow, studs glinting candy-apple through the hematogenous film. He balled his pitching fist and pounded the crook of the arm, once-twice, hitting the vulnerable joint there, three solid hammering hits, four, each impact smashing new pain into his own throat. His head was ripening feverishly with hot concussion and tilted time; he felt humid blossoms of blood warming his chest, flowering adherently and expanding like snaps of scalding grease, each passing second another fireburst in the midst of shellshock and onrushing trauma. His whole network of nerves screamed that he was still alive, but wouldn't be for long unless...

He twisted and brought his elbow down hard into the bend of the invading limb, as though chopping tough foliage. The fingers on his throat popped free with a meaty click. His voicebox was dented. He could *feel* it, by damn, feel just how close his own funeral was as the impetus of his sudden release tumbled him ass-first over the hassock next to the loveseat. His head clipped the standing lamp, which hinged floorward and crashed like an axe into a headsman's block. Two of its three bulbs burst with carbon-blue detonations, spitting sparks and glass across the rug. He stopped several splinters and felt pain in his ear, just as he could feel chilly air seeking his esophagus through the puncture in his neck.

The surviving bulb in the lamp began to blacken the rug fibers, adding thin smoke to the air and a horror movie cast to the upward-slanting shadows.

It was like watching a thief sneak through a slit in a circus tent, except the barrier had gone the consistency of thick flesh, tucks and folds erupting crookedly and exsanguinating as it was rent. Hands sheathed in rotten leather heaved against the bloody lips of the rupture. The forked arch lanced toward the room's high ceiling as a blood-sodden Army boot kicked out more egress and left a cleated red print on the floor. A shoulder oozed through.

Edgar seemed to lack adequate time to regain control of his

own arms and legs. He was losing too much needed blood. His brain was swimming like boxer shorts on the ring-rinse cycle.

He saw sharp things.

Chains and pins glittered, starched in moist organic rot, binding a decayed leather jacket to a denim vest, all of it immersed in the same autopsy dye. Zippers and medals swung, scattering rust-spiced blood droplets. Darker lettering on the saturated jacket read KILLER PUSSY. STONER'S EVIL. What god knew what they meant?

The attacker possessed no actual face, to speak of. But it grinned, still stuck halfway inside the wall. Then it pulled out a switchblade. The stress of the grin pulled loose a dripping gob of cheek and chin which smacked the floor with a meaty splash, exposing gapped yellow teeth.

Red drizzle blinded Edgar. It was a torrent now, funneling from the rip in the wall with faucet force, pooling gelidly and coming in an eager tide for his outstretched feet. So much blood.

The corroded Italian switch opened with the sound of steel, committing. It was a sound that knocked Edgar back into the real world. If he rolled for his front door he'd get seven inches of bye-bye in the backside. He tried to yell for help. His modified throat would not permit this.

His pulped nose was a dysfunctional ruin; it forced him to gulp air orally. The creature was nearly free of the rubbery wall. Edgar thought of a film seen long ago. Live birth.

Cry for help, indeed. Before him, for whatever reason, was an embodiment of everything he thought screwed up in this not-so-brave new world: A knife-waving punk in leathers with a sneer and an attitude. Kenilworth's grubworm populace condensed into one hideous, wet red amalgam, come to drive him out at last.

He heard a clogged noise like gargled phlegm. He finally got his eyes open.

The son of a bitch was laughing at him. Without a mouth, unsleeving its left leg from the spurting fissure in the wall, readying its pathetic little wop toadsticker for its debut taste. Laughing at him.

Edgar crabbed backward. The interloper lunged for the

front door, to block. That was that Edgar had counted on. He rolled fast to one knee, came up running, and in three deft steps made it to the bathroom.

By the time the thing had slid over to bar escape from the tiny closeted passage, Edgar had unfolded his straight razor.

He felt his voice betrayed him. The only sounds in his room were his own labored respiration and the shuffling of his slippered feet as he feinted and bobbed. His attacker mirrored, parry, defense, making slick wet noises. To Edgar it was wartime once again, and he intended to be just as unrelenting as he had been in 1942. This would not be the first time he'd used cold steel to speed an enemy to Hell. He had wrapped his shield hand in a towel.

Back at the wall a skinny black cat squeezed through the bottom of the gap, seeming startled that its transit had gotten it bloodied. It crouched behind the steam coil, in the space that had not been there before, and began to meticulously lick itself clean. Every so often its golden eyes would flicker up to keep track of the fight going on near the bathroom.

Edgar saw at once that his opponent was blind. The bathroom light jabbed into the vacant concavities of two empty sockets, crusted but eyeless. It was tracking him some other way.

He put up his toweled forearm. He'd learned the move decades ago and instinct had not deserted him. If the enemy strikes and sinks his knife into your forearm, you could twist your wrist and trap the blade momentarily between the bones, buying you an instant to deliver your own *coup de grâce.* He made another preliminary jab. The thing in the biker jacket ducked, though sluggishly, as if remote-controlled.

It tried to come a step nearer, its reek cumbering the confined space. Edgar fought against taking an equivalent step backward; he did not want the bathroom wall against his butt. He slashed laterally and the Swedish edge split air a millimeter from the monster's naked jawbone.

It recoiled, reeling back just a hair. That meant it feared the razor. Edgar could win.

Now they danced, commencing the serpentine weaving that lays groundwork for serious stab wounds: The swift flash of honed metal, penetration and damage, victory for one of two. The mocking grin remained to dominate the lower quadrant of the thing's head but it was not a grin. It was the absence of skin and muscle, the permanent mirth of a deathshead's dentition. Edgar thrust and withdrew, snaky-quick. His opponent tossed his switchblade lightly from one hand to the other. Webs of tacky blood seemed to join the hands in midair. Showoff.

Edgar tried to carve in low and was detoured. Then the zombiatic thing fisted its weapon, blade extending from the pinky finger end—the worst possible position in which to hold a knife in combat, Edgar knew, since it severely restricts the angle of a good strike. He saw the long black nail on the pinky finger of the knife hand as it rose high for a downward blow, a killing charge. Seeing that move, Edgar felt the contest was his.

With a strangulated yell he rushed forward, trapping the attacker's knife overhead with his towel hand. With the other he ribboned the stomach in brutal slashes, making Xs over and over. The squared tip of the straight razor bit easily into rotted clothing and putrescent tissue, cleaving and splitting. Slops of fluid glurted forth deep brown, chased by spirals of ripe green bowel.

He saw the festering visage alight, all bugs and bone, eyeless pits, bloodskim and gassy rot, the insectile bristle of dead hair, the skeletal grin fixed forever. His hand was engulfed as he dug in and gutted his adversary. He heard the switchblade clatter uselessly to the floorboards.

I got you.

The thing grabbed a tight fistful of Edgar's hair. He realized it was not panting with effort, nor gasping in death. It wasn't breathing at all.

Edgar's grip on the razor weakened. It hung in the voided trench of evacuated stomach, sunk deep, doing as little harm as it had seconds previously.

Edgar's feet left the floor as he was lifted. He felt his slippers drop off. He squirmed and it did not change history one smidgen. The skull-grin unhinged. Then came pain, warm and far away, slamming to maximum as Edgar's throat was bitten out, the gristle of his Adam's apple spit free to bounce around the tiles of the bathroom.

The towel fell and piled up on itself, drinking blood. Edgar kicked.

The cat watched the rolling knot in the bathroom; it might be a toy to be chased for sport.

Edgar's last cogent thought was the burning wish that his unhuman assailant was not a Jew. For motivations entirely irrational, Edgar had always been very vocal about despising Jews ever since moving in to 107. Privately he knew that Jewish people were no better or worse than the human race at large. But he made it part of his Kenilworth persona to hate them, and it was a role he partook with as much gusto as his self-imposed status as night watchman for the ground floor.

He dearly hoped he had not been done in and beaten by a Jew, even a living dead Jew.

Edgar hit the floor, dead as spoiled cabbage. His fall drove the switchblade deep into the meat of his shoulder but he would never feel it.

The sounds of Edgar's leaking corpse were all that came to violate the abrupt silence.

Then the intruder began to tremble. It reached quaking claws to steady itself against the narrow walls of the bathroom corridor as its moist jackstraw framework rocked and rolled with the rush of its victory. Clabbered mucoid paste voided from the raw hole of the esophagal tube in thick, pumping spasms. A sweat of free blood shuddered forth to lubricate the parched facial tissue; it ran moist, yet steamless and cold. Old blood. Used blood. It dyed the cracks and runnels in the hideous face like ink on spoiled leather, then dripped to similarly tint the actual leather of the decayed biker jacket. Unabsorbed speckles glittered in the bad light.

Imbued in wet red, the jacket nevertheless creaked when the intruder bent stiffly, using dead man's hands in fingerless gloves to gather up its own slithering offal. The load was messy and undisciplined; it was heaped back where it came from and shreds of the jacket were crudely knotted to keep it there. The zipper was oxidized to uselessness, frozen fast in rust. The jacket remained slashed to tatters in front. A few more knots and it would be damned stylish.

Cautiously, the intruder bent one more time, as though aware it could fold this way so many times before falling apart into a goulash of rent meat fiber. It used its long, coke-snorting pinky fingernail to spoon out one of Edgar's eyes. Spaghetti tendons trailed behind. It was duly plugged into an empty socket, where it displaced a squirt of ochre pus and swiveled until the pupil faced front, expanding suddenly with new visual signals.

The intruder only took one eye. Only one was needed for seeing.

It stepped over Edgar's corpse and entered the bathroom to pry the plywood loose from the boarded-up airshaft window. Feeding time, now.

But first it stooped one more time, using the stump of one mealy finger to scrawl EAT ME in the coagulated red still thick on its newest victim's forehead.

Nineteen

The sheer cold left Jonathan breathing hard, and tonight he was panting better than a pair of hound dogs. The Garrison Street corridor was a wind tunnel of blowing snow; the mean temperature, far enough below zero to keep the snow particles hard and stinging as dermabrasive grit. The act of respiration, let alone locomotion, sapped core energy. Forget coherent thought or politeness to strangers. He began to sympathize with the elemental nastiness of Chicago natives.

The cabbie wanted to drawl about the weather. Stupid asshole, of course it was cold enough for Jonathan. That was like sticking a loaded gun in somebody's mouth and going, *scary enough for ya?* He tossed a ten at the idiot and did not hang for change. He had to close the back door of the cab twice and thought he might have heard the driver mutter some sexual epithet between slams.

Fuck him. Maybe he'll die tonight.

Jonathan had snorted coke twice more between quitting time and snagging the taxi at Bash's place. In the Rapid O'Graphics bathroom he emptied the drinking straws into one of those black plastic 35-millimeter film cans that were all over the office. The little black cans, with their firm-snapping grey caps, were one of those items Jonathan had always thought should have more uses. When you bought film you kept them, then never found anything to do with them and ultimately trashed them so that they didn't hang around to frustrate you. They seemed invented for drug applications. He remembered the guys and dolls at the U. of Louisiana frequently kept a sociable amount of pot on hand in such containers.

He tapped out each straw carefully, not letting any of the contents go to waste this time. He was thankful. The blow had helped him navigate the day at Capra's. He almost had to cop a second container, so he sniffed the top-off then and there.

He'd treated himself to a second blast in Bash's bathroom, after dinner. He ruminated on how people who repaired to the lavatories to do drugs always wound up seeing themselves in mirrors as they performed. Hi there you devil you—*snukk, snorf*—ahh, nice day—*sneef, schlork*—how about dem Cubs?

There is no more vocal expert than a rookie.

The coke helped blunt Bash's apparent middle-class sellout. Fine. Bash-man could enjoy his broadening tushie and toast his status as a brand new Butt Person by letting Camela jab a 24-karat circle pin through his ballbag.

Jonathan realized why you chopped lines with a razor blade. Coke chunks in your nose could *hurt.* They could also fall out to spatter your shirt like big white cornstarch boogers. By the fourth or fifth session he felt professional. No drug tyro, was he.

He still had most of his little can of coke left. This stuff beat coffee all to Hades; even Terminal Turbos.

He hit the eiderdown, so to speak, as soon as his door was bolted. He slept soundly for about two minutes, then jackknifed awake with his heart racing. He smelled sweat, unlovely and oil bound, oozing from his pores. There was a sporadic commotion below him—hard to tell whether this was building noise or storm noise. It stopped soon enough. Noise above, like someone walking around in Cruz's room, but it ceased too soon to tell, as well. He decided to shower off before conking out, and got out of bed to remove his clothes.

All quiet, above and below, as he padded into the bathroom.

It was late enough that a decent feed of hot water was all his for the hogging. The steam did him good, the spray tenderized his clenched back muscles, and he emerged pink and scrubbed and toasty, his eyelids drooping and his legs insisting on the horizontal. For good measure he drank a bolt of milk from the fridge. Drowsiness in a cup. More white stuff.

The towel he wore was one of the purloined Holiday Inn numbers, also white. Perhaps this was some subtle conspiracy.

Doing coke before bedtime was probably a stupid idea. Nahh. Let it wait.

He was two steps from the bed—hell, in this room you were only two steps from *anything*—when Jamaica knocked on the outer door of the airlock. Jonathan did not have to guess at who this late visitor might be. Still clad in his towel he admitted her, saying nothing, which was itself an indictment.

"Hi there." She made a point of smiling tightly. "I brought back your Overkill shirt." To play the uberfemme now was not a winning strategy. She breezed into the room. By now she knew the drill with the various doors, and where to try sitting down. Jonathan, for all the guilt he wanted to disburse, could not help watching her cross the room. It was that kind of walk.

Tonight she wore acid-wash jeans tight enough to make his groin ache. Flat-heeled soft leather boots. A crisp sweatshirt with BEVERLY HILLS HOTEL stenciled in glitter, gold on burgundy. She shed a bulky brown bomber jacket with tufts of aged wool at the collar and a flaking insignia depicting the Flying 8-Ball Squadron, Euro Theatre, crew of the B-24 Sweet Eloise.

"You know," she said, "when I was little, my mother told me the way to get boys to think I was fascinating was to get them to talk about themselves. It worked, too. Then I discovered a much quicker way to get boys interested in me. Then I got, like, more mature. I decided to mix both approaches, and that worked out pretty okay. It beat busting my buns to capture a diploma, you hear what I'm saying?"

"You want something to drink?"

"Beer's fine. Some more of that special coffee you made would be great." She knew the things driving him to act impervious and icily polite. She was already cold enough tonight. "Jonathan—listen to me. I do what I do and I rarely put up with shit about it. Normally I wouldn't bother to come over here and—"

"Never mind." He waved a hand, the classic gesture of striking down an imaginary barricade of bullshit. "I'm just being a jerk. It's my night to be a jerk. I *know* what you do."

That brought a hopeful smile forth. Not happy, but pleased for now. "What say we skip the part where we argue?" She extended her hand in good fellowship, mustering a comically military set of jaw.

They clasped and shook. Contact with her skin nearly drove Jonathan insane right then and there. He brewed more of the Columbian Supremo, ground medium coarse at the market.

Next step. "After all the crap that went down this weekend, I just wanted to mention that if you truly didn't like that scene, and were serious about doing something, you can. You can help. Cruz, me, all of us. Jesus, you think I *like* doing the nasty with Bauhaus? You think I'm crazy or have no taste? No way, hoser."

Whatever hold Bauhaus had over her, whatever history they had racked up, however black it got, it doesn't matter, Jonathan thought. I have her there. I have her now.

"Your mom coach you in the other stuff?" He tried to sound wry.

"Hm!" It was a laugh. "How much did your parents tell *you* about the beast with two backs?"

"Topic never came up."

"Never?" The pun set her to snickering. "You've been doing some of Uncle Bauhaus' comedy dust, haven't you, my friend?"

"Am I?"

"Am you what?" She crossed her ankles, leaned back to use her coat as a cushion, warming now. Outside the wind raised hell, scouring the stone, making threats so that the wood within the walls groaned and ticked in fear.

"Am I your friend?" He stopped the hot plate busywork to look dead at her.

"Sure." It was that simple. "We've been through so much together, wot?"

No matter which way he turned he felt jumpy, nervous, uncomfortable. Jamaica's presence, so close, untethered him. Maybe this was backwash from the cocaine.

Water boiled. "So what's the status report on our pal Cruz?"

"Hospital kept him for a day. Fill him full of drugs, most likely. What a joke." She had not actually seen Cruz, but had heard X-rays were necessary for some of the injuries he had sustained at the Oakwood pokey. She half reclined on the cot, chocking a wrist beneath her chin. Her elbow sank into the pad.

She eased in like a sleepy cat, having fun watching Jonathan putter about, wearing his towel.

"What do you take?"

"We've already done that one." She enjoyed being playful, partially because playfulness seemed to perturb him so much. "I take...everything."

She got the Moon mug again, Jonathan's "company" cup. She wondered if it was something astrological, peered close. Nope, science. Kind of the same, really.

To make a place for himself on the cot next to her would be going too far. He decided to clear a yet-unpacked box from the wicker seat of the rocking chair.

Jamaica saw him make up his mind. When he turned to the chair, she snatched off his towel.

"Ooh. Good buns." She grinned evilly.

"Goddamnit—!" Cold air goosed him. He tried to play normal, holding out a hand for the towel while a volcanic blush tinted his entire nude body a uniform red.

"I like that."

"What?"

"You didn't cover your crotch with your other hand."

"Seems kind of stupid. I mean, it's nothing you haven't seen, right?" His arm beckoned; he might have been posing for a Grecian sculptor. *Ding-Dong in Search of a Fig Leaf.*

"You dress to the left."

"What...?" He almost made a move to grab the towel; she wadded it defensively to dissuade him. His voice had gone up high. It was absurd, this badinage in the buff. It was more than comic. Nearly burlesque. "Uh...please?"

"One of my favorite words." She stood up, held out the towel...

and tossed it into the bathroom, out of range.

Before Jonathan could fade for it, she eliminated the distance between them, collecting his rising penis gently in one hand, the back of his neck in the other, and drew him bodily into a lush kiss.

She found his lips tight, his teeth locked, his brain lying to his entire body.

She had blindsided him. He wanted her so badly he was incapable of composing a coherent sentence. The lies melted like sherbet in a microwave oven. He hardened below, softened above. He willed his arms to enfold her.

He expected some grotesque orgy of pumping and suction, a stroke film thrill ride that would have force-fit her into the character part of whore. She could live up to the label he'd slipped on her when assaulted by the sight of Bauhaus' blow job.

She knew this, and played against stereotype.

The hand holding his cock did nothing but maintain its loving grip. He came up stiff as a railroad spike, scrotum contracting, balls aching to give to her. For the nonce she avoided the lewder tonguework, softly kissing his neck, his earlobes, his blissfully closed eyelids. She rubbed her face against his bare chest, feeling his heart slip gears, hearing his breathing become precipitous.

No rush.

Calmly, mildly, she grazed him until he was quivering. His legs refused to hold him standing any longer.

Jonathan found himself lying slowly back on the cot, the cool leather of the bomber jacket against one calf. Jamaica made sure he could see her peel her sweatshirt inside-out. She was free of her boots and pants in a second, and over him, her fine large nipples tracing an electric geometry on his flesh. She moved astride him and crawled forward, foxy and languorous. He felt her explicit outcrop of pubic hair examine his navel, then his sternum, then his lips.

He opened his eyes. His cognizance overloaded with her, blowing off free champagne bubble sparks and firework lightning. Her face was what he saw, benevolent, benedictory, far above and looking down at him from between the hard coffee nipples, and when their eyes locked she accepted what she saw, and shifted oh so subtly, a wealth of precision and control there in those schooled leg muscles, and she offered herself to his ready mouth, the rosewater tang of labia unexpected and exhilarating.

He had been starving, bereft for so long.

"You haven't done this in a while, have you, baby?" She was concerned.

"It's been tough." He chuckled. "I was about to say it's been hard."

"No drawbacks in *that* arena. You seem—*ah!*" She sucked air sharply. "Like that. Like that. *Just* like that."

She had been reaching rearward to fondle him. She lost herself and her grip became indecisive. Jonathan did not speak for a few liquid moments, and she mashed downward onto his face a little rougher than she intended.

He felt her trembling.

When he could next see her face, it was turned far to his right, her graceful deer's neck arched, mouth open, eyes shut. She paced her breathing. Her eyes glowed like emerald candles, and suddenly she was in a great, urgent hurry, moving and seizing him and before he knew it he had been swiftly guided all the way into her and she was making the sort of noises a thirsty person makes between big gulps of water. She moved fast and it felt too good to last. He tipped over and came his whole life out.

When she reached for her coffee mug she found the contents still tepid. She and Jonathan had accomplished a hell of a lot in very little time.

"Can you be bribed?" She stroked his chest.

"Can't everybody?" He loved best of all the feel of her legs against his, moving idly. "Everybody has a price tag. On some people you need to find out where it's hidden. On some the price is too high. Most people are too eager to sell their souls when it's buyer's market." His groin was entirely juiced. "What do you need done?"

"Besides my back, again?" She drew breath deeply.

"No—you said I could help. Before."

"I came down here from Cruz's room. Tried you earlier, but you weren't home. Guess you were somewhere else, still busy being a jerk."

This amused him by now.

"Bauhaus. That asshole. Had Cruz's apartment turned over. Marko probably buzzed over here as soon as Cruz got his first

sedation. He slipped his keys to me before we all walked into
Bauhaus' place. Upstairs, it's a professional search job, but it's
still obvious. Bauhaus is taking potshots at Cruz's story about
flushing the dope. To see if it sprouts holes and bleeds."

"How did you get over here tonight, anyway?" The flesh of
her calf was smooth and perfect against the sole of his naked
foot.

"Bosco."

"Come again?"

"I do have a car. Not much of a car, but it's transportation,
they say. One of those little Jap skateboards. I call it Bosco.
After..." She furrowed her brow. "I don't remember. That's
weird."

Jonathan was from Texas, and had never used Bosco. "I
didn't see a car the first night you were here. The night of the
jail stuff."

"Bosco was in the shop. Maybe he likes it there because it's
warmer. Or something. He's spent most of the winter there. I'm
always losing a belt or blowing a hose or something. I always
remember to put all the fluids and water in, but..."

"The guys at the repair bay probably sabotage the car so
you'll keep coming back, so they can hang around and gawk at
you."

"Bosco is usually fixed by a woman. Adela."

"Whoops. You're right. Unwarranted sexist assumption.
Unless, of course, Adela's gay."

"No, she...wait." She actually thought about it for a moment.
"You know, I have no idea. Suppose it's possible. Personally, I
think the solution to all this is to get a new car. Quite American,
thinking that way. I genuflected to the energy crisis and bought
a car, used, that conserved gasoline for the entire country. Now
its paintjob is down to the gray. It's full of road dings and there
ain't much tread left. It's on Adela's lift most of the time, and
nobody worries about gas shortages anymore."

"We're about due for a new one. Just as soon as everyone
cycles back into muscle engines. Then, *pow*—right in the wallet."

"Bosco made it over here tonight, though. Whether he'll start,
after being buried in snow, is another proposition altogether."

The storm heaved against the windows as punctuation.

"I just came in out of that," he said. From ice cakes and carbonized slush to the warm taste of Jamaica lingering on his lips.

Right now Jonathan's recall was scant and fuzzy where their trip to Bauhaus' was concerned. He had overheard many details, but was able to interpret precious few. Cruz's mouth had not been in top form for storytelling.

"You told Bauhaus that Cruz dumped the stuff into the toilet. Two kilos."

"I lied. File a lawsuit. I didn't mention the gun in the candy box, either. Cruz wrapped it up pretty good. We need to go get it out, now, before Bauhaus invents any more options. Cruz is in no shape to fetch anything; that guy in the jail really did a job on his arms. And Cruz knows this guy in Florida named Rosie. He can translate the dope into cash."

"The bag is really at the bottom of the airshaft, right?"

"Gun, dope and all. If the bag didn't break."

"You want me to fish out the bag?" He was surprised to discover himself postcoitally overprotective. No one had been inside Jamaica as recently as Jonathan. He was randified, territorial and hot to maintain his front-running position. He supposed it was all grandly primitive. Some hormonal imperative.

"Cruz dropped that bag from the third floor, and there's a damned good chance it got punctured when it hit bottom." The longer they waited around, the greater was the likelihood that their potential freedom egg had decomposed into worthless white goo. "Do you know if there's some way to get into the airshaft from the basement?"

"No. Not that I've seen."

Jonathan had made a single sortie down to the icebound laundry room. There were many heavily hasped doors, some with bolted steel fascia, and a few grotty basement studios. Occupancy was full. Cold water dripped to pool near the center of the cement floor. The severity of the winter had rendered the washer and dryer useless; the winter itself would soon jeopardize the incumbent mayor's tenure. There was no earthly reason, Jonathan saw, for the airshafts to have below ground access. The floorplan was confusing enough that, down there, he lacked any idea of which direction he was pointed. Each floor seemed skewed, its halls and doors and stairs in slightly variant positions.

He thought it out. "If I ask Fergus, he'll just ask questions. *Boolsheet sunvabitch*, he'll say. It might be better, quicker and easier to just climb down the shaft and get it."

"What? You mean like mountaineering?"

"From the second floor it's only one story down. The bathroom windows looking out onto the shaft are all soaped up or boarded over. Up. And down. And nobody suspects anything. Might be better. Safer."

She stared as though his forehead had just sprouted a finger. "You can *do* that?"

He clenched both fists tight, to pop the hamstrings. "I've always had more strength in my arms than my legs. Did some flatrock scrambling in Texas and some caving in Arizona. With the right kind of rope it's just a bit more strenuous than going up and down stairs. Besides, if I can shimmy down there and hook goodies on to the line for you to pull up, we don't risk anybody catching us in the hallways with, how you say, incriminating evidence. We can Mission Control the whole recovery from behind my own locked door—*two* locked doors—and nobody has to know. Even if Bauhaus has somebody keeping an eye on Cruz's place, he still won't suspect. Yes?"

He savored this sudden feeling of control. He was steering, for a change.

Jamaica was not about to question a windfall. "When could we do this?"

He saw it coming. "Why not right now, tonight?" He was well-fucked and giddy with potential. He could impress her with forthright action. "You're here, I'm here. I even stole a flashlight from work today so I could take a peek down there myself. We've got magic fairie dust for those critical energy boosts. All we need is a rope."

"Any ideas about that?" Her expression said *dumb question, I'll wager.*

"I thought you'd never ask."

"Wait." She stayed sly. "Who says I'm done with you yet?"

He moved his hand up the curve of her flank, caressing the roundness of her ass, cupping one breast to thumb the nipple, and gathered her hand in his, lacing the fingers and bringing it up to his mouth for a kiss. "That's nice. You can be my reward, so I'll have incentive."

He was off the bed and moving. Time again for him to do something, as opposed to his standard operating procedure. In an eyeblink he felt his life hit the groove and accelerate. This was a streak that could alter all that was bad, and it insisted on being played out.

"So what about the rope?" She beat him to the bathroom.

He pulled on a pair of layabout fatigue pants. Where the hell had those been when she'd denuded him? He thought of her sitting on the toilet and hoped not all of him went down the drain. "I need to hop downstairs for that. Is there anything you need while I'm...?"

"Mmm." Her voice resonated against the tilework. "Maybe just you, inside me, again."

That dried up his throat in a hurry. It couldn't have been that good for her. "Give me a break," he said, warily.

"Jonathan." Again that chastising tone. "You made me come, babe. Half the men in the world don't even know what a clitoris *is*, let alone *where* it is."

She knew this would send him off just brimming over with himself. She needed to keep him high-spirited and energized right now...but not merely to play pawn and retrieve Cruz's stash. His friction and pressure had been filling and good. She could feel her pussy throbbing with each heartbeat. Jonathan had been considerate and capable. Her orgasms had been genuine, though distanced and slightly out of true. She could bring herself off harder and more furiously; still, this had been pleasant. The part she liked the best had been a couple of nights ago when they had just snuggled and slept, even though she could feel his erection and sense the discomfort rolling off him in psychic waves. He was in no hurry. With most clients it had been strip *now*, fuck *now*, leave *now*. Jonathan had been willing to wait, so hesitant that she'd finally had to seduce him, now *there* was a switcheroo. With tutoring, he had the raw chops to become a hurricane of a bed partner. It might be fun to teach him.

She heard the apartment doors unbolt, open and close in sequence. Another hot bath might be just the tonic now. The bruises she had acquired were on the wane. She was glad Bauhaus had not chosen to punch her around, as he sometimes enjoyed as part of his humiliation scenarios.

As she got the hot water going, the bathroom door was nudged open behind her. The skinny black cat slinked in, leaving a wandering line of small, bloody footprints.

Even before he got to the basement stairwell Jonathan could see his breath in the air as he moved. He suspected that Fergus the super was not a resident of one of Kenilworth's subterranean cubicles, which were probably too clean for him. He did, however, maintain a seedy downstairs office where Jonathan had put his signature to a one-year lease. The commitment made sense in a metaphysical way: If you stayed here for more than a year, you were trapped; if you were smart, you used that year to better yourself, and escape.

Jonathan noticed the lights still on in 107, the apartment below his. That would be the old guy who was forever railing against the Jews. Maybe he hit the bottle and hurled junk around once he got sufficiently lubricated. The noise, earlier, had been that sort of disturbance. Now the ruckus had run full course and it was time for sleeping off the injustices of the rotten world at large. Jonathan heard no television going as he passed the door, downward-bound.

On the first floor someone had put masking tape across the nonworking elevator doors, like a low budget movie's version of a police line.

The steps turned to stone and the wallboard fell away to the crumbling strata of the building's foundations. Down here were inadequate bare bulbs and more sealed doors embalmed in paint. These latter were chipped, gouged and scored as though some clawed monster had attempted forcible entry. Another door that led who knew where was blocked by warped lumber stacked to one side of the corridor. These smells included paint, solvents, wet rug, mold, sewage, all forming a toxic industrial mulch.

Jonathan knew Fergus' eyrie to be a crowded junkyard of building maintenance—buckets, tools, boxes of greasy plumbing knicknacks, bags of plaster and patch. He'd had to move a power saw off the desk to sign his papers. The desk was a military job in battle green, all metal and no nonsense. Weighing down the honeycomb of shelves on three sides were cartons of dusty lightbulbs, jars of screws and bolts, a drain snake, paint-clogged trays and rollers, more power tools...and maybe, just maybe something Jonathan could press into service as a climbing line. The weirdest item he had noticed in the office before were two huge twenty-five pound sacks of dog kibble sagging together in one corner. A staple of Fergus' diet, from his aroma.

The office might also have a secret hatch of some sort, leading to the airshaft. The possibility was enticing but Jonathan was not going to invest too much hope there.

Far away, but forever ambient, was the noise of Kenilworth. The heartbeat. The ghost. Whatever.

Jonathan scanned the rest of the corridor, peering around corners as though expecting to be shot at. Nothing.

He pulled the roll of drafting tape from the pocket of his parka and rapidly smoothed out a crosshatch pattern on the window of Fergus' office door. Then he checked the passage again. More nothing. He planted his elbow sharply into the double-X of tape, dead center. The glass snapped and the tape web sagged quietly into his grasp, laden with trapped fragments. Three more seconds and he was inside.

Three minutes more, and he was out.

He took time to stow the taped mass of busted glass in one of the trash dumpsters, which were stationed beyond the laundry room at the far west end of the lot. To get there you used an exterior door that let onto a trench-like breezeway. At about eye-level there was a gap of two feet that permitted a mole's eye view of what Jonathan supposed was a small backyard. Right now the open space between the bottom of the first floor and the excavation of the basement level was plugged up by snow. It was like the inside of a glacier, a frozen tunnel iced solid with leakage and polluted stalactites. It reminded Jonathan of a circular chute in a cave, but of glass, not rock. Light rainbowed off the tessellated, curving veneer of ice. With his shadow blocking one end it would make a great poster for a journey to the center of the earth movie.

The illusion was spoiled by the crudely lettered sign Fergus had posted on the laundry room door, proclaiming the obvious.

Jonathan reconsidered all the locked doors down here. No time to jimmy them all in hopes of chancing across a grate or lid leading to the airshaft. Hell, down here he might waste an hour burgling his way into the wrong shaft. Knocking on doors to request neighborly egress had never struck him as an option, let alone an intelligent idea. This was something no one should know about.

Besides—the climb would impress Jamaica.

The prize from Fergus' rathole was a pair of figure-eight coils of heavy duty electrical extension cable, 25-footers with grounded plugmold outlets every eight feet. Both were sheathed in groove-textured, bright orange insulation that made the wire more durable and bulked it out to a diameter of half an inch. It had been the strongest, most practical stuff to be stolen from the super's lair.

The best way to test it would be to unreel it out his window and go outside to hang on it for a moment. This would additionally help him determine whether the lines should be linked end-to-end or braided together. Twenty-five feet, plus his own height, should be the right length unless the shaft was much deeper than the basement floor, which wasn't likely. Some of the length would be used up by knots, anchoring, and play over the bathroom sill. One of these cords were surely adequate to the task of holding his weight.

When he re-entered 207 he felt the heat buffet and knew Jamaica had drawn herself a hot bath. He liked the role-reversal. This time, he was clothed and she would be clad in the towel...

The spoiler he had not foreseen was the amount of blood that would be soaking her towel when he walked in, smiling.

Blood on her hands.

When she showed him, the cat on the towel in her lap tried

to break, displeased with all this undignified probing and wiping.

"Jonathan, he walked right into the bathroom; he was just *covered* in blood..."

At least one towel was a goner. Jonathan was about to ask if the blood was real; another puerile Jonathan-type question. In such amounts blood looked bogus. A half-tub of hot water steamed, unused. Jamaica would need it; there were even smudges of blood on her face.

It ain't my fault. I'm innocent, I tell you.

"Is he hurt?"

"Not that I can see. But look here." She released the animal; at least its paws were clean now. She and Jonathan backtracked along the trail of sticky crimson pawprints to a place four feet from the steam heater.

There was a vertical slit in the wall near floor level. Semi-coagulated droplets oozed from it.

"Ho...lee..."

"Shit. That's what I said."

It was as though a careless butcher had carved an arm-sized hole in a side of beef with a dull cleaver. The edges of the cut folded inward. Layers of paint had broken to reveal deeper layers still flexible enough to cling to the folds, curving with them back into darkness.

Jamaica extended a hand.

"Don't touch it!" She recoiled before he could smack her hand away. From his drafting box Jonathan got a steel ruler, a cork-backed job that would make a nasty offensive weapon if correctly brandished. He poked the outer edges of the slit. They flinched, shrinking back, splitting new hairlines in the paint and liberating fresher, redder drops of blood.

The anodized steel sank eight inches before he withdrew it, red now.

They interrupted each other with assorted biblical and scatological expletives. The hole stayed. The cat rejoined them. Warmer with the humans. It poked its snubbed triangular nose forward to sniff the bloodstuff.

Jonathan batted it away, angry. Control had been his until this ugliness had reared. He had to say something, mark this anomaly with commentary, to reassure both himself and Jamaica that they weren't hallucinating.

"Cat showed up bloody the other night, too. Just as bewildered." He said this in an outpouring of breath more like the admission of some guilty secret. "I couldn't figure out how he got into the room. The doors were closed. You sure he wasn't in here when I left?"

"No idea." Her voice was a whisper. She unwound the towel from her waist, tried to find a clean spot, and blotted her face. "I just...you know, assumed he was napping in a box or something."

"Same here. But what if *this* was how he got in?"

All eyes sought the bleeding gash in the wall. Of course this was not happening. Sure. No way.

Her logic circuits still would not accept it. "No, Jonathan, just look—it's all bloody and moist and confining. No cat would just walk into something like that. They're fussy. They hate getting mussed or wet."

"Yeah. But what if it isn't this way on the end where he goes in?"

"I don't get it." She looked again. Uh-uh, no way.

"Jamaica, this isn't a tunnel behind a secret panel. You may not have noticed, but this is an exterior wall were looking at.' He was right. "Oh. Shit."

Now that the offending towel was not manhandling him so fiercely, the cat felt like jabbing at it with one paw. Then he wanted to curl up and snooze on it.

"Little fuck. Wish he could talk."

No way, Bubs—not with your nude ladyfriend here.

He unlatched the for-show brass catch top of the nearest casement and slid the window up. Crumbly sill wood creaked and aged caulking fell loose. The cold hurried greedily in. Pellets of hard snow shot in to sting Jonathan's hands and melt on contact, leaving freezing water to trickle back along his wrists, driven by lashes of wind.

"*Jonathan, for fuck's sake!*" Jamaica sprang away and hugged herself as if suffering a bad cramp. She was still unclothed, and not so eager to embrace the elements in all their pissed off Earth Matriach splendor.

"Yow. Sorry. Listen—you still want to fetch Cruz's little package, then throw on your sweatshirt and help me with this. Please?"

She knew there was little time, stayed practical and decided not to make a mad, though the power welling up in her alluring green eyes told him it would be easy. "Okay. What do I do?"

He was leaning out the window. The storm was incredible. "First come here and take a look." His hair was thickly spiced with snow.

She saw there was no bloody hole on the outside of Kenilworth Arms, two stories up. The bricks were cold and uniform, braced for future assaults of weather and pollution.

"I know for a fact the wallboard can't be more than an inch thick, because I knocked out a chunk while I was moving in. The insulation is shit—prewar, and I don't mean Vietnam or Korea. Fire hazards galore in this dump."

"I believe it." Her teeth chattered. Thirty minutes ago she had been so hot on the outside, so warm on the inside, so frisky and wet and eager. Right now was like waking up in a frigid shower. Jonathan closed the window and she let out a gasp of thanks. Sometimes your whole body could goosebump to the point of dermal pain, a core chill that might never burn off.

Jonathan tied the female end of one extension cord through the feed pipe for the heater, which he knew was incapable of generating heat serious enough to damage the wire. Jamaica had her jeans and sweatshirt on and had wrapped herself in the unzipped sleeping bag like an Indian. He reopened the window and unreeled the cord. It did not quite reach to the first floor windows; the ceilings were high ones here at Kenilworth. With fisherman's patience he wound up the cord on his forearm, attached the second cord, and tried again, making the center binding knot strong. There wasn't enough cord to braid it along its entire length, as he had hoped.

He crunched outside in his parka and found that he had about eight extra feet to play with. He doubled the wire around his wrist and did a deliberately slow pull-up. He felt the line tauten and he sank back to snow level. While Jamaica watched from the window, her face a white mask in a chrysalis of down nylon, he grabbed above the slack and repeated. The cord went arrow straight and he did a leisurely count-off to thirty as he hung, hitops braced against the snowmelt-slippery bricks. The cord would breathe, stretching, but not much, under his 155 pounds. He walked up the building to head height. He wiggled around. The insulation took a firmer bite and tightened his knots. He stopped before he could unmoor the heater from his floor, which would be no surprise tonight.

He could trust this stuff to a two-way climb.

Jamaica was in the bathroom immersing her hands. The cat was asleep, having licked and cleaned itself to its own satisfaction. The gooey crimson incision had condensed to a maroon hairline; the blood below it on the floor had dried to skim.

"God! It must be thirty below out there. Colder, with the wind chill."

"Everybody says that. Like: 'It's not the heat—'"

"It's the stupidity." He traced the line of the slit with his finger, something he would not permit Jamaica to do moments before. It was still moist, but receding by the second. It was only half its original length now.

She caught him. "Jonathan..."

"It's like *skin*. Like a cut healing in fast motion." Near the center it had the consistency of modeling clay; at its periphery the wall had resumed normal solidity. The paint now lay clean and uninterrupted. "Did you see anything like this in Cruz's room?"

"No!" Like she wouldn't have mentioned it if she had. "Yuck. But I can't say it was something I was looking for. You just said the cat might've walked in here through that hole and *you* missed it."

He shook his head. "It wasn't there before." He was almost certain. "And it's not gonna be here in another minute or two." She folded her arms. "You were going to say something like, *you're not gonna believe this, but.*"

"Hm. *But.* But there is something decidedly bent going on in this building, and I'm not talking about the police raids, or the domestic punch-outs, or the occasional burglary-in-progress. Right now I'm beginning to think that maybe that Mexican kid got lost by crawling into a hole exactly like this one here."

"Oh yeah." She rubbed her face slowly, as if topped off by the world of pain. "Can't you just see us running down to the police station to give them the skinny on what really happened? Yo, Barnett, we figured it all out, man!"

Their mutual laughter was rueful. Jonathan collected in the cord, shut the window and dropped the blind. The process had gotten him thoroughly wet.

"Cruz thought there was some kind of ghost in the building. Said he could hear it moaning and groaning. *I* never heard a damned thing."

He decided to let her in on it. "When we were sleeping together, I was thinking there was an airflow or vibration, something that sounds like a heartbeat, but only if you listen really close. A definite cadence, a repeating pattern." *Boom-cha-boom-cha-cha.*

"Can't hear it." She held her hands toward the heater, flexing her long, elegant fingers.

"No. It's never that easy. It's one of those vague noises, almost subliminal. The kind that makes you doubt your sanity, but only when you're alone." He began tying large, pretzel-shaped climbing loops every four or five feet along the cord.

"You weren't alone. You were with me." She grew catty. "Why, we've been alone together a lot."

"*Tch.* I was never more alone, I think now, than the last two years I spent with Amanda. Quite an opera, that."

He traded his Reebs for snowboots. Capra had lent him the cash to buy the footgear, and Jonathan was quick to appreciate their utility. Steel-toed and gum-soled, they laced firm up to the calf. The reinforced toes were not absolutely essential, but he had never owned such boots, and thought it cool to walk around with the same protection that miners and construction wildcats had.

"Ah, but you still love her. I know that tone." She watched him work. "She still makes you mad."

"Like I think I said before, subtlety doesn't seem to be my forte these days. Yeah. Losing her was like tearing tissue."

"Not Kleenex, but heartmuscle, eh? Sounds like love." She

was not trying to be cruel out of meanness. She just knew better, and sensed he might permit her to be a realist. He was not a little boy, and he'd better be able to handle someone knocking down that *nobody hurts like I hurt* garbage.

"If you define love the way Bierce did," he said. "When you don't have a lot of new input, I think you start recycling the memories, old emotions, until they spoil from overuse and begin growing mold. You hit the point at which the original emotion will no longer make legible copies."

"You're an idiot romantic," she said. "Either that or you're so goddamned possessive that you'll never let go. Equally unhealthy."

"My buddy Bash suggested I just find a new girlfriend. It's so easy for him to say that." But Bash, Jonathan knew, had his own factory-fresh set of problems now. He might as well have Camela's engagement ring through his own nose.

"I would've made the same suggestion. Let the old bitch go. When it's over, it's over. A lot of people never learn fundamentals like that. They hang on to all the memories because a few of them were good. That sounds suspiciously like letting one apple spoil the basket. I'm running out of clichés. The bitch is history. Move on."

Now that was a sublime concept. Let her go. Move on. Try to get on with your life, dummy. He needed an outsider to put it so baldly, to say it in simple words he had been unwilling to aim and fire at Amanda. *Bitch.* Yeah, you've got your own petty agenda, bitch, and firebomb anybody who countermands it, even if they love you, right? There was no oblique way to deliver the message. No one had ever said, just let the BITCH go. Let her go on her bitchy way to toxify and cripple someone else's life instead of clinging to yours like a sourpuss ghost of recrimination and culpability. Jonathan had protected her more than anyone. He had done so overlooking the core fact that Amanda was, you know, one of those. A bitch. That he ought to, well, just. *Let her go.* She wants to go, so *let* her. Don't ever try to love somebody against their will; that's how you make a wasteland where nobody wins a prize, ever. Let her go. Amanda had been a bitch.

And Jamaica—she was a whore. What the hell did *she* know about Amanda? Nada.

You're doing it again, he realized. Why did he need Amanda to bonk him repeatedly on the head with the club of bad memories? He did it so well himself. And covered for his tormentor, to boot.

Instead of snapping at Jamaica, defending some inviolate, rosy memory of Amanda, he tried to think of a better answer for her. This strategy was new but pleasant.

"Uh...well, I didn't let her go. She kind of let me go. Sort of. Maybe that was it: Being the dumpee instead of the dumper." In a rude flash slingshot by abrupt and intense anger, he saw Amanda get pasted by the toothy grille of a speeding Coca-Cola truck. From Waco. Yeah. *Splat!* A disfiguring traffic mishap might really be a windfall for her. A catch-all blame basket for everything bad that ever befell her. At least it would erase the smugness from her demeanor.

"Male pride is an ugly thing sometimes," Jamaica said. "Makes you stupid. Makes you do stupid things."

"My fault." He shrugged. He'd have to stop that. "I didn't bother amassing new events to put in front of the memory of her. Growth doesn't really block out past pain but it can erect a scenic divider so you don't have to *look* at it. I just held at a constant pain level, like a computer refusing new data. When I finally overloaded, I took a chance on coming to Chicago."

"And look at you now!" She smiled and that made him feel better. Normally he hated being made fun of.

"That's how I wound up in this palace." He waggled an imaginary Groucho cigar. "So, my dear, what's *your* story?"

She was up now, and next to him.

"Jonathan. I think you're basically a nice guy, I really do. Misguided, and over-reactionary, but at the core a nice guy. You let people fuck with your head too much. You dwell on bad shit too deeply. You *think* about feeling too much, instead of just *feeling*." She frowned. "And I think you just asked me your own special variation on the dumbest question in the universe: *What's a nice girl like you.* Etcetera."

"Oops. Shit. Sorry." He blushed. It was endearing.

"Don't apologize. Jesus, that's another bylaw you're going to have to learn. *Stop sorrying.*" She rubbed his neck muscles, standing behind him. She had sincerely tried to cheer him without compromising. Or lying. What the hell did she think she was doing?

"Time's wasting," she said. "What's next?"

"Humph." He gave his head a courtly shake. "*That,* madame, must wait until after I have completed my climb for the record books."

He was so...Jamaica hunted for a word. Mannered, around her. Good god, did getting laid open him up that much? He was considerate, attentive, and once she had given him a goal, determined and goal-oriented. Or, as the illiterates would have it, goal-orientated. This near-stranger was about to descend into an icky cold dark shaft to salvage all their lives, merely because she had told him their lives needed salvaging.

He exchanged his parka for two sweatshirts atop a T-shirt—more maneuverability—and tucked his pantlegs into the boots before lacing up. From one of the kitchen boxes he grabbed a pair of utility candles and a matchbook from the coffee shop he frequented over on Weedwine Street. He wanted a backup light source in case something moronic befell the nine-volter he'd borrowed from Capra's. Jamaica knew the coffee shop; it was called the Bottomless Cup and it was just across Broadhurst Avenue, the eastern borderline of Oakwood. Jonathan told her that the waitress and all the locals referred to the place as Weedwine Eats, for obvious ho-ho reasons.

Jonathan yanked out a yard of filament tape and twisted it into a sturdy lanyard which he threaded through the flashlight grip, then around his belt.

"Just call me Tensing Norkhay."

He still had the trucker's gloves from Bash's, and slipped them on before attempting to pound his bathroom window open again. It remained as jammed and cantankerous as every other window in Kenilworth. Knocking out his cardboard patch would not suffice; he needed the leeway used up by the window frame. After a bit of violence it surrendered.

He saw more of the fecal residue on the outside of the sill, caked there as though someone had scraped their bootsoles.

The eagle claw feet of the bathtub had settled not on top of the floor tiles but through them, actually penetrating them. The tub was heavy and immobile enough to provide a solid and reliable tie-off. Jonathan's confusion of electrical cord resembled alien macramé. He choke-knotted the anchor end around the claw foot nearest the window and paid out the line a few feet at a time, so as not to tangle it. A cockroach, irate at this intrusion upon its under-the-tub domain, decided to make a run for it. Jamaica pulped it as soon as it was into the light.

Standing in the tub, he clicked on the lantern and wormed his head and shoulders through. This was the first time he had gone so far into the mysterious adjunct to his apartment. Darkness gulped his breath vapor a foot from his nose. A loamy odor hit his sense of smell in a definite updraft. Rigor gone over into dry rot, as much spicy or neutral as fetid. He thought of the preserved redolence of opened tombs. After the initial olfactory shock it wasn't as bad as the spoiled hamburger effluence of the blood that had spilled from the wall in the next room.

He cleared off the sill, already married to the idea of getting filthy during this incursion.

The light exposed the corrugated metal as glistening with gravid moisture. Sagging, arrested droplets glinted the gemlike green of corruption, the color of botulin or nuclear waste. The vertical face of the sill was greased. Going would be dicey.

"I guess you don't have a folding fire escape ladder in your saddlebag?"

"Sorry, babe. I could go camp out in front of the Oakwood hardware store till opening time and charm the hired help into a loaner. But it's five to three in the morning, and by four o'clock I'd really like to kiss this place adios forever—you know what I mean?"

The fantasy jackhammered Jonathan. A few thousand bucks in-pocket, and hit the happy trail with Jamaica. Thrills and adventure. California, maybe.

"It's more than twenty feet." The end of his line did not quite graze the surface of the pool in the bottom of the shaft. "I see water and what looks like a floating Glad bag. Other junk down there. Smells like a dead squirrel. A whole family of dead squirrels. Several generations."

That made him think again of the missing Velasquez kid. Jonathan's nose did not wish to process the aroma of dead baby marinated in slime.

Jamaica had read his mind. "Jesus, Jonathan, you don't suppose that kid is...?"

"I *do* suppose," he said rigidly. "But that doesn't change our travel plans, now does it? And if I do find him down there all waterlogged, or with a split plank in his mouth and out the back of his head, what are we supposed to do about it? Call the police? Give me a break: *'Oh, yes, Officer Robot Cop? We were engaged in a mid-morning cocaine hunt when we stumbled across this expired individual. No, we don't know anything else. Can we go home now?'"*

"Calm down. Calm down. It's probably nothing. The kid was upstairs and on the opposite end of the building."

They could have argued but it was an unneeded luxury. They were well over the dare line. Criminals never called uniforms for assistance the way dogs never stepped in dogshit.

He snapped off the light and let it hang from his waist. Descent would be made in the dark, on the off chance that some insomniac tenant might see a wildly swinging UFO light through their window as they were taking a dump. If the gut of the shaft ran much deeper than the basement floor, he'd have to grab the bag while hanging one-handed on the line. Not recommended. Once you start a suspension climb, a little meter runs up a body bill on your arms and legs and muscle coordination, and it doesn't stop ticking from courtesy. He was counting on exertion to keep him warm.

Jonathan imagined Kenilworth as a living entity long past its prime, yet still sternutatious. Too sedentary, its tenants huddled or hiding or sleeping, raggedly coexisting in fear and pique. Disruptions would be like gastric incidents. A domestic quarrel was a fart, a slamming door a twinge of tendonitis. At least this would explain the rhythmic vascular pumping only he seemed to be able to hear.

He thought of a tiny daredevil poised on his own tongue, readying to slide down the long, wet esophagus on a line of dental floss. He saw the black cat as a roaming parasite, a benign infection that traversed gaps of integrity in the building's venation. It might have nosed into one of those dead-end iceboxes on one floor and emerged from a raw, hemorrhaging wall slit on another. They came and went like blemishes— temporary one-way passages with an inside and an outside, the building's heartbeat still vigorous enough to push that blood ever-forward.

The Velasquez kid might just as easily have fallen into a fissure where Kenilworth's memory had lapsed or gone lax or just been forgotten.

The deeper the *madman* probed into the House of Usher, the nearer he drew to the insanity ruling all. And in the end when Roderick Usher loses his mind, the house—Poe's paradigm of Roderick's actual head, the skull of the doomed and hypersensitive man—splits right down the middle and caves into the tarn.

He'd bring it up to Jamaica when they next had leisure. Right now it was climb baby climb. Jonathan would just be one more errant corpuscular lump crawling down the wrong tube. He should zip out before he made Kenilworth Arms sneeze.

Which reminded him.

"Get me that little black plastic vial out of my parka, would you please? Right-hand outside pocket."

She brought him the coke with some amusement, watched while he laid and snorted thick lines from the back of his hand without spilling any, and then helped herself.

"Cheers," she said.

Jonathan heard the peculiar dog-whistle squeak in his ears. They popped. He felt the top of his palate dry, setting off coke's special form of post-nasal drip. He sniffed and swallowed twice.

All the internal renovations done here, he thought. All the nails driven, doors removed, walls altered. Bones broken, then splinted to heal in new directions, to grow new bone where none was needed, to function improperly. Like someone who has suffered too many operations.

"Help me with this." He established a push-up brace against the far rim of the tub and backed his legs out the window. It was the only safe approach; no way was he going out head first to slam and dangle. This way he could hang by his elbows on the sill and catch traction.

Jamaica knelt, taking advantage of his defenseless position. "Kiss for luck?"

"Absolutely." He smiled, not expecting to.

She took his face in her hands and laid one on him that nearly collapsed his grip on the tub. They made pleasurable noises back and forth, their hunger resurging. When she broke away, her resinous amber-green eyes tried to swallow him. He would have been enveloped willingly, but for a small chore yet undone.

"I think you sucked the breath out of my lungs," he said, woozed.

She spotted him during his exit, hefting him by the shoulders. The toes of his boots banged the steel lining and slipped. He spread his legs and got a foothold.

She snugged the red glove-pulls around his wrists while he hung from the sill.

"Okay. No talking. It'll echo like hell. When I get to the bottom and give the line three tugs, haul up the bag and feed the line back down." He did not want to tuck it into his belt and then lose or break it halfway up.

She nodded and took her post at the sill. He felt her lips give him a peck on the forehead.

"Go," she said, and he did.

Twenty

When Cruz crawled out from under the sedatives he found himself flatbacking it in a hospital bed with crib rails and staring at Marko, who bore a brotherly resemblance to the gorilla that had tried to mangle him in the Oakwood slammer.

"About time you woke up. I was getting tired of reading that fuckun *Sports Illustrated.*" If it had been the swimsuit issue, of course, things would have been different.

The TV shined down godlike from a wall bracket. No sound. It filled the dim room with an eerie cobalt glow that made Marko's tack-head eyes iridesce. Cruz saw that his dislocated arm was expertly taped to a bedrail and that IV leads were plugged in and dripping glucose. He was wearing a johnny and could feel its butterfly knots pressing into his spine.

"Helluva shiner you got there."

Seen from the inside, the eye injury was frightening. The TV light made it tear.

Marko was wearing a tweed jacket with leather elbow patches. It stretched tight across the tit. His curly blond hair was kinky and wet; he looked like Gorgeous George, the wrestler from Rosie's heyday. Marko's face was the sort that funnybook artists, lacking time or ability, hastily sketch in for background thugs, disposable bad guys, all square jaw and piggy eyes and sloping brow and no human character whatsoever.

"You were in the bathroom," Cruz said. He remembered Bauhaus asking questions, his expression that of a man who has lost a major lawsuit and been advised by his attorneys against showing any emotion. He had most likely put the screws to Jamaica to see if their answers harmonized.

"*You* are on drugs," Marko returned.

"Time is it?"

Marko consulted his Casio. Entry level brain scans a hundred-function display. Now that technology had provided precise digits, it was easier for people like this to tell time. "Two thirty; thereabouts. Two thirty-three."

"What does Bauhaus want?"

Meaning: It took grease to get you in here at this time of night, and has my tail sprung a leak I don't know about? Bauhaus smacked his lips when people dug their graves with their own tongues. Pretend you know everything, say you're just double-checking, and let your victim spill his or her guts right out. Just like Emilio, back in Florida, posing innocent what-ifs and toying with his platinum razor. Sing off key and we customize your face, easy as carving white meat or dark off another kind of turkey.

"Bauhaus just wants to be sure you're okay." The butt of a large-caliber auto pistol in Marko's left armpit spoiled the line of his overstressed suit.

"If that's true, then you must've searched my place already." Cruz's eyes sought the toupee commercial marching silently across the screen above. He wanted his monogrammed shirts, he wanted his Miami mugginess back. He wanted out. As soon as this goon hulked away, he'd hazard a mayday to Rosie on the bedside phone...

...which Bauhaus probably had bugged.

"Your place was clean. You're smart, not to try and fool Bauhaus. You shoulda seen what happened the last guy tried to fuck with him."

"He told me. Guy's laid up at Menard Penitentiary for raping a minor."

Marko smiled. It was not a jolly thing to behold. "Maybe you ain't so smart." Lightning logic in action.

That upped Cruz's vital signs a notch. "What are you talking about?"

"*I* knew that kid. He ain't in prison. He's gone. He's history."

Cruz could see conflict shading the bovine eyes. In this exchange, Cruz was supposed to reveal all the information.

Marko was not here to clue him to the ins and outs of Jimmy McBride's leave-taking. But he had played a key part, oh yeah, and like most sadists Marko got hard by recounting nasty details. The hideous pains he had specially engineered, the moist and inglorious deaths he had precipitated. This man had killed more times than he could count even with his size thirteens off. And he got high on the act. And when you have something you love so much you cannot keep it all to yourself...you brag.

"So? What's the scoop?" Cruz tried hard to broadcast annoyance, a fed-up air that this creature, this killer with his blunted sensibilities and narrow range of emotions, could receive legibly. "You just here to jerk my dick, or play watch puppy, or threaten me, or what?"

The chiseled eyes flared crimson. Had an insult just been hurled?

"C'mon, ace, read my lips. Bauhaus told me Jimmy McBride got shitcanned for twistin' piston inside some junior high school gash. Now *you* tell me Bauhaus had him killed."

"Stupid." It came out *stoopud*. Marko's knuckles went bloodless on the rail as he leaned to loom in Cruz's face. "Ain't no fuckun Jimmy McBride. Guy before you, his name was Boner. That's what we all called him. If he had a real name I didn't know it. But it was him, and he got killed, and you just better watch your fuckun ass and be glad Bauhaus' two keys din't turn up in your fuckun apartment or you'd be suckun the air conditioning in the fuckun morgue right now." He jabbed a thick finger as each noun was expelled; pithecanthropoidal punctuation.

Having said his thing, Marko lifted the bedside phone and punched in. It was amusing for Cruz to watch someone else steam at hurdling Bauhaus' telephonic obstacle course. Perhaps it was just a morphine notion—whatever the ladies in white at St. Jude's had jammed him with for the pain was mellow, like brown writing on yellow paper—but it seemed goofily simple to fill in Bauhaus' half of the ensuing conversation.

Marko the body-buster went: "Yeah, it's me, Mister..."

And Bauhaus would say: *Skip it. Did Cruz tell you where that guy Jonathan lives?*

"Uh, nossir, not yet. I..."

Well FIND OUT, asshole, and get over there and search and I do mean right goddamn now!

"Yes, sir. I will. Does...?"

And find out where that rent-a-cooze Jamaica got to. Make Cruz tell you. Pinch his IV lead shut or find a hypo and fill it with Windex...

"Yes, sir. I'll get right on it."

Marko hung up and paused to seethe. A good, foamy head of anger would stab hellfear right into Cruz's heart.

But Cruz slid home ahead of him. "Say—did you question that guy, whatsisname, Jonathan? Can't remember his last name. Bauhaus saw him, though. I'm sure he told you."

"Huh? No. I mean, yeah—of course he did."

Cruz tried hard to keep Marko off balance, to pretend a brilliant solution had just landed. "That Jonathan guy lives in the same building, man, how could you miss it? Apartment 323. Go down the hallway past the elevator. It's on the far side of the building. Use the Garrison Street entrance. You'll see the apartment numbers on the mailboxes downstairs."

"What about that whore? Bauhaus said she was with you when—"

"Well obviously she's in bed with me right now globbing my knob," Cruz interposed. "How the hell should I know? She's probably off hitting the bricks, doing what ladies of the night do. If I was you, I'd worry about nailing Jonathan down first... you know what I mean?"

Marko shot a gaze of daggers and disfigurement. In a moment he'd stomp away to patch the cracks in his shoddy shakedown, or Bauhaus would feed his weenie to a Rottweiler.

"You better fuckun be right."

The sight of Marko's back, rushing out, hit Cruz like a shot of Jack Daniel's and made him feel perversely good. Marko's grimace was akin to the scrunched expression of a stone Mayan idol taking a dump.

In a moment he heard the elevator ding. All quiet on this ward, tonight.

The night nurse had left a pocket spindle of gauze on the bedside tray. Cruz checked his chart and found out he was due for a peek in five minutes. Once the nurse had done her duty, he unplugged his IV lead and bandaged his arm. He had not needed another injection. Taking along a syringe might be a good idea, for later.

His clothing would be in the closet.

Victor Stallis lent the weather a barrage of choice cuss words. Since midnight the blizzard had been knocking calls around like bowling pins on the police bands.

Flurries whiplashed inland by monster salvos of air rolling unstoppably off the Lake Michigan chop now lifted free snow and pitched it maliciously into any object dumb enough to stand against the storm force. It was abrasive and torturous. The blizzard was hungry, and insisted on grabbing nourishment directly from the psyches and property of all Chicagoans, from the Division Street junkies to the penthoused worthies on Lakeshore Drive. Wouldn't want to own their picture windows tonight, Stallis thought. Open the curtains and it would look like an impossibly big TV screen filled with roiling static. The cost of replacing the glass would equal his wages for a year.

His unit was faced into the wind. The frontal attack of the storm strobed his wipers. Useless. He did not dare roll along at more than a steady thirty on this late tour. The Oakwood patrol grid measured about five square miles. The most persistent drawback here was boredom. At least that was better than the panic ulcers of most of the officers that worked in the Loop.

Victor Stallis was a policeman in decline. He had let his exercise regimen slide ever since Liz had left that stupid note on that stupid dresser. The one her stupid mother had bought her at antique store mark-up, as a fourth anniversary gift. Liz was a closed case now not because Stallis was a cop, but because his ideas of sexual progress and hers had dovetailed late in their third year together. He had begun to suggest things. Calisthenic alternatives. Jellies and devices. Submissive-dominant positions. New orifices. The kind of lovemaking that left the marks of a severe interrogation. Handcuffs and pimp sticks.

Stallis rode the brake and tried to grind the sleep from his face. He was unsaddled, his belt and gear dumped on the shotgun seat. Five of Oakwood's twenty-man force were downed tonight by bugs and the runs, the numbing depletions that came of working too many double shifts in blizzards. Tonight he had rolled solo, with nothing to look forward to except B&E calls and a domestic or two; wintertime cabin fever made people pull the weirdest shit.

He thought about tearing off a piece with the hooker the station guys had nicknamed Little Oral Angie. Things were slow, so he went through the motions. He reported a vagrant with a head wound needed to be dropped at St. Jude's. Then he went on the prowl for a vagrant. Angie held forth from a condo two doors from the turn-in for St Jude's emergency bay. Usually you could get a sympathetic orderly or nurse to chase the paper. In the time it took, a cop with a good sense of schedule or an alarm on his watch could fly by Little Oral Angie's and get his torpedo sluiced.

But Angie had been riding the rag tonight of all nights, bloated and surly, her glands puffed with some busily incubating infection. Stallis had bid her a hasty adieu, cursing the snow and the cold once more. He had dealt the baton to his chosen vagrant smartly. The head injuries were convincing. But his side trip to the ER had been a total waste of time, not counting the paperwork.

Victor Stallis' assessment of his own sexual condition was sympathetic and rationalized. Police were exposed to so many tough scenes over a decade of service that the accretion of emotional callus was inevitable. You got so you required more and more stimulation to feel basic reactions. His own genital appetites had become afflicted as a byproduct of his sensual neutrality. In his own words, these days he needed to swing much wider to hit the sweet spot. Liz had not been understanding. Hell, Little Oral Angie could comprehend this sort of psychology without needing it explained chapter and verse. Stallis had even given her money. Twice. He tried to be a decent guy.

Now alone in the AM, he sat in his cruiser, a hard-on inflating, then ebbing, then retumescing as he thought about what he'd missed with Angie, the poor bitch. There was certainly no street action on Oakwood's ice-encrusted sidewalks *this* night, and his stuck-up mate was far gone.

The radio blipped, chasing channels, then crackled and fuzzed completely out. It was like trying to listen to punk music, for godsake. Stallis thumbed the volume down to minimum. The scanner LEDs continued marching. It was too freezing to coop; if he tried catching some naptime he'd wake up an icicle in the St. Jude's morgue. Three o'clock seemed continents distant. After tonight's run he'd be switching shifts from day to night. He'd get off at three and wouldn't have to go back on duty until midnight the following day.

He had *so* counted on Little Oral Angie.

In the middle of this stormy night, the glacial mounds of snowfall reflected sizzling bright. Tornados of flying snow inched visibility to zero. Even using his low beams, Stallis could not see more than a few feet ahead. The street lamps were at full power and he could not see them, only their hazy light, coming and going like clouds dashing past the window of a jet. High beams would just throw his own light back in his face. He thought of a high-mountain whiteout. Fresh snow piled up in the poorly plowed avenues.

It was too goddamned *cold* for criminals to be afoot.

He was not even sure of which street he had wheeled onto until he recognized Jamaica's beat-to-shit Honda Civic, half-interred by a rising summit of white. He reached over to crank down his passenger window and looked up at the Garrison Street entrance to Kenilworth Arms.

Now *there* was a notion.

If Jamaica was holed up in Kenilworth tonight, it would surely have something to do with the aftermath of the bust in which Stallis had partaken. Maybe the dopers were massing to flank, or that scumbag Bauhaus had ordered a relocation. Retreat and regroup. Stallis enjoyed the game; dope dealers and their idiot operatives were always so predictable. He could say he spotted suspicious local activity, to justify a follow-up. If Jamaica was inside, she would squat-thrust this beef bayonet just to avoid more jail, more hassle, more black copy on the big bad yellow sheet. She'd take it up the ass and bark like a whippet if he ordered her to.

He dismounted, buckled his gunbelt and zipped up his

high-collared, insulated coat. A grim smile above, a loaded gun below. Stiff upper lip; stiff lower tip, as Reinholtz incessantly joked.

Curtains fluttered wildly from an open ground-floor window, one of the corner ones. Inside it was totally dark, and through the blizzard the window looked smashed. If anyone was sleeping in there they would have blocked the window up by now, he thought.

Even in this craven-cur weather, it looked like a burglary, by god. Maybe a death.

Both in the military and on the force, Stallis had seen a heavy helping of dead people. He had killed two or three himself; it depended on what you counted as people. Death, he theorized, was one of the things that had hardened him...as opposed to making him hard.

Damn Liz anyway. Wives were supposed to be supportive.

He waded over and found the windowsill to be a couple of feet higher than his eyebrows. No obvious clues visible from his position. Should he call this in? Should he bother?

To protect and serve. He thought it would be better to protect once he had been serviced. After his below the belt needs were taken care of, he could get official.

The storm's wild tarantella provided peachy cover noise. He grabbed the sill and hoisted himself up for a fast peek. The likely answer was that this was a vacant room whose glass had been blown in by the blizzard. His boots thunked the slippery bricks and his hardware clattered. It was all subsumed by the howl and pelt of the wind. Snow stung his cheeks so hard he wondered if they were bleeding.

He swung his baton flashlight to bear. The first thing his sight registered was blood, lots of it, smeared all over the walls and floor as though a gallon jugful had been lustily slung by a drunken vandal.

When the smell hit him, he lost his grip on the sill. A catalogue of profanity slugged up in his mind. His chin *thocked* hard against the cement overhang; he tasted tooth enamel shavings and his own blood for real. None of his awed words made it into the refrigerated air.

His fall was arrested by strong arms.

It took Stallis a second to see this. His jaw felt like it had stopped a good hook that had jarred his gray matter and caused him to drop the flashlight. His eyes teared and the tears froze on contact with the slipstream of iced wind.

When he cracked his eyes open he felt the skin rupture in papercut slits. Pain slammed his sight dark again. Two seconds ago this had not happened yet. Reflex made him think to claw his .357 from its holster. Another nook of his brain fought to decide whether he should holler protest or thanks at being grabbed by the scruff.

His toes never got the opportunity to touch the cold crust of ice blanketing the sidewalk. As he was hoisted up he finally got his eyes open and his senses ordered. The smell that had galvanized him was the battlefield fetor of messy death. Those schooled in proximity to the lifeless will tell you there is no smell quite equal to it, and once you know it, you're stuck with it, close as a lover, ominous as the glinting edge of goodbuddy Mr. D's waiting scythe.

His knees struck the brickwork as he was dragged upward. His scrotum got mashed. His skull was an airtight can with a rubber ball bouncing madly around inside, making dings and dents.

He saw the face of the person who had dared to mess so physically with a police officer.

Not a person. Not a face. His hand hurried to draw the revolver.

Stallis saw a moist visage awash in discharge and blood, looking peeled, or overbaked. Skinless sinews cuddled a good nine inches of jaw in which hundreds of pencil incisors were crookedly seated. At the crown was a pulsing wad of cauliflower brains topped by a froth of bloody white hair. The arms supporting him were naked bone enwrapped in hanks of muscle like a derelict's clothing held together by electrical tape.

No eyes looked back at Stallis' in the chancy storm light.

This was not real. It was a ghoulish caricature, ineptly architectured, holding him aloft with strength that was not structurally possible. It was all wrong.

It was wearing a bloody necktie, loosely knotted at half mast. No body, no legs, just a solid caterpillar column of flayed and oozing flesh all the way to the floor, covered by a red-soaked shirt just as long. The bone haft of a switchblade jutted like an aerial from the thing's right shoulder.

Stallis had to get to his radio. Call in a Code 34—officer needs help. He still had not pulled his gun all the way out. If he died in this room the call would be a 10-19. If he blew this obscenity away, he would be asked *what was your backstop?* You were not supposed to fire a round from your weapon unless you made damned sure it would not pierce whatever waited behind your target, and thus possibly hole some slow bystander.

Fuck all that jive.

Stallis freed the Magnum from its roost, cocked on the upswing, jammed it into the breastbone of the creature holding him, and snapped the trigger. The gun went off with a muffled *kowkff!* and remained mired to the trigger guard in the quicksand clay of sternum. It hung fast even after Stallis' grip slackened and fell away.

Impact. Impact. By the fourth time Stallis' occipital smashed into the casement he was thoroughly insensate. Thin splinters fell from the molding. Bits of glass were embedded in the back of his head.

The sluglike creature sneezed, causing the revolver to catapult from its chest and skid into a gelid bloodpool on the floor, smoke still wisping from its muzzle. Stallis was propped against the inside wall. His body refused to sit, lolling drunkenly.

The thing wearing the necktie was confused and slow. It knew it was supposed to be the occupant of this room. It knew the building had intended for it to be this room's occupant. But what was it supposed to do next?

A skeleton claw rose, badly puppeteered, and closed on the bone handle of the Italian switchblade, feeling it the way a teenager might probe his first facial hair. Yes. Remembered behavior was the cue.

It unsheathed the switchblade from the meat of its shoulder with a juicy sliding rasp. Then it sawed a jagged, leaking line, ear-to-ear, across the crown of Victor Stallis' head. Bony fingertips immersed themselves, gripping the lips of the gushing fissure, and peeled back firmly. Wet treats aplenty were unveiled.

The thing could not think. Its drives were tidal, elemental, orts of memory like jigsaw puzzle pieces in an unruly pile. Part of it wanted to coil back into the humid sanctuary of the tunnels. Part of it was hungry. Part was satiated and beset by incomprehensible nightmares—images impossible to assimilate, as strange and alien as telepathic impressions from a different species.

Another part of it wanted its eyes back. Its fine, clear-seeing, Jew-hating eyes.

Twenty-One

Heights did not scare Jonathan. Nor the dark. The close press of the shaft was no threat because he was not a claustrophobe. Its confinement was illusory. The downward rappel was going to take him back to his caving days, during which he had inched down chutes larded in clay mud or wrist-deep in batshit.

He thrilled to the fact he was going to such cliffhanger lengths. He felt alive to the core and in charge of his own destiny. This was a missed sensation, and welcome.

Going down would be the easy part. His biceps and forearms were equal to such a short hop. Jamaica watched him tip outward from the bathroom sill and brace his gumsoled boots against the waffled metal. He eased his weight on to the makeshift extension-cord line and it went taut enough to play a solo on.

"Shh," he cautioned. Jamaica was hanging on to the cord.

He anchored with his left arm and felt for the next climbing loop with his right. Almost immediately his toes skidded against the slick, wet surface of the airshaft's lining. This was going to be like a series of short falls from one pretzel knot to the next...and the next was down near his knees.

Despite his tight grip the free line smoked through his gloved hand with alarming acceleration. He felt air rushing upward. He fisted leather around insulation and lurched to a lung-compressing halt when he hit the next pretzel. Momentum bashed his face against the corrugated steel and flung shock lightning across his inner eyelids. His heart freaked, punching too much blood furiously through his brain, flooding it with an assortment of nasty thoughts about his own abrupt termination, like defective cars smashing together in a freeway pile-up.

He hung. He pendulumed. He felt nasal blood dotting his upper lip.

"Jonathan!" Even her aphonic whisper was loud in the vertical tunnel of metal.

The orange insulation did a hangman's rope squeak against the windowsill and Jonathan's hair collected a chaff of paint flakes. He kept his eyes shut and tried to stabilize by feel.

"I'm okay, I'm okay—shh!"

The rusty brown steel that had mashed and scraped his ear open was an inch deep in slime—probably snowmelt and particulate grime from the roof, basted by the building's warmth. It seemed much more slippery than dirty water. If Jonathan was going to play Batman and live, his next step would have to be more cautiously taken. Being cautious would lose him time. Jamaica was watching. He did not want to look bad in front of her, either.

He re-established his footholds, toeing in to penetrate the goo and make a solid friction bite on the metal before he backed his full weight out from the wall a second time. His breathing equalized. Calm. Calm. He was okay. He opened his eyes.

He had stopped eight or nine feet below the pale, yellowish light shining from the bathroom window. Jamaica's head, in silhouette, watched. Her hair was a backlit gray nimbus; no facial expression was visible.

"The bathtub moved," she rasped at him.

He hung steady. Better this time. After-images of the bathroom window receded and he could see oily droplets wandering groundward, broken loose by the tremors of his passage. It reminded him of the cold, greasy gel in which Spam was canned. It had air bubbles trapped in it and was the color of nicotine. Maybe that was just the yellow light, from above. He backed down and extended his foot, planting it. *Katoong.*

A couple more pretzels and he might be able to relax his muscles on the sill of 107's bathroom, right below him. It was the middle of the night and the old anti-Semite had better be snoring by now.

Hand over hand he lowered himself. Going was smoother where the line had not brushed against the wall and gotten coated. He judged drop and tried to make his boots meet the sill quietly. He hung by cocked biceps, unflexing one buoyant foot of distance at a time.

His toetips grazed the sill and swept debris. Slowly he swept his left foot across, and heard shavings and crumblings patter into the water below. An unpleasant snapshot came and went, of him hitting bottom and sinking lip-deep into the same soft, sucking paste he had found smeared across the flip side of his window cardboard. That would be boss.

Wedging heels against the sill, he walked his hands down the line and rocked back, angling away. His knees popped like carrots snapping. From the darkness within the window, cold air meandered. The sweat on his back chilled. There was no bathroom window here. From the jut of splinters he judged the window had been inelegantly battered out from the inside.

Jonathan was too enwrapped in his mission to notice, at first, the mortuary taint of opened corpses and aired blood. Below he saw the faintest glints of still water, its depth unguessable. He could feel the pretzel knots constricting all along the line as he hovered. Time to invest in a fast reconnoiter. It took two loops of cord to lock down his forearm this time; his gloves were wet and the line was lubricated. It tried to shimmy through, then tightened. He tilted the nine-volt lamp down for a sneak preview.

Greenish barnacles of mold edged into peaks on all sides of the shaft, two-dimensional stalagmites appliquéd to the corroded steel. Jonathan thought of cave paintings. Their luminous peaks gradated from the color of oxidized copper to a battery-acid white just beneath his perch. Random ripple patterns petered out on the surface of the turbid water. Somewhere above him a toilet flushed, booming distantly with a sewer-pipe echo. At the far side of the pool—by his reckoning, the south side—he saw a beachhead of compost. Random garbage, fallen junk and human refuse had piled against one side of the shaft to form a trashberg. Perhaps he could light on its tiny peak to avoid getting dunked and stinky.

Nearby bobbed Cruz's Hefty bag. A huge air bubble had ballooned one corner into a huge plastic nipple. A shard of wood like a bamboo skewer had rammed through the bag, its top aimed right at Jonathan's ass. He could barely make it out in the wavering light, a hair-fine needle of wet, earthen stuff more mineral than wood.

He swung the light up. Even at his bad angle it was impossible to miss seeing all the blood in 107. Impact splats ideogrammed the whitewashed walls and a wide widow's peak of red reached toward the sill. The sill itself was wet and crimson, like a bad cherrystain job, and ruddy clots edged broken glass and wood alike. A congealing swath twice the width of a dunked and dragged mop traced an erratic byway of death up and over the rim of the tub, across still-wet tiles and out the wide open door. Hanks of shredded garments and saturated clumps of organic matter despoiled the purity, the abstract symmetry of the sanguine sheen.

From the belly of the tub a straight razor winked at Jonathan, cocked into an L-shape. It appeared to have been dunked in somebody's heart and thrown to its current roost with considerable force; stringers of gooey crimson glued it to the porcelain.

Now he smelled it, full kick. A stench that demanded torching to the ground; the tilling of ashes.

He prioritized rapidly: The decision to look had been his. If he continued taxing his body by hanging and gawking, pretty soon all choices would be stolen. Once he had recovered the trashbag and Jamaica could tell him what they'd won, then he could meddle wherever else he wanted. He had just told Jamaica that if the dead Velasquez kid was afloat down here he would ignore it until Cruz's cache had been salvaged. Rule One. He had to stick to his agenda.

He lowered away...sincerely hoping that nothing poked any part of a head out of 107 to say howdy-do.

It got a lot messier a lot faster.

An attempt to Tarzan closer to the sloping shoreline of silt merely dumped Jonathan dead center. His foot struck the canted surface and skidded as though packed in adipose. He went face-down into the slime, his head missing the pointed stick by about three inches. The lamp swung, submerged and broke surface, making lightning. He had just enough time to slam his mouth and eyes shut before the trashberg crumbled and sank him, arms flailing.

It was like cold vomit hydrotherapy.

Jonathan felt clammy ooze infiltrate his clothing, seeking and finding openings, soaking through layers at about the temperature of the Quietly Beer in his fridge. He touched bottom—it wasn't deep—and clawed madly for the fragile support of the trashberg's peak. It went to gelatin in his grasp. He scrabbled and splashed, blind in a concrete slop trough over four feet deep. He thought of pond scum, verdant and suffocating, hiding quicksand. The junkpile flowed away at the thirty degree angle and bristled with sharp edges—glass, split wood, slatting, rusty wire. He sank one boot as deep as it would go, and, once anchored, grabbed for the line. His fingers, packed with oleaginous glop, found a climbing pretzel and clamped.

He pulled himself up, sucking air, scared.

He achieved tension on the end of the line and was able to hoist himself free to waist-depth, boots engulfed in the muck of the trashberg. No way he could climb back now. He was slipperier than a fish dunked in motor oil. The only escape option was getting out through 107, which seemed empty, whatever violence it had witnessed now past.

But still. All that blood.

Again he chided himself. Cringer, coward, pussy. His ears hurt from clenching his teeth.

The lamp secured to his belt was still alight. Leakage had not yet subverted it, but the beam was already sputtering. He knew the matches in his pocket were now doused and useless.

Hurry.

One-handed he untangled the Hefty bag from where it was gaffed and knotted it through one of the pretzels. Then he fell back against the slick slope, feet mired, arms seeking the corner in cruciform after giving his three pre-planned yanks on the cord. Jamaica hauled up the prize and Jonathan hoped he did not sink further than waist deep.

The bag spun, blocking the glow from above and dripping on his head. He did not sink but could feel how precarious his footing was. Slowly he moved to get his lamp out of the water. The muck roiled in slugging waves, capturing the artificial lamplight like luminescent paint. On the side of the shaft common with the broken window of 107 Jonathan could just make out a fat strip of riveted iron, just kissing the top of the waterline. It might be a welded-up sub-basement window, or maybe Fergus' secret hatchway. Perhaps he crawled down here to geek pigeons and sodomize pre-schoolers.

The glop beneath his left boot lost all mock of cohesion and gave way faster than hot taffy. His hands scraped the corrugated metal, gathering brown gel all the way, forestalling his immersion for another few seconds. The lamp went under again. Now the waterline cut across, from the bottom of his ribcage on the right to his left collarbone. His left hand sought solidity and fished up several stubs of wood so waterlogged they sank as soon as he dropped them. His fingers clasped something harder, cylindrical, too smooth to be part of the pulpwood he assumed was the basis for the trashberg. An impromptu walking stick to keep him from swallowing more sewage. He got it unstuck without seriously jeopardizing his balance. He felt a knob at one end. In the light he saw it was a bone, porous and glistening. An ulna—the longer of the two crossed forearm bones. Once upon a time the knob had been somebody's elbow. Somebody with arms just a bit longer than Jonathan's. This was not the remains of a dead rat or drowned cat.

He stopped breathing, terror making new grabs at his nerve endings.

Almost any surplus movement would slip him face-down into the goop again, and he did not hanker to die that way, no thanks. His body was immobile with conflict. What he wanted to do was thrash and holler and get the hell away as fast as his parts could propel him. He was keeping his nostrils from vacuuming up diarrheic mulch solely by virtue of standing on some stranger's skeleton. Maybe two or three bodies more, beneath that, deciding, right now, whether to reach for the gum-soled boots and the living flesh they packaged.

He heard the knotted extension cord bonking and feeling its crooked way back down the airshaft. Ten more seconds, and he could grab it, scatter-ass up to the first floor, and just run full tilt past whatever might be lurking there to scare him into a padded cell.

He dropped the bone. It sank. It had been the afflicted color of diseased eyes, stained by the cloudy water. Tough little strings of cured meat still clung to it. When he shut his eyes he could still see it, dissolving to yellow motes at the edges in his vision.

The water moved by itself, rolling heavily toward Jonathan's face, slopping his chin and tightly pressed lips. It floated detritus free from the trashberg and receded in a massy, tidal movement, the way a full bathtub shifts when you climb inside.

Something big had just changed position in the sump at the deep end of the pool. The water rose to immerse the strip of rivets, then came back for Jonathan.

His breath was misting free in whimpers now. All he could think of was being trapped down here, his rope out of reach, trapped with something that wanted to make him into a jumble of feces-clotted bones. Something big.

His coke bang crested. The ice sealing his throat cracked and cleared.

"Hurry up! Hurry with the fucking rope, goddammit, *hey!*" Just now he gave not an earthly burp who heard him or what they might think was going on.

Elsewhere in Kenilworth, someone Jonathan would never meet shouted *shut the fuck up* in response.

The swaying end of the extension cord hastened down. A Greek chorus. A safety line from God his ownself. Jonathan backslid and sloshed clumsily.

When he mopped his eyes clear, he was looking into a bullet-shaped, eyeless head that had nosed out of the water between him and the hatchway of riveted iron. It was the girth of a Navy torpedo and so was the triangular, turd-colored body that uncoiled behind it, slopping greasy waves against the walls of the shaft. Shadows danced as the water surged to bury the trashberg.

Too many drugs scampered through Jonathan's overloaded brain *too many* like a scorpion stinging itself to death in mad circles *too many fucking drugs, Jonathan!*

He screamed for help in the wet darkness, grabbing the bottommost climbing pretzel at last, pushing off from the trashberg and slamming bodily into the opposite wall. He spun as the blunt face backed into a striking curve and darted in to bite him.

Twice. Hot pain stapled his kidneys to his lungs.

He had a deathgrip on the line and did the fastest unbraced pull-up in sports history. He dealt the thing a firm kick in the snout. It backpedaled in the thick water.

He hit the shaft with a noise louder than the Notre Dame cathedral bell tolling the half hour. His boots slipped but he was moving fast, driven by the most primal motivation known to the human species. In seconds he had hooked one forearm over the sill to 107. Waiting glass sliced open his fingers. New blood introduced itself to old. He winced but who cared. It hurt but who thought pain was going to stop him?

Which struck him as peculiar...because from the waist down, he was dead air. He could no longer feel his legs ascending. He wobbled on the line.

A pleasing, novocained numbness rose to squelch his signals. He hung by one arm on the sill and tried to collate this new data. All he could vocalize was a drawn-out *uhh* noise. I've become the ghost, he thought. Cruz's ghost, moaning in the night. An inky-black cloud of sedation pushed upward, gently, toward his eyes, to mist them over.

The lamp's bulb shorted out with a snap.

Far above him, miles overhead, a silhouette watched from a tiny yellow rectangle, waving arms. Calling for someone named Jonathan. The undulating orange of the extension cord caressed his face. He tried to shout again, made a purring noise.

Relax. His arm did.

Jonathan watched the light above whip around crazily as he fell. He knew his head whacked the shaft on his roll downward, but felt no corresponding impact or sting. The pain had blotted away first. Then the terror. He felt the coolness of water, closing over his face. He only made a few bubbles because he had forgotten to breathe any more.

He had an erection. He thought of Jamaica, making love with him. That, too, had been fuzzy-good this way. His cock pressed hard against his fatigue pants as his arm slid down the incline of the trashberg and went under.

He tried to say Amanda's name. He would have liked his last thoughts to be about Amanda, but as the sliding, sinuous weight embraced him, he could no longer remember what she was supposed to look like.

Twenty-Two

Cruz could feel his bones grinding with every step. The cold coaxed his aches into handicaps and the boreal air helped to pound him awake. The downside was that it also helped him shake off the painkillers, which made his recent pummelings resurge vengefully, with teeth.

An efficient sling of web straps and shiny aluminum buckles cradled his arm in a soft white pouch that was downy on the inside, like baby clothing. It kept his wrecked arm immobile against his chest and put him in mind of a color-coordinated shoulder holster. In the closet at St. Jude's he had found his fatigue jacket on a hanger. About fifty bucks in tatty bills was still hiding in the upper front pocket.

Somewhere between jail and the hospital, his dogtags had gone AWOL. Whoever thieved them had taken more than indulgent gold jewelry; Cruz felt unmanned and unmoored without his gift from Rosie. Another vital link to Florida had been stolen from him. Pieces of his identity were dropping away.

He remembered blacking out in Bauhaus' shower stall. Waking up lashed to the hospital crib. Marko, of the shotgun shell mug. Cruz did not need a watch to know his time was pissing away posthaste.

Catching a cab at St. Jude's back dock had been easy. Finding one willing to drive to Oakwood in the worsening blizzard was a matter of mean bribery.

Before sneaking from his room at the hospital he phoned Jamaica's number and got her machine. He had no idea what he might say that would not clue Bauhaus to his movements, and he assumed Jamaica's phone was hot. He had hoped she would pick up in person...but again, what would he say?

Bauhaus' electronic ears were everywhere. Given Marko's special wake-up cheerfulness, Cruz decided no messages were good messages and hung up. Sorry.

The only thing left was to try linking up with that Jonathan guy and find out what had gone down at Bauhaus' place. Jonathan could be quizzed on the brisk and destructive search that had most likely taken place one floor right above his head.

His arm stabbed at his brain, restive, reminding him that none of this movement was a stellar idea.

The cab inched up Garrison and tried to deny the force of the storm. New snow had taken a recess. Ship-flipping winds of hurricane strength careened inland. The unmelted dunes of snow were whipped into new, traffic-snarling, pedestrian-interring, civilization-stopping configurations. That toddlin' town. It toddles because it cannot walk, lumbered as it is by ton upon ton of excelsior from the sky—blanched water the thickness of cremation ashes.

Cruz shivered in the inadequate kickback from the cab's heater. He was already cold and hurting, and once debarked, he'd be nearly broke. They pulled abreast of a police car, double-parked next to another vehicle beached on a plow-tide of filthy snow. Add fear. Cruz's heart began to bump so hard it hurt his throat.

He muttered *goddamnit* several times and ordered the driver to drop him around the corner, on Kentmore, out of sight of the cruiser.

Tip? Fuck you, too.

The Kentmore door was locked. At night all entrances were supposed to be secure; tenants were keyed. Generally the doors hung open all hours anyway. Snow had drifted into a pile against the steps and door. It had been this way for a while. Tonight, of all nights.

It took a bit of painful choreography for Cruz to unzip his jacket's tuck-away hood and snug the drawstring around his face. He hoped the snowblow would keep him anonymous. He tried not to act the spy when he peeked around Kenilworth's northwest corner.

It looked as though there might not be anyone inside the police car.

Three steps closer. The dash and running lights were burning. No head silhouettes. Was the cop sleeping inside? Not bloody likely—not parked this way, not in this storm. Inside, then, pounding on doors, running down the scents of drugs and bad guys and missing children.

Cruz drew closer, one more hunched trudger in the predawn blizzard. Slow pace. Curious citizen. *Oh, look, the police. Everything'll be okay now...*

The car was vacant. Snow was in the process of piling up, grading smooth the sharp juncture of hood and windshield. The driver's side window was down and more snow was melting on the seat. The cruiser's heater was still running. No keys, though.

His first thought was to sack the unit, and quickly. But his lame arm was a hindrance. The cop in charge would probably mosey out the Garrison door and book him as soon as he reached into the car's cabin. Did police cars have car alarms? Sure, they must. Now was not the time to find out for sure. Not now, when Cruz needed a bookful of other questions answered first.

The Garrison door was cracked open a foot or so and the temperature in the foyer hovered just shy of zero. Cruz noticed curtains flapping recklessly out of a broken ground floor window. Another abandonment, he thought. They sneak off, clear out in the dead of night, taking the lightbulbs, taking the switchplates—even the ones dipped in Fergus' all-purpose white paint. Lights out. Nobody home.

He had no way of seeing the blood on the windowsill. It had already frosted over and whited out.

From the Garrison side he had to use the stairs at the end of the hallway. The subdivisional walls in Kenilworth were so mazed that many rooms shared no common access on the same floor. While you could walk from the Kentmore stairwell to the Garrison stairwell on Jonathan's floor, you could not make the same direct trip on the first or third floors. On the ground floor you'd run into a blank wall and another Fergus slapdash paintjob. Up top, you'd hit an off-center door where part of the corridor had been retrofitted to enlarge a room that otherwise would not have had a window.

If Fergus would just fix the goddamned elevator a lot of agony could be circumvented. Cruz had never seen it budge, not once, the whole time he had lived here. The masking tape across the single-wide sliding door was old and crumbly. OUT OF ORDER. Maybe Fergus had painted the elevator shaft so thickly that the car could no longer slide up and down. Maybe he had lost the car. Pawned it, perhaps, for several cases of formaldehyde aftershave.

Cruz passed more columns of disused icebox doors in the ground floor hallway. Now and then other small doors, three feet high and hasped, like special entrances for midgets. A wall where a door had been sealed off by Fergus. Kenilworth specialized in doors that led nowhere.

No, wait.

Here was the elevator: Outer door retracted, interior light on, apparently in working order. Cruz thought he heard a faint hum. Perhaps the lift inspectors had come round and Fergus had gotten his toe caught in some legal jam.

Cruz was unsure. His aching arm urged him to give the elevator a try. When he stepped inside the car wobbled minutely with his weight; that was expected. It was the size of a single closet, and while the smells of disinfectant and wet carpet lingered, he had not expected to find it so clean, its walls so smooth and undirtied. It contradicted Kenilworth's demeanor. It did not even seem like an elevator, he realized, because there was no chrome, no rails, no framed advertisements. Just a box with doors, an inner one of scissors gate that slid shut when the outer one was secure. He could see into the hallway through a lozenge-shaped port full of wire-mesh glass. Near his head was a grille the size of a paperback book. A tiny service hatch was set flush with the ceiling about six inches beyond his good arm's reach. The function buttons were old-fashioned spring knobs, one for each floor plus a painted-over toggle switch that he assumed could stop the car. He pushed 3 and noticed that the bottommost button was embossed with an *L*. Lobby, that was a hoot.

Machinery whirred to speed and the car lurched, bumping

against the sides of the shaft as it rose. A crooked gap of light wavered against the rubberized join where the two doors did not quite agree.

Cruz gave silent thanks to the god of elevators. In here it was warmer. He leaned against the wall. Hauling his half-dead glutes up all of Kenilworth's Dr. Seuss stairs would nail a fresh jab of pain into his skull for every step ventured.

The car halted at the second floor. Apparently *all* the bugs had not yet been worked out.

He pressed 3 a bunch more, annoyed. After some deliberation of wheels and cables, the car decided to labor upward again. It rose three feet, then jolted to a crooked standstill that shoved Cruz off-kilter, as though the floor was a boat deck on choppy surf. He piled into a corner and remained standing. The lines had fouled, or the car had changed its batty mechanical mind and decided now was siesta time. It was no longer wobbling. It felt as stuck as a fat man in a skinny doorway.

Cruz cursed Fergus again and flipped the STOP button. Up-down, click-click, *nada.* Of course.

He hauled open the inner door. He had to angle in his boot to succeed, and muscle spasms forced him to wince with the effort; every tendon in his neck seemed sprung. From his knees down he could see the second-floor elevator door. The floor of the car bisected the mesh window. Dim light played across his feet. All he had to do was drop to a sitting position, shove the door open with one foot and bail out. He hesitated because his attention was drawn to what he saw at the top of the open inner door.

The masonry stopped. He saw a four-by-four vertical support post, and beyond it, blackness. The wall was not continuous; there was a gap of two feet or more between the second and third floors of the building, like horizontal dead-air soundproofing...though in a roach ranch like this one, nothing so sophisticated was ever intentional.

He could just reach it. He backed across the car, going on tiptoe to see further. Conceivably this lightless gap could stretch to the limits of the building itself, and that was enough for Cruz's mind to classify it as a bootlegger's hidey-hole. A dry, cured smell rolled from the gap to bypass Cruz and seek the open elevator shaft. It was like old attics, mummy spices.

This, he thought, would be a primo tuckaway for several tons of Great White.

Dope, as a concept, punched new urgency into his chest. The gap was perfect, probably forgotten. It could be turned to advantage later, after more immediate accounts were updated.

Something thumped smartly against the roof of the car, like a big tomato falling twenty feet and hitting. *Splat.* Chiquita came back to haunt him again.

His sense of discovery flip-flopped with common sense. The elevator, regardless of appearances, had to be kin to everything else in Fergus' empire—worn out, ancient, dangerous and unpredictably finicky. Now it was jammed in the shaft, hanging on air, and things were raining onto the roof...

...so get your gnarly ass *out*, already.

Worming his legs downward was creepy enough, given the potential drop of the shaft just beneath him. The second floor door resisted a simple kick. His numb arm picked this moment to begin throbbing. The last of the injections was rinsing clear in his bloodstream.

Cruz knew he would not curve, like smoke around a corner, to fall, but he thought about it anyway, the same way anyone on a high enough roof thinks about going over the edge. Gravity would provide freefall. Then positive impact with concrete and gears and stuff with sharp protrusions. So nice, to precipitate Bauhaus' jelloid bulk down such an avenue. Cruz wanted to witness the touchdown, revel in the shattering of bones, point out the curds of exploded brain.

God, but he could do with a twin-bore blast of the White Stuff to clear the rooms of his head. Sharpen his reflexes; knock down the damnable pain in his armpit.

Somewhere behind closed doors a woman screamed on the second floor. B.F.D. I've got problems of my own, lady. He wondered if Kenilworth's theoretical ghost was up late, a-haunting.

Another *thonk;* a big fist, or worse, hitting the roof of the car. Cruz held back the inner door and hung, putting his boot to the edge of the wire-mesh window below. Now he kicked, not pushed.

New thought: The elevator works were eating themselves alive up there. Falling to pieces. The car would unjam and plummet any second.

If it dropped now, his legs would be guillotined by concrete and steel. Crushed bones. Legs severed. He would be cut in two like a fingernail.

The whole goddamned building was going nuts.

On his second kick the door below banged back wide and Cruz squirmed free, battering his elbow against the floor as he fell out and rolled. The door swung shut and slammed loudly. He stayed spread out on the floor a few beats, smelling cat piss, his heart trying to pound itself into a new shape. Whatever else, he was still alive and breathing.

Options reran.

By now Marko had dropped by apartment 323 and realized it was a dodge. Having already trashed Cruz's place at the opposite end of the building, he would report immediately to Bauhaus. They would both have tipped to his absence from the hospital by now. Jamaica had to be warned, but not by phone; Jonathan had to be briefed if not cautioned. Cruz felt Jonathan was in no real jeopardy, just as the possibility of a fall down the elevator shaft had been no danger.

He pushed hair from his eyes and scanned the second floor hallway. One more scream, from the far end, his end of Kenilworth. Some bitch getting slapped around because she won't put out during her period. Some mommy who can't control her brat, so she shrieks at it like that Velasquez *puta*. Some screamer who doesn't have all the wordly goods the universe of TV game shows tells her she should have, so she vents off at her live-in peasant boyfriend. Who cared.

Or maybe she wanted out. Just out. Cruz could get behind that.

The thought of Marko and Bauhaus gave Cruz another potential for the gap between floors. A genuinely desperate person might hide himself there, coming and going through the roof hatch of the elevator. It would require tools and supplies and some prep, but past that it was foolproof. Who would even look? Between the cellar rooms and the walled-up corridors and the subdivided apartments and the unexpected turns, Kenilworth had more forgotten convolutions than a mystery novel had secret panels.

No doubt, if Cruz searched long enough, he'd find bones.

Across from the elevator door was the uneven end table, its Folger's coffee can still holding a bounty of dusty plastic flowers. On the floor with Cruz were gum wrappers and cigarette butts and the nondescript stains of animals or children or incontinent drunks. The ground-out butts had left burn commas in the prehistoric carpeting. There was a gray oval on the wall above the table where a mirror had once hung. Gentleman callers may perform a last-minute grooming inspection before delivering their calling cards at the doors of ladies of quality.

Uh-huh, yeah, right.

He backtracked to the eastern stairwell, walking right past Jonathan's closed and locked outer door. The sounds of hopelessness had ceased. Cruz paused.

Nothing encouraged him to knock, so he took the stairs one by one. Let Jonathan sleep ten more minutes, if it was going to come to hairy late-night commotion.

As he made the final turn, ascending to the third floor, a black face glared at him from apartment 304 and was instantly supplanted by a slamming door. Anger and hostility in that gaze, plus bumps. Not my bitch, not my connection, not my main man, so piss off.

Cruz edged toward his own apartment, 307, like a good spy. That was his role tonight. He found the outer door closed but not locked. The inner door of the airlock was still open by three inches, admitting light to the cramped vestibule. As he eased it open, tensed to flee, he tipped to the extra ingredient in the fierce stare of that black guy, a man he had never seen and did not know from Martin Luther King.

A disgusted projectionist played the whole scenario in the theatre of Cruz's mind. Dummy. Can't you guess?

Marko invades, probably using keys or a good Lockaid gun. His turnover of 307 is rapid, methodical, professional. He knows the federal investigator search routine and flows from gag to gag like a dancer being judged. He's out in three minutes flat. While Cruz is trying to con a cabbie into driving to Oakwood, the asshole from 304 stumps home after an evening of petty theft and sees the door to Cruz's place ajar. After a skittish second, he peeks. Sees the ghetto blaster, the tapes, the camera. Marko would have taken the film from the camera already. The black guy decides to enrich one of Chicago's finer pawnshops with Cruz's untended property. He is sloppy, taking three times as long as Marko and leaves a hellacious mess. Between the pro and the amateur, Cruz has been cleaned out, utterly.

He slumped onto his bed, dejected. Even the beer had been liberated from the fridge. He hoped it had boiled. Something new broke.

Not Kenilworth, busting another stitch. Not Cruz's shabby fourth-hand furniture. He felt the actual *give* inside of himself, like a taut rubber band relaxing.

Bauhaus, Marko, the pain, the burglary, the hasslement— none of this mattered a damn. Cruz glimpsed, for perhaps the second or third time in his life, a bigger picture than the world as seen through his own baby browns.

What mattered was that he take action. Something to cut Jamaica free of that slug swine Bauhaus. Something to ensure Jonathan would be in the clear. Jonathan, who Cruz knew barely at all, yet who had *done* for him. A stranger who did not need any of Bauhaus' psychic sewage smeared across his life. Cruz needed something with which to strike a detente with Emilio, back home. Absolution was impossible...but a deal was never vetoed without scrutiny. Even before he was King Stud of Miami, Emilio was foremost a dealer. Cruz had to offer a deal. He also had to exorcise the ghost of Chiquita, falling still; scour her from the space she had appropriated inside his head.

He had to arrange a life that did not require him to constantly look back over his shoulder in unending fear.

The need to phone Rosie's emergency number swelled up and burst and filled him now, overriding even the agony of his ruined arm.

Abruptly he felt uncomfortable up on Kenilworth's third

floor. He no longer belonged here. It was too high. Too far to fall.

He did not have to strain to hear it now—the ebb-and-flow moan of Kenilworth's ghost, the signature noise of the building itself.

He used what the intruders had left him inside of his own apartment. He found a sweatshirt and spent several minutes gingerly wrestling into it, adding a layer to his insulation, then climbed back into his nightfighting jacket. He resecured his sling, snugging his arm above the jacket's waist drawstring. He had to use his teeth to retie it. When he zipped up his arm felt locked down, safe.

He abandoned 307 to the fates and headed back for the stairs, avoiding the cursed elevator. When he rounded the second-floor corner he collided with Jamaica, who had hustled posthaste out of Jonathan's apartment, to hell with closing doors.

The wild look in her eyes attacked Cruz's congratulatory self-effacement, stomping it down, rolling over and swiftly killing it.

Sure enough, she found Playtex rubber gloves in one of Jonathan's kitchen boxes. This was a lifesaver.

Once she hauled in the knotted extension cord she had quickly become a mess. It was caked and gravid with some gelatinous discharge. She tried wiping her hands and only spread it around, as cloudy and slippery as olive oil yet lacking that distinctive olfactory presence.

The odor of the slime was a kissin' cousin to the stench of the grainier, fecal stuff. This was not alarming. The gunk on the line held swimming soot, the stale tang of bad seawater, and assorted particulate matter. Jamaica thought of a gobbet of industrial lubricant left on a dusty floor, then mixed with rancid fat plus that canned blue jelly they made you wash your hands with in jail, plus a healthy scoop of droppings from a very diseased dog.

Then fermented.

The water took its time warming up, as usual. She held her hand under the faucet. The glob resisted for a moment, then slid off to thicken the drain, leaving a film on her palm. She scrubbed at it with a paper towel, then hunted up the rubber gloves in a hurry because Jonathan, not her, was the one down in the shaft wading in this shit.

Her guess at depth was doomed to remain a guess. In the dicey light from Jonathan's lantern she could only perceive tilting shadows from two stories up, like trying to follow a gunfight at the terminus of a dark alley. Her perspective was completely disrupted. The ghostly acoustics of the shaft hampered true sounds the same way. No sensory evidence was trustworthy.

Cruz's garbage bag came up with a ragged tear in one side, and was so inundated in organic grease that Jamaica knew she would leave it in the bathtub. With gloved hands she widened the tear, then undid Cruz's knots. The slime made that pretty simple.

Whatever had punctured the bag down there had taken one kilo of cocaine with it. She lifted out a taped brick with a wide, wet mouth…and the mouth was empty, its white bounty lost to the water. Half the take, stolen already.

The weight of the gun in the Whitman Sampler box had saved the other kilo strictly by virtue of trapping it within a twist of thick plastic. Jamaica unwound it and it had become so convoluted that she felt encouraged. The candy box, astonishingly, was as dry as the night she had delivered it. The brick held speckles of water but its seal was inviolate.

Do your part, she thought, and hurriedly fed the line back down to Jonathan.

By the time they were finished, his bathroom would be a total loss. Best to shower and scrub and leave the cleaning of inanimate objects to some future, less fortunate tenant.

The pretzel knots slipped and slid past her grasp, all the way until the line was paid out. She heard sloshing coming at her from the shaft as she placed the kilo and the candy box on top of the toilet tank. Real stupid, to risk getting them wet *now*.

One kilo. Forty grand, maybe fifty—they could cut Bauhaus' pharmaceutical grade almost thirty percent before its orbit of potency began to decay. That would gram the load out to approximately…

Shit. She'd need a calculator just to estimate what the flake was worth.

She held the line, poised over a fouled bathtub in a subhuman tenement, blizzarded in, fearful and desperate and suddenly incapable of the simplest add-up, and that made her so mad she wanted to kick down the wall. Life in the lightspeed lane sure was a hoot. Do you know me? My name is Jamaica—this week— and I used to be a human being.

More heavy sloshabout echoed toward her. She tried to keep track of Jonathan, who was listing awkwardly in the muck below, but the updraft had dented her nostrils two times too many. It was the smell of dead animals and rot heavy with parasites. The extension cord groaned against the moldy casement. Fortunately the tub had slid all the way to the wall and could scoot no further under Jonathan's swinging weight. She had watched the topmost pretzel loop squeeze shut like the eye of a sleeping cat.

She had known what was in the candy box. She had known from the first, even without seeing. The heft of that box had told her stories. In a twitch of unexpected clarity she saw the gun representing just as much freedom as the kilo of coke sitting on the toilet tank.

They had all talked of changing things, of steering their lives. Now she was on the brink of implementation, feeling something inside of her shy back. No. Better to stay where you are. To hold what you have rather than risk it. When you risk, you gamble, and when you gamble you can lose. Embrace the security you've built and don't dare to ask for more. You've walled yourself into such a nice fortress; it would be stupid to walk away and leave those walls, and their safety, and…

"Hurry up!" It was Jonathan. "Hurry with the fucking rope, goddammit, *hey!*"

He had broken his own directive and was shouting, his voice superamplified by the tunnel of metal, hollow and lost. A misfire. Something had staled for sure.

The line was completely paid out. Jamaica stepped into the tub, her boots skidding on moisture and residual gunk from the Hefty bag piled near the drain like a dead manta ray, deflated yet still lethal. She wriggled through the window, braced at the waist, to agitate the line. If Jonathan did not have it in hand, it had gotten hung up or tangled. There was no slack on her end. Light from his lamp darted across her face and stung her eyes. She averted her head, blind for a second. She had recorded a glimpse of how lubricated the entire shaft was, in the play of the lightbeam over the thickly coated walls. Genuinely gross.

Climbing loops had fouled to form a big knot. She felt it shake free.

By now the two of them were scaring up a beastly racket. She heard another voice in a distant apartment yell back. *Shut the fuck up.* One more tenor in the tenement symphony.

The light below danced. The line swayed, then drew taut. She heard the gong noise of Jonathan's boots hitting the corrugated steel, then a less controlled gong of impact. When she looked she saw only the light, veering in circles, slicing burn tracks across her vision and illuminating nothing.

She heard Jonathan scream. Not a *help* noise. Worse.

More thuddings and splashing. The line remained weighted, telegraphing his ascent to her.

To hell with decorum, she thought. Why should she start following rules today?

"Jonathan?" They'd already announced themselves to the building at large anyway. She leaned further out, head and shoulders into the fetor of the shaft now, and grabbed the extension cord with her gloved hands. It was too heavy for her, but she tried to pull it in, to help him closer.

Below, the lamp bulb vanished, a lone star in a black void, finally embracing death itself.

"Jonathan!"

The line went slack in her grip. She could not know that the next sound she heard was Jonathan's face striking the shaft as he did a backward somersault and picked up speed. Then he splashed and sank.

Panic endorphins flooded her, turning Jonathan's name into a yell. Jamaica had never screamed before and did not now.

She heard him make a low noise. *Uhh.* Like Cruz's imaginary ghost, the off-key inhabitant of Kenilworth. It was a quiescent purr, almost sexual.

She pictured him fallen, the back of his head caved in, with whatever had holed the Hefty bag now jutting through his chest. Or throat.

All her thoughts changed nothing.

She hung. Fifteen seconds more. She heard bubbling. She called his name once more...but softly this time, realizing he was gone, taken away in an instant.

On the tank the gun awaited her pleasure, a scepter of power. *You do what I say.* Point the scepter and they do what you say. It gets you into the apartment on the first floor with no credentials or questions. It lets you pass so you may shine a light. Solve the mystery. Then move your fine symmetrical butt, lady, because you're packing an illegal firearm plus enough even less legal dope to put you in the state hotel until your fucking *eyes* turn gray.

A big part of her wanted to stick, and continue calling uselessly out the window. A bigger part craved lights out and deep, irresponsible sleep without dreams. She forced herself to move; it was like wading.

The candy box was sealed in clear packing tape. When she tried to muscle it open she only succeeded in ripping off the box lid, exposing a grooved butt in matte black. When she tipped the box she felt the packet of cartridges slide heavily. Taped to the inside of the box were also two magazines, already loaded, the blunt copper noses of the headmost shells peeking out. Minuscule phallic symbols all in a regiment. She withdrew the pistol and got the clip in right on the first try. She thought she knew how to use this weapon.

She was on her way out the door, determined, decided, gun in hand, when she nearly collided with Cruz, who looked like he had just wandered out of a freefire zone.

Twenty-Three

Sometimes the place remembers holes. The cat knows this. The cat does not know the concept of a building. Merely place. It cannot know the building is older than its own span of years, the very bricks that comprise its walls themselves the remnants of other buildings, long demolished. The cat has no notions of age or death or time, or a time for dying. These are human conceits.

Kenilworth Arms has been mortared together from the components of buildings long dead. To the cat the bricks smell unstable.

The cat pauses in its latest exploration of the basement, endlessly questioning, yet never extrapolating. All it knows is that new avenues of passage come and go in the place like sunspots. There are holes that exist for a moment to link ground floor to rooftop, or east fire escape to west corridor. Then they close up seamlessly. The cat is learning how to employ these deliciously random doorways. How to pull clear of them before the place recalls its own structure accurately enough to put solid walls back where they belong.

Sometimes the cat squeezes through the far end bloodied or filthy. The cat dislikes this, but not enough to shun the curious holes as they open and close like blooms beneath a sunlamp.

Just now the cat freezes on alert. It senses the proximity of another living thing. It crouches low and proceeds paw over paw to reconnoiter the corner.

A large, sleeping animal is blocking the tunnel. The cat already finds the tunnel inhospitable. Too hot, too damp, too slimy down here. It is lost. It wants a new hole to iris open so it may go somewhere else. To its rear is nothing but more horizontal tunnel, terminating in a thick iron hatch that is bolted shut from the opposite side.

The thing is coiled, sleeping in a pool of its own amniotic juice, and it looks enormous to the cat. The cat acknowledges the presence of quite a few long, needle-like, nasty teeth. It does not desire combat, but if cornered by the iron door, it will claw and hiss and attempt to inflict as much damage as possible in order to buy a chance at running around the big creature. Escape lay ahead, not behind. Just now, to pass the sleeping thing, the cat will have to squeeze around it or walk over it. This is not worth the risk of waking the creature up.

The cat will wait, but never for long.

The cat sits, feels dampness, rises back. It watches the creature breathe. It smells identity spoor: The blood of a recent kill, the hydrochloric waft of digestion and elimination. The place takes no more notice of this creature than it does of the cat; no more notice than the cat itself would lend a tapeworm.

The cat lifts one paw and shakes it fastidiously. Hopeless. So much grooming to do, once it gets out. If.

The cat has rapidly cultivated a sense of trust that a hole will open soon. But it feels the tilted equilibrium of the place. The place has become fitful and unreliable. The place has remembered to make the elevator function, then forgotten its purpose. The car remains jammed, doors agape, near the second floor. The cat knows this because it has padded to the edge and peered into the darkness of the shaft. The cat has heard some half-living thing, wet and angry and incomplete, wallowing about on the roof of the car. The cat did not check into that one. It did not want a fight then any more than it wanted to agitate this even larger creature sleeping some ten paces distant, blocking the metal tunnel with its bloated brown bulk.

The creature is rather like a snake the cat had once caught and eviscerated, only lacking the serpentine symmetry. The only other applicable physical comparison the cat could dredge up—its attention span is extremely limited—is of a stale sausage casing it had once thrown up. This creature was like that, too.

Dented and fat and stinky, exuding smells of grease and fat, curled into itself like a braid of excrement.

Only this is much bigger. And alive.

A measure of careful respect was to be accorded here. The cat would wait.

The sound of slowly dripping water, to the rear, made the cat check quickly to see if another of the place's holes had decided to open up.

When the cat looks back, the creature is shifting. Dreaming, perhaps. Its fatty hide hangs loosely, as though a sleeker corpus is trapped within a baggy monster suit. Gravid flesh drips from the hump of back to pool around the creature, blocking the cramped accessway even more.

Sleeping, it regurgitates bones, yawns wide and toothy, and resumes dreaming.

The expelled bones are waxed in adipose and stomach acid. Curls of steam twist up into the cooler air. Broken rib struts, thin wings of calcium, airy and light. A human mandible with porcelain and silver fillings.

The cat holds at ten paces, disinclined to assume the role of dessert or midnight snackeroo. For this creature, the cat would not even be two bites.

When the creature yawns again the cat sees that the lining of its circular maw is ribbed and tessellated, with pimply bumps. It is a startling uniform white. The luminescent mold slathered about the metal tunnel makes this last observation possible. The cat cannot see colors so it does not see all the red. It can smell the blood, however, and recognizes it as recently fresh.

The cat's feet are genuinely wet and uncomfortable now. It backs off nearly all the way back to the metal hatch, high-stepping and shaking each paw in turn. It is warmer back here. It stretches against the wall, out of sight of the sleeping creature. The wall yields. The cat sees its claws open scratching-post furrows.

The cat's brain is not sophisticated enough to posit that perhaps it *willed* this opening to happen. It knows only to take advantage. In moments it has slashed the hole wide enough to

David J. Schow

permit passage. Worth the discomfort and damp, this time, just
to get away.

As was its nature, the cat forgets about the sleeping creature
just as soon as it is gone.

Twenty-Four

"Calm down!"
    The first thirty seconds of hysteria were loud and useless.

"Calm down! *Shut up!*"

Strangers screamed for quiet. Threats were hurled from behind tilt-bar locks, but no one actually emerged to rumble as Cruz and Jamaica shouted in each other's faces near the second floor stairwell.

"No, no!" Jamaica was prattling, rapidfire. "*You* don't understand; he's *hurt*, he's *down* there; we've got to help him—!"

The gun, forgotten in her own grip, was randomly aimed right at Cruz's groin while she spoke. He snatched it right out of her hand. "Will you just wait one second!"

She overrode and shoved him back roughly. "*You* wait. He could be drowning while you just *stand* there!"

With a sound like a growl she shoved past, colliding with his injured arm and spinning him halfway as she lit down the stairs. *Drugs*, Cruz thought. She acts like she's on something.

Who was drowning?

He wanted to chase her then, but the cocked door to 207 deterred him. The gun in his hand offered bravery. He squirmed around the airlock doors and poked his head into Jonathan's place.

Maybe *Jonathan* was drowning?

Inside: Boxes, clutter, the cot, more boxes. Bloody footprints. He trailed them to the bathroom and saw his own Glad bag slowly deflating in the tub. Blood and shit were smeared everywhere and the window was open. It looked like an open mouth. When he saw the orange extension cord feeding out and down, he thought of plugging it in to perhaps electrocute the ghosts of Kenilworth and sterilize the dead or dying things down in the shaft.

When he saw the kilo of coke stationed on top of the toilet tank, Cruz forgot all about poor old Jonathan.

Half the stash had been salvaged. Half at least. Whatever else had gone down while he was trapped in hospital dreamtime, half his payoff was here, now, and it was good enough. It would need hiding. Bauhaus' pet mugger, Mr. Marko of the fullback body and golf tee brain, would return here just as soon as he found out he had been foxed.

And five minutes ago Cruz had just accidentally discovered the perfect hidey-hole.

On the closed lid of the toilet seat was the candy box, ripped open. Inside were a clip and a box of cartridges. *Gun's in your HAND already, homeboy,* Cruz's brain informed him.

He lurched, vision spotting momentarily. His arm pounded. He hurt and couldn't quite deduce what the hell had transpired during his brief absence, and by the way...

...there is still a police car parked on Garrison Street, right outside, and you are standing here like a dickless mannequin with a gun in your hand and enough pharmaceutical cocaine to get you butt-fucked by convicts for five or six more lifetimes.

Chaos thundered back from the stairs. He tried to whirl and draw a bead. The muzzle didn't dip when he knew it was Jamaica, knew it was his name being called.

You could always toss the kilo back out the window. It was time he stopped repeating mistakes. In an instant he decided that he was capable of blindsiding a lone cop. Knock his ass down the stairs. Run like hell. Disappear into the blizzard. Stop someplace where he could dope it all out. Later.

No time.

He thought of Rosie's crisis cool. The shit was flying grandly now. He had to be careful not to inhale any.

She was at the bathroom door. "Come on, come *on,* you've gotta *come,* hurry UP!"

One-handed, he lofted the kilo onto Jonathan's cot and got a positive grip on the Sig Sauer. He wouldn't be able to shoot worth a tick fart with his left hand, but life's rich cornucopia of options did not afford him a choice. Sidewise, gun drawn, he edged down the stairs to 107 right behind Jamaica. Dark in there. Cold. He saw her hesitate at the threshold. She had come down here, seen stuff, and bolted back up the stairs. Twenty seconds, tops. Too much for her mind to process without distance.

He saw the look on her face as she urged him ahead.

The only light that seemed to work blazed from the bathroom. Cruz saw the dried blood all over the living room walls by its pale, canted luminescence. Some splashes reached nearly to the ceiling. Blood stained the blinds and soaked the flapping curtain in the busted casement window. Broad smears of it across the floor. Gelid little ponds, still tacky, where gravity had pooled it. The furniture was overturned and sundered.

He stepped carefully around the blood. The bathroom vestibule, identical to those in his and Jonathan's rooms, was like the drainage gutter of an abattoir on beef bashing day. There was an eye on the floor, roots already dried stiff. The bathroom itself was even worse.

Cruz could not make his lips and tongue cooperate enough to ask stupid, obvious questions. This was nothing like seeing Chiquita perform her swan-song dive. This was an overload of unending meat and fluid and carnage; a corpse pit empty of corpses, yet retaining plenty of clues.

Wadded into a corner and soaked with blood was a policeman's hazard jacket bearing an Oakwood patch and single hashmarks. In the far corner there was a cap, upside-down, with some bloodied hair still inside. Cruz crossed to the broken Garrison Street window and sure enough, the cruiser was right outside. Still vacant.

Jamaica's face held the expression of a woman who had just been punched out by her one true love. Or punched from the inside. Only now did Cruz notice she was wearing a pair of bright orange Playtex rubber gloves.

This was the old Jew-hater's apartment, he realized. He

spotted an open dresser drawer and purloined a handkerchief, folding it to mask his nose and mouth from the stench. His throat wanted to gag. He had zero desire to look at what he might chuck up, thanks.

The bathroom was awash in dry maroon. A cleanup challenge worthy of Mrs. Bates' best boy, Norman. The airshaft window was smashed out and there were bloody bootprints marking the exterior sill. The extension cord hung in the blackness, pretzel loop swaying dreamily—a Daliesque component of weirdness texturing this tableau of slaughter.

Cruz saw the straight razor in the bathtub and shivered. It had nothing to do with the biting cold. The bloodied razor stuck to the porcelain was Emilio, raising his platinum shaver and saying, *remember me?*

He was shaking now, trembling with that bone-deep loss of control that heralds the shudder you cannot suppress. It takes you and shakes you until it is done with you.

The storm backhanded Kenilworth with a blow of sub-zero air. The curtains sucked out, then blew inward. Both Cruz and Jamaica felt the building shift. The metal in the airshaft clicked and groaned. When air is cold enough, it fails to carry odors, and that, at least, was a small relief.

Jamaica moved closer, equipped now with her own bandana, unable to close her eyes or avert her head. She gaped at the bathroom window, not dumbly, but with the opposite of any expression—empty, drained, null.

"Jonathan," she said. "Is..."

The silence did the rest for both of them.

Cruz leaned out to case the shaft and found the corrugated steel dense with slime. Below he could just make out the bobbing red and white plastic of the dead lantern. A handful of wooden matches floated on the surface of the water, which looked thick and mulchy. He reached out to stir the extension cord; matches were drawn to its wake. When he reeled in the free end he found nothing attached. Just one more climbing loop.

"If Jonathan is down there, he's underwater. He's past tense."

It was too dark for Cruz to perceive the muddy crimson tint the water had assumed.

When he looked back, Jamaica had drawn away and the blizzard's howl and keen had dropped a notch. The living room casement had not been broken, and she had closed it.

Somehow it was better *and* worse that there were no actual dead bodies, or parts thereof, to step around in 107. The blood, so much of it, only reminded Cruz again and again of Chiquita, fallen woman, dead center in her personal pool of lifeblood, a liquid corona of bubbly red, expanding.

More Red? No thanks ever so much, I've had enough. (Clink.)
Cruz had never liked wine much.

With the window closed the cold air in the living room settled, bringing the raw meat stench back for a powerful encore. It sent Jamaica back to the hall.

He found her in the corridor near the foyer—the place where they had all been rousted two nights before. Her knees were bent, her back to the wall, and she hugged her saddlebag purse to her chest like a shield. Her striking green eyes were fixed and wet but no tears had broken loose. She looked to Cruz like a person teetering on the brink of circuit fusion.

He took her arm. She still wasn't seeing him.

"Come on. Back upstairs. For just a minute."

She shook her head *no*, vigorously, pulling away, her shoulder blades thumping the wall. Distantly, somebody thumped back.

"Jamaica." He softened his tone. "Hey."

Amber cooked hotly through the green, and now the eyes had him targeted. "I'm fine, goddamnit, just don't touch me. I am fine." She sniffed hard, as if blasting mildew from the crannies of her head. The cold air cleared her sinuses.

He started to move his lips again. To talk shit, to try evening her keel, because with typical macho lead-headedness, he thought he had a Hysterical Female burdening his flight path. He needed to get Important Stuff done and here Jamaica was, falling to pieces.

She met his gaze and saw that she wasn't special, wasn't anything apart from a panicked whore.

Fuck *that*, she thought.

Bloodbaths infiltrated her brain, immersing it and whispering *you'll never forget me, babe.* She used anger to shove the images away. Time enough for them later; they'd be with her the rest of her life.

Before Cruz could even commence his calm-down speech she interposed. "I don't need a pat on the head. And I don't need a Valium. Get your ass back in there and close those doors. Bauhaus had your room turned over tonight; he wants to nail your ass, and if I was you I'd devote some serious meditation time to your potential for being dead within the next few hours."

He blew out a frustrated breath. "Marko. That fucking meatball. When I first got here I thought Marko had gone on a rampage and killed everybody—"

"This isn't Marko's style." She pictured the methodical way with which Cruz's room had been dealt...before some amateur had done a smash 'n' grab mop-up. "But I told you: Nobody *takes* from Bauhaus. He never forgets."

O.D. City, thought Cruz, of Bauhaus. Guy's on so much chemical he thinks he's some kind of deity, just like Emilio. All the subterfuge and behind-the-scenes double-dealing made Bauhaus smarmier. At least Emilio's straight razor was a plain threat, and Cruz almost longed to face it rather than continue this secret agent crap. Take Emilio mano-a-mano and *resolve* something. Don't call in Rosie. Do it yourself.

He wanted a blast of toot very badly now, and knew just where he could ease that craving. It hollowed his stomach and made his temples bang.

"You've got to stash that kilo," she said. "That's all we've got left and we're about to lose *that*. Company's coming."

"Any second," he said. "I know just the place." He motioned her back toward the stairs but she resisted.

"I promised I'd be at Bauhaus' tonight. If I don't show he'll know something stinks. He probably already knows you've split from St. Jude's. Marko has been here and gone."

"I sent him to check out Jonathan. To buy time."

Her eyes might have accused him of selling out a near-stranger, but she knew that given the options she might as well have made the same choice. "I've *got* to go. Give me a couple of hours and a place where I can meet you."

"The Bottomless Cup will be open at dawn. On Weedwine."
She nodded.

Back in Jonathan's apartment Cruz examined the climbing set-up in awe while Jamaica re-donned her bomber jacket and zipped up for the tempest. He did not want her to see him slicing open the kilo and vacuuming a palmful of Columbian Cremora up his snoot. He wanted her to leave so he could get on with the nasal action news.

"Better give me 'til noon," she said. "Christ knows what Bauhaus has planned, and I don't want him to tip for the better part of a day."

Get out of here, he thought, pretending to pay attention.

"I'll meet you and we can bug outta here. Pass the dope to your pal in Florida. Nobody'll be expecting your unannounced flyby and we'll be gone before your buddy Emilio can do anything about it."

"And before Bauhaus can nail my ass to a flaming tree."

"So resign yourself to the idea of being a fugitive for a piece, bud," she said. "Maybe your pal Rosie can introduce us to a new city."

When Cruz nodded Jamaica thought: *Jesus, it worked!* Cruz was so anxious for a short snort that he didn't care how flimsy her story was. He was set to tuck into that kilo before she was past the front door.

Fine. She left him to it. Dope dealer, damn thyself.

Jonathan, sorry I got you into this mess. She pulled shut the door to her late friend's apartment.

As soon as she was out of Cruz's sight she unzipped her jacket, hiked up her Beverly Hills sweatshirt, and transferred to her bag two items she had collected downstairs while Cruz was busy trying not to smell the gore drenching the bathroom: A ring of keys belonging to Officer Stallis, who was still MIA. And a matte-finish .357 Mag with one shot fired and five still in the cylinder. Also Stallis'.

No time for eulogies to Jonathan. His life would have to serve by salvaging her own. Time enough for appreciations later, when she knew if she *had* been salvaged.

Five slugs should be plenty.

Her original plan was back on track. And the key ring made her think of other, more brutally subtle embellishments.

It had been like a million years of waiting, compressed into his brain, itching to inflate. Cruz's thumbnail fumbled against the steel teeth of his Swiss army knife. His knuckle was jabbed open in his vast rush; he licked off the dot of blood. Finally he pried up a blade and used it to carve an erratic incision across the top of the kilo package. He'd used toilet paper to blot the beads of moisture from the plastic first. The brick reminded him of one of those vacuum packets of coffee, hard as a kiln tile yet slightly yielding, like the business end of a padded sparring staff.

Fssss. Product of Columbia.

The brick grew a smile for him, frosted with white granules. He jabbed the knife blade and lifted a miniature Everest for each nostril.

Like the kilo that had died in battle, this blow was Bauhaus' hit-single 90% cut—extra-extra dry, barely stepped on. There was just a hint of some light stimulant. Methylphenidate, thought Cruz, though he couldn't have spelled it if a Luger was stuck in his ear. Or phenmetrazine. Nothing that would seriously hurt him if he topped off his tanks, so he destroyed about a gram. He matched the blizzard raging against Kenilworth with a blizzard inside the snow globe of his skull, and felt his metabolism slam to stride. *Boom-cha-cha;* good music in his heart and thunder in his hyper-caffeinated highway of veins.

The ache in his arm turned itself down to MUTE and his brain was hang gliding. He felt near optimum again—alert, primed, attentive, satellite eyes ready to target and dispatch deadly laser judgment, ready for goddamn anything. The next act would be critical and he needed to remain on this plateau of efficiency. He could feel calories burning while he stood there.

He found Jonathan's Excedrin in the sink cabinet and crunched up five, swallowing the chalky powder with a palmful of sink water. These pills, too, would be his ally against the constant headache and the staplegun pain that possessed his ruined arm. He pinched running water and rinsed his septum with a hard sniff. He found he could now focus with extreme clarity on each particle of dust swimming down the saline in his eyes.

Perfect.

He was breathing harder and faster now, the cold air feeling good, cleansing, sharp, bracing, biting, goddamn *good*. His exhaustion had been shucked like a dirty shirt.

When he felt the thing clutching his leg he thought first of a living dead hand, and that nearly springboarded him right through the ceiling. He yelped, screwing to one side and barely avoiding a head-cracking fall into the bathtub.

Cat. Just the cat.

The black cat he had seen in the corridor a few days ago was at his feet, rubbing insistently against the lace eyelets on his army boots. Perhaps this was Jonathan's pet; it certainly seemed to have mistaken Cruz for a friend.

At first he thought the cat was injured; it had tracked in some blood. But it did not seem to be in any pain. Cruz checked the door and found it still closed. It sure as hell hadn't come in through the bathroom window, as the song went. No cat, not even presuming cats had brains, was good enough to shimmy up Jonathan's improvised rope against all the slime and rot Cruz had seen in the airshaft.

"Okay, Cat Man. Where the hell did you come from? You been in here all along?"

No response. Stupid cat.

It followed Cruz back to the living room—like Cruz's apartment, the box with the biggest window was, by default, the "living" room. It was the *only* true room apart from the bathroom. Jonathan owned more books than Cruz had ever seen in his life. Still boxed from the move; fated now to stay boxed until someone who didn't give a damn about Jonathan's reading taste recycled them piecemeal.

Cruz had not been inside a library or bookstore since the fourth grade. He checked out a few spines. *Collected Wilde. Jujitsu for Christ. Winner Take Nothing. Whores.* Something called *The Diamond Bogo. Cold in July. The Simple Art of Murder.* How in hell did this guy *know* which books he'd like; how did you even decide to buy a book without fucking *reading* it? The covers were all confusing and didn't help. Just another aspect making books an impenetrable codex to Cruz: You couldn't even judge them by their covers. Where the hell did you even *start?* He opened one at random and tried to make flyby sense of Nietzsche. On a Post-it note stuck to one page Jonathan had written: *No more distance from fear / Now it's in your face / Deal with it or DIE.* It was all like trying to read alien UFO symbols.

It was with this comparison—imaginative, for Cruz—in mind that he glanced up and saw the bloody fissure in the wall near the window. It had shifted about three feet from its original position, though Cruz could not know that.

He muttered something automatic and indecent.

The fissure was akin to a cut in thick flesh, dermal layers of plaster and lath and wallboard and pressed ash. It exuded blood like sweat. Not from a rupture—it just kind of beaded forth, to drip. If you stressed the edge of the split you could make it ooze a bit more vigorously.

Cruz lifted one of Jonathan's paperbacks and pressed it into the lips of the fold; it was about that size. Blood gathered to lubricate the entry. Cruz released Jonathan's copy of *The Last Good Kiss* and it was wetly swallowed. *Glormp.* And gone.

Then, as if transit in the opposite direction fulfilled its purpose, the fissure closed and faded, leaving a scar on the wallwork and a speckle of blood on the floorboards. While Cruz watched, it zipped up. He did not blink. The cat watched, too, bored. Old news.

Cruz's squat went away and he fell buttwise.

More meaningless invective. As in: *What the godfuck is going ON here?*

The standing ovation in his vascular tract began to sit down. An encore was demanded. Cruz dusted his septum and used the lees to work his gums. He ransacked Jonathan's kitchen box, found plastic wrap, and resealed the kilo. After more search and seizure he appropriated Jonathan's rucksack and stuffed in the coke, the Sig Sauer, and the extra ammo.

He did not want to carry the dope into the streets for his

rendezvous with Jamaica. Stash it in the elevator cubby until Bauhaus has his fit. Come back in the dead of night, liberate it, and take off. A plan, was that. He'd have to figure out a way to convince the elevator to stop in mid-shaft. Maybe he could just climb through the ceiling hatch from the second floor and reach the mystery gap that way. He'd need a chair or something to hoist himself through. His arm hurt less right now and he might be able to unsling it for a single life-saving pull-up.

He closed the apartment door behind him and heard the latch click. If the elevator cooperated by rising to the second floor when summoned, Cruz figured it was trustworthy...for now, at least.

Machinery ground and he listened while the lift clunked and wheezed upward. Christ only knew what shape the cables were in.

When the doors parted, Cruz aborted his plan to walk right in. The missing Velasquez kid was waiting for him there on the floor of the car. Half of him, anyway.

Twenty-Five

Just when had this movie tipped over into comedy? What was the equation, Jamaica wondered, for stuff so absurd that your only sane response could be slackjawed hilarity...until you became the one taking the big bow for precipitating that absurdity?

A serious gust rocked the car and she jogged the wheel in response. A nonslip pro driver's sheath wrapped the wheel and the car had power steering. Cabin fans breezed out good heat in thick drafts. Mechanical air. Another benefit of civilization.

She didn't even want to ponder the riot shotgun by her knee. The hat was what made everything a giggle-fest.

Welcome to the Comedy Dungeon our special guests: Groucho, Chico, Harpo...and Bimbo!

Her brain speed-reeled tidbits in terms of her yellow sheet: Accessory to homicide. Culpability in possession of narcotic substances for sale. Concealment of an unregistered loaded weapon. Theft of firearm. Accessory, again, to homicide, again—this one a police officer. Grand theft auto. Willful theft of police property. Leaving death scene. No phone calls to Mom.

Impersonating a police officer. Ha. Ha.

She had perched Stallis' service cap far back on her head, lest it dump forward to blind her. Stallis had owned a lot of headbone. It wasn't the first time Jamaica had worn his cap; once or twice he'd forced her to model it while enacting his own sordid form of speed bail. In her life Jamaica had definitely seen as much of Stallis below the belt as above the neck, even counting the leer.

The storm made it absolutely impossible to perceive who

might or might not be piloting the Oakwood police cruiser. Visibility was double-ought. Guilt and paranoia supplied the mean justifications for donning the hat.

Trying to see through the unrelenting assault of blowing snow was like trying to steer through a tidal wave. The left front wheel broke through an iced-over pothole; the jounce made Jamaica grip the wheel hard enough to snap a fingernail. Gray slush splashed to freeze on the windshield, where the wipers bumped over it until the de-icers coaxed it free. The cloudy scab broke apart and ran.

Alibis scampered through her mind similarly. Furtive excuses; ratlike.

It was improbable that she would actually be caught on a night like this—spotted and pulled over by Oakwood's minions of right and might. The knowledge did not ease her fear or make it less rigid or consumptive. What was she supposed to say to the men with a thousand questions, if busted? That blood and violence had transacted at Kenilworth Arms...that she could not locate a phone...that she had dashed into a blizzard and there was the patrol unit with keys waiting, and that maybe they'd take her wild story seriously if she brought home the cruiser as proof?

In sum, she'd tell them she panicked.

They were all such macho jerks at the Oakwood station that they would jock-itch to believe little Jamaica, hardcore penis wrangler, had spilled her cool and bolted like a frightened deer. Hah. *Women.*

Even given the power steering, hanging corners had proved the hardest maneuver. She felt the heavy backside of the cruiser slide around to ding curbed and snowbound cars. She could not muster the nerve to employ the lights or siren. To what purpose? No traffic to clear this late. She had sought out the switch for the base radio and clicked it off. The company of voices was something she did not desire just now. Transmissions had bled sporadically through the banshee howl of atmospheric interference. The voices on this channel were all bad, and she had no mouth for ghost accompaniment that would make her feel as guilty as she unequivocally was already.

Nearly blind. She cranked hard right.

She banged her lip against the wheel as she felt the crash bumper stave in the driver's side door of a Lincoln Towne Car half-buried in a rising bank of street snow. Impact reverberated in her spine. Now she had to shift, back out, renegotiate. She had not yet topped twenty-five miles per hour for this entire excursion...nor would she. The fifteen-minute haul to Bauhaus' winding driveway took nearly an hour.

She was sweating now. The back windows were totally iced. The perspiration that oiled her back was a fifty-fifty mix of nerves and heat. Had she fogged the back windows herself? There was a strong chance that after tonight she might have to spend a couple of decades in a cell with a lidless toilet. She was wagered in for the whole kitty, and if she was fated to fail and fall, then a few items were going on the record, by god, before she got pushed off the diving board.

Item #1...

Only a fraction of people in the world knew how to handle the rudder of their own future. To the rest, life was a mystery. They sat and waited for exterior miracles to render their options academic—death, divine intervention, addiction, winning a lottery. Her tiny apartment in Elmwood Park was a "working woman's studio." In it, she slipped on stale workout clothes and did stretches before a JVC television that needed to be replaced. In it, she wore ankle weights and brewed hibiscus tea and looked forward to maybe buying herself a CD player for Christmas. In it, she never read the paper nor watched the news. She slept, wrapped up in print sheets on a second-hand queen-size that she'd bought from another prostitute. Asleep, she sometimes suffered nightmares. They were never sexual.

Jonathan—poor Jonathan, goddamnit—had never learned how important it had been to her *not* to return to her working woman's studio the night after Cruz had gotten busted. Contact, that night, had been paramount. Contact with another human being. No one else Jamaica knew counted.

In her apartment, she took very long showers, never baths. At Jonathan's, the bath had not been a threat. She spent a lot of time naked in front of angled mirrors, vigilant for any hint of

stress or age so she could mount a cosmetic counterattack that
would intimidate the offending obsolescence into retreat. Let
stretch marks and varicose veins bushwhack the weak of spirit.
Looking at herself in her mirrors, she thought tragicomic
things. Assessed her own vagina as "fit." Wondered how many
liters of semen she'd "processed." How much mouthwash would
be used up by the end of her life. If she would ever get sufficient
sleep on a nightly basis.

If there was any such thing as love, outside of fiction.

Chemical entertainment, and its availability, were a big
minus factor. A touch too much Equatorial Sneeze-Whiz. How
many kilos, when her life tallies were toted? Bauhaus and his
phylum were overjoyed to play generous, ushering their pets
toward flameout. People were toys to Bauhaus. You wound
them up, they did their tricks, and eventually they broke.
Especially if you played with them hard and frequently. You
laid your hands upon them, yet never touched them, except on
a mercantile level.

Unfair, it seemed, that Bauhaus would most likely be
wheeling and dealing long after she had eaten grave dirt.

To Bauhaus, *she* was no different from his onyx bar top or
his projection TV or his fleet of limos and sleek, overpriced
urban speedsters.

Item #1 peeled down to a simple imperative: *Shed Bauhaus.*
And parasites like him. Hadn't she swallowed enough fast-lane
horseshit to know how superficial glitz was, and what the true
costs were?

Item #2: Stop your own stagnation, she thought. Change. Get
out. Save yourself. Look what happened to Jonathan.

Item #3: If people like Jonathan had to die...shouldn't it count
for something?

Item #4: If *you* die, will anybody give a damn?

Her emotions were no longer individualized. The fear, the
anger, pain and confusion had all melded seamlessly with her
exhaustion to yoke a weight of conscience to her neck and cinch
straps tightly enough to bestow a sledgehammer migraine. No
longer could this circus of events be idly noted, and it was no
good to pretend her reality had not been coarsely disrupted.

The pileup demanded a climax, a capper. A definitive act of will. She had to *do something* about all this, and her actions would alter the matrix of her whole existence. It was time to move to new digs. You either packed in advance or you blithely waited for your old place to collapse around your ears.

Her catalyst, more than any single wrong, had been the look in Cruz's eyes just moments ago. His pathological, barely suppressed desperation to dig into that kilo of blow on Jonathan's toilet and metabolize it, *arriba, arriba,* posthaste, goddamn now before I die.

Cruz's eyes no longer saw the coke as a nest egg. Their plans, born grandly of panic and jailbreak desperation, had drowned with Jonathan and were now so much melted sooty snow. She had to pull herself clear of this death-dive. Save Cruz only if she could. If the drugs got in her way again she'd have to brush him away like lint.

She nearly missed Bauhaus' slanted driveway altogether; the cruiser was against the wind now and its low beams bounced swirling whiteout off her retinas. It was dark and noiselessly snowbound.

Better to pace up there unannounced.

She killed the running lights and ditched the car keys under the floormat. Stallis' revolver, one shot spent, was tucked into her waistband beneath the Beverly Hills sweatshirt, its bulge concealed by the bulk of the bomber jacket.

After a fast camera ID she was buzzed through Bauhaus' security by one of his coke ornaments, Chari or Krystal; she never could remember which was which. Bauhaus himself was holding court from the cushioned circular pit of the living room. Silk smoking jacket, baggy velvet pants, new Bambi-hide mocs on bare feet. Eight or nine grand in slush gold was tangled up in his graying chest hair. Chari or Krystal—the *other* one— was squinting like a nocturnal rodent at MTV on the video projection screen. It was all fast cuts, flashing motion, eye-searing color—the acid hallucinations of a psychotic. She wore an open towel, one hand at her pubes as though it had forgotten its mission, the other lingering in a bowl of cheese popcorn. She was starting to sprout zits around her mouth from all the junk food, and pretty soon Bauhaus would flush her.

Kill her, if she was lucky.

Closer to Bauhaus, now turned towards Jamaica's entrance as though interrupted in the midst of a critical exchange of information, was a guest she had never seen before. He stopped talking and smiling when he saw her; it was a baring of teeth marinated in olive oil. His hair was thick, layered, virulently black. He was one of those men with a permanent facial shadow of stubble and vast fields of dense body hair. His forehead was high and wide. Good cheekbones narrowed to a pointed chin, lending a mantis aspect to the whole face, which had been tanned by ultraviolet to an unnatural bronze that made his eyes seem to bug. Whites were visible above the iris. He looked mildly insane.

Jamaica smelled a man who would slap down cash money for her, here and now, and not be nice.

"Speak of the devil," Bauhaus began, fat and happy. He halved the sound on the TV remote and recrossed his thick legs with a grunt. With a flourish he lifted a Cuban cigar, nine smoldering inches, from a quartz ashtray and sucked on it. "Trot on down, babe. Got company here you need to meet."

Need to *meat*, she thought.

"This here is my good pal from Florida, Emilio."

Emilio rose, courtly, did a semi-bow and squeezed her hand. Contact lingered. When he bent she could see the platinum straight razor on its chain around his neck. His grin was having a hard time not being predatory.

Bauhaus tried to make a smoke ring and failed. "Emilio and you have something in common, my dear."

Oh, shit—here it comes, like an arrow in the back.

"Simian ancestors?" She smiled sweetly.

They missed it. Bauhaus puffed. His end of the cigar was too soggy. "Our good compatriot Cruz. You wouldn't happen to know where he is, would you, cookie?"

"Last I heard, he was in St. Jude's. You should know; you booked him in after you and Marko finished with him."

"Mm." Bauhaus was uninterested in the recap. "Yesterday's news, I'm afraid. Marko went to check up on him, in fact. I'm afraid Cruz gave Marko mistaken directions to your friend Jonathan's apartment. Remember your little waif friend, Jonathan? Am I going too fast for you?"

She shrugged. "So what?"

Lord Alfred flounced in, doe-eyed and spaced out. He delivered a mug of black Colombian coffee to Emilio, who had not yet graced this confab with a word. From an inside pocket of his Versace jacket he produced a carved vial of black jade. A tiny golden spoon was attached to the vial's screwcap by a delicate chain. Two spoonfuls vanished into the coffee; he noticed her watching and a tight smile twitched up one side of his face.

Not coke. Crank. More kick than Sweet 'N Low.

Bauhaus snapped his fingers and Lord Alfred stiffened. His toes drummed the shag like he didn't have enough to do. "Get out of here," Bauhaus said. "Take your leave. Go fuck yourself."

Lord Alfred hurried away to do as he was told.

Bauhaus resumed his James Bond villain pose. Now was his time for speechmaking, to highball toward a *bon mot*-laden denouement. "Sweetness, do remember that certain drugs fog the memory."

"What about Jonathan?" She watched Emilio drain the coffee mug all at once.

"I don't need you to give me his address because I'm sure Marko has it knocked by now. But do you know what the funny, funny thing is?"

She was supposed to ask. She didn't. Bauhaus frowned.

"Why, as soon as Marko left the hospital, our stout associate Cruz just...vanished. It was as if he'd risen from his sickbed and, I don't know, *strolled* right out of there. You wouldn't have any notion of where he might have gone, would you, my jewel?"

Jamaica's eyes narrowed. "You mean you sent Marko to choke Cruz and he gave you the slip."

"In sum, yes." His gecko eyes flickered up, warning her not to laugh. Bauhaus' good pal from Florida, Emilio, was reddening with each mention of Cruz's name.

"I haven't seen him." To miss a beat now would be fatal. "Jonathan either. What do you think I'm doing here? I figured everybody would wind up at one of your parties. All things considered, Kenilworth isn't exactly the safest place for Cruz to hang just now."

"And what, pray tell, became of Jonathan?"

"He went to the movies. He fell down a hole. How the hell should I know?"

"You seemed a touch *protective* of him the other night." He took one more fat puff of his malodorous cheroot before abandoning it. "Fuck him last night?"

She held her tongue.

"Ahh." He sounded as though he'd just loosed a satisfying fart. "Look at her face, Emilio. She did it. She let young Jonathan jam his bat up her gooey little twat. I think she's holding out on us." He drew the sibilant out into a hiss of mean pleasure.

"I think we should give the lady the benefit of the doubt, and our understanding," Emilio offered smoothly. "Some things, don't forget, are won of kindness, Bauhaus—not intimidation."

She looked from one to the other. From oil to grease.

"Tell us, dear," Emilio said. "We only want you to help us to help Cruz. Is there anything else that might clue us in as to where he's gone? Bauhaus says he was injured. That worries me. If he left hospital in a sedated haze, why, he might...have an accident."

Chari made a blind grab for Bauhaus' groin. He shoved her back and she began to search for her clitoris.

"Like I said, I haven't seen him since I saw him here."

Bauhaus nodded. It was the expression of a high school teacher working his way through *my dog ate my homework.* "The other night your friend Jonathan stole some merchandise from me. With your help."

"What?" This was getting wearisome.

"I'll play back the tapes for you, if you wish. They depict, clearly and in spite of the low light, your own sweet self filling several straws with my finest Number Four and hiding them in Jonathan's parka. Remember now?" he snorted. "My party favors *are* for the guests, dearest, but I think you really should have asked."

"Gimme a break." The pistol nestled against her hipbone nudged her, gently suggesting fast solutions. "He sampled. I primed him for you. You'll have another budding user beholden to you in a month. What the hell do you care about an ounce or so?"

"Seems I've been giving away too much free lately without being consulted. Like those two kilos Cruz says he donated to Chicago Public Works via the sewer system. Emilio informs me that Cruz may be highly motivated to turn that big a taste around—into cash—and leave our fair state without compensating his benefactors."

Just when Jamaica wanted to ask why Bauhaus gave a pinch of shit about helping some out-of-state 'caine slinger, she spotted the Halliburton case on the dining room table. Dealers who watched too many movies just loved them. This one would be full of dope or greenbacks or both.

"Relax, Bauhaus." Emilio stood up. He was shorter than Jamaica. "Shelve it. I'm positive that little Jamaica—that *is* your name?—only wants to help and dislikes being grilled and threatened. Here." He clasped her forearm gently. "Let me show you something that'll make you wet."

He led her to the Halliburton, clicked the combination latches and flipped back the lid. Inside both shells was wall-to-wall money. Seven stacks across, three vertical, Treasury-banded Franklin notes.

"Nice." Jamaica kept her eyes on Emilio.

He slipped a hundred dollar bill from one of the stacks, rolled it into a tube as though preparing to whiff a line, and instead slipped it behind Jamaica's left ear like a reserve cigarette. He paused to grace her feathered earring with thick, dark fingers. "Nice," he said back.

Her stomach tried to clench. No way. Not with this guy, not ever.

USE me, the gun insisted. *Jam me into that overpriced dentition and blast his slug brains across one of those abstract nightmares Bauhaus bought as a tax deduction.*

"Such gorgeous green eyes," Emilio said to his good pal. "Green attracts green. Your girl likes money, Bauhaus. I don't think we'll have any difficulty."

She suffered his touch as long as it stayed around her face.

Seeing the money made her consider an alternate angle of attack. "Inhospitable outside tonight." Bauhaus' tone was blasé and bored now. He was so sure he steered, all the time. "Too late for the better private clubs. The drive would be inconvenient. Hazardous, even. Please feel free to employ any of my guest rooms; they're all made up." He jerked his head in the direction of the black, lacquered doorways beyond the kitchen. "The red bedroom's the nicest in cold weather. Champagne? I'll have Lord Alfred fetch it for you."

"P.J.," said Emilio. "I like the flowers on the bottle."

"Chilled and ready."

"You got cameras? I'd like to run some tape."

"Every room. In fact, the tripod is in the red bedroom just now. I am delighted to have anticipated your excellent tastes."

Bauhaus had smelled Emilio's anus and was making a happy face. Jamaica realized it was critical for Bauhaus to impress this creature. Was Bauhaus *afraid* of Emilio?

"You may lead," Emilio said to Jamaica.

She clicked on her work face. They had to buy it. Emilio's hard-on for her had put the Cruz mission on hold. Eyes lidded, now sassy and feral, she reached into the Halliburton and peeled away two more century notes, crumpling and tucking them into one of the snap pockets on her bomber jacket.

She did her strut toward the red room, making them watch. Chari started snoring on the couch, popcorn crumbs in her pubic hair.

Emilio grinned like a mandrill. Plenty of time to deal with Cruz; all the disadvantages were his. Chicago was a happening place.

He did not want his reckoning with Cruz to come swiftly. He wanted the payoff to linger, savorably. He had faith in his power over women, and it would be sporting to win Jamaica's trust, then run her betrayal past Cruz seconds prior to the whistle of the axe. Emilio loved the reactions of patsies and suckers when they tipped. They made the funniest faces. Then he made the faces even funnier, and more garish, with his razor.

He might slice this bimbo just for laughs. Cut her while he was shooting off into her. That was a pleasure he had not availed himself of for a while. Chiquita had been born to bleed for him, and Cruz had thieved away that joy. Other women had suffered fast because of it.

Jamaica led but did not take Emilio's hand.

The choice of rooms in Bauhaus' tacky mini-motel really didn't matter. Jamaica had, at one time or another, fornicated in all of them.

Twenty-Six

I'M A LITTLE STINKER, read the T-shirt worn by the glistening thing pasted to the far corner of Kenilworth's creaky elevator. The shirt was pink with watery blood and the logo was darkened wetly. Mid-sternum it trailed away to tatters, exposing an undercarriage of dorsal plates and pitted moist tissue like some mad amalgam of snake and slug. Puckered pores secreted mucoid lubricant; dry tracks of it shined silvery on the walls of the car.

When the doors opened and it saw Cruz standing there it recoiled, its idly twisting tail making wet dishrag noises as it slapped the floor and close walls, leaving stains.

It had Mario Velasquez's face, sort of.

The child's eyes had been reproduced too large, as though inspired by a velvet painting in a "family motel." The irises were copper, lacking pupils. The mouth was too wide, too big, a downturned lipless slash, an overstated clown-frown spoiled by the crowd of needled fangs ganged within. The slim points meshed crookedly and jutted like thorns in a hedge. An ill fit all around.

While Cruz stood there, mouth agape and doing nothing, it yawned back, imitating him. The sounds it made were nasal and congested. Cruz thought of a python's jaws, dislocating to swallow prey wider than its head. He thought of the savage meat-gob with steel teeth he'd seen in *Alien*, his favorite party flick back in the real world.

No fucking way, dudes.

As he stood rooted, still doing nothing, the slippery little beast sucked in one more labored wheeze of breath, then looped its segments up the wall of the car and out the open ceiling hatch. Its blunt, olive-colored tail-tip flicked through last.

Cruz remembered his bumpy elevator ride to the second floor. *That's when it fell on top of the ascending car, maybe got hamstrung in the cables; that was why the car had convulsed to an unscheduled halt between floors. Maybe its bottom half had gotten pinched in the gears and torn away. Maybe...*

Yeah, and maybe he wasn't really seeing any of this. He forced himself to move cautiously; go slower. Remember Spider Man and his fate by blowtorch. That guy's clear sensorium had left him with absolutely no doubt he was seeing and feeling dozens of icky spiders crawling all over his spiderless body. What *else* had he seen before he flinted his flame? What visions accompanied him into the emergency ward, his lung tissue fried golden-black by freebasing? What had he been looking at seven days later, when he died wearing a straitjacket?

Cruz opened his eyes. No monster prawn in the elevator. The bloodslime trails still gleamed in the car's wan light. A clot of gunk collected on the service hatch dripped free and hit the car's grimy floor like a warm pat of butter.

Time did its elongation trick. Bustworthy as Hitler, Cruz stood there, thinking with a perspicuity awesome in its precision and focus: *It lives in the gap between floors; that's where it hides out, and if I want to stash stuff there, I've got to kill it.*

Still, all those teeth.

The sun was on the rise. If he looked out a window right now he'd see a filthy bedsheet of sky snugging taut to ruin everyone's morning. His eyes felt red, the lids pinned back. His sinuses were petrified; his joints called in sick. He could feel his neckbones grate when he turned his head. He was aswim in that insomniac anxiety that six lines of really good coke—or ten of bad—could deliver, out-of-tune brass band and all. Did the dope make him nervous? Nahh. The thing that made him nervous had just scuttled into the elevator shaft, a head on a body that had no physical right to exist.

Simple, then. It flashes mug, you blow it away. The Sig Sauer was loaded with smooth-bore subsonic rounds, flat-nosed motherfuckers that could tear away pounds of meat wherever they hit.

Instead of a rumble, Cruz could just burn ass out of this dump. No reason he couldn't just split.

Hide the kilo. Oh, right.

His nape hairs rose like fog-stirred reeds and he caught the prickle of eyes monitoring him, as though he was still in range of Bauhaus' security cameras. Any second now a stampede of cops would buzz all over Kenilworth Arms in a pushy search for their stolen brother in blue—the cop whose coat was stiffening in several quarts of blood down in 107. It would be a spectacle...but not one Cruz could afford to hang for, because he had just watched a book vanish into a bloody slit in the wall of Jonathan's apartment, a fissure that had folded petals and erased itself, leaving a scar on the wall. He hadn't believed *that*, either. And now another monstrous joke had just slid contrary to gravity and hoisted its coils into the darkness of the elevator shaft. These were not hallucinations, not paranoia, pain, nor drugs. He had *seen* these things.

Powerful persuaders were held in his hands. He could power up that shaft, blast the Snail Pail Kid to filets and tuck away his dope wherever he goddamn well *wanted* to stash it! Electricity fired in his extremities, hot, pure, insistent. Two more toots would kick him into high-burn and he could play superhero.

He dug in with his index finger and did the fun thing, feeling his ears pop as he snorted. Ice-white contrails climbed nimbly, then Stuka-dived to cannonade his brain, one salvo for each hemisphere.

He lifted the hall table to use as a temporary step-up. The Folger's can with the plastic flowers went rolling, clanging too loud, too long, too much.

An accusatory face poked out about three doors down. "Hey, stop making so much noise out there, man!" The face was youngish, brownish, dirty.

Cruz's lip spasmed. He hauled the Sig Sauer full out, aiming like a killer and bellowing. *"Go fuck yourself, asshole!"*

The door slammed shut with amazing speed and lack of further protest.

What hey, this stuff really *works!*

His mouth worked, chewing what was not there, yet chewing it well and fully. The table would easily allow him to poke his head through the service hatch for recon.

Trap, he heard a voice warn.

He tossed the Folger's can through underhand. It fell back and clattered. He already hated the noise it made. With the table chocked in place he eased up, gun-first. More nothing.

The shaft was dim, faintly viridescent, showing shadows but few details. Cruz's eyes adjusted and pain stroked rearward from his temples. The thin table legs wobbled. About ten feet above the car he thought he could discern the band of dead blackness girding the shaft.

Nobody knew about this secret gap but him. Well…him plus one other tenant, soon to embrace past tense.

There was no practical way to ascend, one-armed, and cover himself, short of asking Slug Baby to lend a tentacle. He heard the table leg snap just before the jolt of upset snatched away his balance. His hand flailed for the hatchway, missed, then captured it just as the arc of his fall had begun. He caught the metal lip with his fingertips, hearing the knuckles wrench apart and feeling the sharp edge bite through the bone. They slipped free and down he went, collapsing into the corner where the monster baby had started out.

He hit the floor with his fist clenched, hot blood seeking the inside of his coatsleeve. The car jounced like a bad mattress and the back of his head skidded against the wall with enough friction to scalp him.

God, but he hated the sensation of being cut! The feel of that thin edge shivering through to kiss your skeleton. He thought of the way a blade tasted the pruny, delicate pad of your wet thumb when you perpetrated some dumb accident in the kitchen. Perhaps that was why his fear of Emilio's straight razor had always been elemental, a fear beyond mere retribution. Cruz *knew* what that pitted platinum would feel like, penetrating him to cut loose the running red stuff, carving tissue with no pressure at all, slicing deep because that was what that stropped end was *supposed* to do and do smartly, cut, and cut, and…

The elevator car was moving. Going down. The doors had not bothered to close. Just as Cruz thought to roll out, the first floor dashed upward too fast and was lost. He clenched his bleeding fist tight and watched his escape opportunity come and go in a fingersnap. Fresh blood trickled through the interstices of his fingers and provided his sole coloring; in the last fifteen minutes or so his pallor had gone ashen. The car stopped with the ease of a sofa flung from a fire escape. Cruz had not even regained his knees when he was pitched forward by the stop, to whack his cheekbone hard against another wall of the car and crush his wounded arm in its sling. The broken table and Jonathan's rucksack slid toward him; the car was stopped at an angle. He heard springs and cables squeaking. Had he just fallen two stories in an elevator? The mushy splatting noise, he already knew.

Anger gushed in to bursting. He clawed the dropped automatic out from beneath him, flipped off the safety with a bloody thumb, and fired at the service hatch just as the goggle-eyed thing that looked like the Velasquez brat got its toothy face up for a peek. One, two, three shots. Ejected brass rang and rolled while the explosions of report bashed in Cruz's eardrums in the confinement of the car and punched the air from his chest. His too-clear sensorium permitted him to see the first shot plowing into the creature's right eyebrow. It whipcracked backward and stayed down. The ceiling of the car won two more smoking punctures while a can-can line inside Cruz's head tried to kick out his eyes from behind, one-two, *boom-cha-cha*.

The gun slipped from his grasp, lubricated by his own bloodshed.

Again the goddamned car had stopped where it wanted. Only a crack of free space showed near the foot of the door track. If Cruz wanted out, he'd either have to widen that opening or force the car to go further down.

He had not considered that the elevator might go to Kenilworth's basement, or beyond.

Cruz surely wanted out, but tried to stand perpendicular to the floor, which was a goof. His own weight yanked him toward the open door and bounced his face off bare concrete, the shock rattling his bones and giving his gray matter one more good stir, kind of like keeping the Hershey's syrup in your chocolate milk agitated. He felt the shiner rise on his face. Downtime in the hospital had calmed it, but now it had been summoned anew to bloat and darken, a reopened wound. The car was hung up at about a forty-five-degree slant. Impossible. Cruz did not care.

He no longer had a "good" arm, so he braced his less injured one against the tilted wall and jumped against the floor, feeling the car lurch.

"*Move*, goddamnit!"

He thumped the panel buttons with the heel of his hand, leaving a thick smear of blood on the L button, which jammed and did not pop back out. Below, the crack of space had widened. Now it was a thin triangle, admitting pale light from outside.

"Come on—come *onn!*"

The triangle grew nearly a foot with a metallic shriek. It was a noise like tomb doors being crowbarred open. Cruz could make out tiny metal shavings littering the door track. Fresh ones. Just a few inches more and he could squirm through to confront his next test.

When he licked his upper lip he tasted coke and blood. Not bad.

Rest for thirty. Capture some breath. He slumped with his butt wedged into the vee formed by the car's slant and dug into the rucksack for some chemical refreshment. Close to two grams were already pushing and shoving in his bloodstream.

Up-down, like being bowstrung and fired. Yes.

His head pulled itself toward his knees. He felt almost as if he were in a hundred-mile freefall toward a pillowy bunch of clouds. The smell of fresh linen. He made sure to hug the kilo close, just in case he happened to pass out.

Emilio jerked awake with a snort, pissed off before he was even fully conscious, angry at the dream that had been piloting itself so weirdly. In the dream, he had built an elemental rage; he simply dragged that rage with him when he felt the callback pull of the real world.

He never woke up easily. Not anymore. Always a sharp start that yanked him to full sit-up with his pump pounding. Rosie had once accused him of getting high on stress. Emilio had laughed; yeah, sure, *riiight.*

Me worry? For what?

Because he was engirded by cutthroats who would greedily appropriate the network he'd built; who would fuck over years of service in his name for the right cash advance? Because the entire federal fucking government was devoted—during polls, at least—to the downfall and incarceration of him and anyone that fit the profile? Because nothing, not even his wealth and power, could stop the reflex tightness in his sternum whenever his limo breezed past a police car on a city street?

Rosie had relaxed. Had *been* relaxed, that old warhorse. Permanently relaxed, once Emilio had gotten the skinny on Cruz.

Sirens, now, outside, and with the sound came the clench of muscle in his chest. Great—that sound would goose him into a coronary someday.

Sirens? At the House of Bauhaus?

The morning had proceeded tastily up until now.

Emilio had always been fond of stripping his bitches personally. He enjoyed the pop of buttons and the patterns in which filmy panties could shred. Party girls were paid to indulge, of course, but he also savored the token protest—the bleat of surprise, or even better, that wistful quiet he got when he destroyed something the squiff had favored. You could read the hate in their eyes and they had to fuck you anyway. Power. You do what I say.

Bauhaus' heroin was pure as the driven...well, Bauhaus sure knew it, and Emilio found out quickly. Just the prescrip to mellow him out from the coke. Emilio had no wish to doze while he had the use of Jamaica, though, so he chased the bitter bite of his crank cocktail with some of Bauhaus' collector's edition scotch. Drugs to go up. Drugs to go down. Pretty soon his body chemistry was going up and down faster and faster. Emilio resonated. He could probably hold oscilloscope leads between his fingers and make a sine wave on the screen.

He had rucked her bomber jacket to the floor of the red bedroom. She understood it was to stay there, so she peeled out of her Beverly Hills sweatshirt while they stood nose-to-nose. Sly, he thought. Practiced.

Just how good was this one?

His eyes indicated the floor. She dropped to her knees and undid the myriad buttons and zippers to be found at his groin. When the sword-pleated Verri Uomo trousers pooled (without the telltale *chink* of loose change; Emilio never carried coins because they were vulgar), she rubbed her face, kittenish, against the stiff and wiry hair of his crotch. Emilio had shaved his pubis for a full year, subscribing to the adolescent theory that it would grow back thicker each sweep. Apparently the myth had paid off. Today he could gather a fistful, pull hard, and feel no pain.

He had grabbed her head to rub her face to and fro around his swelling erection. Sand her down a bit, first.

People had wanted nothing but to *take* from him, all his life. Emilio had spent nearly forty years *en garde* against those who would take from him.

The track lighting in the red bedroom was fed by a rheostat. Jamaica had dialed it low and lit candles, which lent an altar aspect to the room's king-sized waterbed. As she reached for the headboard controls her knee had bumped the comforter and the bed's surface undulated amoebically.

When Emilio *gave* things, he wanted it to be noticed. He wanted his gifts to be appreciated, for the recipients and onlookers to compliment his taste and laud his generosity. When people did not wait for Emilio to be generous with toys or favors and *took* from him, Emilio's balls got frosty.

When Jamaica rose to share the taste of his own cock via a kiss, Emilio had gone for his straight razor. The ball-and-socket link of the neck chain had been engineered for him by a Little Havana jeweler who thrived by customizing trinkets for coke royalty. It separated when Emilio yanked downward, making a pocketknife click. The platinum razor, opening on its original oiled hinge, made no sound at all.

Her hand rose to clasp his forearm gently. A grip that could be interpreted as a lightly whorish come-on...and could also bring her hand to bear for defense if the knife action got funny. His heartbeat shot blood through his brain and back down to maintain the stiffness below decks. This Jamaica bitch was sharp.

His thumb had remained on the trigger-like stud that levered the blade free. Their eyes talked. He snapped his hand upward and halved her chemise a quarter-inch from her flesh. After drawing a quick breath, she told him he was good with that thing, and after panting a bit himself, Emilio agreed.

Cruz had taken from Emilio. Stolen something. It wasn't the petty embezzlement, small change skimmed by the bottom feeders. That was given in any enterprise which employed runners smart enough to avoid street busts. Emilio squandered a lot of folding green on purpose, just to prove money meant nothing to him. His frivolity was casual enough to suggest the poverty of his youth. He flung the cash around, yes—but Emilio knew where every cent got flung.

Cruz had stolen Chiquita, taken her without permission and broken her without excuse or replacement. Stung by his guilt, he had fled to Chicago instead of asking forgiveness and attempting redress. It had been simple enough to barbecue the story out of the other coke droids at the fatal penthouse party. They'd all watched Chiqui take her plunge. And Cruz had not stuck around to pay proper obeisance. A little slapping around and yelling, a bit of work with the razor and all would have been settled. Cruz would have perhaps gained a dueling scar as a permanent dermal record of his fuckup.

Problem was, with Emilio, you could never be sure of just how angry he might get, and to precisely what depth, terminal or not, he might opt to cut. Enter Rosie, the answer man. Exit Cruz, via Eastern Airlines, first class.

This had become a matter of principle and executive discipline. No intramural turmoil could be allowed to slide. Emilio had enough dragons to battle as things were. Some carpet-calling could be run down personally. This gave him a sense of keeping his core smarts honed, of not losing touch with the streets that had given him so much.

It had been a slow week, unfortunately for Cruz. Rosie's replacement was a white guy named Riff who knew how to man the terminals and oversee product flow while Emilio carved a chunk of R&R. Emilio bought out the entire first class section of the flight, so as not to be pestered by tourists or idiots. He'd tipped the first class stewardess a century note and she'd given him a Chicago phone number, written beneath her name, *Stef*, on a card. Emilio had felt boyishly lavish and had come off the flight in a good mood that Bauhaus had done nothing to dispel.

While he admired and enjoyed Jamaica, Emilio kept a running tab of his northward trip. In his mind, Cruz's name was on the bill.

Jamaica was moist and tight and well-schooled and paid not to say no. A touch of bondage, a tot of anal hijinks, a dab of Noxzema, two or three drops of hash oil. A few bruises and a squirt of blood—hers—and Emilio was ready for naptime.

He awoke all at once, hearing sirens.

In his dream, he had been slapping her face. Telling her that in case of virus he would spend a year hunting her, then an hour cutting her throat. Then he would use her blood as lube to jerk off while she died. That was cool. It always scared the hell out of them.

In the dream, Emilio had jump-cut to Cruz and seen him quaking in terror. Wounded, confused, panicked and bleeding, his entire body trying to run, his mind befogged with the dumb animal comprehension of impending death. Emilio had made the dream beg for his mercy. Grovel before you bite the big one, that your leavetaking from this world should mean even less. Your epitaph shall read GROVELER. WEASEL. COWARD. SCUM.

So, so fine. The anger was righteous, religiously pure. An excellent system of corpse disposal awaited, or so Bauhaus guaranteed, should Emilio care to leave enough behind for bagging. Bauhaus—always the thoughtful host.

But the wake-up was as rough as usual, Emilio's heartbeat revving to redline, bringing him to the surface alert and ready to kick ass, take names and do business. The sound of the police siren had tripped his internal danger flags. His body jerked, causing a sloshing within the big balloon that constituted the waterbed.

Emilio only slept four hour hauls at best. His physician had diagnosed bad sleeping habits. Irregular and too-rich meals. Substance abuse and too many stimulants. In the checkup printout it had all been tallied under the exotic designation *aberrant lifestyle.* Emilio was proud of that. Such a status suggested he was the boss of his own life. He desired to always be diagnosed that way.

Long ago he'd quit cigarettes just like that. He'd have to alter his sleep mode next. As much as crank kept him keyed, he'd slam to sleep if he was in one position long enough, which was one reason he was a pacer, a foot-tapper. Force him to sit still and he'd drop off...but only for those four hours.

He had to change that. He did not wish to die a young but very successful man.

His body tried to execute its reflex sit-up but did not make it a third of the way. At first he thought his body had blown some internal gasket untimely, to betray him between checkups.

Then he saw, he felt.

Emilio was securely lashed to the posters of the waterbed frame with the Ace bandages from Jamaica's bag. Hand and foot. The knots were no joke. Jamaica was not in the room. Her jacket was gone.

Emilio started yelling, in competition with the still-howling police siren outside.

...the kilo don't drop the kilo...

The ligaments in Cruz's neck popped audibly when he jerked up his head. No sirens. He thought he heard sirens. Dream hazard signs, most likely. The real world rushed in to re-catalogue his injuries, and pain brought him around like a volume knob being twisted to high-end.

The kilo snugged between his legs and chest was intact. His eyes watched it slide off as he awoke. It hit the crooked floor of the jammed elevator with a floursack crackle and coughed out a blurt of white powder, about eight thousand dollars' worth. Then Cruz's aches started singing.

He did not panic. He swept the coke into his hand and scooped most back. Several dispatches of flake were sped up to Brain Central. Then he tried to work up some spit so he could rinse his nose, which was bleeding anew.

Fuck it. Let it bleed, as the song goes.

Already he'd done enough blow to jump hurdles and black out, though he blamed his wounds and lack of sleep. He did recall that while down he'd experienced some sort of wispy nightmare about Emilio. *Not* recommended. All those evil scenarios, in explicit detail, showing how Emilio's platinum shaver would skin off hunks. Rated X for violence. A couple of years back, Cruz would not have been admitted without an adult guardian.

Kenilworth's Elevator from Hell had gone totally out of its gourd. Dim light seeped through from what Cruz estimated to be one of the basement hallways. The psychedelic, forty-five-degree crack he had sought to widen by jumping up and down was now large enough to squeeze through. There were no elevator doors, merely an erratic rent in the foundation concrete. He saw a wet floor. Pools tossed back the greenish light. The light in the car was sputtering but alive.

Elevator crash. That would explain it.

Or perhaps this was another hidden level, even bigger. Maybe the tunnels where Fergus the super hones his troll skills and collected toejam.

Time. Was Jamaica on her second or third cup of coffee over at the Bottomless Cup, getting impatient?

Just a bit more incentive, before he stashed the brick. He knocked back coke misted with his own blood. At least it went down wet.

He felt for balance with his unencumbered arm after zipping up the kilo. When he opened his hand the slash of scab across his palm broke and new blood emerged to glisten. He could form a fist but not open his hand flat. Good enough for shooting. He eased out and immediately slipped on the slick stone floor. He was right-side up now, and that was befuddling. His cleated boots helped him not to fall and he hugged the nearest wall.

Not water, on the floor. More like the putrescent goop he'd

seen in the old Jew-hater's apartment. Or the gunk secreted by the baby monster...which he was not so sure he had actually seen with his eyes. Not now. Probably just the drugs.

Just say *yeee-hah*. Wasn't that what drugs were for? To fuck with your head and give you public license to be a butt hair. The drugs were there to blame. *I did what? Wow, I musta been fuuuucked up.*

He decided to trail the back of his hand against the wall to keep from falling down, and, head bowed, he carefully negotiated the passage. The odd glow reminded him of some bad fish he'd gotten once from a Pompano Beach vendor, a sunbrowned guy with a portable steam table who sold little paper cups of cooked whitefish. Tasty, but when Cruz had taken the cup into a bathroom he noticed that the fish acted like a blacklight poster. He cupped his eyes, watched the meat radiate a calm blue glow, and two hours later he was barfing chunky white foam. He hated throwing up; hadn't done it since the flight north. All control was thieved from you, plus you lost your lunch (which might have been expensive and delicious), plus it felt like twenty good rabbit punches to the lungs, *plus* you got to taste your own bile and the acrid sewage dripping down from your palate for hours. Thrills.

The mellow illumination in the corridor was just like Cruz's mystery fish, only green. It brought back all the bad associations. He burped and tasted stomach acid. He wasn't hungry—that be the Real Thang again, killing his appetite—but knew he should probably stoke in some food soon, perhaps at the greasy spoon when he met Jamaica. The thought of food made him burp again.

Something standing at the terminus of the corridor burped back at him, just as Cruz was willing himself not to vomit.

As belches went, it was more ambitious, a clogged mortar blast that reverberated against all the concrete down here. It was followed by a congested laugh, then the iron-lung wheeze of labored respiration.

Cruz's head cleared and he clawed out the Sig Sauer. A human-shaped silhouette blocked light about ten feet ahead, hair sticking out wild and cowlicked. The upper torso was outlined by a heavy biker jacket. Cruz saw the slim shadow of an open switchblade in one gloved hand.

He could see a speck of moisture drip from the tip of the knife.

"Have to. Leave." The shadowman's voice was rusty, ruined, hoarse. The words were spaces with effort and mauled phlegmatically, as though a foreign phrasebook was being recited from a tubercular deathbed.

Cruz stayed on stand-down where he was. No strain. Gun beats knife the way rock breaks scissors.

When the stranger took a shuffling forward step, Cruz thumbed back the hammer and felt his hand continue bleeding. Damn.

The next step moved the stranger into the light. Cruz's spine iced up and bells rang in his head.

Eyes glinted toward him. More than two, stuck in places in the face that were all wrong.

The thing's free hand opened and grew a straight razor. Cruz saw it to be the razor he'd last seen in the bathtub of 107, dappled in dry blood. The switch in the opposite hand had a white bone handle. The razor made a slithering wet noise that indicated it was emerging from flesh, not from coatsleeve. The edge shined and dripped.

The front of the leather jacket was shredded and knotted. A baby-sized arm protruded from the center of the mesh and helped hold everything in concert.

Another step forward. Cruz raised the gun.

Now he could see the butchered meat of the face, a suppurating, bloody jigsaw of too many parts. Skull shone through. The thing smiled at him.

At least two of the eyes in its face were Jonathan's.

Twenty-Seven

Just like the Mummy—slow but inexorable—Bash trudged his Toyota truck toward Garrison and Kentmore Streets in the monster face of the storm. Blowing snow belabored the windshield and caked against the wipers, a slushy dybbuk sent to hamper his progress.

He should not be doing this. He should be happy. He should not be making waves.

Chains in front, deep-cleated snow tires lugged onto his rear axle, and he was crawling. There were times when the climate around Chicago really sucked. And blew. Simultaneously.

Bash was not a happy puppy. Not normally given to introspection, he had wallowed in same for two days now and watched the fountains of his rosy future turn to soggy asswipe. All his life Bash had been a genius at talking people into things. Jonathan had bought the Chicago gig on his say-so. And Jonathan had fallen for all the ways Bash had rationalized selling out, a logical, nay, *wonderful* game plan for turning into his own worst nightmare—a genuine Gold Card carrying Butt Dude. And Jonathan had not slapped him upside the head. Jonathan had said *okay friend o' mine—anything that makes you happy.*

Happy crappy.

A white meteor crashed into the windshield on the cab's passenger side and rewarded Bash's perseverance with a cobweb of cracks in the safety glass. Goddamnit it to hell. Now the storm was heaving missiles at him. Visibility was nothing. It was like trying to penetrate a mountaintop *foehn* or a total whiteout at sea. An avalanche from the sky descended to bury and batter while the wind currents did their most devilish to rock the truck, even flip it into a snowbound building or icebank.

At not more than five per, he rolled slowly up behind a municipal plowing rig, a broad, low-slung Trackmaster on treads, the kind used to clear ice runways in the Arctic. Its strobes and yellow flashers flared harshly off all the blinding white. It was not moving.

Once Jonathan had failed to campaign against Bash's impending wedlock to the fair Camela, Bash had felt soiled, as if he had just put a fast one over on an amigo. His justifications lacked obvious blown stitches—this was to become a good and useful shared life. Yet he felt the misgivings sometimes felt by criminals who slip through legal loopholes and think, *You're as guilty as a tomcat with a dead bird in its mouth, but you may go free because you are LEGALLY correct.*

It had taken Camela a scant three days to raise the topic of how large their brood was going to be. Plans had to be fomented. How many miniature Bashes could the universe at large withstand? She was trying, and throwing honest effort toward correcting their relationship for the future good of both of them, but now Bash perceived a clear ceiling on just how long she would make that effort. While she had a lucid concept of just where it terminated—along with her unusually good manners, of late—Bash had not been supplied with clues to the agenda.

He was being steered, however pleasantly. Bash detested having his reins yanked.

Jonathan would no doubt see it as a betrayal. What the poor, solitary son of a bitch needed right now was friends, and Bash had wasted their last dinner together getting roasted and off-loading Butt Person bilge. Stout fellow, that Bash, always covering his own ass.

And this morning, Jonathan had not shown for work. He had stayed under the entire weekend without so much as a phone call. Bash was hoping it was merely the ferocity of the blizzard. Capra had sanctioned a day off for all employees of Rapid O'Graphics, and morning toasts had been hoisted. Bash begged off early to venture into the storm and seek out Jonathan. He had lied to Camela, telling her that he would meet her back at Capra's. Camela's desire to avoid getting fresh snow in her perm did the rest.

There were purging aspects to this quest that Bash's mind could not ignore. What he really wanted to do was herd Jonathan over to that coffee shop on Weedwine for some caffeine meditation. And talk, laced with true things, for a change.

White chuffs of exhaust blatted from the Trackmaster pipes but still it straddled the road, unmoving, impossible to pass. To Bash's left, where he should have been able to make out parked cars and a building wall, he could only register a slope of chalky colorlessness. White was the utter absence of color, he'd read.

He draped his hurricane hood, zipped up and dismounted. His boots sank through about a foot of snowfall before stopping. Moving like a diver through turbid water, he waded past the rear gate of the Toyota and saw the top third of a corner signpost protruding from the snowpack. He rocked it to jar the snow loose, and read that he was one block from the Garrison Street entrance to Kenilworth Arms.

There was nobody manning the Trackmaster. It idled against the tilt of the storm, vacant. So far this had been a winter of some weirdness and much insanity; some of the city's municipal plow operators were dogging triple shifts and occasionally flipping out. One had begun shoving parked cars into Lake Michigan to butt them out of his way. Another, just a week ago, had steamrolled over a citizen in his Porsche, mashing both to bloody tinfoil.

He backed the truck up to clear it from the rearward path of the Trackmaster, should it opt to embark on a backward path of destruction. Velvet Elvis "Hot Damn Tamale" was half-done on the dash's CD player and Bash terminated it. He hoped the Bottomless Cup was still open in blow like this. He hoped the storm did not implode his fractured windshield.

The Garrison Street door was hopeless—locked, iced, impassable. He slogged around to the Kenilworth door, where he found the glass blown inward. Apparently a fist of wind had sheared in, angled deadly, and done the deed. Broken stalactites, fallen from the roof ledge, poked from the dune of snow like some Viet Cong booby trap. He crouched and stepped through the toothy ingress. In his wake big arrowheads of glass jarred free and made no noise as they were gulped by the snow.

The foyer was another sub-zero mess, tracked up, besotted and half-frozen. How could tenants stand this? It wasn't something you ignored by stuffing a towel into a door crack. He pushed through the hallway door and made for the stairs, hands deeply interred in pockets, snow sliding off him like the world's most overstated Head & Shoulders ad.

Perhaps Bash's match had been lit by Jonathan's outrageous tale of arrest and hookers and TV drama jeopardy. People with normal, safe, Butt lives never savored this brand of thrill. You had to taste life…and sometimes the taste was really *icky*. Better to fall in love and have your heart broken, than never to experience it. Some of life's icky flavors demanded mental mouthwash. Some changed the way you did things forever. Jonathan had been hit by a fast, color-saturated sideswipe of excitement in the middle of this colorless void. Bash, snug and secure at home, not to mention bored, had missed out while he was programming ways to insure his life would be even more comfy and dangerless.

He hated it whenever he could feel the grind and shift of his character changing shape. His excuse for coming here on this fine, hellish day was to review things with Jonathan and see if they were still watertight. What he really wanted Jonathan to do was talk him out of it…just hit the road for Vegas…become smugglers or astronauts…

The outer door to 207 moved when Bash tapped on it. It was unlocked, and he stepped through. Door Number Two was also ajar.

"Jonathan. Hey?"

Inside, movement. Heavy tread, crossing to the door just as Bash pushed it back with gloved fingertips. Then the door was wrested from him, leaping wide open.

"Shut your fuckun hole."

Not Jonathan. Someone as tall as Bash, with wider shoulders. Gripping a big-frame automatic whose muzzle sniffed Bash's eyebrows.

"Ass in here. Now. Total quiet or I blow your teeth out through your hairdo. Step in now."

Bash was relieved not to see Jonathan's bullet-riddled corpse in a loose-limbed sprawl on the floor. The big man closed and locked the inner door. Bash swallowed hard. Jonathan's stuff was unboxed and strewn with no regard to order or fragility.

Bash wondered how many hits he could take before his body went and died on him.

"Back against the wall and slide down to a sitting position. Do it now." The gun indicated directions.

Bash did as he was told.

In less than forty seconds he would be grappling with this intruder, fighting for his life.

The most apt image Jamaica could summon was an alarm clock. The old kind, tinny and moon-faced. The kind of clock terrorists employ in shoot-em-up movies to touch off their death packets of plastique. The clock was ticking. Detonation was afoot and the race was on.

Her life was a time bomb.

One more crossed-off square on the calendar march toward the end of life. A wildly blowing blizzard and one more stolen automobile. A new glorious day.

She nudged Bauhaus' cherry-red Corvette into the breakdown lane with emergency flashers blinking. Up ahead she could make out the taillights of another hapless commuter snared to immobility by the storm and a sense of shared catastrophe composed her a bit. Her teeth were chattering in spite of the artificial heat flooding her legs. The gas gauge hung at a quarter tank. How long before *she* was running on fumes? How much more of this cliffhanger crap could she weather before steam came pouring out her ears?

She crunched to a halt in two feet of new snow and put the 'Vette in park. She could see no other vehicles, other than the lost soul up ahead. High beam blinkers came and went like ghosts in the swirls of white. Lights up high would mean plows or tractors. Lights on her level would mean other victims. Like her. Maybe the authorities. Jamaica hated that word, *authorities.*

The downtime permitted her to rummage in Bauhaus' glovebox. Beneath an ungainly stack of CDs and half a lid of makings for stale reefer she found his dented flask. Her fingers traced the light Deco engraving, and her nose told her it was bourbon, eighty proof.

Under the flask she found a revolver. Just what she needed in her life—another gun. Hallelujah.

Jammed endwise against the floorboard on the passenger side was Emilio's Halliburton case, filled end-to-end with money. On the suicide seat was her saddlebag and Officer Stallis' stolen service pistol. It had been fired until empty sometime in the last hour.

The piece she withdrew from the glovebox was a compact, pimpish revolver, snub-nosed and nickle-plated, pure Bauhaus. Perhaps he kept it for plugging traffic cops.

The storm did its damndest to ice the tinted windows and keep the car enshrouded in white—blank, featureless, the color of picked bones. Jamaica caught herself glazing out, staring at the dashboard clock. It was the ticking kind. So many events, crammed into a handful of revolutions on such a tiny clock face. It didn't seem doable.

She smacked herself lightly on one cheek to revive. The heat was making her dopey. She got out of the car to let the snow sting her, and, eyes tearing against the gale force winds, she threw both guns into the blizzard as far as her pitching arm could propel them.

Emilio had been a cinch. Literally.

He is so brimmed over with ego that stacking the sexual deck against him hardly requires a caloric expenditure. She does not fuck him per se—she processes him, on the same mental level she blinks or respirates.

In the aberration department, he has nothing new to offer her. Adroitly she simulates the requisite climax. Emilio is one of those who fancies himself a "giving" creature because he always forces his bedmate to come first.

When they both doze, Jamaica makes sure she is on top. Bauhaus' downers, nicked from the fruit salad dish on the onyx bartop, help.

Almost by rote she handcuffs and hogties him, resisting the urge to separate his hairy balls with a bullet. Make 'em dance. Or maybe pour amyl nitrate all over them...glue him to the sheets...

Getting the revolver free of her jacket before Emilio could burrow into her clothing had proven dicey. She never forgets that cameras are watching. No median for theatrical gestures just yet. Everything has to appear business-as-usual, and tying Emilio to the bedposts qualifies. Only just.

She does not need that much time to act, and plans on moving faster, thinking faster than any of them.

More kink to come, following this brief bathroom break.

Once in the john, she uses Arrid Extra Dry to powder the panel where she knows the camera lens to be and hurries into her clothing. After getting her boots on and snugging Officer Stallis' gun into one of the insulated pockets, she fields an unwanted glimpse of herself in the full mirror over the sink. Her mascara is blotchy, her eyes raccoon-rimmed in kohl, her hair sweated out. The purple streak sticks up like something out of a cartoon. Poster child for the runaways of America. Please save me from those mean streets.

A toot for luck, chopped on the marble counter. For stamina. Bravery, if not courage.

The moment she steps out of the bathroom, the clock begins its countdown.

She rolls Emilio's silk socks into a wad and crams them toward the back of his throat. His breath hitches and he begins to draw air through his congested nose, still out.

She's out the door.

Chari and Krystal are flat-alpha on the sunken circular sofa, curled into each other like sisters at a slumber party, butts exposed, legs splayed unconsciously. MTV rages away on the video screen. Sedative rock, clichéd to snoozeland. Guitar rapists with big hair, throttling their penile fretboards and making faces as though what they are doing is REALLY HARD. *The lead man for Guns 'N Roses is prancing and shrieking. He has no butt—the backside of his too cool leather pants hangs like an airline bag with two empty pouches.*

Jamaica is thankful for the cover noise.

Lord Alfred is not in evidence. Probably ass-up in the master bedroom, dripping Vaseline. Good.

The Halliburton case is still on the dining room table, though snapped and locked. Its mellow aluminum shell makes light abstracts on the two inch glass. Outside the blizzard is still fighting to get in, pelting the bulletproof window with BB-sized hail that shatters on impact. The wind lashes like a penitent's scourge.

Guns 'N Roses stop. Whip Hand starts. "Maneater." Now rock 'n' rollers trash a school lit in aggressive crimsons.

She catches the tang of the coca paste cigarette before she actually tracks him, standing behind the bar, his eyes reflecting steely light from the video monitors mounted in the cabinets.

"Shit." *She draws.*

"Hope you're wearing a napkin," *Bauhaus says calmly. He sees the gun.* "We wouldn't want Emilio's spunk freezing a plug in your butt, dearie." *Probably has his own weapon below the bartop, just out of sight.*

Jamaica pulls the .357 to full cock, hoping that Bauhaus is smogged out on dope and his response time is retarded. She wants him to pull something rash. A provocation that will justify blasting him deader than a T-bone steak.

"I want to see both hands empty and on the bar," *she says, feeling stupid, as though she is playacting.* "Right now."

"Mm, quite. So Miami Vice of you." *Pause.* "You ungrateful little skag. You do forget your place. You're supposed to say, 'Or god help me I'll shoot you where you stand.' Yes?"

"Hands. Now." *She can't help gesturing with the pistol.*

She senses that Bauhaus is playing it perfectly level because he is about to kill her. When his hands rose, one of them would be packed. By the time she can react she will be stopping a bullet.

Fuck it, she thinks, snapping her trigger.

The service revolver jumps like a gator wrenching apart dead prey and a heavy-grain hollowpoint plows through a bottle of Napoleon brandy a foot from Bauhaus' head before taking out the backbar mirror in an explosion of bright silver spears. The noise is spectacular but does not stir the bimbettes snoozing on the sofa.

Bauhaus flinches hard. Both hands are up. He has actually been startled into dropping his own gun. He wants insults, build-up, a stand-off. At Jamaica's shot he has tried to whip-draw. The ramp sight of his big automatic has banged against the bar edge and the gun gets away from him, hitting his bare foot. His face scrunches inward while pieces of the bar glass are still flying.

"Owww, GODDAMNIT!"

She keeps her gun braced in a two-handed grip. Not only does this look bad to the bone, but it helps her keep the muzzle down. Miracle, she thinks.

The ebony cigarette holder hangs slackly from his lips. The cigarette has fallen and is smoldering on the deep blue shag. "Step out." She has regained her nerve.

Bauhaus shuffles sidewise to clear the bar, hands limp at the wrists and crossed before the cleft of his silk lapels, the way a cripple might hold two useless limbs as scant protection. He is not wearing pants, just his smoking jacket, belted loosely over his pendulant tummy. Jamaica sees him wince as splinters of glass pierce the soles of his naked feet. Imagining his blood fires her own resolve.

His eyes seek the dropped automatic one last time. Jamaica says no sternly and he gets the message.

His eyes are wet, red, inset. His breaths are fast and shallow. His panicked body is trying to burn off dope with adrenaline. Too slowly. White legs bowed, he stands before the mercy of the .357.

She tells him to sit on the barstool and cock his legs back around the rail. But for the threat of her pistol she might have been setting him up for some of the usual sex play. Small rivulets of blood pattern the chrome as his feet bleed.

Nimbly she steps around the bar, bootheels powdering glass bits. She fetches the automatic and pulls two bottles of Quietly beer from the fridge.

She offers one to Bauhaus. He stares at it, face ruddy with child's guilt. You spoiled my fun. He is hesitant to actually touch the bottle, sensing some ruse or dumb game of vengeance. His penis, flaccid and white as his chicken-skin legs, lolls from a fold in the smoking jacket.

"Dope's right in front of you," she says, indicating the party bowls of tablets and capsules. A riot of consciousness-altering color. "Help yourself. Start with a big handful."

His eyes flare. He tries his first gambit. "Marko will be back here any second." His tone of warning needs a speck of polish just now.

"You sent Marko to turn over Jonathan's apartment. That was before Emilio and I hit the sack, right? It's too soon for him to be back and you know it. That asshole enjoys his work."

"Just like he's going to enjoy widening your cunt face with a power drill. Emilio will have his bit of fun, too. Your value just dropped to negative numbers. There won't be enough left of you to make a lampshade out of." Flecks of foam have collected in the corners of Bauhaus' mouth.

"Guess I've got nothing to lose, then, by blowing your fucking head off." She is yelling. She cocks again and gets right in his face.

Eat, she tells him.

She knows that in the ratty backwaters of Bauhaus' mind waits the speech of doom designed to convince this bitch all is lost for her. Her life ends tonight. You'll never breathe in this town again.

He looks toward Chari and Krystal. Nobody home. His hand edges toward the pill dish and she knows what he is thinking: buy time.

So odd a sensation, to know the interior of his head.

"I said a handful, not a sample. Between these two guns I've got enough shots to make you scream a helluva long time before you get to pass out or die."

Ludes, loads, poppers, black cats, percs; Bauhaus is infamous for the freshness of his fruit salad. Gyros, highwires, dexedrine, black beauties, red nightmares, crystal blue persuaders, none of them a niggardly dosage. Skimp for guests? Never. About ten assorted pills are gathered in his palm.

"Drink me," she says. "Cheers."

She takes a long pull off her Quietly while Bauhaus chokes down the cornucopia of drugs. Two hard swallows. Something gets lodged and he coughs. Ack ack ack. He washes it all down with beer.

Jamaica makes him repeat the routine four more times, until the bowl is half empty.

Keeping him in sight and making sure his legs stayed wrapped around the stool, she hunts up car keys from the cabinet rack. She does not want him to know which of his automobile collection she is stealing. Backstepping, always holding the pistol on him, she collects the Halliburton case from the dining room.

Bauhaus works on making saliva. He says nothing now.

She is itching to murder him. Make him eat the gun and watch his brains decorate the picture window, to drip down. If he gets loose he'll make her compost in a second. She will be erased from the earth. To Bauhaus it would be an adjustment in a ledger. He has never related to her as a human being, or even a person for rent. To kill him would be to degrade herself to his level of nonhumanity. She does not want to become a robot that badly. What is good, merciless corporate practice is not necessarily a good bottom line for her life. She would relive killing him every day of her life, and he is not worth that much time inside her head.

Bauhaus does not rate her rage. This comes as somewhat of a revelation to her.

She is about to tell him what to do next when he makes his move. He slaps himself hard in the face with his palm. Then he snarls. The snarl becomes a yell; the sound martial artists make when they pop a good workout sweat.

Bauhaus launches himself from the stool, pounding toward her on bloody feet, his muscles fighting their way to the surface of his flesh, and Jamaica has just enough time to remember that among the dope on the bar, lost in the mix, are probably some ampoules of PCP.

Bauhaus has smashed the ampoule right into his face. Pinpoints of glass are jammed into his upper lip.

His charge is clumsy and mad, making up in fury what it lacks in grace. His arms are outflung into claws.

She gets the Halliburton up one-handed and whacks him in the face. Christ but the thing is heavy and all that's inside is paper. Not a good shot, but it has weight behind it. Bauhaus is deflected to execute a spreadeagled headfirst dive into the sunken living room.

Instead of trying to circumvent him, Jamaica sprints for the first bedroom. The green bedroom. Two doors down, Emilio is still faded to black, touring dreamland and getting angry at everything.

Bauhaus yowls incoherently, spraying spittle, the veins in his eyes bulging. He gets an arm and a leg through the bedroom door just as she tries to slam and lock it.

She kicks him in the shin hard enough to lay back flesh and expose bone. He does not feel it.

His hand clutches blindly for her windpipe and she must drop the Halliburton to hold the door. The door seesaws and he skins his wounded leg free to kick at it. Now Jamaica is making her own kind of growl. She shoulders the door hard and hears two of his fingers break as his hand is hastily withdrawn from the jamb. The bursting knucks sound like a party-popper.

She reconsiders having to relieve Bauhaus of his life in the next ten seconds or so. She gets the door lock engaged but knows it won't hold.

The first time Bauhaus rams the door a framed painting jumps from the wall to break frame and glass on the floor. It depicts human skulls in ochre, and is signed in a childish hand by John Wayne Gacy.

Jamaica grabs the case and runs for the closet. When Bauhaus caves in the door it will take him two or three seconds to track and orient. She is counting on that lag of time to save her bod.

If the bedroom had been a dead end she would have had to shoot her way to the front door. Breaking windows to sneak free was a joke in this building—all the windows are security-barred, on coded releases. There are even tiny bars on the intake for the industrial heating/cooling unit. Jamaica is not stupid enough to retreat to a dead end just to be cornered by a lunatic lathered out on animal trank. She has ducked into the green bedroom specifically to enter the closet.

Bauhaus collides with the door. A whitewood crack appears lengthwise through the middle. It bows toward her. The hinges tear halfway free of their moorings.

Jamaica sweeps aside the racked clothing in the closet, mostly coats, slickers, winter gear. She paws around for the big red button she knows to be there. Accelerating fear tries to iris her throat shut.

The heel of her hand skids past the edge of the circuit box. It is further back than she remembers. It is industrial gray with a flexible conduit hose coming out of the top. The button is mounted in the center of the box, within an insulated collar that prevents an accidental trip.

The door of the green bedroom flies apart into matchsticks and kindling sawdust. Bauhaus sprawls in, still clumsy on his injured leg. He stands up, weaving, and yanks a sharp fragment of the door out of his left tit.

Wooden stakes only stop some monsters.

His smoking jacket is torn open, belt dangling. His feet are crimson to the ankles and he has a hard-on.

The button emits a buzzer noise Jamaica has forever associated with the employee doors on bank counters. With that noise the back wall of the closet will retract to the right for seven seconds, then relock. It will release her into the rear of the foyer closet, thence into the room with the mirrored walls and bullet-deflecting glass. She will be exactly two feet from the front door.

If the building's alarms have not gone off by this time, they will as soon as Jamaica employs the escape panel. Pressing that big red button is just like kicking off Doomsday in all those World War III flicks. Bauhaus' legion of backup security, firepower unslung, will come charged and gnashing their teeth. Hell, not so pretty, would officially bust loose.

Evermore the braggart, Bauhaus has foolishly pointed out the button to Jamaica, about a year back, in the afterburn of two hours of mediocre sex and countless lines of excellent controlled substances. Jamaica has joked to Jonathan about Bauhaus' "secret panels." Jonathan is dead now and Jamaica does not wish to join him.

The panel takes its mechanical time withdrawing as Bauhaus slouches across the room to kill her.

She steps through, case-first. He misses her neck but ensnares a fistful of her hair and braces against the closet frame, trying to reel her back headlong. She loses the case; it mashes her foot. How can money be so heavy?

Her hands hang on to the metal hanger bar as she is trawled
backward, her neck tendons snapping tight as thick rubber bands to
shoot pain up and over the crown of her head. The panel is closing.

Fleetingly she wishes that she had the chemical edge.

Bauhaus makes another caveman noise and whips her head back.
Her occipital cracks against the panel as it seals off with a good nine
inches of her hair still in his grasp on the leeward side.

She aches to shoot him now, a craving nearly sexual in its bite and
intensity.

The escape panel is a one-shot option that cannot be triggered
repeatedly. It is designed to foil such pursuit, and will not open again
until five minutes had clocked off on the circuit box's timer. Bauhaus
has told her this, too, never suspecting she would be the one to use his
own system against him.

But he would know that, which means that the only thing holding
Jamaica's hair now is the door. Bauhaus is already on his way around
to cut her off. Perhaps an extra moment, to collect a meat cleaver or
another firearm, to gift her with pain.

The panel flashing is secured with metal brads and rubberized for
a quiet, positive contact. Jamaica steels herself, one, two, three and jerks
her head forward. Roots shed and hair filament snaps like twigs in a
blaze; there is no sound inside your head like the sound of your own
hair tearing away in gobs.

Seventeen years younger, and she recalls the dentist's warm
assurances that this wouldn't hurt a bit, and that he would count to ten
before he did anything. He grabbed a lower molar and rocked it in the
jaws of padded pliers, counting one two three as her tooth was levered
free, roots and all, in a blurt of oral blood that had made her gag and
cry.

Tears came now.

Luckily her hair is still damp from the exertions with Emilio, plus
a flash of panic sweat across her scalp. That helps rend her loose, but
the back of her head feels sanded and bleeding. Her foot throbs and tries
to spill her with a misstep.

She makes it out through the foyer door just as Bauhaus appears on *the other side of the smoky glass. There is blood all over him by now. Neither of them can hear the alarms, though use of the closet panel has certainly fired them off. Just past an inch of armored glass she can see him feverishly punching buttons to override. He makes a hasty error and punches in one more time.*

She recovers the Halliburton with her left hand and cross-draws the .357 with her right. She empties the cylinder at Bauhaus' fat ogre head from a distance of less than five feet. The cleavage glass saves him, naturally, but the spectacle of it fragmenting and webbing as it is stung by the police loads is fearsome enough to make him dive. By the time the echoes of report die Jamaica is out the front door and hobbling toward the heated shell that keeps the elements from pestering Bauhaus' 1971 Corvette.

No alarms outside. Perhaps Bauhaus has inadvertently shut them off.

A security car will slip up the drive. If she roars past them in the Corvette they will assume she is Bauhaus, and the sight of the police cruiser at the foot of the drive will slow them down another critical second or two.

It is easy to hide in a blizzard of disaster area proportions. The load of drugs she has compelled Bauhaus to ingest has to kick in soon. Has to.

Icy air flinted against her cheeks; Mother Nature the sadist. She slams the Corvette's door and cheats the storm. Bauhaus still has not emerged. She spies headlights angling up the drive. A third eye, a door-mounted spotlight, probes madly around in the blowing snow.

As soon as the cherry-red car is free of the port the windows fog up. Good. At least she doesn't have to wear the stupid hat again.

As she veers around the security car she beeps twice. A second unit is close behind. Go get 'em, boys. Defend the house; let the boss (or his car, at least) fly.

They buy it wholesale.

The nose of the 'Vette hits the avenue with a crunch of impacted ice. The leftward slide is unabortable. She broadsides a concrete post smoked in ice, crimping the rear fender on her side. So what.

She stomps the brakes and the Corvette chomps into a berm of snow eleven feet high, huge enough to ski down. The motor thrums while she sits, knuckles bloodlessly clamping the wheel, fighting to detour tears and perhaps a fit of hyper-respiration that can easily black her out.

Five seconds pass. No further assault comes from the house above. She imagines the chaos. Ten seconds.

The idea hits her, tickles her, and she wastes no time jumping outdoors and making it real.

Officer Stallis' Oakwood cruiser was still dark at the foot of the slanted driveway. She has just missed colliding with it. The keys are still under the floormat. No time to marvel. Work fast and get out.

She flips the toggles for lights and siren.

A full bore Code Three of scintillation and noise rips across the snowy dawn. After locking all the doors she flings the keys strong and they cease to exist in the swirling clouds of white condensation and tornado snow.

She feels lighter and freer with each stride back to the Corvette.

The shit is about to come out the shotgun, but she feels okay, like she just might make it.

She took another rejuvenating swig from Bauhaus' glovebox flask and considered just why she had to meet Cruz at the Bottomless Cup. Why bother going back to Kenilworth Arms?

Why not just hit the southbound interchange and keep on driving?

On the floorboard by the Halliburton was the large and ugly automatic Bauhaus had pulled on her. God, so many guns she had actually missed disposing of one.

It was chucked into a faraway snowbank. When she replaced the flask in the glovebox she found the vehicle registration, and Bauhaus' name was nowhere on it. Of course. Such documents would be filtered. The car was owned by a perfectly innocent bank. If she was pulled over by guys with badges, she might just skim free.

She had promised Cruz she would rendezvous. It seemed a promise she could break, no strain.

Bauhaus, if he ever woke up from the overdose, would certainly have Cruz murdered if Cruz was dumb enough to stay in the vicinity of Kenilworth Arms. By now Cruz had inhaled enough of the kilo to hang tough while heavy-caliber slugs ate chunks out of him.

She no longer needed the slice of money Cruz would reap from the kilo...provided he hadn't already metabolized it all.

She had her saddlebag and almost too much cash to carry. Kenilworth was a trap, a pit, a maze of blood-drenched rooms and more craziness than could ever be scared up at Bauhaus' madhouse. Did she really need *more* grief to round out her day?

Silently she asked herself questions in the rearview.

As soon as the storm relented she could burn a hundred miles or more, ditch the 'Vette in a frozen creek, and check into a gorgeously anonymous Holiday Inn for a long soak of exceeding warmth. Warmth that could seep to her marrow and begin to heal her. Room service. The mindless meditations of television.

It could start right now.

She watched the dashboard clockface. Time has become her pal again. So easy, to crank the wheel and cruise your fine moneymaking buns right out of this nightmare. As she drove she would smile and thank the officers as they waved her through collisions and roadblocks. For her safety.

It was daylight now, and no time for nightmares. It was nearly eleven.

Jamaica took another sip from the flask and wandered through the FM band on the radio. The frenzy of snow and ice that danced and spun just beyond the hood of the car calmed. It looked like the storm was letting up.

Twenty-Eight

The ceiling was a better place for the gun to be aimed, as opposed to the bridge of Bash's nose.

Without conscious aim or grace his hand shot toward the muzzle of the pistol, trapping it between his middle and ring fingers just as it went off. The slug singed the top edge of his right ear and took some hair with it into the wall.

The explosion seemed to halt time.

The intruder's dense fist swooped to pulverize Bash's neck just above the knob of spine. Bash's whole world lurched sharply to the southeast. Thoughts of wheelchairs flitted through.

The fumbled gun hit the floor between them.

It was like watching two runaway locomotives collide. It was not a fight of heroic blows and manful recoveries, of skilled tricks and artful kicks. This was more like sumo wrestling between two pissed-off guys who had never actually seen sumo wrestling, all wide groping grabs and clumsy tumbles. Boxes took big hits, got split and mashed. Jonathan's possessions spilled to litter the floor and confound footing like a pouch of spilled marbles.

Bash hit the deck and looked up into another oncoming fist.

He saw the meshed fingers like struts in the grille of a semi zooming large to fill his face; it was the first time he had experienced the vertigo of a 3-D movie live. He saw a lumpy gold ring with a garnet the color of a burn scab. Hair on the knuckles. Definitely this was an inferior offshoot of homo sapiens.

Charging face-first into a bank vault door would have been more pleasant, less hurtful.

He heard the crunch in his gums as his front teeth tried to fold back and his lips were hamburgered. The ring chopped him bluntly open. Blood streaked his beard as he rebounded into the wall. He split open a carton of paperbacks and went down in a torrent of good literature as the forces of illiteracy waded in to obliterate him.

The gun was near his foot. No time for a retrieve. He kicked it and saw it spin beneath Jonathan's cot.

His attacker delivered another head shot. Both men were swathed in heavy winter clothing, their padding and insulation at odds with the damage they sought to inflict.

Bash saw, scattered, the kitchen goods he'd loaned to Jonathan. Spatulas. Plastic lids for plastic tubs. Nothing solid or sharpened or lethal. A shaker boosted from a restaurant (the best place to provision yourself if you're new in town) rolled lopsidedly, spilling salt. Bad medicine, that.

He would, without thinking, absorb another sledgehammer blow to protect his own borrowed property. This was *stupid*.

The dive bomber fist screamed in and Bash jerked his face out of the firing line. A hole was punched in the wallboard an inch from his ear. Proximity made the demolition gunblast-loud.

The hole in the wall began immediately to bleed.

Bash continued his awkward pivot and jacked his elbow into his opponent's open mouth. Even through three layers of sleeve, he felt the incisors.

Chances are, Bash thought, that this was *not* one of Jonathan's newfound buddies.

The stranger's head snapped back like footage of a violent sneeze in reverse. He absorbed the blow and did not fall. Instead he grabbed a potato peeler and tried to add it to Bash's forebrain. When Bash feinted the tool jabbed a neat crescent hole in the wall. That hole, too, began to dribble fresh blood.

Then the entire apartment rippled with a lateral vibration like the first warning kick of an earthquake. Neither man noticed. Behind Bash the wall roiled gently, once, deep waters stirred by the passage of a big maneater, or the single soft undulation of a python. The fist-hole tore at the top and

David J. Schow

bottom, becoming an oval and relinquishing more blood with plaster dust and bubbles in it.

The potato peeler was swallowed by the wall.

And the room began to shrink, retracting as if stung.

Bash felt himself nudged from behind, some unseen coach goading him to bull in there and fight, fight, fight. Across the room the cot scooted toward them by half a foot. The pistol was ejected from beneath it like a spit seed. Blood marred it now.

He struggled to uncross his eyes and get his arm up in time to deflect the boot hurrying to pulp his face. It smashed through the hole in the wall and withdrew trailing webs of blood.

Bash moved. Not friendly in this corner.

He rolled out to the right as the ceiling sagged down to kiss their heads. The naked lightbulb there popped like a pimple, spraying sparks and convex slivers of glass. He blocked his attacker's outside hook and sank a solid, body-imploding blow to his midsection. But for the clothing it would have been spectacularly crippling.

The intruder doubled, saw the gun, and turned his recoil to the defensive by grabbing for it. He was good. He had done this sort of thing before.

At last Bash got to kick him in the face. He felt his boot eyelets split the guy's tongue, spoiling his chance at the gun. But again, the son of a bitch would not fall. He sucked up a winning kick to the dentures and arched straight. This guy is too goddamned tough for me, Bash thought. Thinking of football, he decided to hell with it and charged.

He caught the assassin by the throat and left wrist, in a parody of a fireman's carry. Bash pulled backward and stole his opponent's balance.

Here were two inept ballroom waltzers, falling.

The bigger man's heels crushed another of Jonathan's boxes. His free arm swung wide and grabbed the windowsill. It was the last thing to let go as he went through the glass and out, casement and all, the back of his head taking out the crossbar.

The howl of the blizzard blew half the pieces back into the room. Bash won enough time to get a grip on the guy's ankles and assist his upside-down exit.

Gracelessly, the man fell two stories straight down. The snowpack was almost as hard as the sidewalk buried beneath it, and he hit headfirst. Unmoving, he began to collect snow.

The room ceased its convulsion.

Bash reeled into the wall, blood streaming from his mouth. He sat down hard in the middle of the floor. His skull was swimming. He was hurt. He was bleeding, damnit.

Bathroom. Rinse mouth.

The blood-dappled automatic was still on the floor, and Bash's scattered cognizance caused him to gawp at it as though it was the most obvious clue in the world handed to a guy still too stupid to figure out the Secret Word.

The Kahlua bottle he'd secreted as a sneak gift to Jonathan was on its side, bleeding coffee liqueur.

That, and the exsanguinating wall, made him wonder just what had befallen his friend.

He picked up the gun and turned it over in his grasp. Heavy. Loaded. No mickeymouse. His thumb moved across the grooved hammer and his finger felt its way around the trigger, collecting blood. This was serious shit.

The door opened and his heart hit overdrive. He came within an eyeblink of blowing away the person who appeared in the doorway.

"I just missed Marko on his way out," said Jamaica. "Rather, he just missed me. You've gotta be Jonathan's friend. The guy with the truck."

Fergus had no last name to speak of and three preferred expressions in English: *Boolsheet sunvabeech. Fockeen I dunno.* And *I duit.*

When on foreign shores it is generally accepted that the two most important interrogatives are *what do you call this?* and *how do you say this?* Plying his duties as Kenilworth's manager, janitor and repairman, Fergus found it more useful not to know things in order to avoid labor that the scumbag residents of this roach motel would never appreciate anyway. Or tip for. Why are the second floor toilets backing up? *Fockeen I dunno.* Where's the window glass you promised for 210? *Boolsheet sunvabeech screens need clean.* When are you going to fix the washer in the laundry room? *I duit,* pronounced eye-do-eat, meaning that Fergus was a grand master of the jerry-rig, the patch job, the boolsheet bandaid solution. When tenants got fed up and vacated they usually left him holding a deposit for breaking their leases early. Gravy. Such extra cash could buy economy-sized sacks of dog food, or the odd fifth of Night Train. Bonus bucks were good for videotapes of white people fucking each other in the ass, or the compensated companionship of a female, under fifty, who shaved her legs once in a while.

Fergus just loved infidel women.

His relationship to the occupants of Kenilworth was truly symbiotic. They exchanged rock-bottom sustenance like mutual tapeworms, never taking enough to kill the host. Fergus was an inadvertent authority on parasitism; in a roundabout way it was why he remained as the Concierge from Hell.

Back in 1972 the Boss had pointed out that Kenilworth Arms had been constructed during Prohibition, using bricks and material recycled from outmoded and condemned structures that dated to the mid-1880s. Fergus had noticed at once the peculiar smell of the bricks; a tang of mummy spices, or what old tombstones smelled like when they broke. An American never would have perceived it. A smell of age.

After sight, smell constituted Fergus' principal sensory input. His nose was keenly tuned. It was one of the things that kept him from bathing too often. The odor of American soaps and the reek of hard, piped water seemed toxic.

The building was very special. The Boss stressed that. It contained a tunnel system accessed via the basement level, plus custom-built deadspaces, akin to small attics, between the second and third floors. These had originally been engineered for the concealment of large quantities of bootleg liquor.

Fergus was not particular about accepting the position. The thing inside of him forced him to say yes. Later he reckoned all had been for the best. He decided he did not mind being coerced.

The thing alive within him had begun as a stitch, stabbing in just below his left lung and causing the kind of pain you feel when running too fast or breathing wrong. It tended to linger, pulsing rhythmically.

Stomachaches followed. Then massive bouts of constipation. He swigged Mad Dog and ate a bottle of aspirin to cut the worst of the pain. He thought he had grown a tumor, and if so, why bother? He was not ambitious enough to become a morphine addict, so the pain was a convenient excuse for doing nothing with his entire life. His way of giving the finger to an infidel god.

Never would he forget the evening he had been scanning the papers, seeking custodial work to pay rent and buy wine. His little pet stitch decided to sting him, viciously doubling him over hard enough to bang his broad nose on the kitchen table. Blood ran and his head filled swooningly with its aroma. Clutching his gut, he slouched to the toilet to vomit.

Great torture-rack heaves battered him bodily. It was impossible to draw air and it felt as though a policeman was kicking in his lungs. Internal pressure bulged his eyes. They would pop and smear the bowl with aqueous jelly. Most of the pizza he had wolfed down earlier resurged in vast unmasticated hunks. Whole pepperonis tinted purple by cheap vino flip-flopped from his spasming gullet and glued themselves to the walls of the bowl. He puked blood. He knew there were probably ulcers down there, but this pain was new, compounded, different. The ulcers had never bitten him quite this way before.

He spat blood-ribboned mucus and black gouts of digestive acid, his face as red as Thunderbird port, veins tumescent, breath husking inward when it stole the chance. His sphincter contracted and he loaded his trousers with liquid shit that stank of alcohol. His bladder voided warmly as tears, oily and yellow with the impurities of his metabolism, squeezed loose to drip into the toilet bowl. That porcelain ring had become a life preserver, and he hung on even as his internal seizures bounced his jaw off the rim more than once.

Each time the worst part of the nausea passed, he spat and geared for the next wave.

At last his stomach floated as a solid mass ascended, pushing past his epiglottis and separating his teeth. His windpipe was blocked and at first he thought he was chucking up his own intestines. He had heard of really fucked up people actually doing that...

Except that this mass was squirming too vigorously to be married to his musculature. Something was trying to wriggle free of his throat, pushing against the walls of his trachea.

It fell out into the darkened water of the toilet bowl, and coiled. A blunt, eyeless head, brown and bullet-shaped, rose into a cobra pose inches from Fergus' face. He thought of it as a head only because it resembled the business end of his man-thing, only larger, with a red-lipped vertical mouth that suckled on the bloodstains while he watched.

His first impulse was to flush it away. It hung on to the bowl via oral suction and was rinsed clean.

What he had coughed up was about a foot long, and with a vaguely ridged undercarriage. Overall it was the muddy color of potter's clay, the busily feeding head the same girth as the body, which did not taper. It was six or seven inches around. No appendages.

Fergus' vision swam from the physical strain of his ordeal and he passed out on the filthy bathroom floor. When he awoke, the thing was gone and he dismissed it as an especially vile drunkard's hallucination.

Until it prodded him again, from within.

It suggested he respond to the advertisement for Kenilworth Arms. Destiny or dream? It did not matter because the results were identical.

After settling with the Boss, Fergus explored the tunnel network. When he chanced across the bolted hatch that opened into the garbage-flooded southern airshaft, the thing wiggled free and took up residence as the first new tenant of Fergus' administration.

Throughout the years, both of them had stayed.

As reward, it bit Fergus from time to time.

Venom rocketed through his system like Freon, and an irresistible narcotic numbness settled in for a good long while. The first time, Fergus had simply lain back in the tunnel and given himself over to the rolling waves of fuzzy pleasure. He came to eight hours later and found that he had ejaculated in his pants. The pain of his ulcers had subsided. His stomach had settled. His vision was clear.

He was hooked.

Both of them had stayed, through two decades now. Fergus' arms were a riot of scarred puncture marks, so he wore long-sleeved shirts and kept a stiff upper. Both he and his pet grew with time. They protected and nourished each other. It was the nearest Fergus veered toward genuine love in his life.

When the Boss proposed secret extracurricular duties, Fergus was ready. He did it for love.

The Boss, it seemed, had occasional trash disposal problems, said trash being disagreeable individuals who refused to do things the Boss' way, or tried to screw the Boss somehow. Fergus knew the Boss to be a generous employer, appreciative of his charges. He was eager to help out. It benefited everybody.

His pet relished the meat, the fiber, the fresh bloody calories it could not derive from dog food—even the kind that made its own gravy. Fergus reaped the pleasures of increased venom potency caused by the richer diet. And the Boss was provided with a solution to his human trash-flow problem—one that left little evidence.

Ex-employees were not delivered all that frequently. Fergus refined his pet's feeding regimen. Mixing the kibble with dog or cat blood helped. Now and again he would provide his *own* blood, because he cared.

Lately his pet had been overeating, stealing meals away from Fergus' supervision. Fergus could tell instantly, because it was always bloated and logy after a big feed, and it did not require food that often.

Somehow it had snatched that little kid from the third floor. But how? It had no free access to the tunnels unless Fergus opened up the hatches. If his pet had free run, someone might see it. That would goof everything up.

Today he would investigate the tunnels.

The workday started out badly. He had his keys halfway drawn from his chain caddy when he saw that his office window had been broken in the night; there were still pieces of glass on the floor.

"Boolsheet sunvabeech," he muttered.

He could tell the office had been ransacked but the thefts were not immediately apparent. Asking people in the building directly would be fruitless; no one would know or have seen anything.

He fired up his hotplate, boiled some Cup O' Noodles, and installed himself in his sprung and swaybacked desk chair. Outside the blizzard raged, but in here, in the heart of his little universe, he was content.

Two hours later, around ten o'clock or so, he thought he heard gunshots, booming faintly from some distant part of Kenilworth. So what. If it was serious the police would show up again. It had happened more times than was worth counting. Probably just some brownie or blackie asserting their masculinity because their whores tried to pussywhip them. Big deal. Boolsheet.

It took Fergus another forty-five minutes to slouch upstairs and discover the slaughterhouse mess inside of 107, where Mr. Ransome had lived for five years now. Blood leaking from beneath the door was what attracted Fergus' notice. He stood with hands thrust deep into his grimy pockets, tongue working within one cheek to dislodge cold food. The smell lilting up from his armpits masked the worst of the stink inside the room.

"Fockeen I dunno," he muttered. He would have to clean all this up.

He checked the bathroom and concluded that his pet had gotten feisty, crawled up the airshaft, poked through Mr. Ransome's window and dragged him off for a leisurely dismemberment. Given time to decay in the mulch of the shaft, the corpse would in a few days be easier to wrench apart into hunks that were swallowing size.

But where had the policeman's coat come from?

This entire situation was becoming an annoyance. Fergus was abruptly thankful for the storm. It would help keep nosy outsiders away until he could mop up and invent excuses. He locked up 107 securely.

Next on the agenda was the tunnel check. Fergus knew where the water was low and the humidity highest. That would be where it was sleeping. If it had just eaten, its venom would be notably stronger, and that thought was enough to start an erection swelling in Fergus' grubby pants.

Down in the basement corridor he unhasped a utility door. He had fortified this one personally, lining it with steel and rubber flashing, interior hinges and double padlocks. This closet-sized room had originally been built as the tunnel access. It housed a false rear wall which Fergus had removed. Beyond were horizontal racks of wine-cask size, now empty, and a hatch cover of boilerplate iron held tight by six wing nuts, which Fergus spun with bored familiarity. The heavy hatch opened on oiled hinges.

The odor from the metal tunnel told Fergus instantly that his pet was nearby. He smelled fresh wet spoor on the clammy air.

He was head and shoulders into the tunnel, ready to squeeze around the first curve and stand up inside of the larger branch, when he froze tight with pointer alertness.

Voices were coming at him out of the tunnel.

Twenty-Nine

"You'll live," Jamaica pronounced.

Until he met her, Bash had thought he was sharp. Now he had stood dumbfounded while she navigated, never less than certain. Little glitches like mayhem and corpses did not ruffle her resolve.

Was she some sort of *professional* at this?

Once Bash had lowered the gun he had pointed at her, she darted into Jonathan's bathroom and handed him a damp towel for his staved-in mouth. She checked and informed him that no teeth had been lost—just rearranged.

"Save it." She waved a hand when he attempted speech and mutilated words. "I know, I know you've got a million or so questions, babe, and I'm sure what just happened to you is as gonzo as what's happened to me...but we have got to burn ass outta here, and I do mean right now."

She had hustled him downstairs and into her getaway chariot, a Corvette the same color as the lifeblood of the intruder who had tried to deprive Bash of his old age. That blood now tinted the sidewalk ice the color of strawberry popsicles. Snow dervished around and gradually entombed the guy right where he had fallen to break his neck.

"That's Marko." She stepped over the body to get to the car. "What do I call you?"

"Jeffrey. Bash, I mean."

"Well get it in gear, Jeffrey Bash—'cos we've gotta go now."

At the Bottomless Cup she had marched him in by the sleeve and ordered a booth and coffee while they were en route to the men's room. She preceded him. The citizen they surprised took his time zipping up and stepping away from a urinal clogged with filtered butts and wads of spent gum. The citizen's eyes moved up and down Jamaica and she knew what he was thinking right away.

Some things never changed.

"Shit on a fork," Bash said to the mirror. "I've got a black eye. Cammy will drop a *cat.*"

"Please," Jamaica entreated him. "Reassure me that you don't actually know anyone named *Cammy.* Hold still."

Her comedy was for his benefit—mostly—and he behaved while she dabbed at his face. Reasonably human was the closest they could fix him, given the time and facilities. She plugged tiny wads of toilet paper into his nostrils and assured him they did not have to stay there through the next major legal holiday... just until a bit of coagulation could take place.

He thought such first aid might have been more efficiently realized in Jonathan's bathroom. He asked about this and she shook her head confidently.

"No, no, and no. We had to get out and we've got to stay clear. Major shit is gonna fly into the fan any second back there, and believe me you don't want to inhale any." It was an expression she'd heard Cruz use.

Then she stepped out, leaving him to urinate—it stung and there was a thread or two of blood from a shot he'd collected in the kidneys. He returned to the mirror to stare like a retard. His shiner was the size of a tennis ball and his lips felt like ground round, bloody-rare.

Before he could lament his condition too much she returned to hand him a steaming mug of coffee that smelled like a thinking adult's idea of Paradise. She tipped three pink and black capsules into his palm.

"Take 'em. Trust me."

He did, and in ten minutes felt amazingly right, all injuries considered. Pharmacology could be sooo nice.

Their waitress' tag read *Oh Miss.* Bash would have smiled if it did not feel as though his face would split in two.

"Are you okay?"

Jamaica steered. "Yeah, we had a little spat and I had to

bust him in the chops. Boy meets girl. Fist meets face." Leaning closer to the waitress, she added, "I didn't rupture anything I *need*, if you get my meaning."

The waitress made a face, then ventured a cautious smile. Was she being put on? She was the thin, harried type that would still be taking hash-house orders twenty years and a couple of kids later.

"Eggs scrambled dry," said Jamaica. "Bacon crisp. Hash browns well done. Sourdough toast. We don't know if he's eating yet."

"You want the toast burned, too?" She refilled Jamaica's cup. Bash was nursing his slow and gently, still afraid of spitting out incisors.

"I'm into carbon."

"I'll get this order in. Cook's afraid the storm is gonna blow the power out."

There were only three other checks to pick up. A plow operator spreading a freshet of newspapers around a booth and packing down a huge breakfast. He was gearing up for an endless overtime day. Two booths down sat a couple, a preppie type into shirt-and-sweater combos and a sunken-eyed blonde sparrow who was either his wife or fiancée. They waited for club sandwiches and wondered what they were doing stranded in the belly of this fierce white nightmare. At the counter sat the guy from the restroom. He stank of high school dropout and was here to drink too much coffee and chat up *Oh Miss*.

"She's good," Jamaica said. "Keeps your cup full without you having to flag her down."

"You?" At first Bash had to make do more with pointing and expressions than actual talk.

"I tried being a waitress. Hasn't everybody?" She sipped coffee. "You going to hang on to that gun you're packing?"

Shock drained his complexion. He'd forgotten the pistol sunk into the pocket of his olive greatcoat. He was virtually sitting on it, and it had slipped his brain.

"Okay, wait. Next you're gonna ask why don't we call the cops. And I am going to say that gun is a big part of the reason that you and I don't need to start a Q&A with the police—because once they start asking all the questions they're going to ask, neither of us will get a word in."

"Ask about Jonathan first. I was. Actually." Talking hurt but the dope she'd lent him helped. "But you're right."

Her expression darkened. "Jonathan." A long slow breath carried pain and regret out of her. "Jonathan; oh my poor Jonathan."

It took her an hour to get through the rest of the story. Even if the pills had not worked, her words were enough to make Bash momentarily forget his own pain.

Kenilworth Arms uses what it knows.

It concentrates on keeping itself whole, when it can remember what it is supposed to be. It is unaware of the human dramas unfolding inside of its own aged corpus. The blackout periods run longer, these days.

So many details have already been forgotten. Or are remembered wrongly.

Blood has always been spilled here.

In the rooms and compartments and passageways, blood has been spilled, but never more than would amount to a passing toxin in a healthy metabolism. Old buildings can amortize nearly any aberrancy. They outlast crises of the moment. Elapsed time sands floors, erodes bright paint, force fits doors until they either shut properly or jam for good. The walls process the animal odors of garbage and the piss in the corners. What today is a pool of red, staining wood slats forever, is in a year or two an unremembered vagary lacking even a scent.

Kenilworth Arms weathers, and maintains itself. Its tenants have no idea that their own despair is a protein that helps to keep the building whole.

Lately, more blood than usual has moistened the walls and carpet runners. The dosage is capacious enough for the building to experience the power of blood, and be transported by it.

All this has come to pass thanks to the tapeworm.

The tapeworm has initiated the building into the opiate joy of blood. Infirmity and senility are bypassed. The sensation is transporting. Desirable.

Numbness has reigned for an unmeasurable time, though time is irrelevant. Kenilworth has forgotten things. When it can remember, it shores up its failing wallwork—it recalls the correct components of its identity.

It remembers rooms.

To be complete in all of its parts, it sometimes remembers the tenants of the rooms. Sometimes it misremembers them.

Sometimes it remembers half of one thing, plus part of another, and imagines a working fusion. It does not matter that some of the tenants are long gone, or dead. The building uses what it knows.

Or thinks it knows.

Such efforts somehow helped the tapeworm. And the tapeworm presently provided more of the good, anesthetizing blood. The wallpaper sponged it up; the cement cracks drank it; the lintels and flashings and doorjambs got drunk on it.

Just as a person with Alzheimer's Disease might win a caesura of lucidity and drug himself to avoid the coming agony of affliction, so does Kenilworth now desire more of the stuff that renders it so wonderfully uncaring. What the building remembers can help the tapeworm to provide more.

It did.

Now the tapeworm has augmented the blood with a new intoxicant. When mixed with the blood, the sensation is trebled. The building desires even more, and so helps the tapeworm to feed.

It is nothing akin to human consciousness. Birthed from the discards of elder structures, Kenilworth has spent most of its existence on the brink of shutdown.

Or overdose.

It is long past time to be dead. The long fall of years toward oblivion has been fraught with malfunctions and internal failures. The stabbing pains of dysfunctional pipework. The scores and scabs of vandalism. The ravages of weather. All the losses of tone and tension and strength that come with the extremities of age. The millions of tiny ways bodies can hamper and betray their owners. All transpire now, within Kenilworth's remembered walls.

The walls are breaking down as memory is lost. They lose integrity like decaying flesh.

Kenilworth Arms, self-narcotized, tries to use what it knows. Or what it can imagine, in its final hours.

Drugged deeper than ever before, it has what we might call a dream.

"You can go back there and take a survey of all the blood and busted glass, but I don't see any point. Bauhaus and his squad of monkey dicks are going to swoop down on that place. And probably kill everybody in sight."

The backstory had not hurt Jamaica's appetite. Bash had lost his.

He sat. To keep his hands from shaking he clasped them tightly together. They throbbed. His right one ached from hitting Marko. The late Marko, he of the shotgun shell mug and sniper's disposition, was now interred in his own snowdrift outside Kenilworth. Bash wondered if the body would dissolve to black water come spring, and run in the gutters the way he had described it to Jonathan.

He did not say anything.

"Listen. Listen to me." Jamaica's attitude left him no room for bullshit. "I know what's probably going through your head right now. I am so goddamned sorry about Jonathan. But believe me, there is *nothing* to do right now. There is no action that is takeable. You saw Marko; these guys are serious as cancer when it comes to payback. We need to stay out of their way. We need to not let them know where we are. The only thing to do is wait. Wait and see if Cruz shows up."

"How much longer you going to give him?"

"If nothing happens by noon, I'm hitting the road. If the storm will let me. There's gonna be another storm—a shitstorm of questions about Jonathan. You've got to decide whether you want to be the guy to answer them."

"Damn." The Louisiana accent had crept back, muffled by loosened teeth. If even part of what Jamaica had told him was true, no way Bash wanted to try explaining it all to guys in uniforms. She *was* a hooker...but Jonathan had taken her straight...and why would anybody invent a story as crazy as this?

"I keep thinking it's my fault," she said. "He wanted to help me out, that's all. He did stuff for a total stranger. But I think he never would have gotten trapped in this if it wasn't for that chick Amanda, down in Texas. He gave me the skinny on her. I think *she's* the reason he crawled down that shaft for *me.*"

That made Bash snort and look away. When he turned back there were tears blurring the rich brown of his eyes.

"Oh. Oh, goddamnit all to fucking hell..." He clamped his eyes shut. Jamaica reached and folded his unhurt hand in both of hers. He jerked it back. "No. You don't understand."

"Look at me." She was trying to help, to do for Jonathan, in a way. "Jonathan was..."

"Shut *up!*" He thumped the table and the flatware jumped. Conversation throughout the room hitched. "You're the one who doesn't get it," he hissed. "All that bullshit about *Amanda.*"

"She broke his heart. They weren't right for each other. What's to understand?"

"Amanda does not fucking exist." His tone was low and lethal, his eyes locking Jamaica's. "Amanda does not fucking exist because Jonathan *made her up.* There was never an Amanda in Texas. All bullshit. He invented her. He fabricated her like the Bride of Frankenstein out of bits and pieces of other people's personalities. He created, in his head, an ideal woman to break his heart so he'd never have to risk getting involved with a real person, ever. He was walled into himself to the point where he'd do that. If he always had the Amanda story to fall back on he could forever say, *here was the love of my life and look how I fucked it all up.* He could keep people away from him with that story. He could get pity with that story. Mercy fucks, even. He could justify never bothering to look for anyone because no one could ever be as good as his idealization, as worthy of his love as this *fantasy* he named Amanda. That was why I goaded him into coming here. That was why I refused to listen when he tried to fall back on the Amanda story. I even paid his fucking freight just to knock him loose from Fort Worth. God. If he kept up with that Amanda rap, he would just...don't you see?"

His hands did not know what to do, so they spilled his coffee and *Oh Miss* was there in a shot to put things right.

"You're talking like a guy getting ready to blame himself," Jamaica said once the waitress had withdrawn. "Don't. Waste of energy."

He was fresh out of angles of attack.

"We go to so much trouble to prove stuff to ourselves," he said. "Then, once we've settled, we change the rules and have to start all over again." His gaze clouded, looking through her, not at her. His eyes were like the front windows of the Bottomless Cup—full up with storm. "You know dinosaurs? You got the Brontosaurus. Everybody's happy until some guy decides to more properly name it Apatosaurus. Doesn't *change* what it is. Used to be they couldn't prove why a bee flies. It's totally un-aerodynamic, yet you and I both know it flies. So they spend tons of money and they finally prove *why* it flies. Big goddamn deal for all the difference that made. Now they're knocking down bigger rules—Schrödinger's Cat, Occam's Razor. All riffs on the same basic take. If a tree falls over in the woods, does it make a noise? Would it matter whether there was a human being around to document this? Would it have even hit the ground at all if Newton hadn't given a name to gravity?"

He was upset and babbling. It wasn't designed to track, but Jamaica thought she had grabbed the gist.

"Record this in Dolby stereo, J.B." She nailed him full bore with the potent green of her eyes. "Shit happens. Sometimes with no explanation. Dingdongs call it 'God's will.' They hate thinking, is why. It's possible to not think about anything. Just listen to Whip Hand records and eat at McDonald's and never make a wave. But—hear me, now—you can also think things to death. Just as bad as not thinking at all. And if rehashing Jonathan over and over is just going to cause you to blame yourself, what's the point? Shit happens."

His eyes were downcast, evasive.

"Repeat after me: *Shit happens.*"

His voice leveled off. "Shit...happens."

"Now we're getting somewhere."

A heavy gust bowed the windows and the lights flickered, dunking the restaurant in gray. Everyone stopped eating. Ms. Sparrow, two booths down, said a swear word.

"More shit is happening." Bash's eyes indicated the ceiling tubes.

The blizzard's next big buffet caused Ms. Sparrow to flinch and drop her water glass. The windows were inundated by white-out. Nothing out there but churning cold and a world of hurt.

The radio playing in the kitchen went dead as the power was knocked down to stay down, this time.

"Have a refill," Jamaica suggested. "I think we're stuck here for the duration."

Thirty

"Have to. Leave here."

Cruz forgot. Whatever he might have cried upon seeing the dark figure awaiting him in the tunnel, he lost any memory of it the second it had traversed his lips. His mind tried to resist filling with what he could see in the bilious light.

The shadowman took another broken-boned step, its shredded gloves radiating the organic green glow, one hand a switchblade, the other a razor. From half a face, Jonathan's unmistakable green eyes assessed him.

Cruz's eyes tried to avert. No go there, either.

"Jonathan...?"

The motorcycle jacket was alive with decay, rust-caked, the spikes and pins securing the sundered denim and rotten leather all scarified to the junkyard brown of obsolescence. Within the flaps and tatters of leather was the pale lambency of morgue flesh and the dull russet of stale blood.

Another eye, watery blue, was jammed into the sagging bread dough of one cheek, where the flaccid tissue was about to smother it. The crosscut mess of the throat housed more eyes amid its folds and incisions and fissures. An aquamarine one blazed like a wet diamond. A deep brown one seemed to be dying. One with a cataract of pink blood winked at Cruz. Chameleonic, they all monitored different aspects of this intruder's disposition.

There was only the echo of breathing in the tunnel. It was solely Cruz, panting in short, choppy breaths etched with a distant cocaine wheeze. The figure confronting him drew no air. When it spoke its vocal cords buzzed, a rattle of dry desert air across brittle petals of dead flesh. Cruz could see slime glurting from the down-twisted gash of mouth. It looked as if this creature was speaking, coughing, and vomiting yogurt all at once.

"Cruz." It flooded its chin.

A bloody hank of snow-white hair sprouted where there should have been an ear. A strip of orange punk bristle, up top, was denuded by patches of exposed skull, shiny and scabbed.

"Jonathan?"

"Not." It choked. The yogurt flew enriched with stringers of blood. It took another step and Cruz could see the long pinky fingernail on the switchblade hand.

"Far enough." Cruz had gotten his wits and hauled out the Sig Sauer.

The creature rippled. No other way to describe it. Cruz saw its entire surface shimmy, as if it were an envelope of dead flesh packed with busy bugs.

He had to catch his balance. Had the floor shifted or was the coke doing him dirty?

"You gave," said the puzzlebox corpse. "Give again."

Okay, he'd crested out for sure and wasn't really seeing any of this. Not for real. He hurt. All he wanted was *out.*

"Give," the thing repeated. Cruz knew the voice. It was a zombie mockery of every whining schoolkid who couldn't pony up for this week's dime of crack.

One ragged talon rose to plunge the switchblade into the tunnel wall. The metal parted like porkfat as it was sliced in a bleeding vertical line.

Blood began to pool around the creature's crusted combat boots.

Give. Cruz could ask *give what.* He could waste even more time.

It extended its other arm. The razor bit into the wall to Cruz's left, slicing deep. Cruz shuddered, thinking of Emilio's hobby again.

The tunnel floor was vanishing under a sheen of blood as the long cuts in the wall continued to void.

"Give now."

Jonathan's rucksack held most of the surviving kilo and one more clip for the gun, yet unloaded. That kilo was his whole idealized future, wrapped up tight in waterproof plastic. He wasn't sure he wanted to relinquish this particular pot of gold, and so he gave. With the pistol.

His own incoherent howl was lost in the jackhammer noise of gunfire. His torn finger pulled the trigger again and again and he watched holes appear in the thing with Jonathan's eyes. Pulverized meat jumped free and pattered into the skim of blood.

Cruz fired and fired...

One cheekbone, the one without the eye, vaporized to cloud the dank air. A scoop of worm-ridden fat tore free of the neck and splattered the wall next to the razor gash. One knob of shoulder smithereened to powdered leather and mummy dust. A brown eye popped like a ripe zit.

...and fired and fired and...

It made a hissing little snort with each impact, not even staggering. One flattened Luger round from this gun could turn your hand into pâté. The thing stood and jerked as it sucked up each shot.

...the Sig Sauer's action jammed full back. Empty.

"Give now."

Cruz knew he had more bullets. What a funny; this thing would probably even grant him time to reload.

"Give you what?" It was lame. Dumb.

The creature merely extended its switchblade hand, palm up.

Cruz could give, and meld with the jigsaw monster. Give everything. Or he could give, and conceivably escape. His reservations about Emilio began to look a mite silly.

"You show me the way out of here, and I'll give."

The creature turned left and sank both bladed hands into the fissure begun with Edgar Ransome's straight razor. It pulled the rim wide and the incision tore crookedly, spouting darker jets of venous blood.

The narrow hole had been ripped to head height.

"Out."

"You mean I have to walk *into* that?"

"Out." It stepped back from its handiwork, blood-soaked and dripping. Cruz watched a steaming gob of the yogurt-stuff drip slowly down from the skull cavity to fill the bite removed from its neck by a bullet. It anchored and began to mesh and bind, patching the damage.

A new eye poked through the jellied mass like a surfacing periscope. Smaller than the others, and brown.

One of Mario Velasquez's eyes, Cruz realized.

"Give. Now."

The racketing oscillation of gunshots against metal made Fergus contract, hands over ears, prone in the tunnel. Violence was taking place just around the next turn.

Between that and him his pet had been coiled sleeping, logy and unresponsive from too much of a good thing. It had fed several times outside of Fergus' supervision, and was presently twice the girth he'd ever seen it before. It barely fit the tunnel. That could become a major problem.

But the venom, the stuff that brought on wet dreams without compare, *that* would be at an efficacy Fergus had never before experienced. The sensual feast would almost justify the bother.

At first he thought some invader was discharging bullets to wound his pet. The acoustics were all wrong. The shots came from further down the tunnel, around the curve. So difficult to tell, with all this metal, and the oozing brown bulk of his pet blocking passage.

Even the shots did not stir it, and Fergus had to pound on its tail end to bring it around.

He had not counted on its mood. The torpedo head slithered from beneath the tail coil, and it bit Fergus. Harder, probably, than it intended. But it had just been rudely knocked up, and had lashed out.

Fergus tried to retreat from the bite. No room to maneuver. He saw his drowsy and annoyed pet slide around on itself, breaking up the sleep coils. Fergus had backed off about five yards when the venom piled into his nervous system like a train wreck.

It was what he imagined an overdose of pleasure might feel like. He would have preferred to be on his bed, or in his familiar office chair, instead of banging his head against metal the first time orgasm cut through his stomach. But it was beyond his options to be picky just now.

At least he had located his pet, which did not seem anxious to lose him again.

Fergus trembled. The juice took hold and his eyes filled with brain pictures.

He probably only imagined he saw his pet crawling right into the sheer metal wall of the tunnel. *That* was crazy.

Thirty-One

Come on, addled rodent fuck. Just a bit more.

An antique Italian armoire stood tall at the end of the hallway leading to Bauhaus' color-coordinated bedroom collection. People paid obscene prices for such things, only to retrofit them as bars and buffets; upscale liquor cabinets. Emilio had found this one to be stocked with guns.

Now he drew a short-barreled Wilson Arms Witness Protection shotgun, a heavily-modified version of the trusty Remington 870. This one had rubberized assault grips and a ventilated rib. His free hand supported Bauhaus, whom he'd had to dress for the cold. Bauhaus carried no weapons. No way. Sooner would Emilio trust a burp gun to a drunk Nazi at a Jesse Jackson rally. Or give an ICBM to a Republican.

A galaxy of felony chemical was playing suicide thrash inside Bauhaus' skin today. Red giant, white dwarf, burnout. But he had managed to note that Jamaica would most likely try to warn Cruz, and Emilio needed a native guide.

The riot gun's shorty magazine held two rounds of triple-ought Magnum buckshot alternated with two rifled "Sluggers"—a third was already chambered—making the whole package a very ugly thing to be on the wrong end of. Emilio wasn't into drug dealer guns.

He had slotted in each round thinking of what they would do to Cruz's face. First Jamaica, then Cruz.

One more set of stairs, and Bauhaus could be shucked as well. He was dead already and too high to know it.

Cold pierced to chill the platinum razor against his chest. Once the shotgun stopped them, the razor could kill them. So slowly.

Emilio licked his lips. The silence of the building was acute. His heart thudded at combat speed, goosed by a double belt of crank. His brain raced with humiliation. The shame, as he had been untied by Bauhaus' security guards, who knew a whore had foxed him. Naked, trussed, his own socks in his mouth. He had been unmanned and robbed of his cash. Robbed but not broke.

And there was nothing more worthless than a dead prostitute.

The sentries had come piling in with MAC 10s and Ithaca pumps unslung. There was nobody left to shoot. Bauhaus squirmed and hollered while he received first aid, then vomited into the bar sink twice. Emilio mixed him a special calm-down cocktail, stirring mystic powders into a glass of Perrier. The concoction would sideswipe the overload of dope Jamaica had compelled Bauhaus to swallow. A few moments and one more visit to the sink, and Bauhaus told Emilio he was straight enough to go hunting.

He was still telling him. Naggingly, like a whining child. *No but really I am.*

Emilio had ordered a pair of backups to stand down on the first floor. Their guns were enormous, too, and well made. Begrudgingly they assumed their posts and Emilio took Bauhaus up alone. This was personal, a matter of sullied honor.

He acknowledged a chance, however slim, that he might *not* get the big come of killing both the whore and his sleaze weasel ex-runner. Only if he was beaten and dying would he summon his cavalry.

"307. It's his." Bauhaus' eyes were beginning to track independently of each other.

"Keep your voice down." Emilio hoisted him ahead. He'd be good as a shield, if nothing else.

"Wanna *gun.*"

"Shut the fuck up."

As soon as Emilio released his arm Bauhaus sat down hard, as though bonked on the noggin. They both heard a door close on the floor just above them. Footsteps in a big hurry, thumping toward them around the close turns of Fergus the landlord's rickety landing.

When the black kid rounded the turn he saw a shotgun concentrating on filling his nostrils. He jammed to a stop with the fear of a bust bright in his eyes. He had a sling bag over each shoulder and was not in a social mood.

"Awww, *shit.*"

It was comic but Emilio wasn't set to chortle. "Who the fuck are you? Say now."

"I'm Ajax and I'm moving *out* as of now. I ain't gonna stay here. Too fuckin' many people with guns pointing at me all the time. I don't wanna get shot and dead; I wanna *leave.* Please." He shrugged. "That's about it."

Emilio's voice was kept low, resonant, invisible. "I want Cruz." The bore of the riot gun stayed where it was and Ajax started perspiring.

"Don't know him, man, listen, I got to—"

"Wrong answer." The gun got ready to do something other than protect a Witness.

"Uh." Ajax's reality was hastily redefined in terms of *big moby gun.* "Cruz. Right. Brown motherfucker. Like you. I mean, one of them Hispanic dudes, right? Black jacket, like a, uh, whatcha call 'em...army jacket, y'know? He's number 307. I seen him a little while ago. He's got a goddamned gun too. Pointed it at me, too."

"Where upstairs?"

"Right off the landing. Right around the corner, man. It's like, I look out to see what all this motherfuckin *noise* is and I..."

"Keep your voice down."

"Yeah, right, and I, uh, seen all this *hardware*, all this firepower, man, and I say to myself, I cannot *deal*, 'cos guns scare me, y'know, and I get *confused*, and..."

"Fuck off."

There was just enough room for Ajax to skin past and embrace whatever life awaited him outside of Kenilworth. With him went Cruz's tape player and camera, stolen a while back from 307, which had been left open and empty.

Ajax hit the foyer and fled into the backslapping fronts of
snow. Even the worst blizzard in ten years was preferable to the
brand of white-boy lunacy he'd just ducked.

It was the evil opposite of birth. Anti-birth.

Cruz squeezed through headfirst in a spurt of blood and
discharged necrotic tissue, anointed in smegmatic ichor that
glowed the same color as the coating in the tunnels.

He emerged into the last place Kenilworth remembered him
to be, inside of Jonathan's apartment. Mistaken data. Who knew
from accuracy in matters such as these?

It was a disaster area of staved-in cartons and strewn possessions. The eastern window, facing Kentmore, had been
totally destroyed; a pyramidal hummock of snow was rising on
the floor. The dresser mirror was fogged with the cold. Blood
gleamed from the walls.

Cruz located a towel and mopped at his face. The jellied
mucous clung tenaciously, prohibiting his pores from drawing
any of the fouled air. It reeked of liquid putrefaction. He had
been tackled by the Blob and slimed. It hung like setting gel in
his hair when he raked fingers back through it.

Christ, but this place had been *wrecked*.

The walls had skewed inward. The ceiling had bowed down
far enough for Cruz to bump his head on the light fixture. The
place was unstable and hazardous. He heard water dripping.

When the black cat rubbed against his leg, he nearly threw
a clot.

You have got gook all over you.

Cruz jumped; the shock was a physical pain deep in his
head. How could that be? The brain wasn't supposed to have
any nerves to *feel* pain.

Irate, he refused to tread air in this rat-trap, talking
meaninglessly to a cat and waiting for another tremor to
collapse the entire building. His system was flying loops with
the White Lady; he wished he had the leisure to suck some base
and flower out. He did remember to load the Sig Sauer's spare
magazine.

Then he remembered to put it into the gun.

The dope had been lost, but not the battle. At least he was packed.

His wheezy respiration, his slurred speech had been left behind with the tunnels. He felt amped and in regained control. Back in Dade there had been pals of his—Cobalt, Dice, Klondike—who did five grams a day and pulled *guns* on anybody who talked back. Uncool. Very.

Voices in the hallway. Clumping on the stairs.

He eased around the inside door of the airlock. The cat persisted in pushing through first.

"Piss off, comewad," he whispered.

You smell just lover-ly your ownself, big guy.

Cruz snapped the action—silently—and opened the exterior door to 207, stepping out.

Ajax thundered away in a mondo hurry. Smart people did that when you pointed ordnance at their heads. Even idiots, sometimes.

"Straight. Bet your fucking life I am."

Bauhaus was on the spoil. Emilio's hangover cocktail could do only so much patch work before it was rinsed away by the gusher of drugs presently altering Bauhaus' state at instant-replay speed.

"Shut up."

There was no movement in the second floor hallway. Emilio backed into the turn and swung through, bringing the riot gun to bear on the unknown space. Nada. His eyes moved in synchronization with the bore, sweeping.

The elevator dinged and slid up stable. Emilio spun on it and almost cut loose a round.

The car was vacant. Bloodstains inside.

He backtracked to Bauhaus, still sitting on the stairs, before this whacked-out fun-daddy could start feeling genuine pain and cutting some ruckus.

Emilio assumed the third floor units were configured identically to those on the second floor.

Bauhaus stopped on the landing and slumped where there was more room to sit. He looked like a whipped and pouting child; a whiner. Emilio thought, *for my lack of a silencer, you get to live a while longer.*

He wasn't thinking of the shotgun, but of his backup piece, a matte-finish Bren Ten also selected from the armoire. Only a fool strolls in without a fallback, and he had two staggered box-column clips full of humungous ten-millimeter ammo.

Two guns. Two clips. Thirteen steps. Two primary targets. One secondary plus improvisation. The oranges-and-apples mathematics of firefighting and tactical ops equals so much dead meat. Emilio always tried to score one hundred on his tests.

He hugged the wall. Tight but a clear field.

"Make her eat her own tits," Bauhaus mumbled behind him. "Chomp, chomp, such a fancy meal. Fucking *cunt.*"

He saw the outer door to 307 hanging open. He closed in on it and lifted the knob so the door would not scrape back audibly as he entered.

The figure standing in the room turned as Emilio booted the inner door wide and cut loose with the shotgun. By the time the shooting started downstairs, he was too busy to hear it.

The damned cat had to dart out ahead of him. Goddamned animals, Cruz thought. Little booger-flicking monster.

Bauhaus was already staring in his direction, his attention drawn by the cat, and here was Cruz stuck dead bang, framed in the doorway to 207.

Sugar-tit son of a bitch! He should have kicked its black puckerhole down the elevator shaft when he'd had the chance.

If Bauhaus had drawn down on him it would have been lights out. When the fat man got angry instead of western, Cruz realized he was unarmed.

He also got a closer look, in that instant, at Rosie's best Chi-town bud. Bauhaus looked freshly rolled from the compacting bin of a garbage truck. His clothing was askew; all wrong for someone so natty and fastidious. His eyeballs hung in caverns of purple darkness. His face was the color of bread dough misted with fever sweat. Cruz smelled fresh feces in the air.

Bauhaus sat there and tittered.

"You look like shit, kiddo." Blood antiqued his dentition.

You double. Cruz neglected to speak.

"You are a lot of fucking trouble, my laddie. You are death. Why pick me?"

Now was the opportunity to declaim, to testify, to bring home to this bloated leech some of the agony he had paid out. Cruz could not locate a single word. He couldn't even make his facial muscles editorialize for him. He raised the Sig Sauer a foot from his ex-boss' veiny nose.

Bauhaus had already lost command of most below-the-neck motor functions. He could still loll like a beached bass, and flop the aimless paddles of his hands. His stink was bovine, primitive, and his gaze was the zombie stare of a sheep watching the oncoming sledgehammer.

"Shit punk." A spasm twisted his head to the left. "Gahhh." His tongue was gray and inflated.

Cruz thumbed back the hammer of the automatic. He wanted no secret codes, no confessions. He was not starved for a neat homily that could right his world at the last minute. He pointed the gun. It was all he had to do.

"What are you waiting for?"

Cruz swallowed. So dry, his mouth. That would be all the dope. Yeah.

Dope. *That was how Bauhaus looked—strung out to the max. Blood and brain cells were dying by the millions in there. His mind was slamming shutters.* CLOSED: SORRY WE MISSED YOU. *His head would burst like a cantaloupe from the internal pressure.*

Capillaries were rupturing in Bauhaus' eyes, making their sclera the red glass tint that Cruz remembered from the Corvette. Soon his vascular plumbing would fill his lungs with blood and he'd drown from the inside out.

Bauhaus stared down the barrel of the automatic. That prissy, pissy, put-upon expression Cruz knew so well resurfaced.

"You haven't got the dick." Pink froth speckled his lips. One nostril blew a languid bubble of saliva. "Lame. Limp. Dead meat. You're a corpse...and you don't even know it."

A horrid phlegmatic noise convulsed him briefly. Then he grinned with bloodied teeth. When he laughed in Cruz's face, foam slopped onto his chest.

Cruz shut his eyes and fired four times.

Emilio instantly tried to kill the creature he saw. His snap of the riot gun's trigger was instinctual, a survival reflex. The thing on the receiving end demanded to be erased from the earth. The good, sane earth of coke royalty, drug addiction and murder for comedy.

The "Slugger" round blew a baseball-sized hole through the upper left tit and made a wide, messy exit. The northern casement behind it was noisily terminated and a sleetstorm of glass knifed into the room, followed by the equally cutting attack of the blizzard.

The thing grunted. The foot-poundage of the slug knocked it back one step. It looked up at Emilio as though it had just been hit with a turd snowball. Pique misted all of its eyes.

Emilio skipped simple shock, pumping and firing again. The buckshot round hit with the force of ten thirty-eight caliber bullets all at point blank range. Shreds of clothing and flesh erupted in a violent rearward spray. The hair on the back of the creature's head twitched and wet stuff hit the wall.

Emilio could see through its chest, and it was still standing there. He saw the eyes, too many and in the wrong places. He saw the blood dipped switchblade, then the razor.

Fresh hot blood began to issue from the pellet holes in the wallpaper. Blood leaked from the casement to mar the fangs of glass still depending from the frame. It steamed in the furious cold.

Emilio shucked and fired for every step it took toward him, snarling an incoherent warcry. When the magazine ran dry the thing was reaching for his throat.

Emilio felt his shoulders hit the corner, felt his trigger elbow knock the door shut. He had not been aware that he had been backing away. He did not back off from anything. Still thinking artillery would rescue his ass, he cross-drew the Bren Ten as one black claw vised around his neck.

He snapped the trigger professionally, then convulsively, until the pain made him stop.

There was no leeway to puzzle what this thing could be, *how* it could be, or how it absorbed bullets like hand lotion. Emilio did not know it. It seemed to know Emilio, though.

Pain in his throat. His shoes were off the floor. He felt his neck muscles herniate, dark patches of his own blood blossoming beneath his flesh.

His hand found the platinum razor beneath his shirt, jerked the special chain. His thumb levered open the blade and he began to slash into the rotten chest and neck.

Spitting into one of its eyes would have been as effective.

The face leering into Emilio's own was an inept quiltwork of components—nose, eyes, mouth—disrupted by a diagonal fissure. Topside the flesh was pale, mottled with liver spots. The eye was a murky green. The other eye was a turquoise color, poked into mulatto flesh. Another eye in the left cheek was bright blue.

Emilio could only reach to the thing's neck, where his razor bisected the gray eye of an old woman. Vitreous humor spurted like snot. His vision was beginning to flower with snaps of bright yellow light. He tried to kick but could not feel his legs.

In the dresser mirror he saw his own face turning maroon, eyes bulging whitely. He saw other portions of himself through the perforated torso of the monster holding him up against the wall.

The switchblade, growing from the hand that gripped his neck, sniffed toward his carotid artery and began to press. The thing was hacking back with its own razor now, as Emilio's thrusts and death-dealing surgery weakened.

An arm, baby-sized, snaked from the thing's chest cavity and arrested Emilio's razor hand, python-tight.

Emilio felt himself opening up downstairs.

Fuckers. The world was choking on fuckers all lined up to take from him. His whole life. All takers.

Hydrostatic pressure unmoored his eyes. He saw, in the mirror, jets of blood shoot from his ears and nostrils. He died two seconds after he was blinded.

The monster released its deathgrip on Emilio's neck, and began taking, and taking, and taking.

As Cruz pulled the trigger of the automatic he heard powerful gunfire upstairs. None of his business. He had his mind and hands full just shooting at Bauhaus.

ONE: *Chiquita wobbling barefoot on the rail, just out of reach as she teeters, then turns the fall graceful by pretending it's a high-board dive.* TWO: *She falls, arms swanned, the whole descent more fearsome because she doesn't make a sound all the way to the concrete.* THREE: *He rushes to the rail, leans, follows her with his gaze, tracking her like a NASA dish all the way to splashdown. His mind tries to force his eyes not to look. It is impossible to turn away from—*

FOUR: *Impact.*

The shooting above comes faster, panic fire, then stops altogether. The sound is submerged in the riptide echoes of Cruz's own gunfire. The shots are nearly simultaneous.

Chiquita's bikini bottom, the only thing she is wearing, snaps apart when she hits. Her ebony hair spreads to corona her head. She lands face down, twisted; Cruz can see her naked ass from ten stories up.

"*You're probably wasted and stupid enough to jump off, Chiqui. Go on. I dare ya.*"

Bauhaus' damning gaze had dared him to shoot, and he did. Four times.

When Cruz opened his eyes he saw Bauhaus cringing, his body trying to roll into a ball like a dung beetle. He was quivering, eyes gone in tight wrinkles of closure that leaked tears. His mouth was soundlessly agape.

Four bullet holes formed an arc in the wall just above his head. They began to bleed.

Shivering, his hands bunched beneath his chain, Bauhaus opened his eyes. Cruz was still standing there with the gun, and that was the worst scenario he could envision. It made him want to cry even more.

"Bang," Cruz said, and Bauhaus flinched as though shot in the ass.

The red-lipped bullet punctures tore. Bleeding cracks in the wall stretched to connect with each other. The sound was mealy and meaty. Blood dripped to soak Bauhaus' winter coat.

"You're not worth it," Cruz said.

He was not a killer. He was not to blame for the death of Chiqui, or anyone.

"Hear me? You're not worth my time or ammo, Bauhaus."

Bauhaus was easing back into the wall. Being swallowed by it, as the cracks connected and sagged away. His eyes had rolled to whites; it was unlikely that he could even hear Cruz's big discovery as his head was engulfed.

"Hey! You're not worth it!" His lips were peeled back. Bravery had rolled in too late, as usual. Now it did not matter.

Bauhaus had cheated him one last time. When Cruz had finally worked up the spit to yell, Bauhaus was beyond hearing his comeuppance.

Cruz hung around long enough to see the first coil of Kenilworth's resident parasite loop around Bauhaus' midsection, to pull him into the wall like a hooked fish. The greasy dun-colored body slid and cinched. Bauhaus died with his mouth hanging open and his pants full of shit. The drugs probably put him under before he felt much pain, or before the beast could bite.

Cruz backed down the stairs and ran for the next landing. The flight impulse ruled his whole body, even atop the overdose of coke poisoning him.

Home free, he thought as he barreled down the last set of stairs.

Down in the eastern foyer of Kenilworth, the side of the building facing the street where Bauhaus' deceased hit man, Marko, lay entombed in snow, Cruz found that the doors and windows of the building had been forgotten.

Mailboxes. A bulb on a dangling cord. No windows, no grate and no front door.

There was no way out.

After the creature with Jonathan's eyes appropriated Emilio's, it rose as erect as its crooked carriage would permit.

The baby arm protruding from its chest relinquished Emilio's platinum razor for inspection. The arm withdrew and the head poked through the chew and swallow with its hundred teeth.

The creature turned the razor over in its own razor hand. Amalgamating with this prize seemed superfluous. More than needed had been taken all around this time; more blood than the building could use, more of the extra new ingredient Cruz had willingly provided.

Emilio's forehead bulged, puffy with black blood. When the creature pressed the razor's tip into the forehead, the gelid flesh split from internal pressure in one big squirt of red. The blade wandered through the flesh and decided to carve letters there.

The narrow tusks in the baby face tore a hole in Emilio's shirt, then his chest. It began to worry morsels loose. Children need protein.

So much was fading to vapor. The hand wielding the razor faltered. Blood trickled from the forehead to fill the eyesockets and spill downward.

EAT M

That was all it could remember.

When the smaller head finished its last three bites of heartmeat, it withdrew into the chest. Tiny hands poked through to knot the shreds of jacket. Another parasite.

There was enough lampcord in the room to suspend Emilio upside-down, for better drainage. Of what the building wanted to do next, the creature had no clue. It would return to its room, close the door, wait. It kept Emilio's razor; perhaps a use would occur.

Vague recollections, also fading, saddened the monster. It wanted to go out into the night. To ride the trains again.

Thirty-Two

*K*enilworth Arms has never felt this way before.

Tonight its gluttony has allowed it the perception of time's passage, from one second to the next. The amplified awareness is excruciating.

For the first and final time, the building gains a notion of just how aged it really is.

From the basement up...doors meld with their seams and blend into the walls, assuming a uniform hue in accordance with the paint used by the caretaker. Injurious glass is sneezed free of window frames, which then darken and unite the same way they did, by accident, in Elvie Rojas' apartment, early on. Settling cracks close themselves. Stray blood is giddily osmosed. Ruptured brickwork fuses whole again. The lines and details of decades of makeshift architecture flow into one another until there is an uninterrupted sameness to the surfaces.

In moments the entire structure clenches, airtight.

The errant black cat is nearly decapitated as it pads from an icebox door which slams by itself and fades out, embracing the featureless symmetry of the ground floor corridors.

These hallways are now very hallway. Totally hallway, pure, unadorned.

The elevator doors smash shut with the speed of clapping hands. The joins differentiating door from shaft and car from floor blur and are gone. Very wall.

Kenilworth has forgotten most of its own third floor. Entire sections are blanked. There comes a vague, gnatlike pain impossible *for it to register as the remaining tenants, running low on oxygen and beating in terror on walls that no longer have doors or windows.*

Presiding over this is the numbness, such a high, so dreamy.

Kenilworth's hallucinatory misremembrance of itself is only a dream. Parts of itself flinch or make ghost movements, just as people do when having a nightmare.

It can feel the tapeworm, fattened beyond all precedent. No matter. It has provided.

So good, this feeling.

The cat senses deep in its brain that there is no wakening from this dream. With a growing urgency, it begins to seek a way out. In another moment it will be frantic.

Cruz was staring directly at the gangbox of mail drops when all the thin metal doors sprang open at once to regurgitate their contents.

The instant the front door and windows had ceased to exist, the omnipresent noise of the blizzard outside dwindled. In the sudden and engulfing quiet Cruz could hear movement, massive, elemental movement, like tectonic plates warming up to work some creative topography. The floor buckled and shoved him closer to the ceiling. He kept his balance but banged his injured arm one more time. His vision was beginning to lag visibly whenever he turned his head to follow something.

Flyers, crap mail and coupon books hit the slanting floor like a thrown deck of playing cards. From the slot numbered 307—Cruz's apartment—a shiny object fell to clatter floorward and slide according to the changing whims of gravity in this insane place.

It was, Cruz saw, Emilio's platinum straight razor.

It might as well have been Emilio himself. Just add blood and he inflates to full size, eyes afire with vendetta, rips out your fucking heart and slaps you in the face with it.

Cruz's brain did a fast rewind that made him dizzy. Bauhaus had showed up. Emilio had been here, too. How had he been lucky enough to miss that number?

Was Emilio still here, and headed for the front door, as

Cruz had been before the door decided to take a time out?

He moved like a landlubber on a rolling deck to retrieve the razor. It was the only thing that had ever appeared in his mailbox in which he held the slightest interest. He did not receive such deliveries at home.

When he lifted it closer, his thoughts of the thing with Jonathan's eyes dissipated. He had seen the razor growing right out of the flesh of its hand. This was not that razor. Definitely Emilio's.

His body informed him that he could not stay on his feet very much longer. He had already done enough coke to bring on the wheezing, the pallor, and he had finally passed out. That he was up and moving now only meant an intermission.

He levered open the razor. There was blood on it, on the chain, on the blade, on the handle, all over it. That was all he could see before the power quit and he was thrown headlong into mineshaft blackness.

The dark was sudden and total. No daylight; not even the pale radiance of snow or the sickly green of the decay on the face of the thing with Jonathan's eyes.

If the razor had not been a last-ditch gift from whatever remained of the original Jonathan, Cruz would consider it such, knowing straight mortal history would never give a shit either way.

He groped toward where the front door had been and imbedded the razor, plunging deep and hacking himself an emergency passage, hoping that the skewed rules remained in force for ten seconds more.

In the darkness, sinking his arm into that wet incision was like feeling up the innards of a beef carcass. He pushed his good arm in as far as he could. When he hit shoulder depth, he felt cold.

Cruz got a grip on the outside edge and began to feed himself to the hole he had sliced open. Tepid fluids splurted into his face. He got a mouthful of what he fancied to be the gooey yogurt slime. He got his chest in as the floor lurched behind him and tried to snap his leg.

This was crazy, he thought as he pulled himself into the

moist tissue, feeling it trying to heal, to close and seal him up forever. This was nuts. This was something you did on a game show so they gave you cash.

This was a major shitstorm, and he was sucking it up both nostrils. Poor Rosie.

A slit of brain-numbing white. Like looking into the sun. He pulled himself toward it.

The freezing cold attacked the moisture on his hand. The stinging pain was almost a relief; an affirmation of life. He came through, his effort akin to a one-armed pull-up from a tar pit. The snow welcomed him with blinding brightness and pain and soul-killing cold.

He had no idea where he had emerged. Everything was inundated in glacial pack, and the blowing snow reduced eyesight range to his own hand in front of his own face. He watched it ice up in an instant.

When he tried to clench his fist it cracked. His wounds from the elevator reopened and red declared itself against all the whiteness.

Somewhere within a five-block radius was Weedwine, the Bottomless Cup, and Jamaica, tapping her foot and thinking all this rendezvous business was strictly James Bond time. She probably had a cup of hot coffee and a newspaper; read what evolved newswise in the real world during more personal adventures.

Behind Cruz the fissure lanced upward and its peak was finally lost in the fogbanks of whirling snow that hid the top of the building. He had started a crack that tried valiantly to split the entire Kentmore face of the structure. The viridescent glow was just barely discernible. You had to be right next to the building to see it emitting from the fissure. Cruz wanted away from it, and thus never saw it.

Each step away from Kenilworth sank Cruz to the knees in new snow, a bog of adherent crystals that mired his boots and sought to abrade his eyes until they were opaque and unseeing. He slung his free arm ahead, an animal trying to bludgeon down nature. He waded, emplanting each step and dragging himself forward to the next, the bee-like swarm of blowing particles skinning into his eyes with a malevolence more than a mere turn of climate.

Everything outside of the building was buried in snow to regulation cemetery depth, plus a few feet extra. Insurance, perhaps, that the corpses here would never rise.

Cruz whanged his arm hard on a streetlamp pole. Affixed above was a sign sealed up in a caul of ice. He was pretty sure this was the corner of Kentmore and Garrison. Pretty sure.

The stone pole rose like a giant stalagmite of ice, a straight, true fang. By hugging it Cruz could keep the blow out of his eyes for a few crucial seconds.

The moment he squeezed them shut they flooded with harsh tears and froze solid. When he peeled the ice away, skin came with it. New dots of blood froze instantly around his eyes.

He had to sit down.

This was dangerous going. You could get lost ten feet from your own stoop, if the blizzard was ornery enough. The wind chill factor could knock the cold down to sixty or seventy below zero under the right conditions. That could steal your core heat in a matter of minutes. Or your body would run out of water trying to generate warmth. You would dehydrate to nothing about the time your fingers and toes released themselves to the anesthetic of frostbite. Tissue crystallizes and dies, becoming the same autopsy color as the bleeding walls of the building.

Cruz used Emilio's razor to hack at the snow near his waist. The platinum edge punched through crust to softer layers of pack. He had heard of people hastily carving themselves little igloos and waiting out storms of half this ferocity.

When he sat, he had to rest. He had slashed himself clear of the building. That was what mattered. The blizzard was just an inconvenience; everyone in Chicago treated blizzards that way. Minor setback.

The coating of bloodslime he had gained by oozing through the moist fissure linked up and scabbed solid. Every movement of his broke ice.

More than anything, he had to rest before he could continue beating the odds.

He regretted the loss of his dogtags. Without them no one

would know who he was. No identity. Emilio's razor was scant compensation, even though it had saved his life.

This is called irony, he thought.

Ever since Chiquita's death Cruz had feared that his last sight, before dying, would be Emilio's razor.

He turned out to be right. But he was no longer afraid.

Cruz dreamed of being nothing, a thing with no identity. Like water, clear and pure and guiltless. There would not even be clothes to be found, come spring and the thaw.

The worst blizzard of the decade did not ease off until after dawn of the following day.

Thirty-Three

A manda Roberti took one look at the blizzard through the cameo glass of her front door, and made a face. No mail run *today*, she thought.

Mail was important to Amanda. She generally made two trips a day to the Oakwood station, knowing that the postal workers were there around the clock, sorting and bagging and filling each PO box as new material came into their grasp. Amanda ran a mail-order clipping service out of her home, and mail was her lifeline.

The downside was that there was no social life to be derived from her job, as other people, even postal workers, seemed to enjoy as a fringe benefit of a normal life.

Snow was piling up on her front porch. Even through the latched storm door she could feel the pulse of the cold, its insistent invitation to come out and suffer.

Behind her a branch crackled in the fireplace. Earlier in the fall she had collected all the twigs and deadwood from the trees in her backyard, hoarding them beneath a tarpaulin on the back porch for firemaking. The fireplace was modest but the tiles were vivid; it lent both heat and light to her tiny living room.

Most of the upstairs was given over to the stacks of paperwork that defined her job. Magazines in Chicago and New York remunerated her nicely for keeping an open eye and a ready pair of scissors. Amanda Roberti was one woman who was never short on newspaper.

She slept in the downstairs bedroom. She lived downstairs and worked upstairs. She appreciated the clear-cut separation of job and...

What social life? she asked herself again.

Her own ghost, in the translucent reflection of the cameo glass, helped her ask.

She had tilted back the lace drape on the cameo door with a pencil, since her nails were still wet. Sculpted nails, perfect polish, undercoat plus lacquer—who had the time to make their nails so perfect? Only people who were never seen.

The only color the glass held was the color of her eyes, a striking cornflower blue. Cruz had noticed them right off. Amanda had forgotten Cruz.

Twenty-nine years old, and already so much gray in her curly black hair. It was a family thing. All the kids were full of gray by thirty. Her younger sister, Jenna, had gone *white* before she was out of high school. Her hair was full and healthy, but it was totally white. Jenna was sometimes called Jean the way Amanda was called Amy, a name she hated, and one that nonetheless stuck through most of her primary education.

Amanda got the grades. Jenna got the dates.

Each of them had been given a home by their parents—a catch was, of course, that it was a home near where *they* lived, over in Russett Run. Jenna had sold hers as soon as the papers cleared, taken the cash and fled to Colorado. Occasionally she phoned from Boulder or Denver or someplace she had side-tripped. The calls petered out. Now Amanda usually got a call on her birthday. Jenna hadn't bothered to show up for the last three Christmas to-dos.

Amanda's house represented a certain security and stability. She had her backyard and her porch and her driveway. She did her nails perfectly. Seams always lay straight when she made her expeditions to the market or the post office or her parents' house. Here she had her job and her books and her fireplace and hot tea to keep the cold at bay. Cable TV was her window to the world. Installation had been a Christmas gift from her parents. When she got a car she would make the first payments with the help of her parents.

She was a spinster, almost thirty, and sometimes she thought that Jenna wasn't so crazy after all.

She dreams of getting away. At her age she has begun to

admit to herself that dreams don't necessarily represent future reality. She needs to get away. That realization has done little, thus far, to buttress her resolve.

This state was not entirely her fault. She was attractive and had gone out with men. That had started happening later. College was as horizon-expanding as high school had been insular. No cliques, no hierarchies were to be found at the university. In college everyone started at zero.

She had not slept with a man until she was twenty-one. She did not sleep with another for more than a year. Then came a furious compensatory catch-up. Two more years. Then college was over.

Why were men so fucked up? She'd asked Jenna that once, after an evening brandy.

"Because people don't always act in the roles you cast them in," Jenna had told her.

Amanda thought about that one for a while. She liked to invest time in consideration. Weighing her options.

It was when she thought of her bed as a spinster's bed that she got flushed and wanted to break something.

She finally decided the problem did not rest with her. It was Chicago. So difficult to meet kind, eligible men here. Especially in dog weather like this.

Tea mug in hand, she watched the storm. Snow blew and whiteout ruled. No features, no details; it was impossible to see the huge apartment building down at the corner, which she knew to be red brick. Invisible now. She could easily fool her eye into believing the building had vanished entirely from this world. Nothing out there.

Steam from the mug fogged a tiny oval on the glass.

Her parents were no help, asking constantly who she was *seeing*, dear. The question waited like a live landmine in every phone call, every outwardly casual conversation. Goddamned if she was going to let them *intimidate* her into picking up with the wrong partner. When circumstances conspired to force an introduction, her parents usually hated the guy she was with. They never forgave her for "losing" one they had actually liked, a couple of years back.

Losing. As though Michael had been misfiled.

That was how the gentle lying had begun. Survival fibs, non-toxic, offered up for the preservation of her own sanity. She would indicate via assorted conversational subtleties that she *was* seeing someone, thanks for your concern, and yes, he was very nice, and then she would change the subject.

She fantasized itineraries for her imaginary dates, lending her parents just enough detail to make it sound real and offhanded. She knew how important details could be from all the newspapers she scanned and culled. Who, what, why, where, when and how all in the first paragraph. That was the sign of good reportage.

Lately her mother had begun pressing for more facts. She stored everything and never forgot anything.

Amanda held a latent fear of turning into her mother. Running to the opposite extreme was just as lethal.

No longer could Amanda's dream date be a mystery man. Mother would want a name in short order. Amanda would have to invent one soon.

She drew a quick breath of surprise. There was a black cat on her front porch. Its fur was caked with snow. It spotted her and somehow got to the porch. Tunneled, perhaps, avoiding the storm like a submarine avoids surface gales.

In an instant she had made the decision to let it in. It would die out there.

She threw bolts and undid hook latches. She was not prepared for how cold it actually was outside her door, away from her fire. The wind tried to hit her in the face with her own door and the temperature was arctic and frightening. The cat wasted no time jumping inside, and Amanda had to shoulder the door shut against the wind. She feared for the etched glass, which had misted over from this brief episode. If the storm door was to implode, that would be the end.

She locked up, hoping everything would hold until the storm abated.

The cat parked itself by the fireplace and began its licking ritual.

"Hi, kitty." It did not see her as a threat. "I bet you're hungry."

She brought it tuna from a single-serving can and some milk. It cleaned up, and purred when she lifted it. They rubbed noses like Eskimos.

"Guess you're going to want to hang around, now." Amanda knew what people said about cats, once you let them inside.

It was a male. She didn't know exactly what had compelled her to check.

Clearly there was little to do with this day other than staying close to the fire, making a nest of her comforter which her new cat would no doubt share, and curl up with more tea, some movies, maybe a fat, sleep-inducing novel which she could also page through in search of names to give to her fantasy beau.

When she found the name, it was direct, studious, classic. An American name. A normal name, though a touch academic in its full form. Yes.

She dozed of on her couch, feeling like she had actually accomplished something for the afternoon.

The cat was still around, making itself at home, when she woke up.

Camela was asleep.

The argument that had flooded into the wake of Bash's leave-taking from Rapid O'Graphics had been ugly and persistent. Certain details Bash did not wish to share, such as Jamaica, her whole story, and Jonathan's fate as reported by her, hung between Bash and his fiancée of record. Cammy wouldn't let go until she found out everything.

And if she got the whole unrated narrative...well, *that* was an LSD nightmare waiting to burst, wasn't it?

Camela was asleep, and so Bash felt safe in pulling from hiding the huge automatic pistol he'd kept from the wrestling match with Marko. He kept it hidden in his garment bag, along with two thousand dollars Jamaica had given him at the Bottomless Cup after they were done talking.

God, but she had been on the ball. She had walked him through nearly everything, from the loony-bin cartoon of events within Kenilworth to surefooted first aid in the coffee shop's bathroom.

The gun was an Auto Ordnance .41 Action Express loaded with Ultra-Mags. Quite the deadly mouthful, this gangster hardware. Bash had purchased a box of cartridges and spent a lot of late-night time working the action, checking the parts, loading and reloading the clip. The heft of the gun in his hand was awesome.

He had the phone number of Jamaica's machine but knew it was useless. She was long gone.

The money, she had told him, was for helping out. And because he was a friend of Jonathan's. Bash still wasn't completely sure how to track that.

"First time I've ever paid for a man," she had laughed. "Money, I mean."

He had smiled because he did not want to appear stupid. Feeling the energy transfer from someone like Jamaica could be unsettling enough.

He put the gun on the coffee table and finished his fourth Quietly beer of the evening. It was after midnight. He got so little time to himself at home, nowadays.

He had informed Camela that Jonathan had just left. Up and split, no note and no goodbyes. Chicago wasn't in his lane. Camela asked if he had gone back to Texas to make up with that woman, that Amanda, and Bash lacked the energy to add his own spin to *that* story.

When he lifted his Magic 8-Ball from the stereo rack, it advised him to go fuck himself.

His gaze was drawn back to the automatic. He had colorful thoughts of a world where everyone routinely packed pieces like this one. What they once called the "underworld."

He put the 8-Ball back. It wasn't funny tonight.

He toasted Jonathan with his beer. It wasn't the first time. The good humor had been beaten right out of him.

He moved to shake his special snow globe, the one Jonathan had liked so much. When his fingers touched the glass he decided to let it be.

The snow did not stir. The little corpses stayed buried.

Thirty-Four

Chicago is Hell, and the car is as red as blood.

Jamaica maintains a steady fifty per on the southbound 57. Chicago is no longer visible to the rear despite the flat terrain. The thunderheads of oncoming blizzards shroud it, cerements for a city of the dead.

The Missouri state line is a memory, itself indistinct. Jamaica is a good driver. She checks the rearview as needed but has not looked behind her, not once.

Somewhere between the tailpipe of the 'Vette and Cicero, three unloaded handguns are oxidizing their finish in a bank of snow. Grass will cover them in the spring and eventually they will submerge in the loam. They will retain their shape for more than a century. No one will ever find them. Her fast throw has worked better than all the evasion in the world. Some of the bullets she has scattered will ultimately be collected by curious children. The rounds will be harmless by then, curios for bookshelves, mystical pirate booty.

There are no weapons in the car. There are no drugs in the car, though Jamaica swears she can smell coke.

Ghost cocaine, perhaps, working tricks in her head.

Jeffrey Holdsworth Chalmers Tessier has given Jamaica a business card filled with scribbled phone numbers. Maybe someday, she thinks. He has mentioned Louisiana, East Texas, points south. Sounds like a good direction to her.

Going down on America. She laughs at her own reflection.

Each mile carries her farther away. She sheds the chrysalis of her Chicago self.

The town names en route are quaint and amusing.

Metropolis. Mound City. Cairo. Marked Tree. Truckers in cafes want to know where she's from. Motel clerks smile like old Norman Bates himself, and ask if she is traveling alone. What's a nice girl...?

Jamaica is not a nice girl. She showers alone, without fear.

Such amateurs in the boonies. It is all pretty amusing.

Bodies will be discovered, she thinks. Wants and warrants for her, and for the car she drives. Maybe by tomorrow. Don't trade it. Abandon it, as planned. Give it a Viking funeral in some swamp. After one more day. Right now she needs the distance. Sometimes you *could* run away from your problems. Outdistance them.

It saddens her to think of Jonathan. A nice guy. Considerate. All the right knobs and options, and utterly wrong for her. As an unrequited scenario it is a comfort. That delicious taste of never-to-be-finished life biz. He did not deserve what happened to him, but he had died *doing*, taking action, making a commitment that would matter in anyone's reckoning.

She will not cry *oh woe* for him. He would not want that, she is sure.

She wonders whether any of his sperm lingers somewhere inside of her. A microdot of his life. She knows better, and does not cry woe. She weeps for a few miles, to the sad songs on the radio. She is entitled.

Now and then she pretends his spirit rides in the car next to her.

As for Cruz, Emilio had murdered him the moment he had debarked from Florida, hadn't he? Emilio had killed him long-distance and then shown up in time for the climax. The good parts. Rosie had shoved Cruz out the hatch with no chute. Jonathan had tried to help and had been unable to save him. Cruz had been a dead man as soon as Jamaica had first aimed her potent eyes at him.

So much blood. Cruz had thought he had heard a ghost. Now, for all Jamaica knows, the job is his. That brick of coke had been more important to him than anything. She recalls the look in his eyes when he'd fetched the kilo. The look, after they'd waded through the carnage in apartment 107. That hunger living in his eyes. Jamaica knows now that she had been swapping looks with death, walking.

More death waits, back there in the snow. Death is patient.

She imagines Jonathan in the suicide seat as she drives. His outline is like crushed ice in a clear cup from which the drink has been drained. Bump it and the shape falls to shards, held in concert by its own fragile surface tension.

He looks at her. Just looks.

Now there are only his eyes, next to her. Green, like her eyes. Growing dimmer.

Jeffrey Holdsworth Chalmers Tessier had a look in his eyes, too. Not how he could take advantage of her. Not how he could lie to her. Not a lust for guns or drugs or power or vended sex. More a look of hurt bewilderment. Determination lumbered by confusion. A darting need for escape, for a change that would make a loud and lasting noise…the kind of noise that obliterates interference, and lets you hear precisely once more.

…the sort of look Jamaica has come to recognize in her own face. Time for another name change. Adapt or eat lead. She thinks of Jonathan again, and chooses her new name. Just like that.

And maybe someday she can phone up Jeffrey Holdsworth Chalmers Tessier. Shock the shit out of him. Start something, once she's filed the sharp edges off the breaks she's making right now.

Soon. For something they both would be needing.

Low beams to cut the snow. State line to Arkansas. One more down.

She has her smile back. It is her last smile as Jamaica. Her lips still bleed.

Soon.

After decades of travail and unavailability, this first-ever American trade paper edition of *The Shaft* is brought to you by the good offices of Crossroads Press and Macabre Ink, courtesy of the Two Daves, David Wilson and David Dodd, who deserve your thanks. Mine, too.

DJS / April 2020

About the Author

DAVID J. SCHOW is a multiple-award-winning West Coast writer. The latest of his ten novels is a hardboiled extravaganza called *The Big Crush* (2019). The newest of his ten short story collections is a greatest hits anniversary compendium titled *DJStories* (2018).

He has been a contributor to Storm King Comics' *John Carpenter's Tales for a Halloween Night* since its very first issue. In 2018 Storm King released his five-issue series for *John Carpenter's Tales of Science Fiction*— *"The Standoff."*

DJS has written extensively for film (*The Crow, Leatherface: Texas Chainsaw Massacre III, The Hills Run Red*) and television (**Masters of Horror, Mob City, Creepshow**). His nonfiction works include *The Art of Drew Struzan* (2010) and *The Outer Limits at 50* (2014). He can be seen on various DVDs as expert witness or documentarian on everything from *Creature from the Black Lagoon* to *Psycho* to *I, Robot*, not to mention the Rondo and Saturn Award-winning Blu-Ray discs of *The Outer Limits* (Seasons 1 and 2) from Kino-Lorber.

Thanks to him, the word "splatterpunk" has been in the Oxford English Dictionary since 2002.

Curious about other Crossroad Press books?
Stop by our site:
http://store.crossroadpress.com
We offer quality writing
in digital, audio, and print formats.

For Prince Sirki
Who never loses, ever.

I want my stone to read:
Not Dead – Just Resting My Eyes

Made in the USA
Las Vegas, NV
23 November 2020